THE PORTOFINO
DECEPTION

Jeffrey S. Stephens

ibooks

New York

ibooks

1230 Park Avenue
New York, New York 10128
Tel: 212-427-7139 • Fax: 212-860-8852
bricktower@aol.com • www.BrickTowerPress.com

Library of Congress Cataloging-in-Publication Data

Stephens, Jeffrey S.
The Portofino Deception
   ISBN-13: 978-1-59687-850-1
   ISBN-10: 1-59687-850-9
   Library of Congress Control Number: 2007937215

   Fiction/Suspense, Adult/General
   Espionage/Adventure

Copyright © 2007 by Jeffrey S. Stephens

First Edition

Cover design by Matt Drace
Typeset by The Great American Art Company

10 9 8 7 6 5 4 3 2 1

To the memory of Ben Conway, a true believer.

ACKNOWLEDGMENTS

A mere "thank you" does not seem enough of an acknowledgment for those who have stood by me for so long as supporters, critics, ersatz editors and eternally optimistic friends. Chris Beakey, Maureen Benic, Randi Conway, Jackie Covell, Jim Covell, Carol Garinger, Larry Garinger, Linda Kaye, Jennifer Korona, Nicky Lewis, Steve Marks, Andy Moszynski, Dr. Bart Pasternak, Ginny Peluso, Carl Portale, Ron Rosa, MJ Rose, Dennis Rowan, Ed Scannapieco, Dr. Robert Stark, Jean Stone, Caroline Sumner, Scott Sumner, Laura Sutton, Eric Thorkilsen, Melissa Thorkilsen, Frank Wilson - I cherish each of you.

My sincerest appreciation to a very dear friend, necessarily unnamed, who told me the truth about covert operations and explained how the world is a safer place because of the many heroic deeds that will never be revealed.

My gratitude to the publisher John Colby; my brilliant young editor and erstwhile lunch companion Maureen McTigue; and the relentless agent and soon-to-be single digit handicap golfer, Bob Diforio.

And in the end, of course, there are Trevor and Graham and Nancy, without whom the curious passages of life would have no real meaning.

Grazie.

VX is a substance developed in Great Britain in 1952 and remains the deadliest nerve gas ever created. VX—known by its United States Army codename—is a clear, colorless liquid with the consistency of motor oil. A fraction of a drop of VX, absorbed through the skin or inhaled through aeration, can kill by severely disrupting the nervous system. Although a cocktail of drugs can serve as an antidote, VX acts so quickly that victims would have to be injected with the antidote almost immediately to have a chance at survival. VX is the only significant nerve agent created since World War II. VX is a weapon of mass destruction that spreads from impact point killing all in its path . . .

Foxnews.com
cfrterrorism.org
chem.ox.ac.uk

ONE

Jordan Sandor had no reason to expect this quiet autumn morning to erupt with the familiar sounds of his violent past.

It was nearly ten, the air crisp and cool, the calm sky bright and clear and blue. The two-lane blacktop in upstate New York was deserted, except for Dan Peters' old station wagon. Sandor was slouched in the passenger seat, a casual observer of the passing countryside. He and Peters had been riding in silence when a pickup truck came into view, then turned across their path as they continued straight on Route 32.

"That's practically a traffic jam around here."

Sandor nodded. "Not much doing."

"Nope, not this time of year. Summer you get the tourists, hiking, camping, all that bullshit. Winter they come up to ski." Peters eased the wagon along a wide curve. "Fall, some people drive up on the weekends to see the leaves turn color, other than that you get nothing."

They passed a makeshift billboard that boasted authentic home cooking at some nearby restaurant. The poster looked so old Sandor wondered if the restaurant even existed anymore. "You don't miss the city at all?"

Peters thought it over, surveying the barren road. "Sometimes. The places, you know. Not the people. The food, mostly. When I get a taste for good Chinese or Thai, and especially Japanese, that's when I really miss New York. No Sushi Yasuda up here."

Sandor smiled at the road ahead. "Still need your sushi fix."

"Old habits die hard."

"You were the one who convinced me to try it, remember? Raw fish, for Chrissake. Man, how many years ago was that?"

Peters didn't answer, and they fell quiet again.

"Well," Jordan said after another mile or so, "I give you high marks.

1

Looks like you've done a good job of making the transition to the quiet life."

"Quiet everywhere, except up here," Peters said, then pointed to his head. Embarrassed by the confession, he fell silent again.

"You're entitled to some peace," Jordan told him.

"What I saw over there, pal—it never gets peaceful for me. Sometimes I manage to ignore the noise, that's all."

The two men had fought together in the Gulf War, the first one, when they drove the Iraqis out of Kuwait, leaving behind a mess that needed to be cleaned up a dozen years later. Before that, Peters had seen duty in Vietnam. He had been a career soldier, almost fifteen years older than Sandor, but Jordan outranked him when they served in the Persian Gulf.

"Well," Sandor said, "maybe peace and quiet are overrated."

"Yeah, tranquility is a bitch," Peters said, then uttered a short laugh. "So what about you, how do you like your new gig? What are you supposed to be, a reporter or what?"

"I'm a journalist, if you don't mind."

"Oh yeah, a journalist, beautiful. You talk about transition, man. I suppose you don't miss the good fight, eh?"

Sandor faced forward again, toward the road ahead. He had an uneven nose and a jaw line etched in a strong, firm line. His complexion was tanned and a bit weathered for a man not yet forty. His hair was brown, and cut just long enough to allow him to run his fingers through the waves, front to back, which he habitually did when he took time to consider a question or reflect on something that troubled him. He was doing that now, his dark, intense eyes visualizing something beyond their line of sight. After a few moments, he said, "I gave up the good fight and came home the day they left those men for dead in Bahrain."

"Yeah," Peters said as he shook his head, then added, "Bastards."

Jordan nodded without a reply.

After his tour in the Middle East, Peters returned home to finish out his military career and take his pension. Sandor remained abroad, working on special assignments until an undercover team he was assigned to in Panama was exposed. It had been more than a year now, since that incident in Bahrain. The day after they pulled him out and left the others behind to die, Sandor submitted his resignation from government service.

"Not everyone comes home."

Jordan nodded without giving a response.

"Strange, how things never work out the way you figure."

Jordan let that go too. "So what about this Ryan guy we're going to see?"

"What about him?"

"What does he think of this quiet life, now that he's back?"

"You're the journalist, you ask him."

"I will," Sandor said.

Peters rolled down his window, a cold breeze whipping through the car.

Jordan said, "If this guy was really in the mercenary business, he's got some explaining to do before I'll believe a thing he tells me."

Peters turned to his old friend and showed him a crooked grin. "Good old Jordan, Mr. Black and White. The mercenary business is immoral, but if you put on a uniform and shoot someone, that makes it okay."

Sandor shook his head.

"You sure did wave the flag for a while, buddy."

"Yeah, I suppose so," Jordan said. "I still do, in fact. The flag isn't the problem."

Morning sunlight sparkled on the trees, an October spectacle of colors lining the road as they continued on Route 32, towards Jimmy Ryan's house.

"Close your window, will you Dan?"

Peters chuckled as he put it up half way. He was a burly man, with wide shoulders and thick arms. "Blood a little thin these days, Sandor? Winter's coming, you know. Time to bulk up." He patted his ample stomach, evidence that he no longer bothered to maintain his service physique.

Sandor, who was still trim and fit, eyed his friend's gut. "If it's all the same to you, I'll pass on the donuts and put on my jacket instead." He grabbed his sport coat from the back seat, pulled it on, then rubbed his hands together. "So how well do you really know him?"

"Jimmy? I told you, I only met him last month, when he first got back from Europe."

"I thought you said he was in North Africa."

"He was. Spent some time in France before he came back to the States."

"Uh huh. And how'd he find his way to you?"

"I met him in a bar."

"Picking up guys in bars, Danny?"

"Funny."

"You still a Bud man?"

"Loyal to the end. You still going steady with Jack Daniels?"

"Ever faithful."

Danny laughed.

"You think he was looking for you, or was it just a coincidence?"

"Jesus, I don't know, Jordan. Looking for me? I don't think so. We were watching a ballgame, talking, found out we were both in the service, started gabbing. Save the fucking third degree for him, will you? We'll be there in ten minutes."

"Just curious. Occupational hazard."

"New occupation, new hazards. I think I liked you better in Amman."

They approached an intersection and Peters slowed the station wagon slightly, then swung into a left turn that led them onto another two lane road. It was a narrower stretch than Route 32, but just as quiet—until a piercing noise rang out through the clear morning air.

"What the hell was that?" Even as Dan asked the question, they heard a second brief explosion, the sound unmistakable.

"Gunshots," Sandor replied flatly.

"There's no hunting this close to 32," Dan said. "Someone might be shooting off rounds on their property."

As they came around the next curve they discovered the answer. Just ahead, off to their left, two cars were stopped on the grass shoulder. One was a police car, the other a sedan parked in front of the cruiser. Beside the driver's door of the sedan an officer had fallen to the ground in a leaden heap.

Dan instinctively jammed on his brakes and brought his station wagon to a screeching halt.

Jordan hollered a warning as a small, dark man jumped from the passenger side of the sedan and leveled an automatic pistol at them. They were less than fifty yards away.

The first shot smashed through the windshield, covering them in a spray of fractured glass. The second round tore into Dan's left side, piercing him with the awful, numbing sensation of jagged ice slicing through his flesh, giving way almost at once to a searing shock of pain. He lurched backward from the impact, then fell heavily forward onto the steering wheel. His foot slipped from the brake and the car began to roll slowly forward, moving steadily towards the approaching gunman.

As Jordan dove below the level of the dashboard, a third shot exploded through what remained of the windshield, another shower of broken crystals of safety glass covering the two men. Sandor struggled to pull his friend off the steering column and out of the line of fire, keeping himself as low as he could manage, even as another round whistled above him before it went crashing through the side window. The car was still traveling forward, now no more than thirty yards from their assailant.

As another shot was fired, Jordan managed to yank Dan onto the seat. Then he managed to take control of the wheel. He extended his left leg across Dan's ankles, straining to reach the accelerator pedal. He jerked the steering wheel, pressed down on the gas, and the car surged ahead.

They careened wildly to the right, and Jordan knew that if he ran them off the road into the woods they would be finished. He tugged the wheel slightly to the left, guessing at his position with the help of a quick look above the dash. They were even with the two parked cars now as the wagon veered sharply left, causing the gunman to jump backward as Jordan accelerated past him. The man fired again, through the driver's side window, sending more glass cascading across the front seat.

Sandor made several reflexive adjustments, turning quickly left and right, back and forth, guiding the station wagon swiftly past the two parked vehicles. He heard yelling in some foreign language, which he tried to make out as he reached up to tilt the rear view mirror for a look behind them.

The driver of the sedan had gotten out of the car and was waving his arms, ordering his companion back inside. Sandor saw in the mirror that the driver was tall and blond, as dissimilar in appearance from the short, swarthy gunman as he could have been.

Jordan remained low in the seat, peering just above the dash now, doing the best he could to forge ahead, to put some distance between his car and theirs. Several more shots exploded from behind them as he headed down the long, straight stretch of road, but then the firing stopped. Jordan checked the mirror again, surprised to see that the two men were not turning around to pursue him. Instead, they had hurried back into their car and were speeding off in the other direction, towards the main highway.

Jordan realized the driver and gunman might be working a decoy. He watched as they disappeared around the curve from where he and Dan first spotted them. Sandor knew they might spin a turn and come back after him at full speed, but he brought Dan's wagon to an abrupt stop and threw the gearshift into park. If they were returning, he would have no chance to out-run them unless he got behind the wheel.

"Dan, can you hear me?" He tried to raise Peters, to lean him against the driver's door if necessary.

"My side," Peters muttered. "I'm hit bad."

"I know," Jordan told him, relieved to have him say anything at all. "Can you move?"

Dan nodded slightly and Jordan checked behind them again, making sure the sedan did not suddenly roar back into view. He helped his friend slide towards the middle of the seat, then scrambled over him to get behind the wheel. He turned to have another look back, but there was no sign of them, not yet.

Sandor checked his friend, a growing stain of blood running onto the seat amidst the shards of glass. Jordan was experienced enough to guess that Dan was not suffering any major arterial bleeding, but he could see the wound was serious. He pulled off his jacket, folded it up and reached out to place it under Peters' head.

"Don't worry," Sandor said, "I'm getting you to a hospital. Here," he said, grabbing Dan's parka from the back seat of the car, "hold this against your side."

When he had made Peters as comfortable as he could, Jordan swung the car into reverse, completed a high speed u-turn, then sped back, braking to a sudden stop beside the fallen cop. There was still no sign of an ambush. Jordan listened intently, but heard nothing except the hum of the station wagon's engine as it purred through the empty frame where the wind-shield had been. The quiet was eerie now, unsettling after the explosion of gunfire, the shattering of glass, the wailing of tires that had resounded along this desolate strip of roadway. Sandor became aware of the pound-ing in his chest, took a deep breath to steady himself, then stepped quick-ly from the car and knelt beside the wounded officer.

"Can you hear me?"

The man gave no response, but Jordan could see he was still alive.

Sandor removed the pistol from the trooper's holster, all the while returning his anxious gaze ahead, searching for what might appear with-out warning from around the turn. He pulled at the slide and drew a round into the breech of the officer's automatic, then ran back to the police cruiser, picked up the radio mike and spoke into the open channel.

"We have an emergency. Officer down, just off Route 32, repeat, officer down, emergency."

He released the button on the side of the microphone, waiting only an instant before a voice crackled over the speaker, and Jordan knew that for now, at least, it would be all right.

TWO

Sandor was finally alone, seated on a vinyl sofa in the waiting area of the local hospital. He had spent the day being subjected to the repetitive questions of a preliminary police interrogation, treated to a series of medical updates on Dan Peters and the wounded officer, and praised for his courage by a seemingly endless stream of strangers.

The wounded trooper, Jack Collins, was in the intensive care unit. He was only alive, according to all accounts, because of Jordan's reaction under fire. Dan was also out of surgery, in the recovery room, patched up where the bullet had torn into his side and again where it exited through his back.

"Unbelievably lucky," the surgeon had explained to Jordan, "I can't begin to tell you how close this was to a lethal injury. They just missed his spine, his heart . . ."

"I didn't know Danny had a heart," Jordan interrupted with a smile, hoping to be spared further detail, but the surgeon was not deterred. He went on to tell Sandor everything, and at great length.

Now Jordan was sipping lousy coffee out of a paper cup, feeling an immense sense of relief to be alone while trying to sort things out, when he heard someone say, "Mr. Sandor?"

He slowly raised his head to see a broad, stern-looking man wearing a State Trooper's uniform and a chest full of medals. "Yes."

"I'm Captain Reynolds," the man said, his speech as stiff as his posture. "Jack Collins is one of my men."

Sandor stood, his lean frame just a little over six feet tall bringing him eye to eye with the trooper. "Jordan," he said, offering his hand as he made a quick assessment of this authoritarian old cop.

Captain Reynolds looked like one of the tough, leathery, career officers

Sandor had served under, certainly a man who had experienced his share of fighting in the military. Now, years later, his weary, grey eyes said he had spent too much time in a rural area chasing after too many drunk drivers and too many petty criminals, not seeing enough real action. His moments of glory were in the past.

Reynolds' grip was firm, and he held Jordan's hand as if he didn't mean to let go. "They tell me you saved Jack's life."

"Bit of an exaggeration, I think."

"I'm not so sure. If you left him there, doctor says he would have bled to death as easily as anything else. You took a real chance, going back for him the way you did. Could've run for it yourself, right?"

Jordan was embarrassed for about the twentieth time that afternoon and, since Reynolds was obviously not the sentimental type, he figured he should put an end to this part of the discussion as politely as he could. "Look Captain, I figured Collins had a gun, I didn't. I thought going back for it might not be a bad idea."

Reynolds showed him as tight a smile as he'd seen in a while. It was one of those official smiles Jordan would get from a commanding officer who wanted to demonstrate his appreciation for something Sandor had done, without getting emotional about it. "That's a lotta crap," the Captain said, making the statement sound as friendly as hell. "I know a combat vet when I meet one, Sandor. You didn't go back for a gun, you went back because you were trained not to leave your men behind."

"Homework, Captain?"

"Yeah, we do our homework. Checked up on you some. Sorry I never met you overseas. Could've used you in Nam."

"Before my time," Jordan said. Then he shrugged. "Wouldn't have mattered anyway, right?"

"Probably not." Captain Reynolds shook his head. "Buy you a real cup of coffee?"

"Thanks, but I wanted to stop by to see Collins, if I can. They tell me now's the time."

Reynolds nodded. "We'll catch up a little later then. I have a few questions for you."

"Right," Jordan said.

Reynolds stood there for a moment, just to let Sandor know who was in charge. Jordan thought about asking if he was dismissed, but Reynolds turned around, executing something close to a smart about-face, then walked away.

*   *   *

As Sandor strolled down the hospital corridor, it seemed everyone there recognized him. Small town, big news. He stopped at the nurse's station where he exchanged smiles with a comely brunette who was sitting behind a long, white counter.

"I wonder if I might be able to have a short visit with Trooper Collins now. I understand he's feeling a little better, and I'm . . ."

"He's in the ICU, Mr. Sandor," she interrupted. "His only visitors should be immediate family. But for you," she added with a self-conscious tilt of her head, "I'll speak with the doctor right away."

She lingered an extra moment to smile into Jordan's dark eyes, then stepped inside a glass enclosed area behind her, picked up the telephone and, watching Jordan through the partition, made her call. The discussion was brief, she hung up and came out.

"Follow me," she said.

*   *   *

The intensive care unit was a jungle of antiseptic technology, with large, complex machinery dwarfing the patients it surrounded. Strange beeping sounds and audiovisual monitors animated the peaceful, impersonal infirmary. The nurse led Jordan through a maze of medical computers and stainless steel apparatus to Jack Collins' bedside.

"This is Mr. Sandor," she whispered softly to her patient. "The man who saved you."

Jordan could have done without that introduction. "They're the ones who saved you," he protested mildly as he gestured toward the equipment and staff around them. "I just kept you company till they got there." Collins looked about twenty-five, a young officer who had made a rookie's mistake that almost got him killed. Jordan figured a more experienced trooper would never have let them get the drop on him that way, his gun still snapped into the holster.

Collins did his best to smile. He was rigged up to intravenous tubing, his head and neck bandaged, his complexion the color of the white sheets.

All things considered, Sandor thought he looked better than he had earlier that morning, oozing blood, crumpled in a heap along the blacktop.

"They told me what you did," he said in a hoarse, unsteady voice. His tired eyes searched Jordan's face for something, then looked past him.

"Seems you're already on the mend," Jordan said cheerfully. "I just wanted to stop by, see how you're doing."

The nurse, who had remained at his side, told Jordan, "He's doing fine, Mr. Sandor, but he needs his rest. Just a minute or two, please."

Jordan nodded. "Right," he said, then watched as she walked slowly away, giving him a good look at her exit. "Nice girl," he said.

"Yeah," Collins agreed. "Grew up right nearby, in Saugerties. You're not from around here, are you Mr. Sandor?"

"It's Jordan, and no, I'm from the city. Came up to visit an old army pal, Dan Peters. Know him?"

"Not really. Think I heard the name when he moved into town. It's been a while since anyone rented the Larsen place."

"But you never met him."

"Don't think I ever laid eyes on him." Collins winced, the combination of pain killers and medication balancing him on the edge of sleep. "I hear they did a number on him too."

"They did."

"Captain told me. Coulda' been both of us gone, hadn't been for you."

"Forget it," Jordan said.

"How'd it go . . . down at the barracks?"

"The questioning, you mean? All right, I guess. I gave a description of the little guy with the automatic. I only saw the driver for a few seconds, caught a glimpse of him in the mirror."

"Driver's the one who plugged me."

"Tall blonde guy," Jordan said.

"Yeah. Captain tells me you gave a pretty good I.D. on both. License plate too. How in hell'd you manage that?"

"Instincts, that's all."

"Sure," Collins said, sounding like he was about to pass out.

"Strange looking pair, weren't they?"

Collins opened his eyes a bit. "How do you mean?"

"The little guy was an Arab. From what I could see, the driver looked like an All-American linebacker."

"Yeah," Collins said with a slight nod. He was fading fast now.

"I wanted to ask you something, Jack. All right if I call you Jack?"

Collins tried a smile again, his lips dry and uneven. "Ask away."

"They tell me you stopped them for speeding. How did it happen? You give them the siren?"

"Uh huh."

"And they stopped right away?"

"Sure. Probably knew they were gonna blast me." The idea of that seemed to rouse him. "No way to outrun me in that rented car. If they took off, they had to know I'd go for the radio too."

Jordan nodded. That was precisely how he figured it. "Did they say anything? Anything at all?"

Collins took a long, hard swallow. "Not a word. Sonuvabitch just nailed me." He hesitated. "I never even got my gun out of the holster."

Jordan frowned.

"Why?"

"Nothing really," Jordan said. "I just heard them yelling to each other, couldn't make out the language. I thought maybe you heard something."

"Nothing." He paused again and drew a shallow, awkward breath. "Now you say it, though . . . I think I heard something when I was on the ground. I wouldn't have known French from Chinese by then."

"Don't worry about it. They'll get picked up soon enough."

"The car," Collins said, his voice growing weaker. "Captain said they found it."

Jordan nodded, pretending to know what Collins was talking about.

"Down by the reservoir. Another set of tire tracks. Second car waiting for them."

"Right," Jordan said.

"Professionals," Collins muttered.

"We were all lucky to get out of there," Sandor said.

Collins reached out and took hold of Jordan's arm. "You were the luck."

Jordan nodded. "Just one more question, Jack, then I'll let you get some rest. Know a guy up here, name of Jimmy Ryan?"

Collins started to shake his head, but that hurt too much. "No. Can't say as I do."

"Never mind." Sandor patted the man's hand and offered a reassuring smile. "Don't worry, your boys will catch up with them."

Collins looked up at him in a way that told Jordan he knew it was a lie. "They knew what they were about," he said. "They're long gone, aren't they?"

"We'll see."

The young man hesitated, then said, "Take care of yourself."

"You too," Jordan told him, then turned away. Collins was asleep before he left the room.

THREE

Sandor found Captain Reynolds just outside the ICU, where he was quietly giving instructions to two troopers standing guard in the hospital corridor, assigned to protect Jack Collins.

"Captain."

Reynolds turned from his men.

"When you're done, I was wondering if we could have that cup of coffee."

Reynolds told his men he would be gone a while, then took Jordan by the arm and led him down the hallway. "How's Jack?"

"I think he's doing all right. Tough to tell, with all the medication."

The Captain nodded. "Come on, we'll take a walk."

*   *   *

They sat across from each other in a booth in the small diner a couple of blocks from the hospital. Reynolds was telling Sandor about his days in Vietnam, with the 101st Airborne, information Jordan had not requested, but the trooper wanted to share all the same.

"Ran that computer check on you," Reynolds told him after he finished his personal reminiscence. "Like I said before, saw some of your service record."

Jordan waited.

"Not all of it, though. Some major gaps. Looked to me like CID blocks. Where'd you disappear to after your first tour? Military Intelligence, am I right?"

"An oxymoron," Jordan replied.

"Like 'civil servant'?"

Jordan smiled.

14

"So you were still in some kind of government service."

"Some kind."

"And now you're some kind of reporter?"

"Some kind."

"I'm not a big fan of reporters."

"Neither am I."

Reynolds gave him a look that told him saving Jack Collins was not a license for any smart mouth crap, not if he knew what was good for him. "So, what happened to government duty?"

"Got old, Captain. Too many friends got sold out by too many fat-ass bureaucrats."

"Too much crap, am I right?"

"You're right."

"Lapsed patriot, eh?"

"No, still a patriot," Jordan said. "Just that too many people made it too hard to believe in the things that matter to me."

Reynolds shook his head, making a face like he just remembered something he never wanted to think about again. "Yeah, lost my taste for those games myself. Got fed up, took my retirement, came back home. Got this nice job, working towards a second pension. Local politics are a piece of cake, once you've done the Potomac shuffle. It's funny though, even now. Always thought I'd spend my entire life in the military."

"Wish you had?"

"Sometimes. Nine-eleven happened to all of us, know what I mean?"

Sandor nodded.

"Especially when you've worn the uniform. Made me want to re-enlist."

Jordan nodded, leaving the next thought unspoken.

"Tough world, am I right?"

Sandor stared directly into Reynolds' eyes. "After this morning, who am I to argue?"

"Very true."

"So what really went down today?" Jordan asked.

"Good question. Maybe I should be asking you."

"If I knew, I'd tell you," Sandor said.

"I wonder." The Captain retained his erect bearing as he took a drink of his coffee. "I suppose I should get over to the barracks, see what they've turned up."

"Tell me about the second car, Captain, the one they had waiting near the reservoir."

Reynolds took a moment to study Sandor. "Where'd you hear that?"

"Let's just say there are a lot of rumors flying around here today."

Reynolds frowned. "They were professionals, that much is certain."

"That's exactly what Collins said."

"They had the second car waiting, made the switch and took off, God knows where."

"I bet your trooper and my friend weren't their only stop today."

Reynolds nodded slowly. "Who else have you been talking to?"

"Does it matter?"

"It might."

"Okay. Call it a guess, then."

"That the truth?"

"It is. I heard about the second car at the hospital. The other part is just common sense. Two shooters didn't come up here to nail a cop for a speeding ticket, did they?"

Reynolds nodded again. "You're right. They took out a guy, name of James Ryan."

Jordan said nothing at the mention of the name, the man he and Peters were on their way to see. Reynolds searched Sandor's expression for any sign of recognition, but Jordan had been trained too well to blink at this point, even if he was a year out of practice.

"Ryan just moved up here a month or so ago," Reynolds said. "We're running it down now."

"Uh huh."

"My men backtracked from where Collins first spotted the car. Didn't take much, the house this Ryan was renting isn't far from there."

Sandor waited.

"My men tell me they caused that boy some pain before they did him."

"How's that?"

"Tied Ryan up and beat the living crap out of him, then put two in his head."

"You been there yourself to have a look?"

"I'm going now, soon as I clean up some of the paperwork at the barracks. Need you there too, look through some of the mug shots they brought down from Albany, the usual routine."

"Mind if I go with you afterwards? To this guy Ryan's house?"

"Not regulation, you know." He paused. "What the hell. Maybe you can help out, somehow."

Jordan smiled. "It's good to be on the right side of the police."

"Troopers, not police. And I'll be interested to see what side you're really on, son."

"I just want to know what happened."

Reynolds nodded.

"I was going to visit my friend first, if that's all right."

"You do that, then we'll get you a ride to H.Q. And Sandor . . ." Jordan was already standing. "I may be from a small town in upstate New York, but I'm no yokel. You follow me?"

"I never . . ."

Reynolds stood up. "That's okay," he said, giving Jordan a slap on the shoulder. "You just keep it in mind, is all."

FOUR

A t the same time Jordan was having coffee in the diner, a uniformed waiter at the Waldorf-Astoria Hotel in New York was delivering a meal to one of the suites on the seventeenth floor. The young man wheeled in a large tray containing fresh orange juice, poached eggs, several rashers of bacon, wheat toast and a pot of espresso. Also at hand were the pleasant incidentals this grand hotel provides—fresh marmalade and preserves, poppy seed rolls with sweet butter, and a fine setting of flatware and china. The sitting room was decorated in a sedate yet affluent style, an elegant motif featuring the cool blues and greens of the drapes, warm woods and the rich brocades of the upholstery.

"Will that be all sir?" the young man asked.

The dapper Saudi gentleman seated before his mid-afternoon breakfast did not look up. One of the two men attending him pressed a tip into the waiter's hand, then escorted him out of the room, closing the door behind him.

Mahmoud al-Rahmad removed the cloth napkin from the serving cart, then stared down at his decidedly American meal. He did not speak until his assistant returned to the room.

"The timing was truly unfortunate," Rahmad said, still without looking up. His English was polished and formal, an accent produced by a fine British education. His features were smallish and soft, his complexion dusky, and his eyes were as dark as his black hair, which was combed straight back and kept in place. A man in his fifties, he obviously took great care with his appearance. "However," he continued, "it was a mistake to leave those two men behind." He poured himself a cup of the dark coffee while his two subordinates watched in silence. "Mustafa was wrong not to have completed what he had begun."

18

"But sir," his younger assistant protested, "Kerrigan called him back to the car. Surely Mustafa could not risk being left there."

Mahmoud finally looked up, taking a moment before he spoke, his young aide uneasy under his gaze. "How concerned you are for Mustafa. Do you really believe our American friend would have driven away without him?"

"I do not know Kerrigan, sir. I am sorry."

"That is quite all right. Kerrigan is a skilled operative, and he will also be made to answer for his actions. Nevertheless, the problem now created yet remains." He began to poke at the eggs. "In England they serve kippers," he observed with a smile, which amounted to a slight parting of his lips, revealing white teeth that gleamed in contrast to his brown, oily complexion. "I came to enjoy kippers. In many things I have become infected by occidental ways." He laid down his fork, apparently too perturbed by the notion to continue eating. "Here, for instance, we have thought and discussion when action is at a premium." Rahmad sat back in his chair. "Are we certain that the man they eliminated was McHugh?"

"Yes sir. He was using an assumed name."

"Very well. And they elicited everything they could from him?"

The senior aide assured him with no little satisfaction that James McHugh, who was hiding under the name of James Ryan, was made to talk before he was murdered.

"Which presently leaves us with the problem of these other two men. And the policeman."

His aides nodded.

"Mustafa is certain these men did not reach McHugh first?"

Again, his aides confirmed that he was correct. "McHugh was going to meet with them this morning. Our men arrived first."

"Which is the reason, of course, they were on that road. Unfortunate timing," he said again, then shook his head.

"No, sir," the senior aide disagreed. "It would only have been unfortunate if they had reached McHugh first."

Rahmad raised his eyebrows, as if considering that notion. "But these men might have had previous discussions with McHugh. Who knows how much he told to the intermediary . . . what was his name?"

"Peters," the young man replied. "Dan Peters."

"Yes, Peters."

"Mustafa assures us that McHugh told Peters nothing. They were very persuasive in demanding answers of McHugh."

"I am sure. And this Peters, he was only the go-between. He was to introduce McHugh to Sandor?"

"Yes sir."

Rahmad mulled it over. "Well, Kerrigan is on his way out of the country at this very moment. Mustafa is quite capable of providing for his own safety. Even so, Peters and Sandor must be removed."

"What of the policeman?" asked the younger assistant. "How should we deal with him?"

The senior aide interrupted, saying, "The trooper is under guard."

"Yes," Rahmad agreed. "The officer may prove more difficult to reach while he remains under special care. Amazing, how this country reveres its wounded policemen, as if they should be praised for their incompetence rather than being held accountable." He shook his head in disgust. "No, for now the risk would outweigh the purpose. The trooper Collins, he knows nothing of us, or of McHugh. He has no information, except the remote possibility he could identify Kerrigan or Mustafa. If he poses any such threat, we can deal with him later. Sandor and Peters are the problem." He turned to his younger aide and pointed at him. "You see, there are things that experience can teach you, the most important of which may well be patience."

The young man frowned.

"For now, the other two men pose the real danger. They were to meet McHugh, which means they may know something of our operations, no matter how inconsequential. We must be rid of them, especially Sandor."

His aides responded to the last comment with puzzled looks. Rahmad smiled.

"You don't know of Sandor?"

"A reporter of some kind," the younger man offered, repeating what had been reported in the media.

"Yes," Rahmad said with an indulgent chuckle, "so Mr. Sandor would have it appear. We are gathering current information on him now."

"Sir?"

"Jordan Sandor has, shall we say, a history. We will come to that."

"Yes sir."

"So, we must assign the situation in Woodstock to someone subtle.

Peters must be dealt with immediately, but it will require finesse. He is in the hospital, there are police everywhere, so there is risk." He uttered a short, hollow laugh. "Perhaps we should choose another blond, blue-eyed friend for the job," he said. "No reason for our Arab brothers to receive all the bad press, should something go awry."

Mahmoud al-Rahmad, Saudi diplomat and unofficial *Charge d'Affaires* for al-Qaeda espionage activities in New York, returned to the business of his mid-afternoon breakfast.

"Sir," the senior aide asked, "to whom should we refer the other matter?"

He considered that for a moment. "I am informed that Sandor lives here in New York." He reached into his pocket and handed the senior aide a slip of paper. "This is the address. Have his apartment searched before he gets back. Look for anything that pertains to us. Notes, research, tapes. Anything that mentions McHugh or this assumed name, Ryan. Any information about Sandor's visit to Woodstock. Anything, of course, that refers to our activities. Also find out if Sandor has an office. If so, conduct the same search there. Determine who his contacts are, how he and Peters found McHugh."

"What of the man himself, this Sandor?"

"Complete the searches first. Once we eliminate him, the police will render it impossible to get into his apartment to learn what he has discovered."

His aides nodded at his obvious logic.

"After you've accomplished that, the matter should be handed over to Tafallai. I want to speak with him. He will know what to do."

FIVE

"You look positively beautiful," Jordan said as he entered the room.

"Oh yeah," Dan Peters responded weakly, then shot a disgusted look at the intravenous tubes that stretched from his arm and shoulder to the apparatus standing alongside his hospital bed. "I'd feel a lot better if I could borrow someone else's chest for a while."

"Don't look at me," Jordan said. "My chest isn't broad enough to fill your clothes." Peters was a raw-boned type, several inches shorter but much broader than Jordan. "You'd look lousy wearing my torso, pal."

"Funny man," Peters groaned.

"I don't see why you're making such a fuss. Doctor says it's just a flesh wound."

"Yeah. It's my flesh, though." Since being wheeled into the ambulance that morning, Peters had undergone a battery of tests; had suffered through emergency surgery to stitch up the entry and exit wounds; had various doctors and nurses poke and examine him; and he was still under mild sedation. His speech was slow and measured. He asked Jordan about the trooper, and Sandor filled him in on Jack Collins' condition.

"Good thing for all of us you didn't get hit."

Jordan nodded. "So much for your peaceful existence in upstate New York."

Peters attempted a deep breath, grimaced at the effort, then asked, "What the hell is really going on here?"

"Like what?"

"Like what happened to Jimmy Ryan?"

Jordan walked to the large window that overlooked a grassy courtyard in front of the hospital. The autumn afternoon had become unseasonably warm, and he watched as two young men in shirtsleeves entered the building. "You need some rest."

"I heard two nurses yapping out in the hallway."

"And?."

"Why don't you tell me?"

Jordan came back, moved the metal armchair beside the bed and sat down. "I'm not sure yet. It seems the two shooters were on their way back from a visit with your friend Ryan. We were unlucky enough to run into them on our way out of there."

Peters worked that over for a moment, the narcotics muddling his ability to think along a straight line. "Maybe not just unlucky."

"Meaning what?"

"Gimme some time, I might sort it out. I'm kinda slow today." He shifted slightly and uncomfortably in bed. "Maybe Ryan told them we were coming. Maybe they were waiting for us."

"Doesn't look that way. Collins said he stopped them for speeding."

"That so?" He took a moment to have a sip of water, then settled back again. "What about Ryan?"

"What about him?"

"Come on, damnit."

Jordan leaned forward in his chair and, speaking very softly, said, "Way I get it, they did a number on him, then killed him."

"Christ."

"Listen, I haven't told the police we were on our way to see him. Better not share that, not yet. All right?"

"Why?"

"It could mean more trouble for us than we need right now."

"More trouble then getting shot?"

Jordan smiled. "I'm going out to see Ryan's place with Reynolds, the trooper in charge."

"He asks you something, you gonna lie?"

Jordan sighed, then sat back. "I don't want to lie to him. I also don't want to be a volunteer."

"Yeah, I guess not," Peters agreed. "So what about me?"

"What about you?"

"You going to keep lying to me or you going to tell me the truth?"

"I guess that depends, too."

"Come on, Jordan."

Sandor pushed back his dark, wavy hair with the palm of his hand. "You go first."

"What the hell do I know?"

"That's exactly what I'm asking."

Danny's pallid complexion seemed to flush for a moment. "You figure someone found out we were going to see Ryan?"

"That's what I figure."

"Look, I admit our timing was lousy. You think it's more than that?"

"That depends on what else you have to tell me."

Peters struggled to keep his focus. "I already told you. I met Ryan when he first got back from Europe. Real quiet guy at first. Met him in the local saloon, drinking beers. Got to talking about the service, you know how it goes. What branch of the service are you in, what division, where did you tour, all of that bullshit."

"Go on."

Peters' words came a little bit easier now. "He was like a lot of the guys who did time overseas, except more so. Always looking over his shoulder, like an old gunfighter."

"And how old was this old gunfighter?"

"Not sure. Somewhere between you and me. Anyway, we got friendlier, talked about Nam and the Gulf. He told me he did a tour in the Orient, then a stretch in the Middle East. He said he saw a lot, wanted to put some of it on paper, but couldn't write a lick. He was thinking about contacting some reporters. That's when I told him about you. A week or so later, he says he wants to meet you."

"Just like that, he was going to dictate his memoirs to me?"

"I told him you were the best."

"At what?"

Dan answered with a frown. "When he got back to me, he said he'd been to the library, looked up a couple of pieces you'd written. He thought you might be the right guy to help him."

Jordan nodded. "I guess I should be flattered."

"Hey, I'm already in pain here, all right? Anyway, he said he had some dynamite you could put a match to. Worked with people who knew about al-Qaeda, Qadaffi, Iraq, illegal arms trade, bio-terrorism, you name it. Told me he also knew a lot about former G. I.'s who sold out."

"And you guessed he was one of them."

"Yeah, that's what I figured."

"And now you figure that these two hit men found out Ryan was talking to you?"

"If they didn't know before, they must know now, right?"

Jordan nodded. "I would assume so. They worked him over pretty good, according to Reynolds."

"Reynolds?"

"I told you, the Captain heading up the investigation." Jordan had a look at his friend. "You're out of steam, pal. Get some rest." He stood and placed his hand on Dan's arm.

"Okay, but you gotta know, this includes you too now. I mean, if Ryan spilled his guts, he wasn't just talking about me."

"I realize that."

"Whatever Ryan told them, he knew I was bringing you there today, right?"

"I understand."

"You've got to be careful."

"Right."

Peters opened his eyes a bit wider. "So when do you tell me the truth?"

"Later. Take a nap."

"Screw a nap, I want some answers."

"I'm working on some answers, believe me."

"Bullshit. This guy didn't want to see you because you could write an article for him. He wanted to see you because of your connections in Washington."

Jordan offered no response.

"When Ryan said he checked you out, he found more than the articles you wrote, am I right?"

"You may be right."

"So what are you up to?" Peters asked.

Jordan reached out and pinched his cheek. "When I figure it out, you'll be the first to know."

"You're back, aren't you? You're working for them."

Jordan smiled. "Ask me no questions, I'll tell you no lies."

"Come on, Jordan, you owe me."

"Owe you? You owe me, pal. I saved your life."

"Bullshit," his friend responded with a weak smile. "Nothing but a flesh wound. You said so yourself."

SIX

Special Agent John Covington received a call in his Langley office about the shootings near Woodstock, New York. He was apprised of the inquiries being made by local authorities, his own sources having already concluded that the dead man, using the name of Jimmy Ryan, was likely James McHugh. That identification was coming too late, both for McHugh and for the Central Intelligence Agency. Covington's team had been searching for him and, under the Foreign Intelligence Surveillance Act, they might have learned something sooner through wiretaps and other covert technology. Unfortunately, the media was all over the government for using FISA to justify domestic spying, and so now McHugh was dead and the best the CIA could hope for now was that his death would somehow provide them the next lead they desperately needed.

Covington was a slightly built man of fifty, with thinning hair, thin lips, and a slender nose that caused Jordan Sandor to once wonder aloud whether those stingy nostrils allowed in enough air to prevent brain damage. He was wearing his customary white button-down shirt and conservative tie to go with a conservative suit and his conservative manner. Whatever romantic image the public had of the typical CIA agent, Covington provided an accurate picture of the men who actually operated inside the Agency, his appearance and demeanor more like an accountant ready for a tough audit than a man poised for dangerous, physical action. He was part of the large corps of administrative personnel who supported the activities of the men in the field who risked their lives in anonymous endeavors that sometimes succeeded but often failed.

Men like Jordan Sandor.

Covington was Sandor's liaison for three missions before they worked together a year ago on an undercover operation in Panana, capital of the small sheikdom of Bahrain located in the Persian Gulf, just off the coast of Saudi Arabia. Jordan had been assigned to meet with four locals from neighboring Qatar who were sympathetic to American interests, who claimed to have information and possible entrée to a cell of al-Qaeda terrorists. Sandor's orders were to work with the informants to organize a raid on the al-Qaeda camp, taking as many of the terrorists alive as they could safely manage, while destroying the operation. The maneuver would begin with the locals making contact and setting up the CIA play.

It was one of the black ops that the Agency would never acknowledge, especially after the scheme was somehow compromised. Jordan's advance team from Qatar was exposed and then apprehended, kidnapped from their hotel rooms in broad daylight before the counter-terrorism unit finished their arrangements to put an assault team in place. Sandor arrived on the scene half a day too late, then called for backup, demanding a frontal raid on the encampment, intending to rescue his allies, no longer concerned with al-Qaeda survivors or, for that matter, the politics of plausible deniability. Covington refused the request, aborted the mission and had Sandor forcibly removed before any evidence of a United States interdiction in Bahrain might become public and cause an international uproar. Covington argued to his superiors that they had no proof the cell was al-Qaeda, only the word of four agents who had now disappeared. An attack on foreign soil without appropriate supporting evidence would be a disaster.

Sandor's protests went unheard. He was taken out by his own people before he could act, then returned to the States, leaving the local agents to the terrorists.

It was not an incident that the media would ever pick up, the disappearance of foreign nationals in an unstable region. It was just another failed effort by the Agency for which the American sympathizers had undoubtedly paid with their lives.

Sandor demanded an inquiry into how the operation was uncovered, but Covington stonewalled him on that too, closing the file on the matter. That was when Sandor decided to close his own file. He announced his resignation and walked away.

Jordan had never been a Covington fan, and now he blamed him and his boss, Mark Byrnes, for the entire debacle. Byrnes was the Deputy Director of Regional Operations at the time, and he had the authority to override Covington's decision to cut and run. Jordan was extremely vocal in his criticism of both men—vocal, that is, within the Agency. Sandor was both too smart and too loyal to ever go outside the Company with his complaints. Instead, he warned them that he had enough material buried away to provide him the assurance he would never have to see an unfriendly face in his rear view mirror. Not ever. Then he left.

Now Covington and Byrnes would be forced to deal with Sandor again.

*   *   *

Mark Byrnes was waiting in his office for Covington to report. Byrnes was a handsome man of about sixty with well-defined features, his graying hair cut short and combed close, his blue eyes shrewd in a way his subordinates often found unsettling. He was a product of Harvard, Oxford, the diplomatic corps, State Department, and the breeding of a wealthy family that is as close as America comes to aristocracy. In the year that had passed since Jordan's resignation, Byrnes had been rewarded for his hard work by a promotion from Deputy Director of Operations stationed overseas to Deputy Director in Washington. He was a man who always knew what he was about.

Covington entered his office and, after polite greetings, Byrnes asked a few questions. Covington's answers were satisfactory.

"So then, you're up to speed," the DD said.

"I am," Covington agreed.

"And you know that Sandor was there, in Woodstock."

"I do."

"But you don't know why." Byrnes spoke in his customary tone, an economy of time and effort.

"Not yet, sir."

"You're going to have to deal with him, John."

"Yes sir," Covington said.

"In fact, you're the only person that's going to deal with him." The Deputy Director let that idea settle in as he took a look around his large, warmly appointed office. The walls were covered with photographs of Byrnes and the President, Byrnes with various Congressmen, Byrnes with heads of state. He waited as Covington also had a look. It was a reminder of how far he had moved up the chain of command. "This is the only thing I want you working on right now, John. And I want you there right away. McHugh's death may give us the best lead we've had in weeks."

"Yes sir."

"And whatever problems we've had with Sandor in the past, they're in the past. At least from our perspective, is that understood?"

"Yes sir."

"Sandor can be used to our advantage, regardless of any grudge he may still harbor," the DD said, not bothering to articulate his next two thoughts—that Sandor had been his best field agent, and that the debacle in Bahrain had led to Sandor's resignation from the Agency. "The key here is controlling Sandor, using him," the DD said. "This is not about proving a point. You understand that."

"I do, sir."

"I hope so," Byrnes said. "If he can get us the answers we need, it could be useful. Extremely useful."

"Yes, sir. However, controlling Sandor can be difficult, as you well know. We can't afford to have him in a position to compromise our plans."

"Sandor would never compromise the Agency," the DD said.

"It's not the Agency I meant, sir. This is personal with him. He's outside the Company now, and that makes him a risk."

"I know Sandor can be a pain in the ass, but I want to put him in play on this, especially if there's any chance at all he can be of use to us. Damn the risk," he said. "Am I clear?"

"Yes sir."

"All right then. With McHugh dead, we may have a chance to get to his friend, Andrioli. We still have no lead on his whereabouts yet, is that correct?"

"Yes sir."

"We're running out of time on this operation. We can't announce to the media that there are new security threats without a single, positive shred of information in hand."

"I understand that sir."

"I hope you do, I truly hope you do. Now get to New York and find out what you can."

*   *   *

Jordan spent the late afternoon at the State Trooper barracks. A police artist had driven down from Albany, and Sandor worked with him to refine the descriptions he had given earlier. They also reviewed a new series of mug shots on the computer, after being granted access to the federal data-base. They struck out there, but Jordan was not surprised. The more they searched, the more evident it became to him that the two shooters were men who flew below the radar.

For now, he kept those thoughts to himself and struggled to be as patient as he could manage. Matters for the local authorities were fairly chaotic. One of their own had been shot, that was their principal focus. There was also discussion about Ryan, about taking his body to Kingston for an autopsy, and Sandor listened as three junior officers debated the necessity of such action. After all, the youngest of the three argued, there was clear evidence that Ryan had been beaten, then plugged with two shots from close range. They understood that an autopsy was standard proce-dure, the Trooper said, but what was the point in tearing the corpse apart just to confirm what they already knew?

Sandor had answers he was not giving. The ballistics expert would be interested in the slugs they recovered. They would need those results to confirm that the shooters on the road had also taken out Ryan. There would also be questions about chemicals that might be found in the dead man's system. Sandor assumed they would find traces of so-called truth drugs.

While the local law enforcement team debated the possible reasons for the sadistic beating of Ryan prior to his murder, Jordan was certain that he and Dan Peters knew why. Whatever story Ryan had to tell, as Ryan him-self had said to Peters, it was dynamite.

The rest of the available police force, borrowed from neighboring towns and the state, were scurrying around looking for clues, surveying the road-side scene of the shooting and, as far as Sandor reckoned, trying to close the barn door after the horses had galloped away.

"You ready, Sandor?" Reynolds came up from behind, all business in front of his men.

"Ready, sir," Jordan said.

*   *   *

The place rented by Jimmy Ryan was a tiny house set back from an unpaved lane that shunted off an access road leading to Route 32. As Reynolds had explained, it was not far from the spot where Collins and Peters had been shot. Jordan simply nodded, realizing he and Dan had only been a few minutes and a couple of miles late.

The dirt driveway kicked up a cloud of dust in the wake of Reynolds' cruiser. Two troopers were waiting on the small front porch as Reynolds and Sandor got out of the car.

"This is Sandor," the Captain said, "guy that helped Jack."

The officers said hello, then offered their thanks.

"So, what have we got here?" Jordan asked.

Neither of the Troopers replied.

"Let's have a look," Reynolds said as he led him inside. The two officers remained outside, on guard at the door.

Dusk was replacing day, and there wasn't much in the way of lighting in the main room. All the same, Jordan made out the scene immediately. Ryan's body had been removed hours ago, but the chair was there, as were the fragments of rope that had bound Ryan to the wooden seat. Splotches of dried blood stained an oval loom rug.

"Nice, eh?"

Jordan nodded. "I guess you got photos of all this. Before they took him out, I mean."

The Captain responded with a withering look, and Sandor was reminded again of what sort of commanding officer Reynolds must have been.

"Sorry," Jordan said politely. "Of course you did."

"Several rolls, a videotape and a digital camera, if you care to know."

"Right."

Sandor and Reynolds slowly circled the chair in which Ryan had died, viewing the scene from all angles, each of them envisioning what had happened there.

"No sign of forced entry," Reynolds told him, "but around here, who locks the door? Even so, I get the feeling he knew these guys. No sign of a struggle, no overturned tables, no nothing."

"Maybe. They might have walked in, guns drawn, that sort of thing. Taken him before he had a chance to react."

Reynolds grunted. "Main question is, what was the point? Look at this place." He extended his arm like he was displaying the second-place prize on a game show. "What the hell would anyone want? No sign that the place was searched, either. Unless he had the Hope diamond sitting on the table there, what would they be looking for?"

"Information," Jordan said.

The two men stared at each other for a moment.

"Only thing that makes sense."

Reynolds nodded. "They beat the hell out of him, that was obvious if you saw the poor bastard."

"Rule out sodium pentathol."

"What's that?"

"Some of the guys at the barracks, talking about the autopsy."

"Yeah," Reynolds agreed. "You don't pump a guy full of truth serum and then beat hell out of him."

"That was my thought. Autopsy will tell that tale."

"So, not much to see, right?"

Jordan moved slowly around the small room that encompassed the main area of the modest house, the living room, dining area and the entry to the kitchen. "I guess your men have searched the place," he said over his shoulder.

"Thoroughly."

"Find anything interesting?" he asked as he took it all in, looking for something that might be out of place.

"Nothing," the Captain said. "Except one item we thought was odd."

Sandor turned towards him. "I'm all ears."

"This off the record?" Reynolds asked with a wry smile.

"Only if you insist."

The Captain came towards him. They were standing face to face at the doorway to the small kitchen. "One of those electronic tickets," he said in a quiet voice, "the kind you get off a computer. Hidden in his dresser. Plane ticket to Paris."

"As in France?"

"Strange thing. For a guy living in this kind of a shack, I mean. First Class ticket, leaving tomorrow. With a hotel reservation."

"Going back," Jordan said to himself.

"What's that?"

"Nothing. So you tracked it down?"

"We did. The ticket was booked in the name of James McHugh. Hotel reservation also in the name of James McHugh."

"I'm beginning to see a trend. And you already took the man's prints and ran them through . . ."

"The federal databank."

"Don't tell me."

"Our friend James Ryan was actually one James McHugh."

Sandor did not appear surprised, a fact not lost on Reynolds. "I can tell by the look in your eyes it gets better than that, Captain."

Reynolds nodded. "You remember, I told you I did a check on you, saw how they blocked out a chunk of your service."

"Right."

"This McHugh—all I got on him was name, rank and social security number. Finished business."

"Uh huh. So you know we're not talking about a robbery."

"Not even close." Reynolds hesitated. "And something tells me you knew that before we got here."

Sandor gave no answer to that, not yet. "And when you brought McHugh's name up on the computer?"

"I'm sure all the bells and whistles were going off down in Washington."

"That's right."

The two troopers at the door were straining to hear the discussion but missing most of it, as Sandor and Reynolds got quieter with each exchange.

"Sounds like the feds'll be coming in on this in no time," Jordan said.

"I believe that's affirmative," the Captain said. "So what say we cut the bullshit and you tell me what you know about all this?"

Jordan shook his head. "Not any more than you do."

The Captain leaned even closer now. "That's not good enough, son. I've been up front with you. Now why don't you tell something I don't know?"

"Like what?"

"Look, I got one man in the morgue, two men in the hospital and, by some incredible coincidence, you and the dead man turn out to be some sort of federal spooks, all this in a town where six speeding tickets in a week is a crime wave."

"What a mess," Jordan said, doing his best to sound sympathetic.

"That's it? I give you everything I got before the g-men show, and all I get from you is that this is a fucking mess?"

Sandor stared at him without speaking.

"You said something about him going back. What makes you think this guy was ever in France? You told me you never met him."

"And I never did. But I never said I didn't know a thing or two about him."

"Which makes you better informed than I am right now."

"I'm not trying to be difficult, Captain. There are some things I have to do first."

"Me too, like investigating a murder and two attempts. You going to help me or not?"

"Give me a little time and I'll help you any way I can."

Reynolds stared into Jordan's eyes, the younger man's unblinking gaze a match for his own. "Something tells me you're gonna need a friend around here pretty soon. You took care of Jack, you're entitled to something for that, but don't count on it for too much. I can get unfriendly real fast, I think you're jerking me around."

"All right," Jordan said, "let me sort some of this out first, then I'll get back to you. Off the record, right?'

"That's the deal."

Jordan looked around the room again, as if he might have missed something. "What did you say the name of that hotel in Paris was?"

Reynolds smiled. "I didn't say." The Captain pulled a note pad from his pocket. "Something called the Pas de Tour," he said, butchering the pronunciation so badly that he spelled it out. "Mean anything to you?"

"Just that your French is as bad as mine," Jordan replied with a smile.

Reynolds frowned. "Anything else?"

"Not yet," Jordan said. "Not yet."

SEVEN

It was dark by the time Reynolds had one of his men give Sandor a ride back to Dan Peters' house. Jordan was exhausted and, figuring the young officer knew less of what was going on than he did, he managed to keep their discussion brief and close to the surface.

Jordan thanked the trooper as he dropped him off, grateful to be done with everyone and everything for now. It had been a long, draining day and, alone in Dan's small home, he realized how tired he really was. He decided to sleep there, then get an early start for home the next morning. He fixed himself a ham and cheese sandwich and, as he was finishing a second bottle of Dan's Budweiser, he telephoned his friend Bill Sternlich in New York.

"You heard about it already?" Jordan replied to his friend's greeting.

"Are you kidding? You're a hot item, involved in a shooting upstate and all this hero crap."

"Damn, I knew it."

"What's the big deal? You get your fifteen minutes in the spotlight, then everyone can forget your name again."

"Fame is cruel."

"I wouldn't know. I just toil in the service of others."

"Yeah, in the service of the biased media."

Sternlich was an articles editor for the New York Times. He and Sandor met a decade ago, when Bill was on assignment to the Washington bureau and Jordan was still working for the government. Now they were both in New York, their friendship having stood the test of years and the obvious differences between them.

Professional considerations sometimes made it an uneasy alliance. Jordan could never reveal much about his work for the government, and what little he shared with Bill generally could not be printed. That was the first irony of their friendship. The second was the disparity between Sternlich's liberal beliefs, engendered so relentlessly by the editorial leanings of his newspaper, and Sandor's own individualistic views, which would better be expressed by Ayn Rand than anything on the Times Op-Ed pages. The final irony was Jordan's abrupt departure from the Agency and his subsequent decision to enlist in the Fourth Estate, albeit on a freelance basis. Sternlich had given him some help, even getting one of Sandor's pieces published in the paper's Sunday Magazine section.

The main point for Jordan and Bill was that they were friends, which meant something to each of them.

"You really okay?"

"I'm fine," Jordan said. "My friend Dan Peters took a bullet in the side. The trooper was hit pretty hard. You probably know all that. We were lucky to get out."

"That's what I understand."

Neither man said anything for a moment.

"I need a favor, Bill."

Their recent history was a bit lopsided in the area of favors given and received.

"Hey, I'm totally shocked," Sternlich said. "A favor? Like, when was the last time you called to ask me to lunch? Or just to say hello?"

"I need some information on a James McHugh. Likely to be classified, you'll probably need to go through one of your government sources."

"Will I?"

"You'll have to move fast, though, before it comes out that the Jimmy Ryan that was murdered up here today was really Jimmy McHugh."

"That right?"

"Yes. You've got the scoop. Print it right after you get me the dope on this guy."

"And why, may I be so bold to ask, don't you just call one of your old cronies in Langley to get this, whatever, this deep background information?"

"Even guys I trust, now that I'm involved here, they'll balk. You said it yourself. I'm already connected to the shooting."

"Mind if I ask, then, why I would want to do this?"

"Who knows? Full length article?"

"My by-line or yours?"

"I'll flip you for it. Come on, Bill, I need help."

Sternlich issued a long, theatrical sigh into the phone. "I don't know what I can do, but I'll take a run at it."

"You're a pal."

"And what am I supposed to be looking for?"

"I'm not sure, not exactly. See if you can find out where he's been the past couple of years, check out his government service. Get addresses, identification numbers, the usual rundown."

"Uh huh." Jordan could tell that Sternlich was making notes now, a good sign. "And Bill, see if he's got any connection to Paris."

"Paris?"

"I'm coming back tomorrow, call you in the morning at the office."

"I may have to trade favors to get anything, you understand that? You'll owe me for this one."

"I need it Billy. I wouldn't ask if I didn't."

*   *   *

Jordan left Woodstock early the next day and drove south, the bright October sun rising to his left as he headed towards New York City. He guided his aging Land Rover along the sweeping curves and extended straightaways of the Thruway.

Whatever Jimmy McHugh had known, his gruesome death was proof of the importance of what he intended to share. His murderers had inflicted a sadistic beating and, when there was nothing left for McHugh to save, as he sat strapped in that wooden chair facing certain death, he would probably have done anything to spare himself those final moments of pain or degradation, revealing what his murderers wanted to know. That would have included his intention to meet with Sandor and Peters.

Jordan's mind raced as he drove on in silence, the radio and cell phone turned off. He gazed out at the road ahead, his senses keener than they had been in more than a year, since he walked away from a career he had once so believed in that he repeatedly risked his own life to pursue its ends. He felt the familiar sense of that danger again, realizing that he would need to conquer his fears when faced with a reason worthy of putting everything in jeopardy. Circumstances had forced him to rejoin the battle, and he was determined to return on his own terms.

*   *   *

He arrived in the city, pulled his car up to the curb in the "No Parking" zone in front of the old brownstone where he lived on West 76th Street, then placed an expired Press Card in the windshield. He ran up the front stairs and, grabbing his mail, opened the front door to the building, then walked up to his third floor apartment, riffling through the bills and advertisements as he went.

He got to his apartment, unlocked the door and stepped inside.

The place was in shambles. Jordan left the door open as he slowly entered, his nerves on alert as he placed his mail on the foyer table, warily stepping forward into the living room. It appeared that everything had been turned inside out. His brown, tufted leather couch was sliced open, the brass and glass cocktail table shoved against the wall, two chairs and a mahogany cabinet overturned, the contents of drawers dumped in piles, even the Oriental rug lifted and yanked to the side.

Sandor moved cautiously to the bedroom. If anything, it looked even worse. The mattress was slashed, closets and dresser taken apart, clothing scattered all over the floor. The second bedroom, which he used as his office, was a disaster. His filing cabinets had been emptied, the leather chair knocked over, his antique roll-top desk searched, papers strewn across the room.

He remained quiet, his movements studied. He could not be certain the intruder had gone. He checked the bathroom, the small kitchen, then returned to the living room where he looked behind the upended couch. There was no place that had not been invaded, but at least he was sure now that he was alone. He went back to the bedroom, stepped inside the closet, reached up to a hidden compartment, above the top shelf, and pulled away a false panel. He was relieved to find the contents there, including a box containing his small arsenal of weapons, from which he removed an automatic pistol.

Jordan took a deep breath, relieved to have the familiar stock of the beefy Smith & Wesson .45 in hand. He pulled back the slide, drawing a live cartridge into place. The sharp metallic sound provided a measure of comfort, another echo from his past. He walked back to the foyer and closed the front door. Then he returned to the living room, righted a chair, and sat down to make a call. As he reached for the telephone, he saw the line had been cut.

"Sonuvabitch," he said aloud.

EIGHT

Jordan stood up, still holding the automatic, and went to the bathroom. He placed the gun on the vanity counter, then leaned over the sink and splashed cold water on his face. He had a look in the mirror, staring at himself for a moment, studying his dark features, preparing himself.

He toweled off, then went to his bedroom to sort through the clutter of shirts and trousers that were scattered across the floor. He had shaved and showered at Dan's earlier this morning, but was still wearing the clothes from yesterday. He stopped for a moment, thought about using his cell phone to make a call, then decided against it. Too easy for them to intercept the call, if they were already watching him. Whoever "they" were.

He picked up a pair of gray slacks, a long sleeved black polo sweater and found his favorite black loafers, quickly changed, pulled on his leather zipper jacket and stuffed the Smith & Wesson in the waistband of his slacks at the small of his back. He left the mess behind and headed to a local tavern. He knew they wouldn't be open yet, but the owner was a friend and would let Sandor in to use the telephone.

Jordan's first call was to Sternlich.

"How bad?"

"Like a small tornado ran through my place."

"Call the cops, Jordan."

"I don't think so. Not yet, at least."

"What are you waiting for?"

"I'm not sure, but I had enough of the police yesterday. And I don't need another appearance on the AP website. Not now. I've got to sort this out first."

"And what happens when these visitors come back?"

"I don't know yet. Maybe I can ask them to clean up."

39

"I think you ought to make yourself scarce for a while."

"The idea had crossed my mind. What've you found out for me?"

"Nothing yet. Jesus, I'm a reporter, not a magician."

"You're not even a reporter anymore. You're an editor, remember? Use your connections and get me some answers."

"I'll work on it. Please call the police."

"Maybe I will," Jordan told him. "First I'm going to see Beth."

"Beth?"

"We have a lunch date. Thought maybe I should keep it, no?"

"Why not," Sternlich said in frustration. "Give her my best."

Jordan's next call was to Reynolds. He was transferred three times before he finally got through to the Captain.

"I have some news for you from down here," he said, then told him what he found when he returned home. "Please don't tell me to call the locals. You and I know this is no ordinary B and E."

Reynolds couldn't disagree. "You should have the place photographed, dusted for prints."

"I know, I haven't touched much, believe me, but I'd prefer to put that official tap dance on hold for a little while."

"Reason?"

"I'm getting enough attention right now. Might be better if these clowns don't know I've been to the apartment yet."

"That assumes you're not being watched. And these are not clowns, Sandor, you know that already. I've got to advise you that you need to report this. Off the record, I never heard a thing about it."

"Agreed, and thanks. How're the patients doing this morning?"

"Early report, they're both stable. Your friend is in better shape than Collins."

Jordan gave no response.

"Look, you may be safer up here. We've got men all over the place."

Sandor smiled at the notion, and at the paternal tone of Reynold's suggestion. He knew it was not the Captain's natural style. "Any other reason I should come back? More mug shots, maybe?"

Reynolds paused. "Feds are coming in on it this morning. Wanted to know why I didn't hold you overnight as a material witness."

"I see. Who is it, FBI?"

Reynolds chuckled. "So far it is, if you know what I mean."

"I know exactly what you mean." So far, in other words, the feds weren't saying anything. "I'll try to get back there later this afternoon."

*   *   *

Dan Peters had dozed fitfully in his hospital bed, the discomfort of his wound and the intrusions of doctors and nurses throughout the night making it difficult to sleep. All of this was complicated by the confluence of memories and dreams that kept his mind spinning, awake or asleep. The memories would not go away.

It was morning now, but that made no difference. He was still trying to sleep.

His eyes opened slightly when yet another young doctor came into the room and stood over his bed, adjusting the intravenous apparatus that fed a steady flow of glucose solution and antibiotics. Peters closed his eyes again, not seeing the man inject a new substance into the tube that ran from the plastic sack of fluid into his arm.

"Have a good rest," the man said, and Peters was happy to hear the suggestion. Maybe they were going to leave him alone for while.

The man walked out of the room, nodding at a nurse who happened by as he made his way down the long corridor. He greeted her with a friendly smile and said, "Good morning."

It was clear she did not recognize him, and she responded with an uncertain look as he passed. When he turned the corner at the end of the hallway, he saw two uniformed policeman near the elevator. He stopped, made a show of looking at some papers he was holding, then made a gesture with his hand, as if he had forgotten something. He turned back, stepping quickly towards the entrance to the stairway.

One of the troopers had looked towards him, just before he disappeared around the turn. He said to the other officer, "I think I'll take a walk."

The trooper hurried to the end of the hall, but the man was gone. The officer took a quick look into Peters' room, but there was nothing unusual there. Peters appeared to be asleep. The nurse came out of another patient's room and the trooper asked if she had just seen a doctor in Peters' room.

"Yes," she told him, "I saw him coming out of there, just now."

"Did you know him? The doctor, I mean?"

She shook her head. "No," she said. "I don't think I've ever seen him before."

"Call a doctor right away, have Peters checked out," the officer said, then grabbed his radio and broke into a trot, heading back for his partner. "All stations. We've got some suspicious activity on three," he reported into the walkie-talkie. "Cover the lobby and check the elevators for an unidentified man, dressed like a doctor. Five ten, Caucasian, brown hair." The best he could do after a brief glimpse.

The young man they were looking for was running down the interior staircase, removing his white lab coat as he went, the syringe still in the pocket. He dropped the coat to the floor as he neared the door to the lobby. Then he removed the wig he was wearing, his blond crew-cut in stark contrast to the longer, darker hairpiece. He adjusted the brown sport coat he had on underneath the white jacket and put on a pair of eyeglasses. As two troopers were responding to the radio alert from upstairs, he stepped calmly through the lobby. He did not look in the direction of the police as they positioned themselves in front of the elevators. Three other troopers were running to cover the stairwells, but it was too late.

Dan Peters' murderer had already reached the exit, stepped outside the building, then moved quickly to a waiting car that sped him away.

NINE

Jordan arrived at the Algonquin early for his lunch date with Beth. He made himself comfortable in one of the faded armchairs and settled down to wait. He enjoyed the serenity of this old hotel, pleased for the moment to wrap himself in the solace of plush cushions and a stiff drink. He appreciated the connection between this venerated room and the literary lights of days past, which his friend Bill Sternlich found amusing.

Sandor was lost in thought, plotting his next move, then shaking his head at a bad idea, when he heard, "Well, if it isn't our celebrity from the hills."

Her voice startled him. He hadn't noticed her come up from behind. *You're out of practice,* he warned himself.

He turned, then said, "How long have you been there?"

"Boy, that's some greeting," she replied. "I just got here." She looked down at the table. "Whiskey? Kind of heavy before lunch."

"Tennessee whiskey," he said as he stood, then gently kissed her cheek. He caught a hint of perfume, recognizing her fragrance, wondering why he hadn't noticed it as she came up behind him. The scent evoked a flash of remembrances, her soft, warm body next to his, the moments of laughter and anger and passion, and ultimately the realization again of why it was so difficult to let her go. "It's early, I know, but it's already been a rough day. Sit down."

Beth Sharrow took the chair opposite his, easing herself gracefully into the seat. She was always graceful. "Bourbon," she said thoughtfully. "I think I'll go with something a little less potent."

For a moment he lost himself in the hazel eyes, the perpetually healthy complexion that always seemed to carry the glow of recent exercise, her confident but curious smile and the auburn hair that provided a delicate frame to her even features.

"You look like you're in a trance," Beth said. "Not wearing your hero's laurels very well, are you?"

"My heroics are yesterday's news, unfortunately. Boys in the office having fun with this?"

"I wouldn't know."

"Come on, Beth." He had met her years before, on a visit to the New York office of the CIA where they housed analysts, communications experts and a huge retinue of computer geeks. Jordan thought Beth was one of the best inside analysts in the Agency.

"Al Tamucci started a pool," she admitted, referring to one of the computer tekkies he knew.

"For what? For when I'm going to buy it?"

"No. For when you're coming back to work for the Company."

"Not likely," he said. He followed that with a quick shake of his head and a faraway look, as if deciding whether to share something he wasn't ready to say.

Beth recognized the look. "What is it?"

He hesitated, then said, "Someone broke into my apartment."

"What?"

"I didn't want to tell you on the phone."

Beth's smile melted into a look of concern. "When?"

"Not sure. Yesterday, last night, early this morning. They wrecked the place, whenever it happened."

An elderly waiter in a dark, red waistcoat came by and asked if the young lady would care for a cocktail.

"Uh, a white wine, please. Chardonnay, if you have that."

"White wine," Jordan teased. "Here, at the Algonquin?"

"Please, Jordan, tell me what happened."

"All right, but Dorothy Parker must be spinning in her grave."

The waiter was still standing there.

Jordan glanced down at his glass. "I'm fine for now," he said, and the man trudged off to get Beth her wine.

"I don't know what happened," Jordan told her. "I don't even know if it's related to yesterday."

"That's nonsense and you know it. There are no such things as coincidences, isn't that what you taught me."

"Did I say that?"

"Why you?" she asked.

"I don't know yet."

"I thought the problem upstate was just . . . "

"Bad timing? Wrong place at the wrong time?"

She shook her head. "I wish you didn't look so amused."

Jordan took a swallow of the caramel colored liquor. "I'm not amused," he said, "believe me. You should see my living room."

Beth searched his dark, brown eyes for some sign of fear, but there was none. There was only that look of fascination that had always infuriated her so. "What did the police say?" she asked.

"I haven't called the police yet."

"Why?"

"I will, but not yet. There are some things I want to find out first."

"Jordan, you've got to call the police."

"What's the difference when I call? My couch will still be a goner when I get there tomorrow."

"Tomorrow?"

"I thought going back today might be a bad idea." He knew he would go back, but figured it was one less thing she would have to worry about.

"You're right," she agreed, then paused. "You can stay at my place. If you'd like."

"Thanks." He lifted his glass again, but didn't drink. "I wouldn't want to interfere with any of your plans."

"For godssake, Jordan."

He smiled at the sudden flash of anger. "Thanks, really, but I should go upstate today and see Danny, check out what they've found so far. I'm not sure what I'll be doing after that. Maybe I should call an interior decorator."

She shook her head again in that disapproving way he found both charming and annoying. "You know, Jordan, I'd feel a lot better if you seemed less entertained and a little more concerned."

The waiter returned with her wine, which provided Jordan momentary escape from her critical gaze.

"Believe me," he said as the waiter ambled away, "I'm concerned. For starters, I got shot at yesterday. Now my apartment looks like a bomb hit it." He held up his glass and said, "Here's to safe roads ahead," then waited her out until she gave up staring at him and took up her wine. They touched glasses and he drank off a fair sized gulp of his Jack Daniels. "Hey, come on, it's bad luck if you don't drink after a toast."

She sipped some of the Chardonnay, then replaced the glass on the small, wooden cocktail table. "You're not a field agent any more, Jordan. You're not an agent at all. You're flying solo on this, unless you come in."

"That's not happening."

"All right. So tell me the truth. What were they looking for in your apartment? You?"

"I don't think they were searching for me when they slashed my mattress open."

She frowned. "What, then?"

"I really don't know. Papers or something, that's my guess. Something I don't actually have, if you want to know."

"Papers having to do with what?"

"That's what I need to figure out."

"Why not let me take this in? Let us figure it out. Stay with me for a few days, let our people do what they can do."

"I'm not ready for that yet. And you've got to consider that whoever broke in will eventually come looking for me. How safe will it be for you if I lead them to your door?"

"But you need protection. This isn't your fight anymore, Jordan."

"You may be right," he said. Then he leaned forward and took her hand in both of his, softly kissing her open palm. "With everything that's happened, I'm just glad to see you."

She took her hand back slowly. "Sure. So let's get down to it. You didn't keep our lunch date today, with everything that's happened, just to tell me how much you've missed me. What do you want?"

"Want? I wanted to see you."

Beth sighed. "All right, now you've seen me. What else?"

Jordan sat back and looked at her. "Well, you might get me some information."

*   *   *

Tafallai had been strolling in and out of the shops on Forty-Fourth Street, keeping an eye on the entrance to the Algonquin. Just a few years after the attack on Nine-Eleven, and his swarthy complexion and Arabic features aroused no special notice in New York. He was just another young man who had come to the States to make his future. He had an academic appearance, perhaps a graduate student in his mid-twenties, which was in fact the basis for his visa. His skin was olive-toned, his hair curly, long and unkempt. He was not physically imposing, standing only five foot six, slight of build, fine featured. He wore a crew neck sweater and jeans, and a tweed sport coat that hid the 9 millimeter automatic with silencer slung in a holster pulled tight against the left side of his chest.

He was milling around a small poster shop directly across the street from the hotel, pretending to browse through photos of old movie stars, when he spotted Sandor and an attractive young woman leaving the hotel. He waited as Jordan spoke to the woman, kissed her, then watched her walk off before he climbed into a taxi. Tafallai walked slowly out of the shop, just as Sandor's cab went on his way.

Rahmad's search team had made such a blasted mess of rummaging through Sandor's flat, Tafallai had to assume the place would be under surveillance by now, by local law enforcement if not some federal agency. He took out his cell phone and called his man uptown, who informed him there was still no sign of any police response.

Tafallai was surprised, but did not say so. He said he was going to follow the girl, just to see where that might lead, then he would head to Sandor's apartment.

TEN

Jordan and Beth had agreed to skip their lunch together, once he promised to see the police before returning upstate. It was another lie, of
course, and she knew it. All the same, Beth agreed to find out what she
could about James McHugh and, after a second Jack Daniels and several
handfuls of peanuts, Jordan was ready to go back to his apartment, sort
through some things, then head north. As they parted outside the Algonquin, he said he would call her later. Then he hailed a cab as Beth closed
her coat for the walk back to the office. He kissed her on the cheek, climbed
in the taxi and sped off, hoping that she or Sternlich would come up with
some sort of lead while he planned his next move.

Jordan had the cab driver let him out two blocks south of his apartment. In case the building was being watched, he wanted to survey the
area first.

The autumn afternoon carried a damp, gray chill, so he turned up his
collar and hunched his shoulders as he walked along Broadway. It was
wonderful, he mused, how a couple of drinks and the cool air had him
believing that everything would work out, that there really was not that
much to worry about. He smiled at the self-deception, knowing he needed
to clear his head for more serious considerations, pleased to be taking the
short walk.

When he approached the corner of 76th Street, he stopped and had a
look around. The sidewalk traffic seemed normal, both in volume and flow.
The first tell would have been an unusual pattern, like a man slowing down
to look in a window he shouldn't be looking in, just because that was the
shop in front of him at that moment—a women's shoe store, for instance.
Or the spinaround—where the tail decides to reverse direction rather than

stop, or even walk on past the mark. But there was nothing on Broadway that made him suspicious, so he turned onto 76th.

His street was generally quiet by New York City standards, rows of brownstones lining both sides, trees planted in pavement cut-outs, circled by short, wrought iron grating. As he turned onto his block, he strolled at an unhurried pace. Jordan saw that his Rover had not been towed away, although a parking ticket was stuck on the windshield. Then he spotted a man leaning against a railing directly across from his building. As Jordan approached, the man began walking away from him. Perhaps it was the abruptness of the move, or the purpose in his stride. Whatever the reason, Jordan knew why the man was there.

Sandor picked up his pace, but the lookout was half-way down the block and, as soon as Jordan quickened his step, the man broke into a run and disappeared around the far corner.

There was no way to catch him, not with that lead.

Jordan stopped, had another look around, then crossed the street, climbed the stairs, let himself in the building and returned to his apartment. As he unlocked the door and switched on the light, reality was illuminated in a harsh reminder of what had occurred.

He slammed the door shut and walked into the living room, slowly surveying the damage for a second time. Where looking through a cabinet would have sufficed, the drawer had been pulled out, turned upside down and then smashed. Upholstery had been slashed repeatedly, clumps of stuffing scattered all over the room. Small objects were shattered, larger ones broken into pieces. He went to his office, where the intruders had ripped through and savaged the most intimate details of his private life. His writing, letters, even personal souvenirs had been examined and destroyed. It left the apartment with an eerie coldness, as if he had himself been stripped and beaten by faceless strangers, then left there alone to suffer the indignity.

Make no mistake about it, he told himself. *These people are killers, and whatever they want, whatever they think Jimmy McHugh might have told you, they will surely kill you to get it.* He also reminded himself that the man posted across the street would tell them he had returned home.

Jordan went to the bedroom and packed his black leather overnight bag with a few articles of clothing and most of the contents he had retrieved from the hidden compartment in his closet. Right now, he needed to make a couple of calls before he left town. He was still uncertain about using the cell. He had a clean cell in the bag, but he didn't want to use that line, not yet. So he ran downstairs and knocked on his neighbor's door.

Florence Carter was an attractive, young black woman who lived directly below him, an actress of stage and screen whenever she could get the work, a waitress the rest of the time.

It was about one thirty in the afternoon, and she was home.

He told her he was having phone problems. She let him in and said he should make himself comfortable.

"You need some privacy?" she asked.

"No, I don't think so, but thanks."

She offered him something to drink, but he passed.

"Say, Florence, you didn't hear anything going on upstairs, last night, or this morning?"

She shook her head. "I was working last night. What sort of thing you mean?"

"I was away overnight, thought someone might have been in my apartment."

"In your apartment?"

"It's nothing. Just my phones are out, thought maybe there was a service guy came by or something."

"No, not that I know of. My phone is fine."

"Good. Well, I'll just be a couple of minutes."

"Take your time," she told him.

Jordan sat on her couch and picked up the cordless telephone. The first call he made was to his service. There were several messages, some from friends who had picked up the story about the shootings upstate. The most recent voicemails were from Reynolds. He had called twice in the past hour.

Jordan said, "I owe you a buck, Florence, I've got to call upstate," then began dialing.

"Don't be silly," she said as she answered the buzz of the intercom from the front door of their small building.

Jordan was listening to the phone ring somewhere in the police barracks upstate New York. He barely heard Florence's conversation over the speaker, something about a man who said he had flowers to deliver to her.

"Isn't that something," she said with a delighted laugh. "Who'd be sending me flowers today?"

"What's that?" Jordan asked over his shoulder. Then someone picked up his call. "Hello? Yes, Captain Reynolds please. Jordan Sandor calling."

"Mr. Sandor? Yes, hold on."

This time, the Captain picked up the call at once. "Sandor? I've been trying to reach you. You coming up here today?"

"I am. Should be leaving in a few minutes."

"I've got some bad news, I'm sorry to say."

"I'm listening."

Reynolds paused. "Your friend Peters is dead."

Sandor stood up, still clutching the phone. "Dead?" He kept his voice quiet, but Florence was ignoring him as she occupied herself with the prospect of her delivery. "How the hell can he be dead?"

"Doctors don't know what happened yet. They're going to do an autopsy. It appears he had a massive coronary."

"What?"

"One of my men spotted a doctor coming out of his room this morning, someone the nurse on duty had never seen before."

"Did they get him?"

"No, damnit. Whoever he was, he got away."

"Drugs?"

"Guy in forensics says his IV could've been injected with something. We should have an answer by tomorrow morning. Maybe even tonight."

"I'm coming right up."

"Good. Feds are on the scene, by the way, and anxious to speak with you."

"Naturally."

Florence was standing at her door, shaking her head, her smile widening. "Now who would send me flowers?"

As she spoke those words again, Jordan turned to her. "Jesus," he said.

"Listen Sandor," Captain Reynolds was saying, "you're in serious danger. If you get here, we can protect you."

Jordan reflected for an instant on the protection they gave Dan Peters, then he let it go. "Hold on Reynolds," he said, then he turned to the girl. "Florence, is it your birthday or something? Were you expecting flowers from someone?"

She saw the look in Sandor's eyes and her smile instantly vanished. "No, no I'm not," she replied nervously.

"Is your door locked?"

"No," she said, suddenly feeling scared and not knowing why.

"Lock it," he ordered her. "Now."

She was suddenly so frightened by the look on his face that she couldn't move, so Jordan raced across the room and bolted the door himself.

ELEVEN

Tafallai was already in the building, walking up the stairs with a bouquet of flowers in his left hand. He stopped when the metallic sound resonated in the hallway. Was her door being opened or locked?

"Captain," Jordan said into the phone, "I think I've got an unwelcome visitor on his way upstairs. I'll call you back."

"Call the police," Reynolds barked, but Jordan had already disconnected the call.

"Listen, Florence," Sandor said, "just stay cool and quiet and we'll be all right."

Florence appeared stricken, without knowing why. "This has something to do with last night, right? Your apartment? The telephones, like you were asking?"

"Just stay calm, we'll be fine." Even as he spoke the words, he remembered.

The look on his face froze her again. "Jordan, what is it?"

"My door," he said. "I left my goddamned door open. He'll know I'm someplace else in the building." Jordan also remembered the .45 he left upstairs in the leather bag. He cursed himself—a year in from the field and as rusty as an old hinge. "You have a gun here?"

"What? No, I don't have a gun. Look..."

"Be quiet and listen. This guy who says he has flowers, he may be looking for me. He probably rang your buzzer to get into the building. One out of eight apartments, right? And who else is home during the day? If he was really bringing you flowers he'd be knocking on your door by now."

Her face was taut with fear.

"Now take the phone, go into the bathroom, lock the door and call the police. Tell them there's a burglary in progress. Tell them the man is armed. Give them the address. Then get in your bathtub and keep down till I tell you to come out. Got it?"

Florence nodded. She took the phone and punched in 9 1 1 as she hurried into the bathroom.

Tafallai laid down the flowers, his hand gripping the butt of his automatic, drawing it carefully from the holster, the barrel lengthened by a silencer. He was standing just two steps below Florence's landing, having stopped there when he heard her lock turn.

He advanced to the head of the staircase, keeping low to ensure that he could not be seen from the peephole in her door or the facing door of the other apartment on this floor. He stayed in his crouch and waited. There was nothing but silence throughout the building.

Tafallai trusted his instincts, relying on his ability to evaluate danger, and to survive. Would this woman unbolt her door but not open it? Perhaps. Maybe she was waiting for him to knock. Or, he wondered, had she bolted the door shut? And if so, why?

He had planned to deliver the flowers, with a note from 'Your Secret Admirer'. Then he would begin downstairs as she closed the door behind him. She would have no suspicion of him, no cause to retain even the vaguest recollection of his appearance as she took the flowers and read the note. When her door shut, he would head back up to Sandor's apartment, dispose of his target, then return to the street and become lost in the crowds.

He had tried two apartments before buzzing Florence Carter. Single or married, old or young, he knew that women generally abandon caution at the prospect of a flower delivery. The bouquet was his entry ticket into the building.

But now something felt wrong. His man had reported Sandor's return that morning, which meant Sandor had discovered his apartment had been vandalized. But no police had been at the building the entire day. Why hadn't he reported the break-in? Then Sandor met the woman on Forty-fourth Street and returned here again. Yet still there were no police.

The sound of the dead-bolt persuaded Tafallai to move swiftly. His intuition told him to forego the delivery and head directly to Sandor's flat. He turned back for the bouquet, using the flowers to hide the automatic, just in case the woman opened the door. He would tell her he had trouble finding her door. Tafallai nodded to himself. This was the move.

Florence Carter stood anxiously in the sanctuary of her cramped bathroom, worrying in the silence, expecting a sound, an action, a voice. She was whispering into her cordless phone, urging the operator to help.

Jordan was standing at Florence's front door, straining to hear something. He felt the sensations he knew well, the dryness of mouth, moist hands and pounding chest. For a moment he wondered if his imagination had run wild. He told himself he would have quite a laugh over this one, when it turned out to be nothing more than a flower delivery. But if someone was delivering flowers, where was he?

Jordan looked through the peephole and saw nothing.

Tafallai climbed far enough up the next flight of stairs to see the landing. There was Sandor's door, standing ajar. Had Sandor left his apartment, leaving his door open, obviously not expecting to be gone for more than a few moments? Or was it a trap? Where was he? Somewhere in the building? Or was he still inside?

Tafallai crept to the head of the stairwell and put the flowers down. He extended his weapon slightly, keeping it close to his side where he could not be easily disarmed by a sweeping move. He had been warned, when assigned this mission by Rahmad, that Sandor had military and field experience. This was not innocent prey, this was a past professional. But no attack came as Tafallai cautiously and efficiently moved inside and searched the apartment, stepping lightly, still aware that Sandor might be there waiting.

But it did not take long for him to confirm his initial guess. Sandor was not there. He spotted the leather bag on the bed, had a quick look inside, smiling at the sight of the automatic. Wherever Sandor was, he was most likely unarmed.

Tafallai now realized that Sandor's flat was directly above Florence Carter's. Only scant minutes had elapsed since he heard the bolt turn on the floor below. His instincts told him that Sandor was in the apartment Tafallai had selected for his means to enter the building, which he would now turn to his advantage. He picked up the bouquet, left Sandor's apartment and moved back down the stairs.

Jordan listened intently as one footstep followed the next through his apartment above. For a fleeting moment, he thought about bolting from Florence's apartment and making for the street. Unarmed, however, with such a slight lead, he would be too easy a target, especially if the man upstairs had backup outside.

He heard the faint sound of the steps above him leave his apartment and head back down the stairs.

Once this man saw the apartment door was left open, he would have to assume Jordan was somewhere else in the building. Hiding. Or in flight. Jordan considered his options, loathe to do nothing while waiting for the police. It was the obvious move, but not Jordan's style. He wanted to know who this man was, to confront him, to see if he was one of the shooters from yesterday. Jordan knew that once the sirens came wailing down the street, that opportunity would be lost.

But the man was certainly armed. So Jordan stood by the door and waited and listened and struggled to come up with a way to protect Florence and effect his own escape.

Tafallai crept quietly down the steps, resuming his crouch, until he was in the middle of the landing. He reached up quickly and, using the flowers to muffle the sound, shattered the small overhead light fixture with a swipe of his Glock 9 mm, the end of the silencer sending small pieces of the fine glass to the floor, bathing the landing in a shadowy darkness. He then began knocking on Florence Carter's door.

"Miss Carter. I have your flowers, miss." The accent was foreign, the voice sure and unhurried.

There was no response.

"Miss Carter. It's the man from the flower shop." He knocked again.

Jordan heard the sound of the light bulb breaking. A quick look through the peephole revealed nothing but darkness. Now he and this man were alone, separated only by the door and the advantage the attacker most certainly held in his hand. Who knew how long it would take before the police got there at this time of day? Even with sirens blaring, the traffic would be a mess. It could be ten minutes or more. It might as well be days. Jordan considered turning the bolt and yanking the door open, but the door opened in, not out, which would give the other man the edge if Jordan was going to take a run at him.

"Miss Carter, I cannot just leave the flowers here." The voice betrayed a growing impatience. "You must sign for them." Tafallai knocked again, then grabbed the knob and gave it a short, firm twist. The woman who had buzzed him into the building was not answering, which meant he was right. She was not alone in the apartment—she was in there with Jordan Sandor.

Jordan watched as the knob jimmied back and forth. Then there was a loud crash as Tafallai slammed his heel against the door. Tafallai wanted Sandor standing right in front of him, bracing the door shut. He gave a second hard kick, then a third, intending to bring Jordan into the line of fire as he followed the third kick with three shots, rounds spitting though the silencer and splintering their way into the wood surface of the door.

Jordan lunged to the side, on his knees, his body straining to keep the door secure against another series of thrusting kicks. The door had a fireproof metal insert that reinforced it, and so far it kept the bullets from tearing through. Jordan, however, was not about to bet his life on it holding out.

Tafallai fired two more shots, this time targeting the lock, the bullets caroming so loudly off the brass that Florence heard the screeching sound and uttered a scream from the bathroom, provoking Tafallai to spend his last four shots in the nine-round clip. The old door held fast.

Sandor adjusted his position, mindful of what might come next. The man might have explosives, or he might change to armor piercing shells that could rip through. He listened, the momentary silence more frightening than the fusillade that had come before.

Tafallai replaced the clip in his automatic and fired another series of shots. He cursed loudly, knowing that for now he had failed. He had wasted too much time, performed too haphazardly. Police sirens could be heard in the distance, and whether or not they were coming for him, he would not take the risk.

He fired two more shots at the center of the door, then ran to the stairs, past the flowers that lay there, replacing the Glock in its holster before he strode onto the street, disappearing around the corner into the cold afternoon just before a New York City police squad car arrived on the scene.

TWELVE

Less than thirty minutes later, Mahmoud al-Rahmad was seated behind the large, polished rosewood desk in an opulent Park Avenue office he used while in New York. He was glaring at his two aides.

"Perhaps you are correct, sir," said his younger associate, "but Tafallai believes it is only a temporary delay."

Rahmad shook his head. "There are no delays in such matters. There is only failure." His ebony eyes flashed with anger. "And where is this Sandor now? Who has he spoken to? Who is he meeting with? It could be too late already. Wherever he goes, he will certainly not return to his home now, he will seek refuge elsewhere."

"Yes sir, but Tafallai believes we will be able to find him."

Rahmad responded with a bitter smile, his young aide reacting by shifting uneasily in his seat. "And how can that be, my friend? Tafallai has failed at the simplest of assignments, and now wants to conduct a manhunt, is that it? I assure you it will be at his expense, in every sense."

The older assistant, who was leaning on a credenza off to the side, spoke up now. "Tafallai tells us he has a lead on this man's whereabouts."

"Ah. Through what divine intervention?"

"Sandor met with a woman today, sir. Tafallai saw them together. They were very friendly. Tafallai believes he will be successful following that lead. He wants permission to proceed."

"Tafallai should have acted when he saw them together."

"Perhaps so, Rahmad, but the risks were great, and the opportunity did not present itself."

"The opportunity did not present itself," Rahmad mocked him. "Opportunities are created, they do not come gift-wrapped my dear man." He stood and turned away from them, looking out his window to Park

Avenue below. "Risks," he said, still not facing them. "Risks to whom? To our friend Tafallai?" He turned back to them. "Proceed, yes by all means proceed, because the stakes have risen here. We have loose ends that need to be clipped."

The senior aide waited. "Sir?" he finally asked.

"This man Sandor, do you know who he is?"

"No sir. We had his apartment searched. He appears to have no office. He had various articles on political issues concerning . . . "

Rahmad bared his upper teeth. "Forget his papers, you fool. The man was a government operative. Tafallai knew that."

The aide blinked. "Sir?"

"Sandor served in the U. S. military, was assigned to the intelligence service, then worked for the CIA until a year ago." Rahmad paused. "Don't look so impressed at my depth of knowledge. We know about Sandor because he worked for Mr. Traiman."

Vincent Traiman was the man to whom Rahmad reported, a former American agent, now working for al-Qaeda, who was presently hiding in North Africa. Like Sandor, Traiman had been in the United States military, then worked for the CIA. In his final assignment for the Agency, before his defection, he served as Sandor's field supervisor.

In his tenure with Central Intelligence, Traiman was known to be both resourceful and ruthless, a determined man who inspired apprehension from subordinate and superior members alike. Those fears were vindicated four years ago when he betrayed the Agency and his country, turned rogue, and disappeared into Libya carrying a backpack filled with non-sequential hundred dollar bills, a series of numbered Swiss accounts and a folder full of illegal arms deals. He also had a notebook containing the names and address of American contacts and undercover agents throughout the Middle East, just for insurance. His intention to turn traitor was some time in the making.

Traiman was a man with a pragmatic sense of history. He understood that the promise of socialism around the world had been revealed as another Big Lie, not even having lasted the prior century. Traiman had witnessed the triumph of freedom and capitalism up close, as the Soviet Union fell, the Iron Curtain was torn away and the bloc of repressed, satellite nations were left to regain their dignity and autonomy. But then, Arafat, Qaddafi, Saddam Hussein and the leaders of al-Qaeda preached a community of Arab brotherhood, and Traiman saw the coming of new world order.

He realized that only the naïve and uninformed could possibly believe the concentration of wealth enjoyed by the oil rich Mideastern nations would be shared in a Pan-Arabic vision. Dictatorships, monarchies and elite oligarchies ruled the region. There was no real hope for the struggling, suffering masses. There was oppression, starvation and tyranny, all wrapped in the name of Allah and suffocated in the narcotic of religious and ethnic fervor.

Traiman saw an opportunity, and sold out his own country to reap the benefits of the myth being perpetrated by the extreme Islamics. Up to recent times, these Arab nations were bit players on the global economic stage. As the need for oil expanded exponentially, their influence grew, and they began to promote their own Twenty-First century version of world domination. Power through the control of energy, through the intimidation of their own people and through the exportation of terror abroad. None of the princes, generals and statesmen from these countries, or the mercenaries they hired, suffered the deprivation or self-sacrifice they advocated for their zealous constituents. The ideology they espoused was nothing more than a device to satisfy their own greed. It was not a new theme, but there were far-reaching implications in a world that had shrunk through technology, advanced arms and nuclear proliferation.

Traiman recognized the chance he was given, after a tour of duty in Saudi Arabia where he made contacts that sustained him in his efforts to build a force of professional assassins.

As part of his departure strategy, Traiman arranged for the murder of his top agent, Jordan Sandor, knowing that once Traiman's defection was confirmed, Jordan would be the first to come after him. Rather than risk becoming the target of the most talented operative in the CIA's counter-terrorism unit, he attempted a pre-emptive strike. That plot failed, but Traiman had already vanished behind a wall of Wahhabi protection. A couple of years later, Traiman engineered an incursion in Bahrain that, as a bonus, drew the involvement of Sandor. Once again, though, his former charge escaped unharmed. Now, after years in the paid service of al-Qaeda, having coordinated a number of small attacks in Israel and Western Europe, he was preparing a terrorist assault for which he was to be handsomely compensated, and only a few of his closest associates had any idea of the magnitude of the personal rewards he would receive.

He was a man who gave new meaning to words like mercenary and traitor. He was also a man whose existence the Agency could not afford to publicly acknowledge, but who occupied a spot on the covert most-wanted lists compiled by the CIA, MI6 and the Mossad. He was wanted, as they say, dead or alive.

Rahmad's senior aide was staring at him. "You mean, when Mr. Traiman was still with . . . "

"Yes," Rahmad said. "When Mr. Traiman was still with U. S. intelligence, Sandor was one of his subordinates. As soon as his name was mentioned in the news reports, we received word to proceed with extreme caution. Tafallai was warned." He leaned over and picked up a file lying on his desk, holding it up for effect. "Sandor, Jordan, United States Army, Foreign Service after that." He looked up. "This is not some bumbling reporter." He slapped the file down. "This man is an American spy."

*   *   *

While Mahmoud al-Rahmad pieced together Sandor's history and planned to eliminate his future, Jordan was working hard to get out of New York City.

Once he heard the shooter run downstairs, he let Florence Carter out of her bathroom, managing to calm her enough to explain that they were now safe. It's all over, he told her, the man is gone and help is on the way. He said he was going upstairs to check his apartment, but she grabbed his arm, her grip tight enough to leave marks on his wrist. She insisted that he remain right there until the police arrived.

For reasons he could not explain to her, Jordan wanted no part of the local authorities, not now. His friend Dan Peters was dead, someone was now trying to kill him, and Jordan needed to get out of there before he got tied up in hours of interviews and bureaucratic time wasting.

He gently but firmly removed his forearm from Florence's grasp. She was feeling a little less frightened after she heard the police sirens approaching outside the building, so Jordan sat her on the couch, went to her refrigerator and brought her a glass of her own white wine to aid the process.

"It's all right, it really is. The police are here." He was out of time, he knew, if he didn't want to spend the next twelve hours sitting in the local precinct answering questions and looking at another ream of mug shots while explaining things he had no interest in explaining. "Look," he said, standing at her window and pointing at the police cruiser on the street. "They're already in front of the building."

Florence was too numb to move, so she remained on the couch, barely managing a nod.

"I'll be right back," he assured her.

She began to protest again, but was too exhausted from screaming and crying and grappling with Jordan to make much of an effort this time. He did his best to give her a comforting smile, then headed out, shutting her splintered door behind him.

Jordan raced upstairs to his apartment, where the first thing he did was replace the S & W automatic in the back of his waistband. Then he opened the compartment in his bedroom closet and removed a collection of papers, two passports, an envelope with cash and a Walther automatic. He added these items to his overnight bag, threw in his cell phone and went to his front door.

The police could be heard coming up the stairs to Florence's landing, surveying the evidence of the shooting, then knocking on her door. The moment they entered her apartment would be Jordan's only chance to get out of the building, and he took it. Once he heard her door close, he ran on tip toes down the three flights of stairs, then slowed to a saunter as he headed outside towards his car.

He thought about checking under the chassis and hood for explosives but shook that off. They never would have come after him in the building if they were going to blow his car, so he got in, pocketed his cell phone and hid his black leather bag in a concealed metal box he installed years ago, underneath the passenger seat behind a false front. Then he flipped the ignition and was about to make his way out of the city when a black, four-door sedan pulled up alongside him, blocking his escape.

THIRTEEN

The car was so obviously a standard U. S. government issue, Jordan didn't even bother to reach for his automatic. He turned off his ignition and watched as a man stepped out of the passenger side of the sedan, stood at Jordan's window and held up an identification card and badge. Sandor cranked the window down.

"Mr. Sandor, I'm Agent Springs, FBI." The man was about five-ten, sturdily built, with short hair, dull features, and an even duller affect.

"Is this about the parking ticket?" Jordan asked.

"We need to speak with you, sir. Immediately."

Jordan told him he would just as soon speak with him another time, but neither Springs nor the second agent, still seated at the wheel of the car, were budging.

A second police cruiser arrived and stopped behind the patrol car already double parked up the street. While Jordan waited, Springs walked over, spoke to the two uniformed cops, flashed his federal badge, and basically told the locals to mind their own business.

Springs returned to Jordan and said, "I must repeat, we need to see you immediately. Please come with us."

Sandor nodded. "Right. Mind if I take my own car?"

"We prefer you come in ours, sir."

"Prefer, as in, 'let's go', right?"

Springs' sense of humor was as dull as his eyes.

"How about if I make a quick phone call first? Change my plans, okay?" When Springs gave no answer, Jordan said, "I'm actually entitled to make a call if I'm being arrested, right?"

"You're not being arrested."

"Well good, then I'll only be a minute." Without waiting for a reply,

Jordan smiled and rolled his window up. He pulled out his cell phone and dialed Captain Reynolds. When the call was answered on the third ring, he said, "Jordan Sandor here. Looking for Captain Reynolds. It's urgent."

"I can get him for you," the trooper at the switchboard told him, then picked up a radio mike, and called for Reynolds. He said to Jordan, "Sure have our hands full, Mr. Sandor. Guess I don't have to tell you that. Captain's been with the feds all afternoon."

Jordan looked out at Springs, who was now leaning back against his dark blue sedan, arms akimbo, waiting. "That so?"

"Couple of big boys from Washington," the trooper said. "What's all that about, you think?"

"I'd like to know myself."

There was a beeping sound from the trooper's radio, then Sandor heard someone in the background say something about Reynolds.

"How's Collins doing?" Jordan asked.

"Okay, I guess. Still in the ICU. Four guys standing guard for him, round the clock. Tough about your friend."

"Yeah."

"Makes you angry as hell," the trooper on the phone said. "Think those doctors could've done a better job taking care of him, right?"

Jordan realized they were living two different realities. "You would think so," he said, clenching his teeth at the thought of Dan's murder. But he told himself this was not the time to grieve. He knew that time would come.

The trooper said something, but Sandor's mind was elsewhere. Then he heard Reynolds' voice.

"I just got a call," the Captain said. "What the hell happened to you just now?"

Sandor gave him the headlines.

"Jesus," Reynolds said. "You're lucky not to be in a body bag, son."

"Now the feds are here," Jordan told him, "about to take me in."

"You'll be better off," Reynolds said. "They're here too. That's why I couldn't take your call right away. Had to walk out of the room."

"Why? What are they telling you makes this federal?"

"Off the record?"

"As agreed. My friend is dead, remember?"

"Maybe two friends, right?"

"No," Jordan said. "I told you the truth about Ryan or McHugh or who-ever he was. I never met him."

"All they'll say is that it has something to do with Homeland Security. I don't know why, not yet, but that's the way they're playing it."

Sandor nodded to himself, but did not respond.

"They told me I'm not supposed to discuss the case with you. Not even about Peters."

"Perfect. And I bet you just love being pushed aside by a lot of D.C. suits."

"My poker face is probably off a little. One of my boys gets shot in the neck, a local guy is murdered and now they say another has a suspicious heart attack."

"Suspicious? You're kidding, right?'

"I don't need you rubbing my nose in it too."

Jordan gave no answer, which was apology enough for Reynolds.

"They threw us aside like we're the fucking Hardy Boys, just a bunch of hicks getting in their way."

"And now they're here."

"I'm not surprised. Are you?"

"No."

"You and your friend, you were on your way to see McHugh, am I right?"

"That's what they said?"

"That's what I think."

"Okay, off the record, as you like to say. You're right."

"And whoever these people are, they came to the hospital, took out Peters and went after you in New York."

"Looks that way."

"Why? Not because you and Peters were witnesses. Collins was a wit-ness too."

"Collins is under guard."

"Peters would have been under guard too, if you hadn't let me think you guys were there by some lousy accident."

Sandor felt the slap of his accusation. "That's unless you believe Danny had a heart attack."

"Crap," Reynolds said.

"That airline ticket you told me about. It was round trip, right?"

"It was."

"In the name of McHugh?"

"Right."

"What airline?"

"Air France. They confiscated the fucking thing, along with every other paper we had on the case."

FBI Agent Springs knocked on the car window. Jordan turned to him and held up his forefinger. "I better go," he told Reynolds.

"I've got one tidbit might interest you."

"I'm listening."

"Did you know McHugh had a sister?"

"How would I know that?"

"Just asking. She arrived this morning, after we talked. Drove up to the house, met two of my men protecting the crime scene."

"A visit from his sister?"

"That's all I know. By that time the feds were in town, took her away for questioning."

Jordan nodded. "Thanks."

"Remember, Sandor, you didn't hear any of this from me."

"You and I are fine, Captain, believe me."

"Good, cause now I gotta advise you to go with them."

"Trust me, at the moment I don't have any choice."

"And we didn't have any conversation at all, just so we're clear."

"Crystal." Jordan thought about his leather bag with the automatic zipped into the inside pocket, together with his cash and passports. He wondered how long it would be before the feds searched his car and everything in it. "What about Danny's autopsy?"

"I'll let you know."

"You're a good man, Captain."

"I think you are too. Hope I'm not wrong."

"That's it then?"

"That's all I got. Maybe the boys in the button-down shirts can tell you more."

Jordan signed off, then made a show of accidentally dropping his cell phone so he could bend over and take the S & W automatic from inside his belt and slide it under the driver's seat. Then he got out of the car, locking it behind him.

"So," he said to Agent Springs, "you guys want me to drive?"

FOURTEEN

The two FBI agents took Jordan to an office building on West 48th Street, not far from the building where Beth Sharrow and her fellow CIA analysts worked. They cleared Sandor through security in the lobby, had him pass through a metal detector, then Agent Springs escorted him upstairs in the elevator and down a corridor on the seventeenth floor to a small conference room.

There was only one person in the room. He did not bother to look up when Jordan was ushered in. "Have a seat," he said as he continued making notes in a file, "I'll be right with you."

"Sure," Sandor said, "don't rush yourself on my account."

Sandor's tone caused the man to glance up at him now. "I'm Special FBI Agent Prescott, and I'm in charge here," he said. "I know who you are, and I'm not in the mood for any of your bullshit. I said have a seat, so have a seat."

Jordan grinned, then made his way to a small armchair against the wall and sat down.

Agent Springs was standing in the doorway, about to leave. "Will there be anything else, sir?"

"That'll be all," Prescott told him.

As Springs turned, Jordan called after him. "How do I get back to my car? Government going to give me a voucher for a cab?"

Springs looked from Sandor to his boss, but said nothing. His expression made it clear what he'd like to do to Sandor with a voucher.

"Springs will get your car," Prescott said.

"That's all right," Jordan told him. "I'll find my own way back."

"Springs will get your car," Prescott said again, then nodded at the agent who had already taken Sandor's keys.

"Careful driving her, then," Jordan said. "She's a temperamental old girl."

Springs hesitated, then turned and left the room.

Jordan watched as Prescott returned his attention to his file. The conference room was rigged with an array of government equipment. By the look of things, the set-up was pulled together in a hurry. Two telephones were sitting on the table where Prescott was working; a computer station was positioned to the side, the screen flashing code numbers, skittishly awaiting further input; a fax machine was sitting on a box against the wall; a recording machine was in place; three or four devices Jordan did not recognize were lined up off to the side; and a series of cables ran from all this electronic paraphernalia, under the tables, into a strip of surge protectors. He figured Prescott was with the FBI's Counterterrorism Division, and he realized, whatever the feds were doing here, they had only recently set up this shop, but they obviously meant business.

Jordan knew that Prescott's peremptory affect was intended to reinforce the fact that he had all the power, Jordan had none, and on a whim he could toss Sandor in a hole so deep he'd need a steam shovel to dig himself out. He was a typical field office chief and his attitude, as Jordan knew, was standard federal issue. Sandor had been through it all before, on both sides of the charade, and had developed an unwavering dislike for the Prescotts of the world. The entire act was the work of small, unquestioning minds, the consequence of an inability to articulate reason, leaving no choice but to resort to the "because I said so" justification for their actions. As far as Jordan was concerned, no desk jockey had ever won a race.

Everything about Prescott was predictable, even his clothing. His suit was medium gray, his shirt was white with a button-down collar, his tie was red with little blue dots. He looked middle-aged, assuming people live to be a hundred and ten. His nose was wide, his complexion sallow and marred, his eyes pale and hard and cold.

"So you're Jordan Sandor." Prescott put down his pen and removed his reading glasses.

Jordan saw no need to respond.

"We appreciate your cooperation."

"My cooperation?" Jordan smiled. "Your appreciation is evident from the greeting I got downstairs. Now that I've reached the inner sanctum you might want to search me again. I may have a stick of dynamite somewhere your men didn't look."

"Standard procedure, you know that. The important thing is that you're here."

"Well, just in case this interview is being recorded for posterity, I'm only here because I wasn't really given a choice."

"You want us to get a subpoena, I'll have one in five minutes."

"I believe you. So if you want to talk about Danny Peters, let's talk."

"We're sorry about your friend."

"I'm sure."

"But I'll set the agenda for this discussion."

"Look, I've had a rough couple of days, so let's get down to it. Why is the FBI investigating a roadside shooting?"

Prescott leaned forward, which was an empty sort of gesture at intimacy, since Jordan was seated ten feet away. "Mr. Sandor, I realize what you've been through, but I'm going to conduct this investigation. Your questions will have to wait."

"I can ask, right? It's still a free country, as they say, isn't it Mr. Prescott?"

Prescott responded with an undisguised look of contempt. "I told you, I already know all about you, my friend." He tilted his head towards the computer station. "Some of it is fairly intriguing, I must say."

Even in the new order, where intelligence agencies were supposed to work together through the recently created Terrorist Threat Integration Center, Sandor realized that whatever information came up on the federal database would still be laundered to wash out the details of any of the classified work he did in Black Ops for the CIA's Joint Counterterrorism Center. He shrugged at the computer screen as if it were another person in the room. "Let's get something clear from the get-go. I'm not here to intrigue you, and I'm not your friend. My friend was Dan Peters, who got shot in the chest for no reason at all yesterday morning, and today turns up dead in a local hospital with a stated cause of death that a first year intern wouldn't believe. Now if you've got questions, you can ask them, or you can go back to your Big Brother data bank and I'll find my way out of here."

Prescott curled his upper lip above his uneven teeth, as if he just detected a bad smell. "Have it your way, although it may interest you to know that we've already heard from the coroner." He held up a sheet of paper. "Faxed in while you were on your way here. Preliminary blood tests indicate Mr. Peters' coronary might have been chemically induced." He looked at the report. "They suspect a massive dose of potassium fluid was inject-

ed into his IV, which would cause a fatal coronary in less than a minute."
He glanced up at Sandor. "It says that potassium wouldn't leave the kind
of trace other drugs might have. They're still working on it."

The news was not unexpected, but it hit Jordan hard. He felt his eyes
burn, and he took a deep breath.

"How well did you know Peters?"

"We were friends," Jordan said, feeling lousy talking about him in the
past tense. "Fought together in the Gulf War,"

"I know all that. I'm asking how close you were, how much you know
about his activities since he moved Upstate New York."

Jordan was thinking about Dan, not really paying attention to Prescott.
Then, as if finally hearing the question through a haze, he looked up and
said, "Not much. We spent a lot of time together in the military. Only kept
in touch on and off since then."

One of the telephones on Prescott's table rang. "Yes? I see," he said into
the headpiece. Are they here now?" Prescott did not bother to disguise his
annoyance. "All right, no reason to have them wait. Show them in." He
placed the receiver back in its cradle. "We're going to be joined by, uh, others."

"Should I guess, or are you going to tell me who?"

Before Prescott could reply, the door to the conference room opened
and John Covington entered, followed by one of his men, Todd Swedock.
The door was closed behind them.

"Hello Jordan," Covington said pleasantly as he stepped to the front of
the room. He looked the same as the last time Sandor saw him, in Washington, at the debriefing after the mess in the Persian Gulf. His fine features
and cropped hair gave him the look of a bank manager, not a senior CIA
operations chief.

Swedock was taller and slimmer than his boss. He and Sandor had met
in the past, and Sandor had not been impressed. He was not likely to be
impressed by any agent who had yet to attain a position better than John
Covington's lackey.

Swedock sat in a chair near the door.

Jordan said, "Excuse me if I don't get up."

Covington walked over to Prescott, whose confusion was apparent as
he got out of his seat to shake hands.

"You know each other?" Prescott asked.

Covington explained that he and Mr. Swedock were from the State Department, attached to a unit involved with international liaison work. "Mr. Sandor was attached to our delegation at one time."

Prescott nodded, as if that meant something to him.

Sandor had all he could do not to laugh at the bogus job description.

"It's been a while, Jordan," Covington said, taking a seat halfway between Sandor and Prescott.

"And not even a Christmas card since Bahrain," Jordan said.

Covington shrugged indulgently. "Things don't always turn out the way you expect."

"No, I suppose not. It would have been nice, though, if someone told those guys in Panana exactly what they could expect. I mean, they did get their fucking heads cut off for whatever in hell was expected, right?"

Covington calmly turned back to the FBI man, saying, "I don't want to interfere with your investigation, Agent Prescott, but I wonder if we might have a few minutes alone with Mr. Sandor." As an inducement, he offered his pale imitation of a smile.

The effort was wasted on Prescott, who had already guessed that Covington and Swedock were not with the State Department doing international liaison work, and that the background on Sandor, as reported to him by the computer, had been sanitized beyond recognition.

"Not so fast," Jordan interrupted. "Did anybody search *them* before they came in here?"

Ignoring the sarcasm, Covington assured Prescott that "I'll only be a little while."

Prescott studied Covington, knowing he could not refuse the request, but doing his best to appear as though he was actually weighing his reply. "Fine," he said. "But we've got to move this along. We have no time to waste because of your man's uncooperative attitude."

"Of course," Covington agreed genially. He and Swedock even stood as Prescott left the room, a proper show of respect. Jordan remained in his chair. When Covington sat down again, he turned toward Sandor, trying to read something from his impassive expression.

"Nausea," Jordan said, "if that's what you're wondering about."

"Look, I told you before and I'll say it again. We didn't know what you were up against in Bahrain."

Sandor shook his head. "Those people were hung out to dry. You and

Byrnes left them to be murdered because they were politically inconvenient. And what happens? He gets a promotion to Deputy Director, you get a gold star for the effort and those poor bastards get dumped in an unmarked grave by al-Qaeda. Tell me, Covington, what's wrong with that picture?"

Covington's shoulders slumped as he blew out a long breath. "And what if you're right? We were all following orders, including me."

"Following orders? If that isn't the lamest answer you could give, I just don't know. You want some more time, see if you can come up with something worse?"

"Look, the DDO was told to pull the plug, and that was that. What difference does it make what we say about it now?"

"What difference, John? I'm the difference now. You're here because you need something from me, and I wouldn't cross the street for you if it would save your life."

Covington resumed his stiff posture. "Maybe not. But my life is not what's at stake here, is it?"

"Oh, I see. You're going to scare me?"

Covington shook his head. "You're too stubborn and too reckless to be afraid, Sandor. I've had the privilege of seeing that first hand."

"So what do you want, my help?"

"Your help? Is that why you think I'm here?"

"I'll tell you what I think. I think that guy upstate had information you wanted, and now he's dead, and you're hoping I have it."

Covington stared at him. "And do you?"

"If I did, why would I want to tell you?"

Covington started to say something, but Jordan stopped him.

"Save your breath. I'm finished dealing with you people."

"Are you?" Covington asked. "I truly hope not. I hope not for your sake."

FIFTEEN

Mahmoud al-Rahmad had concluded the meeting with his aides, providing them as much detail as he had received about Jordan Sandor and his connection to Vincent Traiman. In the communiqué with this data, Rahmad also received an urgent summons from Tripoli. Traiman wanted to see Rahmad immediately, and so arrangements were made for him to fly back to Libya that night, via Paris, on his Saudi diplomatic passport.

Another message sent from Traiman was channeled from North Africa to a man who called himself Robert Groat. He had been waiting in a hotel room in Washington, D. C. for his orders, and was now instructed to go ahead with his visit to David Fryar, President of the Loubar Corporation. Groat decoded the e-mail, then made his preparations for that conference. He retrieved his aluminum attaché case from the closet, laid it carefully on the table and opened it, removing the papers and files and placing them aside. He then lifted a false panel, exposing the tightly packed contents and a series of wires that ran to a digital sensor. He pocketed a small remote device, activated the sensor, then replaced the panel, the papers and, closing the case, went on his way.

"Mr. Fryar, there's a gentleman here to see you. His name is Robert Groat." David Fryar's secretary was speaking into the intercom. "Mr. Groat says he has an appointment, but I don't show anything in my system." The well groomed, middle-aged woman was obviously embarrassed at the possibility of her inefficiency, and looked up at Groat with an apologetic smile.

Groat was a short, well-muscled man, with a thick neck and grey hair that made him appear older than his fifty-three years. He nodded at the woman, neither forgiving her gaffe nor criticizing her for it. He was simply nodding.

"That's all right," Fryar replied over the speaker, "show him in."

David Fryar was the president of Loubar Technical Assistance Corporation, a rapidly expanding manufacturer of specialized electronics, with offices recently opened in Paris and Hong Kong. Groat had come to the corporate headquarters and, indeed, was without an appointment. He knew Fryar would see him anyway.

The secretary escorted Groat into Fryar's paneled office, where Fryar was standing behind his desk, waiting.

"Could I get you something, Mr. Groat?" the woman asked. "Coffee, water?"

Groat took a moment to survey the oversized room, his heavy-lidded eyes giving the false impression that he was either tired or uninterested. He sized up the man who came from behind his desk to greet him. Close to sixty. Overweight and comfortable. Eyes and chin gone weak with success. Posture a bit stiff, apparently concerned about this meeting, his handshake tentative. "No, thank you," Groat finally replied to the woman.

As his assistant turned to leave, Fryar went back to his chair. Groat took the opportunity to slide his metal attaché case under the desk, then sat down.

"They said I would be hearing from you," Fryar said. "I didn't expect you so soon."

"There was no reason to wait," Groat replied in a monotone that expressed his indifference to the task at hand. "As soon as they saw the problem develop, they sent me here straight away."

"Problem?" Fryar's anxious gaze wandered about the room. "Does Traiman think there's a problem?"

"Yes. Interference with our shipments is always a problem."

Fryar was not prepared for this meeting, not today. He had not slept well since learning the latest cargo destined for the Middle East had been compromised. He had agonized over the possible discovery by Customs officials that this shipment of electronic materiel was being illegally routed, not to mention the consequences of what a full investigation of his company might reveal. He was even more troubled that his decision to hold back the freight was too impulsive. He knew that dealing with Vincent Traiman could be worse than a government inquiry. Far worse.

Three days before, he had received a phone call from one of Traiman's salesmen. That's what they were called. Salesmen. The salesman informed Fryar that his superiors were extremely upset. The shipment of two containers of highly sensitive surveillance equipment had been halted. Fryar would be hearing from their regional representative, Robert Groat. Fryar had not slept since.

Fryar was aware, of course, that the orders placed by Traiman's salesmen ultimately found their way to the Middle East. The itineraries for these shipments had always been obscured by a series of documents and intervening transports that concealed their intended destination. These interim transfers, and a complex network of bills of lading, provided Loubar a veneer of innocence and circumvented federal laws that made such shipments illegal. The cargo was always positioned for delivery to a lawful port, or described as non-military in content. In the past few weeks, Traiman had stepped up the timing, demanding a more direct approach. That was the cause of the error, Fryar believed. One of the forwarding documents had been discovered by an executive in the shipping company, making it apparent that the merchandise was intended for Libya. Discreet inquiries were quickly made through an intermediary, but it was apparent that the man could not be bought off. That was when Fryar feigned ignorance of the true destination for the shipment and made the decision to postpone the exports.

Now, being visited by Vincent Traiman's emissary, Fryar wondered if he had made the wrong choice. What if the shipment had been sent? Traiman could have dealt with the trans-Atlantic shipper later. Some arrangement could certainly be made. Fryar and his company could have pleaded ignorance—they might claim they had no involvement in the actual transfer of the goods, once they arrived in Marseilles. After all, this was the same rationale that had assuaged Fryar's conscience for the past three years. His products were shipped to European ports. What was done with them after that was not his concern. His real concern was Traiman.

When Fryar first met Vincent Traiman, their positions were quite different. Fryar was the Vice-President of Loubar, then a struggling electronics firm. Traiman was an operative at Central Intelligence who possessed considerable knowledge of technology, an understanding of foreign markets and numerous contacts in the Middle East. They met at a promotional party given by Loubar in Paris, then traveled together to Jiddah.

Traiman was already familiar with Loubar products. They were on the cutting edge, and Traiman believed they could have a bright future, especially in countries where he enjoyed some influence. He told Fryar that only three ingredients were needed to ensure his success. First, increased sophistication in the area of surveillance and quasi-military appliances such as deployment of chemical weapons, with which the company had been recently experimenting. Second, an aggressive sales force that could provide proper exposure throughout Europe, Asia and the Middle East. Third, new leadership at the company's helm.

Traiman was both a clear thinker and a man capable of bringing his plans to fruition. Within a year, Fryar was head of the company. Under his stewardship, the sales force had amassed an impressive record of increasing revenues. He was the logical choice to succeed the former president, an uncooperative man whose tenure ended when he met with an unfortunate automobile accident. Fryar had been at the helm since, and the Loubar Corporation continued to grow rapidly in income and international stature.

Now, as Groat sat watching him, Fryar struggled with his predicament. Fryar tried to explain how difficult it would have been to justify a release of the product once the intended port had been uncovered. He attempted to enlist Groat's aid in resolving the dilemma to everyone's satisfaction. He offered to work out the problem, not understanding that it was already too late, not realizing that he, David Fryar, had become the issue.

Groat understood that men like Fryar have no sense of allegiance, and dangerously short memories. He listened as the flabby executive offered a nervous justification for his actions. It was interesting, Groat reflected as Fryar rambled on, how some men will accept prosperity without assessing its true cost, while others will scrutinize both success and failure with an eye on the causes and effects of each.

Fryar was a scientist turned businessman who enjoyed an elevated position of power and wealth he had never imagined. Prestige, luxurious living, fast cars, expensive homes, even women. With the enthusiasm of an irresponsible adolescent, he failed to look beyond his pleasures, to assess the consequences of the bargain he had made. And why should he? As Groat had already observed, men like David Fryar had short memories.

"Excuse me," Groat said, interrupting the litany to which he was paying no attention. "I think we should come right to the point."

"Why, uh, yes, yes of course. Go ahead."

"The shipments have been held past their embarkation dates. The integrity of our operation depends in part on your company." He paused, then said, "It depends on Loubar honoring its commitments." His voice bore no inflection, the message delivered without emotion. "The goods must be released and we must be assured we will not have this problem in the future."

His words hung in the quiet of the overdressed office like a cloud about to burst. Fryar began to explain his concerns again, his desire to cooperate, his fear of what might occur. Then he said, "I simply don't see how we can release these shipments right now."

Groat allowed that last statement to settle over them. What he knew, and Fryar did not, was the importance of this shipment to Vincent Traiman's plan to unleash a series of biochemical attacks in several metropolitan centers within the United States and Europe. What Groat knew, as one of very few men privy to Traiman's scheme, was that Loubar's technology was critical to the deployment and execution of explosive devices containing VX gas, the most lethal nerve gas ever devised. What Groat also knew, was that Traiman was not willing to wait. "Is that the answer you want me to take back with me?"

"No, no of course not," Fryar said. He left his seat and walked to the window that overlooked the Capitol. "What can I do?" He seemed to be asking the question of the city that lay before him.

"You must call right now and tell them to release the shipments. We understand the crates are ready."

"Yes," he admitted, "that's right."

"Fine. Instruct your men to inform the shipping company that the goods are to be delivered to Marseilles. We give you our assurance that once they arrive in Europe, Loubar will have no participation in the transfer beyond the original destination." Now Groat stood and picked up the telephone. His voice had turned cold. "I said you have our assurance, that's all you need. Now make the call."

Fryar stared at him. "I need to think this through. To make arrangements. I'll take care of it tomorrow morning, first thing."

Groat shook his head, holding out the telephone to him. "Call him now," he said. "Unless you call him now, in front of me, I'll have no choice but to report your position to Mr. Traiman. I think you know that would be a mistake on your part."

The threat had been made and now the two men studied each other in silence, until the receiver began beeping. Groat replaced it, but remained standing, staring at Fryar.

"Very well," the older man said dully, the defeat evident in his voice and his posture. He returned to his desk, took his seat and picked up the phone. Groat stood over him as he made the call. Fryar was about to hang up, but Groat interrupted. He insisted on speaking to the supervisor in the Loubar shipping department himself.

Fryar felt the anger well up in his chest, but when he looked at Groat, he saw in the man's eyes that he had no choice. He handed him the phone, and Groat waited for the supervisor to get on the line, then quickly confirmed that the shipment would be in transit that night. Fryar was too upset to recognize the familiarity of their discussion, or to guess the truth—that the supervisor Groat had asked for was already on the Traiman payroll.

At this point, only Fryar, Groat and the shipping foreman knew that the equipment had been released, which was just as Groat had planned. He said, "We have other matters to discuss, but first I'd like to use the men's room."

Fryar began to speak, but Groat interrupted him.

"That's all right, I'll ask your secretary."

Outside, he asked the woman for directions. After she pointed him down the hall, he said, "I think Mr. Fryar wanted to speak with you."

She thanked him, and he walked off, turning down the corridor, passing the restrooms and heading directly for the elevators. Groat rode down alone, stepped quickly through the granite-floored lobby, crossed the street and hailed a cab. As a taxi pulled up, Groat reached into his sportcoat pocket and pressed the button on the remote he was carrying, a device smaller than a pack of cigarettes. Almost instantly, the explosives hidden in Groat's attaché, the metallic case that still sat beneath David Fryar's desk, erupted with a deafening roar, windows shattering, debris and shards of glass falling to the street below. Almost as quickly, a fire spread throughout the large office, consuming the entire space in a searing blaze.

"Holy shit," the cab driver said as Groat climbed into the back seat.

"What the hell was that?" Groat asked.

The driver craned his neck for a better look at the cascading mix of glass and metal. "I don't know, mac, but I'd like to get the hell outta here before something falls on us."

"You're right," Groat said, trying to sound as nervous as he could. "Let's go." He gave the driver an address in Georgetown and eased himself into the seat, not bothering to look back at the confusion and panic that was growing as they pulled away.

Driving along the Potomac, the cab driver chattered on about the explosion. Groat tried to ignore him, though occasionally he voiced his own amazement, and his gratitude that they were safe. He gazed out the window, nodding to himself as he silently reviewed his every move. The only thing that remained of his visit was an introduction to Fryar's assistant, who had undoubtedly been incinerated in the fire that engulfed the room. He knew that even if the secretary had miraculously survived, she would only lead the authorities on a hunt for Robert Groat, a man who did not exist. If this taxi driver were to be asked about a fare he had driven from the building, all he would have is the address of a popular restaurant in Georgetown.

The cabbie paused in the midst of some mindless speculation about the blast.

"Yes," Groat responded to the silence, "just awful," then added a comment about how concerned he was for the people inside the building.

The taxi pulled up to the curb in front of Clyde's Restaurant. Groat paid the driver and wished him good luck, then stood there and watched as the taxi drove away. Groat turned in the opposite direction, walked around the block, tossed the remote transmitter in a public waste can, then pulled out his cell phone. He punched in the numbers of an office in Langley, at CIA headquarters.

As soon as the voice on the other end answered, Groat said, "I know the group responsible for the explosion today." Then he recited the address of an apartment in Washington where three Arabs, from the extremist Wahhabi sect, were in hiding, waiting for instructions from Vincent Traiman for a mission they would never carry out. This was the last part of Groat's current assignment—betraying their own team of terrorists in Washington. Only he and Traiman knew that Groat would expose these men. Only he and Traiman knew the reason why.

Groat ended the call, tossed the cell phone into another trash can he passed, then hailed a taxi and headed to the airport.

SIXTEEN

Sandor was still seated in Prescott's office with John Covington and Todd Swedock.

"Don't worry about me or my loyalties," Jordan told them.

"Fine. Since we can't go on arguing our entire lives," Covington replied wearily, "have it your way. Whatever we say now doesn't change a thing in the past. And it won't straighten out the mess we have here."

"Right. So let's talk about this mess. Like for starters, why are you guys involved?"

"I'm here to monitor the investigation. Let's just say the Company is an interested party."

"Ah, John Covington, always the Company man."

"And Jordan Sandor, always the crusader in pursuit of justice, always occupying the higher moral ground."

Jordan leaned back and stared at him. "The DD sent you here to find out what I know, then put me in play. That about right?"

"Close enough, except for putting you in play."

"How is Byrnes? Still warm and fuzzy as bullet-proof glass?"

Covington responded with a blank stare.

"Bet he misses me," Sandor said with a slight smile.

"If he does, he'd be the only one."

"Now that hurts."

"You're a reckless pain in the ass, Sandor, and we're better off with you gone."

"You may be right, but since you're the ones who flew up from Washington to see me, why not let me in on what we're dealing with here?"

"*We* are not dealing with anything, and I'm not authorized to divulge a single shred of information to you. You're inactive, remember? You want to talk, you go ahead. You want to dummy up, I'll have the FBI hold you as a material witness for as long as a judge will allow, which would suit me fine."

"Come on," Jordan said with a short laugh, "that tough guy act didn't work for you ten years ago, why try to sell it now? Maybe you should let Swedock have a go at it."

Covington and Swedock exchanged a glance.

"It seems I tripped into a whole vat of your problems," Sandor said, "and now I'm involved, whether you like it or not. You can bully me, which we both know isn't going to cut it, or you can ask me to help, which irritates you more than a little bit. Either way, I figure you've got something you want me to do." He turned to Swedock and grinned. "That the party line?"

Swedock did not reply.

"No, not this time," Covington said. "You've been on ice for more than a year. You're not on the team anymore."

"We finally agree about something."

"Good. So tell us what you know about James McHugh."

"Who's McHugh?" Jordan asked, not revealing what Captain Reynolds had told him about Ryan's real name.

Covington gave him a look that said he wasn't buying it. "McHugh was the other man who was murdered in Woodstock."

"Ryan, you mean?"

Covington frowned. "His name was McHugh, as you no doubt know by now. We think he had sensitive intelligence we needed. Our guess is you were after it too."

Sandor saw no point in denying it.

"Why don't you start by telling us how you were introduced?"

"Dan Peters set it up. I never got to speak with the guy." Jordan shrugged. "I don't even know what he had."

Covington paused. "For once, I believe you."

The way he said it, Jordan suddenly had the thought that it might have been Covington who orchestrated the break-in of his apartment. He might have been searching for anything Jordan might have learned from McHugh. Or about him.

"The two shooters got there before I did," Jordan told him.

"So I understand." Covington shook his head. "We were looking for him ourselves," he admitted. "When they got to him, they proved their information was better than ours. Now the only lead we're left with is that the group that had McHugh murdered is apparently after you."

"That's comforting. What group are we talking about, exactly?"

"I'm not authorized to divulge that. Do I have to keep reminding you that you don't have clearance any more?"

Jordan responded with a short laugh. "You're not telling me much, but you want me to be a sitting duck for you, is that it?"

"I'm not asking you to do anything, except tell us what you know. Sitting duck or moving target, that's your choice. We didn't invite you, you crashed this party on your own."

"Really?" Sandor got up and walked around the room, needing to do something before he punched Covington in the jaw. When he sat down again he said, "You're playing me, John."

"I'm doing nothing of the sort. At the moment, in case you haven't noticed, we're not your problem." He pursed his thin lips, giving Jordan the schoolmaster's look of disapproval. "What about the shooting in your building today? What was that supposed to be, an attempted burglary?"

"No. Just a florist with a bad attitude."

"Way I hear it, they'd already turned your apartment into a recycling station."

Jordan sat there staring at him.

"Look," Covington said, "can we try to be civil for a minute?"

"We can try."

Covington leaned forward, resting his forearms on his thighs. "McHugh was a combat vet. He came home, civilian life didn't take, so he heads back to Saudi Arabia, gets recruited by a bad group out of Libya. He becomes one of the play-for-pay boys, working field ops, training these scumbags, probably the same cell that killed those college students for Qaddafi, went after our ambassador in Italy, took out the *Charge d'Affaires* in Paris. McHugh was making a buck, pretending to himself that he's just a guy doing a job until one morning he wakes up and reads the headlines and Presto!, this isn't just a video game in the desert anymore. He waits a while, then bolts for home. They want him, we want him. They got to him first."

"Who? Who was he working for?"

Covington drew a deep breath and let it out slowly. "Answer me this first—and I mean the truth. Did you ever speak with McHugh? Did he ever tell you anything at all?"

Sandor stared into Covington's cold, pale eyes. "I told you the truth, I never met him. Peters was taking me to see him yesterday, you know the rest of that story. But I never laid eyes on this guy McHugh."

"Never spoke with him?"

"Never."

"Well, you're the one being shot at, I guess you're owed something."

"So let's have it."

Covington sat upright in his chair, resuming his wooden posture. "We think he was working for Vincent."

At first, Jordan could not bring himself to respond. His mind raced back to a thousand old images as he tried to reel his thoughts forward again. He ran his fingers through his hair, then scratched the back of his neck. "Traiman?" he finally said.

"We think so."

Jordan felt his jaw tighten.

"Look, I probably shouldn't have told you. I mean, it's speculation so far."

"McHugh was working for that bastard?"

"Imagine, someone you hate more than you hate us."

"You mean someone I hate even more than you."

Covington just shook his head. "That's the only briefing you're going to get. As far as we're concerned, your work with Vincent Traiman is ancient history."

"That sonuvabitch tried to have me murdered."

"Yes, he screwed you, he screwed us, he screwed his country. You want to wave a flag, this is the moment. You want to wage a personal vendetta, you're on your own. Traiman's running arms over there—you have a pretty good idea what he's up to. And we mean to stop him. But you're not an agent. You're not in the Company. We're not asking you to get involved. In fact we're telling you not to. You're a free-lance writer, or a victim on the run, or both, take your pick."

"Actually, I'm a guy out on a limb and what you want me to do is climb all the way to the end."

"Suit yourself." Covington stood up. "All I want from you is information. We know you've been working on a story about Traiman. Come on, don't try and look surprised. If you have something we don't, which I personally doubt, my job is to get it from you. After that, you do what you want."

Sandor stared at him, saying nothing.

"So now our friend Prescott is going to ask you some questions. He doesn't know what kind of work you did with us and he doesn't need to know."

"Still happily sharing information among the federal agencies, I see."

"In this case it could compromise our plans."

"And while I'm dodging bullets, do I get a per diem meal allowance and a cyanide capsule?"

"All I want you to swallow is your sarcasm. The Bureau can lock you up if you like, or you can go somewhere and hide until we sort this out."

"If you ever do, right?"

Covington looked down at him. "Just answer Prescott's questions. Then stay the hell out of our way."

The two men stared at each other, the silence broken by the sound of Swedock's cell phone ringing.

Swedock flipped his phone open, listened without speaking, then responded with a "Yes sir, I'll tell him," and ended the call. He looked at Covington. "We need to talk, sir" he said.

Swedock stood and the two men went to the far corner of the room. Swedock whispered for a few moments, and Covington's look of surprise was no act as far as Jordan could tell. Then they turned to him.

"What now?" Jordan asked.

Covington hesitated, then said, "You'll see on the evening news anyway." He shook his head. "There was an explosion in an office building in D.C. A few people dead, several injured."

"Where?"

"A company called Loubar. Deals in high-end electronics.

Jordan knew the name, recalling it had something to do with a series of controversial military contracts. "Anything else?"

"An anonymous tip led to the capture of three men, believed to be a hit team sent by al-Qaeda."

"Also in D.C.?"

Covington nodded. "I'm going to get Prescott now. You handle him however you want. If the Bureau thinks you're obstructing their investigation, they'll take you into custody, and there's nothing we're going to do about that, just in case you were wondering."

Sandor watched as they headed for the door. "You're a real piece of work, John."

Covington turned back to him. "As far as the Company is concerned, you cannot help, you can only be a liability, which puts you in a different category of risk, if you catch my drift."

Sandor smiled at the threat. "You're still a pathetic little paper pusher," he said, then watched Covington and Swedock walk out the door.

SEVENTEEN

Tafallai knew he must not fail again. He knew the consequences. He also realized that his target, this Jordan Sandor, was now alert to his efforts. He also knew that the authorities were involved. Rahmad would be returning to New York in the next few days. He had to act, and time was short.

Tafallai had never failed before. In one capacity or another, he had been involved in several political assassinations. Not murders, but wartime executions of the enemy. Some assignments had been so expertly conceived and implemented, the deaths had been ruled accidental. Others had been brutal, such as the bludgeoning of a Saudi student in California, or the shooting of the Qaddafi liaison who had become too comfortable with Western ways. In these instances, Tafallai was instructed to use unequivocal methods. His charge was plain—to leave a clear message for others who might be tempted into imprudent action.

In the case of this American, there was no need for subtlety, nor was there any particular reason for his death to bear warning to others. In the matter of Jordan Sandor, the means would be justified by the end.

Tafallai sat in the coffee shop across the street from the building where he had tracked Sandor's lady friend after lunch. It was a tall, modern looking edifice that he knew was home to several floors of CIA back-office workers. *So,* he thought, *Sandor had already made contact with his former friends.* That was too bad. It was a problem, because the offices would be far too secure for him to make his move there. He was left with the woman as his best lead for now, so he stared out the plate glass window into the darkening shadows of evening, and waited.

*   *   *

Coming back into the room, Prescott was determined to restore his sovereignty over the investigation. He strutted in ahead of Covington and Swedock, his bearing and expression intended to convey a message to Sandor—that Prescott was still the man in charge.

Jordan was amused, since he realized that among the four of them, Prescott likely understood the least of what was at stake. All the same, the two CIA agents obligingly submitted to Prescott's show of authority, reminding Jordan yet again why he turned his back on these bureaucrats and their dishonest and, ultimately, dangerous games.

Covington was at his obsequious best, an act Sandor had occasion to witness in the past. Covington agreed with Prescott that the FBI had jurisdiction over the matter, and was certainly in the best position to conduct the investigation. He maintained his ruse about the State Department, giving his assurance that they had only intervened because of the coincidental involvement of their former employee, the insubordinate Jordan Sandor. Covington and Swedock were there to assist Prescott for whatever purpose the Bureau might regard as helpful.

They were joined by an FBI agent who operated the recording device and, as Prescott pursued his interrogation of Sandor, his questions only confirmed the shallowness of his understanding. Jordan saw no reason to educate him. If the Agency wanted to keep the Bureau in the dark for now, that was their business. He answered the questions asked, not volunteering anything, not revealing his past and, for that matter, not divulging anything Captain Reynolds had shared with him. Covington suggested an occasional question, but steered wide of anything that might actually lead to the truth of his relationship with Sandor. Jordan did not interfere, allowing Covington to maintain the deception.

Prescott inquired into the shootings upstate, Sandor's intended visit to McHugh's home, the trashing of Jordan's apartment and the shooting earlier that afternoon. Prescott reached into a file and read off a series of Arabic names, none of which Sandor admitted recognizing as he memorized the list for future reference.

At the conclusion of the interview, Jordan was invited to stay overnight at a nearby hotel.

"Invited?"

"Let's say you are being requested to stay."

"You're locking me up, is that the idea?"

"No, I wouldn't put it that way," Prescott replied testily.

"Just how would you put it?"

"It will only be for a short time," Covington interjected, giving his best imitation of a concerned tone. "You are in serious danger. Your apartment has been vandalized, you've been the target of an assault and your safety is obviously compromised. Mr. Prescott is offering his help. There are agents available, and a night or two under guard might be the best thing for all of us."

"For all of us? I suppose being taken into custody is a fitting reward for saving a cop's life."

"You can stow that hero bullshit," Prescott snapped. "That may go over big with your new friend Captain Reynolds, but as far as we're concerned, you just showed up at the wrong place at the wrong time."

Jordan shrugged. "Who am I to disagree?"

"Hold on," Covington interrupted. "We all want the same thing here, don't we? Let's try to be reasonable."

"You're right," Prescott agreed, his lips curling into something Jordan assumed was supposed to be a sneer. "You go strolling around New York like you're suicidal, and my men can come by later and sweep up the pieces."

"I can see that you're all trying to do me a big favor. Problem is, I'm only looking for a small favor. Why not tell me what this is all about, why the federal government is involved, who in hell you think these people are." He stared directly at Prescott.

"I'm sorry," Prescott replied. "That would be quite impossible."

Of course it would, Jordan realized, *because you don't have a clue.* "That's too bad," he said.

Prescott stood, ready to leave. "We are not here to share information with a reporter, we're here to investigate a situation on behalf of the government."

"That's it, then?"

"That's it."

Jordan stood to face him. "They have a penthouse suite at this hotel?"

*   *   *

Jordan said he needed to get some things from his car, and Prescott okayed the request.

Agent Springs, who had picked Jordan up outside his apartment, now escorted Sandor to a garage a couple of blocks away, where they had parked his Rover. He was several inches shorter than Sandor, but he was also several inches of muscle wider. Jordan was not ready to make a move, not yet. All the same, he wondered at how easily he could take this man out, if the occasion presented itself.

Springs handed Sandor his key ring. Jordan unlocked the passenger door, then made it appear he was looking for something on the floor as he reached under the seat and hit the button that dropped the false front. To his surprise, he saw his leather bag was still there. He hesitated, then pulled the bag out and stood up.

"Clean underwear," he said.

Even more surprising, Springs didn't ask to search through the contents.

Probably found it and had a look already, Jordan figured.

He locked the car but, when he made a move to shove the keys in his pocket, Springs held out his hand.

"My car," Sandor said.

"My orders," Springs replied.

Jordan smiled as he handed him the ring. "I get the feeling you don't like me very much."

Springs offered no smile in response. "Not much, no."

"Any reason? My face, maybe? It's been known to annoy people from time to time."

"You're an unnecessary problem for me, that's all."

"And you don't like acting as my baby sitter."

Agent Springs allowed himself a slight grin. "Not what I signed on for, no."

"Fair enough. How about I make it up to you. I'll buy dinner. On the government, of course."

The grin faded.

"Lighten up," Sandor said. "You allowed to drink on duty?"

*   *   *

The hotel they were using was on Times Square, just one street west of the garage. Springs checked Sandor in on the government tab, Jordan declining the desk clerk's offer to get him help with his luggage.

"I can handle this," Jordan said, holding up the bag.

Springs took him to the elevator and they got in together. "You need this to get off at our floor," Springs said, placing a plastic room key in a slot that cleared access in the elevator to the concierge level, where the contingent from Washington was staying.

"No penthouse suite, eh?"

Springs frowned, then said, "We've arranged for room service, if you want something to eat. Just dial the operator."

"Right," Jordan said. "So I guess dinner for the two of us is out, then."

They got off the lift and found their way to Sandor's room without further conversation. Springs held out the electronic key, which Jordan took and opened the door. He turned back to Springs, who was still standing there, then looked down at the agent's hand. "You're not expecting a tip, are you? I mean, I carried my own bag."

Springs gave him a look that told him how happy he would be to close the hand Jordan was looking at and plant it squarely on Sandor's chin. Instead, he turned and strode away.

Jordan switched on the light, locked the door behind him and went to the small desk near the window. The interview with Prescott and Covington had not provided him any new information, except when Prescott inquired about the series of names. Using the ballpoint pen and note paper provided by the hotel, Jordan wrote the names out phonetically:

Za-goll-ee
Mach-mood al Ray-mad
Sue-are-mar
Moo-stah-fah Ta-gleev
Tal-lel Abdullah Dry-ann
Ibray-am Abass

Most of them meant nothing to him, not yet, but it was a start.

He laid on the bed, studying his list, trying to connect them with any of the research he had done during the past several months. Mahmoud al-Rahmad, some sort of Saudi diplomat as Jordan recalled, was the only name that was familiar. The only name, that is, except for the one he had not written down.

Vincent R. Traiman. Sandor's former field supervisor in the Agency, who had disappeared four years ago, only to emerge as a paid al-Qaeda operative who was allegedly behind a string of terrorist strikes in Israel and Europe. Traiman had reportedly engineered the illegal arms deals that facilitated those attacks, all the while living under the protection of Qadaffi in Libya. After the invasion of Iraq and removal of Saddam Hussein, Qadaffi claimed to have seen the light and made a show of laying down his arms and abandoning his anti-Western rhetoric. Whether his conversion was real or just a convenient pose based on self-preservation, his regime made no admission that Traiman had ever been holed up in Tripoli. Traiman's whereabouts were currently listed as unknown, but rumor had it that Traiman had overstayed his welcome in Libya. Sooner, rather than later, he would be on the move.

Now, as Jordan watched a television news report on the explosion at the Loubar Corporation in Washington, he remembered a covert investigation, a couple of years back, into shipments of materiel from Loubar that the Agency believed were connected to Traiman's mercenary operations. Nothing was ever proved, but the suspicion persisted. So, the day after McHugh was murdered, someone took out the headquarters of Loubar and an al-Qaeda cell in the Capitol was exposed.

Jordan knew that these three events must somehow be related, and he knew Traiman well enough to know that they had his fingerprints all over them.

EIGHTEEN

The evening had begun to grow dark, late autumn breezes blowing a chill through the angular ravines that define the sharp contours of space between the buildings of Manhattan. Tafallai noticed neither the weather nor the passers-by. As people hurried past, he casually finished another cigarette, dropped the butt to the sidewalk and sauntered slowly into the human stream as it moved up the avenue.

Early that afternoon, before his aborted attack on Sandor, Tafallai had followed Beth from the Algonquin Hotel to her office building nearby, on the Avenue of the Americas. He watched as she entered the marble lobby, got into an elevator and disappeared. Now he was back, and he waited across the street until he spotted her leaving the building. He began his pursuit, an uncomplicated task for him. Such a large city, New York. So congested, particularly at this time of day, the relentless rhythm and nearly frantic movement of the people furnishing him cover and providing opportunities to observe.

Fortunately, she was going home, stopping only once in a grocery store. She walked the entire way to east Sixty-Fifth Street, making it that much easier to follow her. Perhaps he would be doubly lucky, and find Sandor at her apartment. That would be too much to ask. At the very least, he would be satisfied with the answers she would provide. That should be enough.

As Beth approached the entrance to the apartment building, he suddenly quickened his pace, reaching her just as she got to the front door. She felt him coming up from behind and turned to face him.

"Jordan sent me," he said before she could speak. "I've been waiting across the street for you."

"Jordan?"

"Yes. He told me you could get him a message if he and I lost contact." His voice was filled with the urgency of the imaginary message. "I haven't been able to reach him all day."

Beth Sharrow eyed him with obvious suspicion. "What exactly did Jordan say?"

Tafallai recognized the look, knowing he could not chance further discussion out here where she had options she would not have once they were inside. In a deft move, he pulled his automatic from inside his jacket and pressed the point of the silencer hard against her ribs before she could react. He said, "If you don't open the door right now, I'll kill you right here."

Beth froze, her left arm clutching the small plastic bag of groceries, her right hand holding the front door key. The training she had received was no match for the 9 mm jabbed into her side. She stared down at the weapon, her face a mask of fear.

Tafallai grabbed the key ring from her. "Stay very close to me, you understand? And don't try anything heroic."

Beth looked into his dark, lifeless eyes, neither moving nor speaking.

"Go," he said.

Beth forced herself to say, "I'll scream."

"I doubt it. You cross me for even a moment and you're dead. Believe me, you're not important enough for me to worry about. Now move." He unlocked the front door and pushed her into the small vestibule. "Where's your apartment?"

"Fourth floor," she said hoarsely.

"You better hope no one is on the elevator."

The car came, and it was empty. He shoved her in, pressed "4", then spun her back around to face him. "Anyone in your place?"

Beth shook her head.

"Don't lie to me," he said, showing her the gun at eye level now.

She shook her head again, and they waited in silence until they reached the fourth floor, Beth staring at the barrel of his gun.

As the elevator door slid open, he grabbed her roughly by the arm and forced her to walk to her door, the automatic again pressed into her side. He told her to point to the right key, which she did without speaking.

They entered the apartment, a large studio with a small foyer that widened into a space that served as both sitting area and bedroom. He closed the door behind them, setting the latch in place. The lamp she always left on in the entry was the only light. It appeared to him they were alone.

He shoved her into a chair, the grocery bag falling to the floor, a tomato rolling across the carpet. He had a quick look around the small apartment, all the while training the gun on her as he moved swiftly in and out of the entryways to the kitchen and bathroom. "Let's keep this simple," he said. "Where is Jordan Sandor?"

"I don't know," she replied in a voice that was now so choked with fright it was barely audible.

Tafallai responded by stepping quickly towards her, then lashing out, smacking her hard across her cheek with the back of his left hand. Her head snapped back, then she grabbed her face with both hands.

He leaned over her, driving the barrel of the Glock into her sternum. "Where is he? You were with him today. Where is he tonight?"

Beth began to cry, her sobs of helplessness nearly strangling the words she tried to speak. "I . . . don't know. I swear it. I . . . I don't know."

He reached down, grabbed her by the collar of her coat and pulled her to her feet. He snarled into her terrified face, then struck her again, this time sending her reeling backwards. She spun, face down, sprawled on the edge of her bed.

"This can't be worth it," he snarled. "He can't be worth it." Tafallai came at her from behind. "Now tell me what you know, and we'll have an end to this."

Beth did not respond. She was incapable of uttering a reply, sobbing hysterically as she crawled onto the bed, seeking some measure of distance from him.

He was right behind her. He pulled her by the shoulder, turning her around. She stared up, her eyes transfixed on the gun. In a violent sweep he crashed the barrel of the automatic against the side of her jaw, the sickening sound of her bone fracturing beneath the blow. She screamed out in anguish, and he reached for a pillow and shoved it over her face.

Beth clutched at the pillow, gasping for air, pain reverberating through her skull in a deafening mix of panic and agony.

"Is it worth it?" he demanded, his voice angrier now. He yanked her coat open, then ripped at her blouse and bra as she struggled to push him away. "Is it worth it?"

Beth writhed convulsively. All that mattered now was getting him away from her, but this small man was much stronger than he appeared. He yanked the pillow away from her—it was stained with blood from her swollen mouth and jaw—then he threw it to the floor.

She shrank from him, curling up, embryo-like against the carved mahogany headboard.

Tafallai leaned forward, his eyes meeting hers in the dim light. "Tell me," he hissed at her through clenched teeth.

She could not focus, her body cold with shock. "Woodstock," she muttered. "It's all I know." She spoke slowly and with difficulty. "Woodstock," she mumbled again.

"When?"

"Today."

"You're lying," he said, raising his hand above her shattered jaw.

"Leave me alone." She was whimpering uncontrollably, her entire body trembling.

Tafallai shook her by the arm, pointing the gun at her face. He realized he would get nothing more from her. "This is the last time I'm going to ask you. Where is he?"

Beth's hazel eyes widened, perhaps sensing she had come to the end. She stared at him, only for an instant, then screamed, "Leave me alone," collapsing under the pain of the effort.

When she heard the sound of shattered wood and twisted metal from the doorway, it seemed a distant event to Beth, a surreal moment of violent action she was witnessing from afar. She could not even be certain if she was again the victim, all she could hear were the gunshots, all she could see was blood.

The door had come crashing open, two men bursting through the opening. Tafallai turned to face them, but he was too late. The small apartment erupted in a barrage of gunfire and bloodshed. Not hers, Beth was beginning to understand, but his. The spray of blood was his, his blood.

The first man through was already standing over Tafallai as the second pulled the blanket from the bed and covered her.

As he leaned forward she shrank away in terror. "Miss Sharrow," the man said, "We're here to help you. Are you all right?"

She reached up and wrapped her arms around the man's neck, then wept as he lifted her from the bed.

Jeffrey S. Stephens

"It's okay," the agent told her. "It's going to be all right."

"She's in shock," a third man said as he came in. "Let's get her the hell out of here."

"They call an ambulance yet?" the second man asked.

"Yeah."

"Okay," said the agent who was still holding Beth, "I'll stay with her."

The two men looked to the first agent, who was now kneeling over Tafallai's body. He was shaking his head.

"No good, goddamnit," the agent said. "The little fucker is dead."

"Shit," said the third man. "Covington isn't going to like it."

NINETEEN

Jordan had not eaten since he munched on peanuts and cashews at the Algonquin, when he met with Beth earlier in the day. He considered room service, calling for a rare steak and a bottle of whatever they claimed to be their most expensive red wine. He decided, instead, that he didn't feel like sitting alone in the room, so he dialed the operator to see what sort of restaurant was available downstairs. He was not surprised to find that his call went directly to an FBI hookup.

"Well," he said "do you think you can at least get me a decent table?"

Yes, the agent told him humorlessly, he was free to go down to dinner, then hung up.

When Jordan left his room, he was greeted by a brief nod from an agent stationed in the hallway. Whatever Prescott and Covington were up to, they were serious about keeping tabs on him.

He rode down in the elevator alone, strolled through the lobby, keeping an eye out for familiar faces, friendly or otherwise. He entered the restaurant and went to the bar. It was a dark room with reflective ceilings, sparkling walls, and black lacquer cocktail tables. The entire effect was about as cozy as stainless steel. Still, Jordan was happier here than sitting upstairs.

He ordered a Jack Daniels Single Barrel on the rocks, then had a seat.

He knew he was being watched. He also knew that any attempt to leave the hotel would create havoc. Even so, he longed for one of the comfortable armchairs at the Algonquin.

His drink came and he took a sip, the first burning taste cutting through a long day's thirst. *Maybe I should skip dinner altogether,* he thought, *maybe I should just get good and drunk.*

He was turning that idea over when he noticed a woman approach. She stopped a few barstools away, standing there, staring at him. She looked to be in her thirties, her trim figure clad in tight jeans and a fitted black v-neck, her arms at her sides, her hands empty. She had sandy, blonde hair and unhappy eyes. In the dimly lit bar he made her for a working girl. He gave her a little frown, then looked straight ahead, hoping she would get the idea that he wasn't the type.

She came closer, and he was about to suggest that she peddle her story elsewhere. Before he had the chance, however, she asked quietly, "Are you Mr. Sandor?"

He looked her up and down now. She had a nice shape, an extremely pretty face, and pale blue eyes that seemed even sadder than they had from a distance. "Who's asking?"

"I'm Christine Frank," she said. "Jimmy McHugh's sister."

*   *   *

The telephone rang. Covington was in his room on the concierge level, unpacking the few things he had brought from Washington.

It was his agent, Swedock. The three men on Sixty-Fifth Street had called in, reporting an attack on Beth Sharrow and the shooting of her assailant. Swedock reported her condition.

"How the hell did they leave her with him that long?"

"They had just arrived," Swedock told him. "Two men were being positioned inside, one at the front. As soon as they heard her scream, they went through her door."

"And the man?"

"He's dead, sir. He was armed. Our men had no choice but to fire."

Covington sat down on the edge of the bed. Holding the phone in one hand, he rubbed his face with the other. "Any ID on him?"

"Not yet."

"Check all sources, find out what you can about him, see if we can connect some dots here."

"Yes sir."

Covington put down the hotel phone, reached for his cell and placed a call.

*   *   *

Jordan had turned on the barstool to face the young woman. "You mind spinning around once? Slowly."

"Excuse me?"

"I've been kind of unpopular recently," he said. "I don't need another stranger making an unfriendly visit. Not up close and personal like this."

She blinked, not moving.

"The way those jeans fit, I don't think I need to frisk you, but just to be sure. If you don't mind."

Christine responded with a confused look. "Are you asking me if I have a gun or something?"

"Or something, yes." Jordan was holding his drink, watching her. "A gun, a bomb, a blackjack, a hidden microphone, anything at all, yes, that's what I'm asking."

She forced a smile and, although it took an effort, it was a very good smile, he thought. It managed to light up her entire face for an instant, even her doleful eyes.

She did a pirouette for him, even lifting her sweater slightly, just enough to expose some of her midriff which, as far as he could tell, was also pretty good. There were no wires, and there was no gun.

"All right?"

"I'm sorry," he said. "Sit down."

She took the seat beside him.

Her features were cleanly drawn, her lips full, her blonde hair tousled, falling to shoulder length, a natural color for her fair complexion. Her pale blue eyes were tinged with red, as if she'd been crying, and she had a slight scar over the left brow that gave a hint of character, or the promise of some story to tell. She rested her hand on the bar, her fingers moving up and down to some beat that had nothing to do with the piped-in music in the background.

"Relax," he said. "Can I get you something? I was going to have dinner. I was thinking about eating right here at the bar, if you're interested."

"No, thank you."

"A drink?"

She appeared to be thinking it over. "All right."

The bartender had come by to see what was going on, especially after Christine did her little one-step rumba.

"New jeans," Jordan said to the man. "She wanted me to see how well they fit."

The bartender appeared unconvinced. "Can I get you something?" he asked her.

"Yes, uh, please, uh, whisky sour. Straight up. And sweet."

"Right," the man said, took another look at the two of them, then went off to mix the drink.

"Whisky sour, sweet and straight up. You're a real boozer, I can tell."

"Not much, no," she said.

"So you're McHugh's sister?"

"Half sister."

"I'm sorry about what happened. I never met him, but I heard."

She looked down at her hands, and he thought she might start crying again, assuming she really had been crying before. "I heard you were here for questioning," she said, almost in a whisper. "Like me."

"How did you hear that?"

"The State Trooper from Woodstock, the one in charge there."

"Uh huh."

"Then I spoke with the men who brought me here, the ones who want me to stay. They said they want to keep you too."

"They told you they want to keep me here?"

"Yes. I mean, they didn't say it was you, they said there was someone else they were helping, but I knew it was you from, the uh . . ."

"I know, the trooper upstate."

"Right."

"So how did you know who I was?"

"The trooper described you."

"I guess Captain Reynolds has quite an artistic way with words. You made me right away."

"No, actually. You're the third man I've approached in the past hour." She gave him another look at her smile. "I think that's why the bartender is watching me."

"Who else is watching you?"

She looked over her shoulder, at two government agents seated at a small table between them and the exit to the main section of the lobby.

"Uh huh, I noticed them when I came in. And they're letting you run free in here, picking up strange men at the bar?"

"I don't know."

"Well, they're not giving you much of a leash, sitting near the door there." He took a sip of his whiskey. "So they offered you protective custody?"

"Yes," she nodded anxiously. "At first they were nice about it, the men upstate. I told them I didn't need any help. Then they drove me down here.

I was in a daze, after finding out about, you know, about Jimmy. They said there were men in New York who wanted to question me. So that's what they did, all afternoon. Question me. Then they told me I should stay here overnight. Think things over." She began to stall out.

"Go on," he said.

"I don't know what I'm supposed to think over, but it sounded like an order, and I didn't know what choice I had."

"You could have just gone home, wherever that is."

She shook her head, as if he made less sense than they did.

"Sit down," he said, and so she perched on the stool beside him. "What else did they say?"

"They said I wasn't cooperating." She looked up from her hands. "That's when they mentioned you. That's why they want to hold us here. They said we're not cooperating."

If she was telling the truth, Jordan knew the accusation was a Covington gambit. If she was lying, he figured Covington could have done better.

The bartender brought her drink and Jordan asked for another.

"You sure you don't want dinner?" Sandor asked her.

"I don't think so. I have no appetite."

"Well, here's to better days," he said, holding up his glass as he watched her sip at the tart drink.

"I went to Woodstock to see Jimmy," she said, then demurely wiped her lips with the paper napkin. *Definitely not much of a drinker,* Sandor noted. "When I got there, I found out what happened, and now I feel like these policemen want to keep me prisoner, and I don't know why." She looked at him, her blue eyes wide, her posture considerably more relaxed than when she first walked up to him. She let out a long, audible sigh. "That's it," she said as she pushed some of her flaxen hair from her forehead.

Jordan shrugged, then finished off his first Jack Daniels in a gulp. "And you thought we were in this together."

"I guess so. I'm not sure what I thought."

He took another moment to look her over. "I have to say, it's not a very believable story."

If he was expecting anger or frustration or upset as a reaction, he got none of that. "I know," she said wearily. "I sort of don't believe any of it myself."

He liked that answer. "All right," Jordan said. "So what do you want?"

She hesitated. "I want to leave. I have to leave."

"Why not just tell them? Call a lawyer. You're not accused of any crime, right? Why come to me?"

She shook her head slightly, as if to say she was not sure. "I don't know. I thought, from what the Captain upstate said about you, and what they said here, I thought . . ."

"That I would help you."

"Yes."

"What did they say about me, the men here?"

"That man from Washington, he said some things, about how you didn't want to stay here. And Captain . . . Reynolds is it?"

Jordan nodded.

"He gave me the idea that maybe you were someone who could help me. I know it sounds crazy."

"It does, since I'm about as confused as you are, and I don't even know what you want from me."

She looked at him again. "I want you to help me to get out of here. I have to go someplace, and even if you don't want to go with me . . ."

"Go with you?"

"Yes."

"Uh huh. Look, Miss, uh . . ."

"Frank. Call me Christine."

"Look, Christine, people have taken to shooting at me the past couple of days. Your brother and a very good friend of mine are already dead. I'm the last guy in the world you want to be standing next to right now. No offense, but maybe protective custody isn't such a bad idea."

She stared at him, perhaps wondering if he might be right. "But you don't believe that, do you?"

Now it was Jordan's turn to stare. "No," he admitted, pushing some of his hair back with his hand. "I don't."

"But you don't believe me either. I can see that."

"Under the circumstances, I'm sure you can understand if I'm a little skeptical of everyone right now. Whoever you are, you've got to tell me something that might persuade me to help you, wherever it is you think you're going."

"All right," she said, looking around, then leaning towards him and speaking in a whisper. "Jimmy had a friend."

TWENTY

Jordan and Christine were seated inside now, at a table in the grill room, beside a large wall of windows overlooking Times Square. She spoke as quietly as she could, Jordan regularly urging her to lower her voice, knowing that Covington, the FBI or both could be remotely monitoring the conversation. The two agents, still seated near the entrance to the bar, did not appear all that interested, except perhaps to block any attempt they might make to leave the place. Even so, Sandor knew they could easily be a decoy.

As he worked on his whiskey and listened, Christine told him about her brother.

James McHugh fought in Vietnam and Cambodia with one of the last groups of Green Berets out of Saigon. He made it home, but his experiences in Southeast Asia cast a shadow he could not outrun. The rest of the country was trying to forget the war, learning to despise the memory of those years, behaving as if the veterans themselves were somehow to blame. McHugh saw young American soldiers murdered and crippled in rice paddies and bomb-pocked fields, and he left every vestige of his own youth and innocence there. The reward for his pain and sacrifice was an ungrateful homeland, filled with people who hated that war and therefore disliked him for reasons he could not fathom. He found himself in a society driven by a seemingly endless contest for more and greater material comforts in which he could not find a way to compete.

Drink and pills got him through the days and nights as he sought to fit into the new order. Finally, when he thought he might never sober up long enough to regain a sense of purpose, an old comrade-in-arms contacted him about work in the Middle East. The positions being offered were strictly non-combat, involving personnel training, equipment and weapon education, flight instruction and technical assistance. The money was good, and tax-free. Why, his friend asked, pay taxes to a country that has no use for you after they sent you to hell and didn't care if you ever came back?

McHugh followed his friend to Libya.

In the beginning things were fine, or so he wrote to Christine. He had money, a certain level of authority and, most important, a reason to get up in the morning. He did not tell her the truth about his work, not in the beginning. He claimed he was working for a foreign company, making a lot of money and feeling better about himself. Eventually he confessed what he had been doing, admitting that he had rationalized his role by being far removed from the actual consequences of his actions. He was a clinical purveyor of military knowledge, nowhere near the bomb blasts in Jerusalem, the assassination attempts in Yemen, the plots to destroy the uneasy balance of power throughout the world's most volatile region. He visited the compound at Bab el-Azziziya, where Qadaffi's disingenuous array of Bedouin tents were actually surrounded by a fortress of walls, bunkers and a sprawling, high-tech military complex. He went into the desert to training grounds where mock attacks were acted out like rehearsals for a bad action movie. McHugh was not part of the fighting, or so he told himself, even as his doubts were assuaged with money and alcohol and women—made available to him and his fellow mercenaries in a society where liquor and pornography are contraband. And so he stumbled forward through the years.

Until one night, when he was watching a cable newscast about the war in Iraq, he saw a report about the soldiers being killed by terrorist assaults. Until he heard the report about a decorated Captain, an old friend, who had been blown to pieces by a roadside bomb. Until that instant, on Nine-Eleven, when he was confronted by everything he had managed to ignore up to then. In a few blinding moments, he was compelled to open his eyes to the contribution he was making to this devastation.

He did not react immediately, biding his time, continuing to perform his duties, waiting several months before requesting leave for some R & R in France. He contacted Christine, whom he had not seen in more than a decade. Christine was going on her summer vacation, on leave from her position as an assistant professor of Art History at Penn State. He invited her to visit, to tour the museums of Paris, providing a rationale for his excursion. He received permission from the quasi-military order of command, then in June flew to Orly, with the secret intention of disappearing forever.

"That was a couple of months ago," Christine said. "When we got together in Paris, that's when Jimmy told me what he'd actually been doing in North Africa."

Jordan nodded. "Go on."

"When he invited me to Paris, he told me he was going to be on vacation. Then, when I got there, he told me he wasn't going back, that he wanted to come home. He was scared, there was fear in everything he said, everything he did. That's when he left Paris."

"And you left with him?"

"No. Oh no. I flew to Madrid and stayed there for two weeks. He insisted on it, paid in advance for everything, the hotel, plane tickets, everything. He wanted people to think we were going there together."

Jordan shook his head as he contemplated the risk she had unwittingly taken. If her story was true, her brother had put her life in danger simply by involving her in his scheme to escape. "And before Paris, you hadn't seen him for more than ten years?"

"Hadn't had a letter from him in more than three."

"Okay. So what happened after Spain, when you got back home?"

"Nothing. Not for several weeks, anyway. I had no way of finding him, no idea where he was. Then I got a call from his friend. He asked me to go to Woodstock and see Jimmy. You know the rest."

"You knew this friend?"

"I only met him once, in Paris this past summer. When he called me the other day he said Jimmy was in trouble, that he needed my help."

Jordan had another good look at her, allowing a brief silence to fall over them as he studied her pale blue eyes for any sort of tell. "So," he finally said with a sigh, "who are you, really? Who sent you to me? Prescott doesn't have the imagination. It would have to be Covington, but frankly, I expect more of him." Christine began to speak, but he held up his hand. "Wait. Let me get this straight. You were supposed to tell me this last bit, about your brother's friend. Then we're supposed to compare everything the two of us know and run off into the night to avenge your brother's murder. How am I doing?"

Christine's eyes filled with tears and she began to cry. She sobbed in a quiet, soulful way that Jordan was sure she calculated for maximum effect.

"Save it," he said, having another pull of his whisky. "I don't melt at the sight of a woman crying. No hard feelings, but the whole act is wasted on me." He handed her a napkin. "Just go back to wherever you came from, and tell them it was a nice try but it didn't work."

She took the napkin, lowered her head and wiped her eyes. Watching her, he had to wonder. If she was acting, she was very good.

"Come on," he said. "Knock it off."

She looked up at him, her eyes red and swollen again. "I don't understand." She spoke in halting fashion now, struggling to take a deep breath. "Those men, they said you were going to leave, that you'd never stay here. That's why I tried to find you. Why don't you believe me? Why would I lie?"

"Why would you lie? There are all sorts of reasons, believe me, not the least of which is my doubts that they would tell you so much about me unless you're working for them. But let's assume you're for real. What do you expect me to do?"

"I expect you to help me."

"I'm listening. But don't say any names, okay?" She nodded, and Jordan knew that if he was being taken, he was being taken but good.

"Okay," Christine said, "this other man, he was Jimmy's best friend over there," she said. "He was the one who brought him to Libya in the first place. Now he's here, in the States."

"I'm still listening."

"These people, the people that killed Jimmy. They'll be after him too."

"And you and I are supposed to save him?"

"There's more to it than that."

"Really? Then why not tell the feds?"

"I can't, don't you see?"

"I'm afraid I don't."

"He told me that if Traiman's men don't kill him, these federal agents will."

The mention of Traiman's name got him to sit up straight in his seat. "No names, right?"

"Sorry. But he was their boss, or whatever, the man they worked for."

Jordan felt his spine stiffen even more. "And what do you expect to do for this other guy?"

"Warn him. Help him. He and Jimmy wanted to speak with someone, someone they could trust."

"And that was supposed to be me?"

"I think so, yes."

"And you knew my name before you got here, right?"

"Yes," she admitted. "I knew your name."

"From Jimmy's friend, right?"

"Yes."

"Who got my name from your brother?"

"I'm not sure."

"But he needs your help? Our help?"

"He does."

"And he has information he's willing to share with me."

"I believe that, yes."

"Where is he?"

"Will you help me?"

Jordan sat there staring at her. She knew Traiman's name. She knew his name. She told the tale and, if it was not entirely credible, it wasn't the worst setup he'd ever heard. He had to figure she was either a plant from Covington or a trap set by the men who had murdered McHugh and Danny. Either way, he had to know.

"Let's eat something first," he said. "I'm starving."

TWENTY-ONE

Covington was still in his hotel room when Swedock called back. "We're getting parts of their conversation," Swedock told him. "They're speaking very quietly, and we'll have to go back and filter out the ambient noise on the tape."

"Cut the techno crap, Todd. Where are they?"

"They're still in the restaurant, sir."

Covington sucked air through his clenched teeth. "I mean, in their conversation."

"Sorry. She told him something about her brother having a friend. She wants him to help her find him."

"A friend? Did she give him a name?"

"No sir. Sandor told her not to use names."

"Any location on this friend?"

"Not yet."

"Well stay with it, and keep me informed. Move Prescott's men out of the way if you have to."

"Yes sir."

"But gently. Move them gently."

"Yes sir."

*　　*　　*

Sandor had a salad, a rare sirloin steak and drank off the best part of a bottle of Opus One. Christine only picked at her salad and barely touched her lamb chops or wine.

As Jordan stood to leave, the two government agents at the far table turned toward him.

"Upstairs," Jordan mouthed towards them, pointing toward the ceiling.

"No reason to have them jumping up and pulling out their guns," he told Christine as he extended his hand to help her from her chair.

He wrote a large tip on the bill and charged it to the room, all at government expense, then took Christine by the arm and led her back through the bar to the elevators.

"I assume you're staying on the concierge floor with the rest of the spooks."

She reached into her pocket and pulled out the plastic pass key.

"Good," he said. "I've got some calls to make, then we'll get together in my room and make a decision."

*   *   *

Christine inserted the plastic card into the slot and they rode up in the elevator. She leaned against the mirrored wall and lowered her head.

"Tired?"

She nodded.

He moved close to her, whispering directly in her ear. "Later, when you come to my room, bring whatever you need to take with you. No suitcase, just a purse and whatever you can stuff in it."

She nodded again.

"We'll tell them we're going back down to the bar for a nightcap."

The door to the elevator slid open and the guard near the elevator on their floor was still there, seated now, waiting for them as they stepped out.

"Good evening," Jordan said to him as they walked by. The agent said nothing.

Christine was staying a few rooms down from his, and he walked her to her door.

"Try and relax," he said. "Take a bath or something."

She gave him a curious look.

"Women like to take a bath when they need to unwind, right?"

She smiled, and he decided that whoever she really was, he definitely liked her smile.

"Stop by in half an hour," he told her in a voice loud enough for their guard to hear, "we'll have one last cocktail." When she was safely inside, he returned to his room, shut the door behind him and flipped the security bolt.

As he stood there, alone in the quiet, his first thought was that something was wrong. *Obviously,* he told himself, *it was all wrong.* Covington would never allow this girl to get to him unless he wanted it that way. She had far too much information, including Traiman's name. And why would they permit him to take his bag from the car, with everything intact?

Jordan took his leather bag off the dresser, tossed it on the bed and went through it again, looking for any signs it had been searched. Everything seemed to be in place, his clothing, his cell phone, the two automatics, even the false pockets inside where he kept cash, the extra passports and his clean cell. That didn't mean it had not been searched. It only meant they were willing to let him keep whatever he had, at least for now.

The obvious question was, *Why?* The answer was just as obvious. They wanted him out there, a moving target in search of Jimmy McHugh's friend. He was still undecided about what part Christine had in that plan.

He used the hotel phone to make his first call, to Captain Reynolds in Woodstock. It was nearly midnight, and the officer on duty told him the Captain could not be reached. There was none of the small talk or cooperation he had from the other trooper that afternoon, even after Jordan said the matter was urgent. It was apparent that Reynolds' unavailability had nothing to do with the time of night. They had cut off that line of communication.

His next call was to Sternlich. Bill picked up the phone on the first ring.

"Sorry to call you so late, Billy."

"Forget it, I wasn't sleeping. I've been trying to reach you for hours. Your cell phone is off."

"I thought it would be better to keep it shut down for now." He did not tell him that he assumed the line was already being tapped.

"Have you heard about Beth?" Sternlich had known Beth Sharrow from the time she and Jordan began seeing each other. Sternlich's wife had become good friends with Beth over the years.

"What about her?"

Sternlich told him.

Sandor had been pacing back and forth in the small room, the base of the phone in one hand, the receiver in the other. As Sternlich described the attack on Beth, he slowly sat into the club chair in the corner. "Oh God," he said.

"It was pretty bad, Jordan, but they say she'll be all right. Broken jaw, shock, a real fucking mess."

"Lunch," was all Jordan could think of to say.

"What?"

"When I met her today for drinks. We were supposed to have lunch, remember? They must have followed her. Used her as a back-up for reaching me. What about this sonuvabitch who . . . ?"

"Dead."

"Goddamnit."

"Yeah. Not good, man."

"Any word on who he was?"

"Nothing yet. Not that I've heard."

"Where is she?"

"Mt. Sinai, but I think a visit from you is rather out of the question. For her sake as well as yours."

Jordan nodded at the phone. "Have you spoken with her?"

"She's under sedation. They said I can see her in the morning."

"Right." Jordan gazed numbly out the hotel window at the brightly lit New York City night. "So here I am, all over again," he said. "And fucking Covington didn't even tell me."

"What?"

"Nothing," he said to Sternlich. He knew Covington's men were listening on this line. His comments were for their benefit. "You get anything for me on that thing I asked you about? Just tell me yes or no."

"Not really. I feel like a doped-up mouse in a rigged maze. Information roadblocks everywhere, courtesy of Big Brother, which tells me you're onto something important. And dangerous."

"You think? I suppose you heard about the shooting at my apartment this afternoon."

"It made the late editions. That's when I first started calling. You're okay?"

"So far. I'm with McHugh's sister. She's telling me a tale, and I'm going to track it down. Meanwhile, I'll get you a number where you can call me. And Bill, drop this thing I asked you about. I'll take it from here."

"You sure?"

"Absolutely." He was concerned he had already involved Sternlich too much. "And let me know what you hear about Beth."

"I will. Where are you now?"

"I'm in protective custody, guest of the feds."

"Well that's good, anyway."

"I'm not so sure. I'll call you in the morning, pal," he said. "And thanks." Then he hung up.

He went to the window, staring out at the city, but not really seeing anything. Peters. McHugh. And now Beth. All that was left to him was to search for a man whose name and location he had told Christine not even to whisper to him, not yet. A man who might lead him to Vincent Traiman so that he could stop him before it was too late. He nodded into the darkness, reflecting for only an instant on an abandoned career revived.

He stripped off his clothes, took his toiletry kit from the bag and went into the bathroom. He brushed his teeth, shaved, then stood in a steaming hot shower, at the end of which he turned the water cold, the freezing rain taking his breath away as it washed away the effects of the bourbon and the wine, reviving him for what he knew would be a sleepless night ahead.

He toweled off, went back inside to his bag and pulled the second cell phone from one of the side compartments. He had to assume both cell phones had been tapped, but this one had an encryption chip that scrambled the outgoing numbers and made it all but impossible to decipher the conversation. When Langley scrambles a call, it was even tough for Langley to make sense of the discussion. He also assumed Covington had the room bugged, so he went back to the bathroom, turned on the shower and the sink, then punched in the numbers for his contact's private line.

"Yes," the familiar voice answered.

"It's me," Sandor whispered.

"I've been waiting."

Sandor gave a brief report, including his discussion with Christine. He spoke as quietly as he could, the noise of the water in the background helping to further mask the conversation.

"What about the interrogation?"

"I didn't get much from them, just a list of names," Jordan said, then recited them.

"Got it. What do you think about this Christine Frank?" the man asked.

"I'm not sure. She might be for real."

"Our background check hasn't turned up anything irregular."

"So I'm going to run with it, then."

"Good."

Jordan hesitated. "I heard about Beth."

"I'm sorry about that, Jordan," the man from the CIA said.

"Let me know how she's doing."

"I will." There was a pause. "So when do you move?"

"I'm out of here with the girl, tonight."

"Good," the man said. "We're running short on time."

"What about the three al-Qaeda you picked up in D.C. today?"

"We're working on them," the man said. "We don't think they had anything to do with the explosion at Loubar. They also don't seem to know much about Traiman's plans."

"Want me to come down and take a run at them?"

"If I thought it would do any good. They were on a need-to-know basis, or that's what it looks like. They were waiting for instructions."

"Then someone flipped them for another reason."

"That's what we think."

"Who?"

"We're working on it."

"Well, let me know what you find out."

"Of course. You do the same."

"Only you."

"Yes," the man said. "For now, it has to be that way. We can't trust anyone else."

"You know it may be a while before I can call you again," Jordan said.

"I understand. You be careful. On all fronts."

"Yes sir."

"Remember, this is not personal, you and Traiman."

"Right."

"I mean it."

"Yes sir."

"And Jordan." The man hesitated. "It's good to have you back."

TWENTY-TWO

It was half past midnight when Christine Frank left her room. The agent on duty eyed her suspiciously as she strolled down the hall and knocked on Sandor's door. Jordan came out into the hall and gave a short wave to their sentry. He received no response.

Once they were in the room, Jordan closed the door, then motioned her into the bathroom. He shut that door behind them, then turned on the hair dryer provided by the hotel, laying it on the vanity counter. It roared and rattled against the marble, making the racket he intended to mask their discussion.

"We don't have much time if we're going to leave," he told her.

She nodded.

He leaned against the wall, arms folded. Christine was dressed in dark blue slacks and a baby blue crew neck sweater. She had fixed her hair and made up her face, though not using much in the way of cosmetics as far as he could tell, which he decided was a good look for her.

"So," he said, "let's have it. Speak quietly and give me the whole thing."

Christine took a deep breath. Then she told him.

Jimmy's friend was a man named Anthony Andrioli. McHugh and Andrioli were in the service together. Andrioli was the one who later introduced Jimmy to the Libyan connection. Christine met him briefly in Paris. When McHugh disappeared from France, Andrioli also vanished.

Christine had not told this to any of Prescott's men, fearing that Andrioli faced the same danger that led to McHugh's death. She did not tell them Andrioli had contacted her with the information that Jimmy was living in Woodstock. She had never even mentioned his name. She lied. Somehow, she explained to Jordan, it seemed the right thing to do at the time.

Andrioli and her brother were in some kind of trouble, that much was clear to her in France. When Andrioli called her he said that the threat came not only from the people in the Middle East who were hunting them, but from the authorities as well. McHugh and Andrioli were criminals, but they had information the authorities wanted. They made an attempt to trade for their own safety, but were turned down. Now they were afraid to trust anyone.

"Why me, then?" Jordan asked.

"I honestly don't know. I only know what Anthony told me on the phone."

"Which was what?"

"That Jimmy was going to meet with you, that he was going to ask you to help them. That's how I knew your name. That's why I asked the Captain in Woodstock about you."

If Christine was an agent working for Covington and the Agency, Sandor figured he might as well go along with her story for now. At least it was a starting point. If she was telling the truth, and Covington was using her to draw Sandor into the game, he was going to take his chances. If she was working for the men who were trying to kill him, and had already murdered McHugh and Peters, he realized by letting her into his room, he would likely be dead already. The compact Walther PPK he had taken from his bag and secured against the small of his back was a reminder of his uncertainty.

"Suppose I buy your story," he said as he carefully studied her, his expression and tone severe as he asked, "Where is this Andrioli now?"

"You'll go with me?" she asked.

"Answer the question."

She hesitated. "Florida," she said. "Fort Lauderdale."

He nodded, the din of the hair dryer blowing and vibrating against the hard countertop filling the small room, frustrating any sort of eavesdropping Covington or Prescott might have arranged. "Tell me where he is and I'll go. You'll be safe here, and I can take whatever message you want me to deliver. All things considered, protective custody is the safest place for you right now."

"No," she said. "I'm scared of these people. And I think Tony will speak with me. He doesn't know you, and he's dangerous."

"Fort Lauderdale," Jordan said.

"Yes. He and Jimmy had information. Important information. But he doesn't trust anyone."

"You said that already."

"Sorry."

"Except he'll trust you, right?"

"I think so."

"Even though you only met him for five minutes or so in Paris."

"He was the one who called me, to tell me to go to Jimmy. He was the one who gave me your name."

"So he's got my name. Why do I need to have you along?"

"I told you already."

Jordan shook his head, reminding himself to be careful, that it was all wrong.

She looked directly into his eyes, the din of the clattering hair dryer echoing off the walls of the small bathroom. "Please, can we get out of here?"

"We can try," he said.

"Will we? Will we try?"

"Yes," he said. "We'll try."

Jordan turned off the dryer and opened the door. He took her by the arm and led her to the bed. He motioned for her purse, then dumped out its contents. It was a large bag, and she had stuffed in clean panties, an extra top and various sundries. He took his soft, black leather bag, removed a few unnecessary items, then placed her things in there. He folded up the sides of his leather satchel and buttoned them in place so the bag appeared smaller, a feature that came in handy from time to time. He moved close to her and whispered, "This is your purse, you carry it. We're going to the bar for a drink."

They left the room, walking at a leisurely pace to the elevator. A new guard was on duty, the midnight to eight shift Jordan surmised.

"We're going downstairs for a nightcap," Sandor said with a smile. "No decent cognac in the mini bar, you know?"

The guard did not smile. "Kinda late, isn't it?"

"Hey," Jordan replied, "you guys can actually speak. I thought this was like Buckingham Palace. Beefeaters. No talking." He pushed the down button on the elevator.

The guard picked up his two-way. "I said, I think it's late."

"Well gee, thanks pop, but it's never too late for cognac. We'll be home before curfew. Call your boys downstairs and wake them up. We'll meet them at the bar."

The elevator bell rang softly and the doors opened. The guard got to his feet.

"Hey," Jordan said with a shrug of his shoulders, "how far can we go in an elevator? We'll see your teammates in the lobby." He held Christine's hand and gently drew her into the lift. "Don't wait up," he said to the agent as the doors closed. The man was already on his walkie-talkie, speaking to someone downstairs.

Jordan hit the button for the lobby. Then, as the doors slid closed, he also hit the buttons for floors one, two and three. He looked down at her shoes. "Can you run in those?"

"Run? Sure, if I have to."

"Down some stairs?"

"Whatever you say."

He took the bag from her shoulder. "We won't have much time. They won't be suspicious when it stops at three, but when it stops at two and then one they'll be all over us."

When the elevator stopped at three, he grabbed her wrist and pulled her out, heading in a trot down the hallway towards the exit sign. He pushed the door open and led the way down the stairs, past level two and one and then past the main floor, racing downward, to the first basement level.

"Come on," he said, urging her to keep up. They reached the lower landing, where Sandor was relieved to find the door was open for re-entry. They would have lost too much time if he had to pick the lock or find another way out. By now, the empty elevator had made its extra stops and opened in the lobby. The car would be empty and Prescott's agents would be already be searching for them.

They entered a long corridor, where the kitchen and room service facilities were located. He turned to the right and they took off. There was still a skeleton hotel staff on hand at this hour, and a heavy-set black woman of about fifty or so poked her head out the door to see who was running down the hall.

"Hello," Sandor said pleasantly, coming to a halt. "We need a quick favor."

The woman gave them a skeptical look. "I'll bet."

"We're not running out on our hotel bill, believe me. I'm rescuing my sister from her boyfriend."

"Sister, huh?" the woman replied.

"Yeah. Her boyfriend's a bastard. Beats her. Won't let her go." As he spoke, Jordan pulled a hundred dollar bill from his pocket. "All we need is a back way out of here," he said, holding up the money.

"I could lose my job," the woman said.

"Who'll ever know?" Jordan asked, pulling a second bill out and giving the woman a closer look at the two portraits of Benjamin Franklin.

"Well," the woman said, "I'm not about goin' anywhere with you two, see? But I can tell you the best way out."

Jordan pressed the money into her hand. The woman quickly folded the bills and stuffed them into the pocket of her apron.

"Right there," she said, pointing down the length of corridor. "Third door on your left, take the stairs down one more flight to the garage, first door to your right, then come back up the ramp and out on Forty-Fourth Street. You run into Louis, he'd be the only one on duty now, at the cashier station. You just tell him Celia sent you, he'll let you by without no trouble."

"Thank you Celia," Jordan said as he turned to head off down the hallway.

"I'm not Celia," she called after them. "Celia's a no account pain in my ass, but Louis likes her and if there's any trouble, it'll be her neck." Then she turned and went back to work in the kitchen.

They followed her directions, through the third door, then hurried down another level where they found the entrance to the underground garage just below the ramp leading up to Forty-Fourth Street. Jordan stopped.

"Hold it. Security cameras." He put out his arm and held her back, in the doorway, as he surveyed the large parking area. "Up there." He pointed to a stationary camera off to their left. "We just need to get around that one. They'll already be checking the monitors."

"Then what? Can we run up that ramp?"

"They might have agents outside by now," he told her. "I have no idea how much manpower they've thrown at this detail."

"What are we going to do?"

"Only two choices, as far as I can tell. We can go on foot, take our chances, hope to get lucky." He paused.

"Or?"

"Or, we can steal a ride."

He led her into the garage, heading to the right, keeping low, staying behind the parked cars. Sandor chose an older model Ford Taurus that was head-in to the wall, dropped his bag to the ground and pulled out some tools. He peered through the driver's window and saw the slowly blinking red light, telling him the alarm system was armed. He checked the car on the other side of him and saw it was also locked. This was a self-park garage and he would need a bit of self-help to get them out of there. "No problem," he told her. He removed a flat piece of metal with a rounded hook at the end from his cloth tool kit. In a few moments he had the hood of the Taurus open and the alarm system disarmed. He used the same tool to unlock the driver's door, then slid under the dashboard, pulling out wires and starting the car while she kneeled beside him on the ground. "Come on," he told her, and she scampered around the front and got in on the passenger side as he took the wheel.

Jordan backed the car out, then drove up the ramp and stopped at the cashier station at the cross-bar. Jordan rolled down his window. The man inside the glass enclosed booth was a trim looking black man who appeared to be in his early forties. He asked for the parking receipt.

"You must be Louis," Sandor said.

"I know you?"

"No, but Celia told us to ask for you."

A slight smile came to the man's lips.

"See, Louis, we've lost our receipt, and we're kind of in a hurry. She said you could help us out."

The man's smile vanished. "She did, eh. And how do I know you're not stealing this here car?"

Jordan turned to Christine. "You hear that, sweetheart? Isn't that rich." He turned back to Louis. "Let me ask you something? If I was going to steal a car from this parking lot, why would I choose this old heap?"

Louis nodded at the logic of his argument. "All right," he said as he began to lean forward, "but lemme see your car key, so I know you ain't pullin' the wool, if you see my point."

"Of course," Jordan said but, instead of reaching for the non-existent key, he picked up the Walther .380, which he had placed beside his thigh, then leveled it at the man's face. "I'm sorry Louis, but if you move a hair, I'm going to have to shoot you in the head. I would really prefer not to have to do that." With his other hand, Jordan pulled a hundred dollar bill from his pocket. "You see, Louis, we have a problem and not much time to work it out. So here's the drill. You open that cross-bar and we'll drive away. I'm also going to ask you to get out of your booth, take this hundred dollars and start running down the ramp in back of us. All we need is a few minutes, after which you can call the police or whoever you've got to call, and in the meantime, you get to keep the hundred. So what's it going to be, because I'm all out of time, and I would really hate to have to blow your head off."

Louis started to move.

"Eh, eh, eh, eh," Sandor responded, waving the gun at the man. "No panic buttons, Louis."

"Easy man, I'm just gettin' outta the booth."

"Raise the bar first. And Louis, if I hear an alarm go off, I'll kill you. Maybe not right now, but Celia knows where you live."

The bar came up, Louis stepped gingerly from his booth, grabbed the C-note from Jordan's hand and took off like a deer in rut down the ramp behind them.

Jordan stepped on the gas and turned east on Forty-Fourth Street.

TWENTY-THREE

John Covington was trying to catch a nap in his hotel room, fully clothed, on top of the quilted bedspread. When the telephone rang it roused him from an uneasy sleep. He had the receiver in his hand before the second ring.

"I just got the call from downstairs, sir. He's gone."

Covington nodded into the darkness. "Good."

"It seems Washington was right about him," Swedock said.

Covington bristled at the suggestion that the Deputy Director, not he, had made the evaluation.

"He's a loose cannon, isn't he sir?"

"Sandor was never a team player," Covington said. "Now he's not even on the roster."

"Yes sir."

"What else?"

"Sandor tried to reach Reynolds. They shut that down. Then he spoke to his friend, the reporter at the Times. He found out about Beth Sharrow."

Covington considered that for a moment. "It might help, actually."

"We think he made another call, on a cell phone. We couldn't get that one, too much background interference."

"That's not very helpful. Let me know if you get a trace."

"Yes sir," Swedock said.

"So it's Sandor and the girl."

"She sure won't make for unattractive company for him, will she?"

Covington had enough of Swedock's unenlightening observations. "Did they leave on foot?"

"No, they stole a car from the hotel garage. We're trying to get a lead on them now."

"Excuse me? You're telling me you lost them?"

"Prescott's men lost them, sir."

"I instructed you to move his men aside, not shove them in a ditch."

"We did our best to stay with them, but Prescott's agents were the gate-keepers. Sandor gave them the slip."

"Do we have any information on the car?"

"We do, but it's no help. It was abandoned, just a few blocks away."

"And then what? Cab, subway, foot, what?"

"We're tracking that down. You think they'll stay in New York?"

"That's what I need you to find out," Covington replied angrily. "Get on it. And once you pick up the scent again, remember, Sandor will be looking for us, and we don't want him to see us, at least not yet. I want him to spend his energy finding Andrioli, not shaking our team."

Covington didn't wait for an answer before hanging up. He switched on the lamp and stood up, having a look out the window at New York City below. Sandor had taken his bait. He probably would not trust the girl, not at first. He might not even buy any of what she told him. All Sandor had to believe was that there was danger and that he could protect her.

As Covington knew, it was a role his former agent would find irre-sistible.

*   *   *

After Sandor had exited the parking garage and turned the Taurus onto Forty-Fourth Street, he checked the rear-view mirror and saw two agents in front of the hotel, one on a radio transmitter, the other frantically look-ing around. He thought he saw one of them point at the car, not certain whether they had guessed right or if they had just received a call from the hotel security office after they were spotted on the surveillance camera near the cashier in the parking garage.

Jordan reached Sixth Avenue, took a quick left, another left on Fifty-Third Street, then pulled to the curb. He left the car running, next to a fire hydrant just east of Seventh Avenue. He told Christine to get out, grabbing his bag as he exited the sedan. He shoved the Walther in his pocket, took her hand, and they hurried on foot to Broadway, then north to Fifty-Sev-enth Street where Jordan hailed a cab.

*   *   *

Covington got another call from Swedock. The FBI had given him some worthless details about the Taurus that Sandor had stolen. They located a man who spotted the couple leaving the car and walking west toward Broadway. Other than that, they had nothing.

Once it was clear that they had lost Jordan, Covington had no choice but to telephone Washington.

The Deputy Director was not pleased to be called at one in the morning, especially to be given bad news.

"Good God, Covington. The FBI and the Agency combined, and you lost him?"

"Yes."

"Without a single lead on where he's going?"

"So far, that's the situation."

"Unbelievable," Byrnes fumed. "This was supposed to be a long leash, not an open cage."

"I know that."

"Well, goddamnit, do something about it."

"Yes sir. What about the Bureau?"

"What do you think? We have no choice now. Explain the predicament, tell them to call in their Homeland Security liaison. And for godssake, be diplomatic about it."

"Yes sir."

Byrnes took a deep breath. "You heard about the takedown of the three man cell, just a couple of hours after the explosion at Loubar?"

"I did."

"Interesting timing. And doesn't it strike you as odd that the informant had a number for the Agency and used that, rather than calling the police or the FBI?"

"The thought had occurred to me," Covington said.

"Yes," the DD replied, musing over the possible implications of that seemingly small issue.

"They could have someone inside, sir. Is that what you're thinking?"

"It's not the most obvious nexus but yes, that was my concern."

"These men are being interrogated now?"

"Of course."

"Maybe that will lead you to something."

Byrnes paused. "We'll see. So far we've gotten nothing. I intend to become involved in the questioning."

Covington did not voice his surprise at the DD becoming hands on at that level.

"Bottom line," Byrnes said, "find Sandor and find Andrioli."

"Yes sir."

"And Covington."

"Yes sir?"

"We need Andrioli alive."

"I know that."

The DD slammed the phone down without further comment.

*   *   *

Jordan had the cab take them to a motel he knew, just across the Grand Central Parkway from LaGuardia Airport. It was the sort of motel where the clerk at the front desk was accustomed to the sight of a man and a woman arriving after one in the morning—none of his business. Jordan paid for the room in cash, and that was also none of the clerk's business. He handed Sandor a key to a room on the second floor and wished them a good night.

Jordan and Christine found the room and let themselves in. It was square, with a large, well-used bed against the wall, one chair, an old television bolted to the top of the dresser and a nightstand. Jordan went to the telephone, set his bag on the floor and began making arrangements for a flight to Fort Lauderdale in the morning.

"Nine o'clock," he said over his shoulder. "That's the first flight I can get us on."

"At least we can get some rest," Christine said. "I haven't slept for two nights."

Jordan finished with the airline, then phoned Federal Express to get an address for the nearest drop box. Next, he called information and got a number and address for a commercial mailbox center in Fort Lauderdale. When he was done, he propped up two pillows and laid down on the bed. She sat down beside him.

"So," Jordan said, staring up at the ceiling, "you want to tell me why you're really here?"

She fluffed up her pillows and leaned on her arm, facing him. "I don't know what you mean."

"What I mean is, Prescott wouldn't have held us, at least not for long. And you could have contacted anyone you chose. An attorney. A family member. A friend. People knew we were there. I have people who knew. Even Captain Reynolds knew. You would have been safe. They weren't going to throw us in a dungeon, you could have found a way to contact your friend."

"No," she said, "you're wrong. We won't be able to reach him unless we go there and find him."

"That's it? That's your whole explanation?"

"Yes," she said, her voice beginning to tremble, "but if you don't believe me, why are you here?"

He turned towards her. "Good question. Wish I had a good answer."

"Try."

"Well, for starters, I'd like to believe you. If you're telling the truth, I have every reason to get on that plane in the morning and help you search for your pal Andrioli. He may have information, as you say, and I want it. I've got one friend dead, another in the hospital, and I'm beginning to feel like a moving target in a carnival game. There's an answer to this somewhere, and he might have it." He let her think about that for a moment. "Of course, if you're lying, there might even be more reason to stay close to you."

"That's it, then?"

"That's it."

"So I'm either a liar or not, and that's why you're here?" The look of sadness in her eyes seemed genuine enough to him.

"That," he said, "and your smile. I'd like to see some more of your smile."

She lowered her head, not bothering to attend to the tear that ran down her cheek. "I only met you a few hours ago, and all I've done is cry."

"And this is the second hotel room we've been in together. Your crying again could ruin my reputation." He sat up to have a better look at her, then reached out and tenderly wiped her face with his fingertips.

Christine forced a slight smile.

"That's better," he said.

Their eyes met, just long enough for the intimacy of that moment to become uncomfortable. She turned away, and he thought she might break down again.

"Come on," he said, "we'll get this all sorted out." He gently pushed the hair back from her face. "It's what I do, you know."

She allowed herself to relax as he held her, nodding as he spoke. "I know," she whispered. "Tony told me."

"Told you what?"

"He told me that's why Jimmy was going to meet with you. That you were a reporter or something, but that you really were something else before."

"Andrioli told you that?"

She nodded.

"And he learned that from Jimmy?"

She nodded again, and Jordan found himself wishing he could speak with Dan Peters one more time.

He waited, not saying anything as she studied his face, his regular features, the strong line of his jaw, the determined look in his eyes. "You really can help, can't you?"

"Yes," Jordan said, "I can. But I think there are still a few things you need to tell me."

TWENTY-FOUR

Mahmoud al-Rahmad reached Tripoli, via a flight from Paris. He was met at the airport, then traveled by limousine to the progressive center of this historic city, oblivious to the dazzling architectural counterpoints that defined this country in transition. Modern design was mixed with traditional structures, less a blend than a dissonant metaphor of the internal struggles this nation faced.

Rahmad, although a man with considerable appreciation for aesthetics, was concerned with the more immediate issues at hand.

He arrived at his destination, a contemporary office building situated in the heart of town, and he proceeded at once to the top floor. The elevator rose without pause to the highest level, where Rahmad emerged into a richly appointed reception area that revealed the occidental taste of its inhabitants. Although most of the international espionage activities in Libya had long been coordinated from the Villa Pietri, this penthouse was another sort of operation. Rahmad was ushered into Vincent R. Traiman's private office.

Traiman was in his middle fifties, with short, dark, nappy hair and dark eyes. He was not quite six feet tall, with broad shoulders, strong arms and the determined posture of a fighter. His features were blunt and hard, possessing something of the brutality of a pugilist or the roughness of a former linebacker. He had, in fact, played football in his college days, from there enlisting in the service, eventually rising to the rank of Captain in the United States Army. Later, he worked as an aide in the diplomatic corps, from which he was tapped as a field operative for the CIA. While he was with the Company, Traiman used his experience and training to land an assignment in the Middle East, cultivating influential friends and contacts along the way. He also found a way to amass a small, private army.

The United States government had provided unwitting assistance to Traiman's enterprise, having created a sub-class of sociopaths among the combat veterans in Southeast Asia. These soldiers had been part of the elite teams trained to become vicious jungle killers, continually exposed to the threat of death; men who were incapable of resuming their normal lives after the fall of Saigon.

Some came home, ill-equipped to deal with a resumption of their prior lives, falling victim to the haunting memories of Southeast Asia. Others re-upped, seeking in military service that sense of danger that had become their personal opiate. Yet the American armed forces could no longer provide what they needed. Even when the United States had wars to fight, they were different wars. The Gulf War of 1991 was typical of this new era of conflict. Scud missiles and stingers took the place of boots on the ground. The public had no stomach for sending men overseas to fight in battles perceived to be the problems of other countries. Vietnam had changed everything.

These impatient warriors were not willing to wait more than a decade for the United States to launch its next offensive in Iraq. They became increasingly frustrated, breaking rules and violating laws, those still in the service becoming insubordinate to younger, superior officers who had no idea what real fighting was about. And each of these malcontents had their names and serial numbers entered into the all-knowing computers of the United States intelligence community.

While he was still with the CIA, Vincent R. Traiman had access to those computers. He knew who these men were, knew that they were candidates for the platoon he intended to build. He offered lucrative contracts to the most talented, enticing men who were not able to leave the thrill of war behind. He used his position not only to create personal profit through illegal arms transactions, but also to build his own forces. These were men he could enlist, not to risk death for God, country or some synthesized ideology, but for money, and the sheer excitement of the battle.

When Traiman departed the CIA, he did not resign, he simply disappeared behind the protection of his own place guard and his conspirators from al-Qaeda. Jordan Sandor, narrowly escaped assassination at the hands of one of Traiman's new compatriots. By then, however, Traiman had safely made his retreat, a mercenary-at-large, the most wanted man on the CIA's secret most wanted list. Ironically, he never armed himself with so much as a pocket knife.

*   *   *

"Your omissions have become dangerous, Rahmad." Traiman's manner was always direct, his speech a potent economy of words. "You will have to rectify these errors."

"This work has already begun. We have placed one of the teams on Sandor."

"You have? Does your team know that Sandor is no longer in government custody?"

Rahamd did his best to conceal his surprise. Just before he left New York, he was informed that Sandor had been taken by the FBI. Now Traiman was suggesting that his intelligence sources, reporting to him in Libya, were better than Rahmad's, right there in New York. "We suspected that he would be released. Our team is on this."

"Are they? We'll see. Are you also aware that your man was killed last night in New York? In the process of attacking a woman Sandor worked with at the Agency?"

"I've been flying all night. I . . . "

"Yes, I understand that. But in the meantime, your principal concern remains unresolved."

"Andrioli," Rahmad said tentatively.

"Of course."

Now Rahmad's eyes averted Traiman's. "I must be honest and report that our men have been unsuccessful in locating him. If McHugh knew where he is, our men were not able to extract this information."

Traiman's laughter had no trace of humor as it cut through the tension of this interview. "Very noble of you, Rahmad, to admit the failure of your men. And what of you? What part do you have in this failure?"

The Arab did not respond. He suffered Traiman's anger in silence, still averting the cold gaze that bore down upon him. He only looked up when Traiman stood and walked to the wall of windows behind his desk.

"It has become increasingly difficult to recruit skilled men." Traiman spoke as he looked out at the city, his back to Rahmad. "We have had to increase salaries and bonuses, and to give assurances we prefer not to give. Revelations from our friend Andrioli could compromise our plans, not to mention the efforts of the teams we have already put in place. The longer he remains at large, the greater the risk."

"I understand."

"We are at a crossroads, and time is a luxury we do not have. You understand that too, I presume."

"I do."

Traiman turned to face him. "Well, it happens that I do know where we can find Mr. Andrioli. We have a team ready to depart for the United States today."

Once again, Rahmad was rocked by the news of Traiman's information. He began to wonder if one of his aides was playing both sides. "Where?" he asked, straining to sound composed.

"Don't be concerned," Traiman said with an abrupt wave of his hand.

Rahmad wanted to know where Andrioli was and how Traiman learned of his location, but held his tongue. Instead he asked, "What can I do to assist you?"

"You will meet with the team this morning. Right now. They will debrief you. Tell them everything you know about Andrioli, all the information your men have gathered."

"Of course," Rahmad agreed quickly.

Traiman replied with an impatient look that said he did not expect much to come from the assistance Rahmad was going to provide. "Our teams are moving into place in New York and San Francisco. They're already situated in London and Rome. However, we received some other bad news. The group in Washington has been compromised."

"I am aware of that," Rahmad said, grateful to finally be told something he already knew, even if he had learned of it from Fox News before leaving New York. "A tragedy."

"Yes," Traiman said, not revealing that it was his own man, Groat, who had betrayed them. He also kept to himself the pressure he was receiving from Qaddafi's regime to leave Tripoli. Traiman was becoming a political liability, and he was preparing to abandon his bunker in Libya for a yacht that would take him to anonymous safety on the Mediterranean.

"How were they discovered?"

"We're investigating that now. Their cell is being blamed for the explosion at Loubar."

"Is that possible? They had nothing to do with that, did they?"

"Of course not."

Rahmad's eyes narrowed as he watched Traiman now, but he said nothing.

"We also have the matter of the technical supplies being shipped from Loubar. Since the problem with Mr. Fryar has been resolved to our satisfaction, we'll need to monitor the situation until a new chief executive of that company is selected."

"Of course."

"Your assistance may be required in that process. If you are contacted by a man named Groat, you are to give him your full cooperation."

TWENTY-FIVE

It was nearly two in the morning by the time Jordan and Christine finished talking. She claimed not to know any more of importance than she had already shared with him, but Sandor had encouraged her to go over everything again, filling in some blanks along the way.

She told him that Jimmy McHugh was actually her half brother, which explained why their last names were different. He was more than ten years older than Christine, the result of a mistake their mother had made when she was too young to take care of him herself. Jimmy had been raised by foster parents, and Christine never even knew about him, she explained, until after both of her parents had died and Jimmy began writing to her from Vietnam. She had no other brothers or sisters, nor did he. Christine was just a child when he shipped out, by then living in the care of her mother's sister, Aunt Sarah. Jimmy figured he had no other family back home except his mother's sister, and so through her he finally discovered he had a sister living in Wilkes Barre. Christine met him a couple of times when he came home after the war, but he was moving around a lot in those days, and they lost touch again for several years.

Christine had difficulty speaking about her family, seemingly unable to look directly at Jordan, or to keep the chronology of her personal history straight. Jordan kept her on track, not revealing his continuing skepticism, eventually leading her back to the events that led to her last meeting with McHugh, in Paris.

Christine said that she began to hear from Jimmy again about a year ago. There were some phone calls and letters from overseas. A few months ago he wrote and asked her to come to France.

"And you didn't share any of this with Prescott?"

"Not really. I just told him that Jimmy was my brother. He didn't seem very interested in my past."

"What was he interested in, then?"

"Mainly about anything Jimmy told me, how I came to be visiting him, that stuff."

When she visited her brother in Paris, she really believed it was going to be a family reunion and a vacation. "The day after I arrived, that's when he told me the truth. At least most of it. He said he needed me to help him get away from the people he was working for. That's why he sent me to Madrid. He wanted them to believe we were going to visit the Prado and all that. I'm an art history professor."

"You mentioned."

"Well, an Assistant professor."

"Right. But he put you in harm's way. They could have come looking for you, to find him."

She was sitting up against the padded headboard now. "I know," she said. "What else was he going to do? He needed me."

Jordan realized he was becoming angry at this dead man's thoughtlessness, the selfish risks he took at her expense. Then he thought of Dan Peters, and of Beth, and exhaled slowly. "I guess he did," he said.

"He still does," she said softly.

He let that go. "And you told Prescott about Paris and Madrid?"

"Yes. Actually, it was the other man who asked me about it."

"Covington?"

"Yes."

"You told them everything?"

"Everything except about meeting Tony."

"Andrioli?"

She nodded. "I didn't say anything about helping him. I told you, I never even mentioned his name."

"Did they?"

She shook her head.

"Well, we'll find out how much help we can be to Mr. Andrioli in a few hours. Let's get some rest."

She got up from the bed and pulled back her side of the covers. "I don't have anything to sleep in," she said.

Jordan stood up and turned down the other half of the bedspread. "How about I turn around, you get yourself ready and climb under the sheets?'

She laughed. "What a prude you are, Mr. Sandor." She began to undress. "You going to just stand there and make me feel ridiculous?"

"Sorry," Jordan said, his back to her now. He stripped down to his underpants, then dialed the automated wake-up call mechanism. He climbed under the sheets and switched off his light as she did the same on her side of the bed.

"Just one last thing." He spoke quietly into the darkness. "Who is this Andrioli to you? Really."

"I told you, he's Jimmy's best friend."

"That's it?"

"That's it."

"And you're willing to risk your life to get to him, to warn him?"

He waited until she finally said, "No. That's not what this is about. Not for me. Jimmy wanted to do something. He and Anthony, they have information they wanted to give to someone they could trust."

"And that's us."

"Yes," she whispered.

"All right."

"But, what you just said. About risking my life."

"Yes?"

"It's hard for me to think of it like that. I still can't, you know?"

"I understand."

They let the darkness fill the quiet.

"It's hard for me to believe Jimmy is gone," she said.

He didn't respond.

She paused again, before saying, "You'll watch out for me, won't you?"

"Oh yes. I certainly will."

He heard her utter a sigh, felt her relax a little beside him.

He wanted to believe her, but he did not. She had just lost her brother, and yet she hadn't even mentioned a funeral. Her family saga was sketchy at best, delivered in a staccato fashion that spoke more of invention than remembrance. He could feel that she was truly frightened, but he had no idea what was driving her.

"I know you're scared," he said softly, "but it'll be all right."

"Will it?"

"Yes," he whispered. "Now try and get some sleep. Tomorrow's going to be another long day."

*   *   *

Prescott found Covington in the hotel lobby. It was the middle of the night, and there were no polite greetings as he approached. His lousy complexion and homely face were not helped by either the late hour or his sour mood.

"Well?" Covington asked.

"Still nothing," Prescott admitted.

"I wish I could understand this, I really do. You were alerted that they were on the move, then your men lost them fifty yards from the hotel."

"Save it," Prescott barked back at him. "You can throw your weight around someplace else. My men know their job."

"Of course."

"We're working on a lead. They may have been spotted on foot, heading up Broadway."

"Look, don't misunderstand. I'm not here to criticize the Bureau's procedures. We have a shared problem. We need to find them, or it'll be an embarrassment to both of us."

"Not to mention a danger to this girl, if your friend Sandor is allowed to run amuck."

"Yes, that too."

Prescott gave him a quizzical look. "So when are you going to drop this State Department bullshit and tell me why the CIA is involved?"

Covington pressed his thin lips together and nodded. "You need to make a phone call," he said. "And so do I."

TWENTY-SIX

As Sandor struggled to find a couple of hours sleep in the middle of the New York night, Rahmad was completing his early morning interview with two men who had been brought to Vincent Traiman's office in the center of Tripoli.

One was an American, tall and trim with straight, dark hair and pointed features. The second was an Englishman who stood a bit shorter than his companion, with reddish hair, a wide nose and pale, inert eyes. They were each neatly attired in suits and ties, ready to pose as corporate types who would soon be en route to the United States.

Traiman was in attendance as Rahmad provided the details of the information he had gathered on McHugh, Andrioli and the events of the past two days in New York.

The two assassins listened without speaking, their taciturn affect nettling Rahmad.

"McHugh did not know Andrioli's location," Rahmad told them. "My men were extremely persuasive in their methods of extracting information. McHugh's sister was appointed their go-between. This way, if either of them was taken, each had no way of giving up the other." He looked from the American to the Englishman, but neither reacted. While Rahmad shared what he knew, he also wanted information from them. That was his business, after all. Information.

He had no way of knowing that these men were under strict orders from Traiman to reveal nothing. Neither was even authorized to disclose their ultimate destination.

Rahmad proceeded with his monologue, going over things twice at Traiman's prompting. Then Traiman stood and announced that the interview was at an end. He and Rahmad bid the men good fortune, then had them escorted to a car for the ride to the airport. There, they would board a flight to

Paris, the first leg on their journey to Miami International and then Fort Lauderdale.

Rahmad retook his seat, satisfied that he had finished his work. He had furnished all the available intelligence, especially what Kerrigan and Mustafa had been able to coerce from James McHugh.

"Your report was woefully inadequate. What you did not provide," Traiman told him, "is Andrioli's location. We were obliged to discover that for ourselves."

Rahmad quickly changed the subject. "What about Sandor?"

"Yes, Sandor. Out of view for the moment. But we'll undoubtedly find him again very soon."

*   *   *

At first light, Bill Sternlich got out of bed without waking his wife, pulled on his old, white terrycloth bathrobe, then shuffled his way into the kitchen and put up a pot of coffee. His laptop was on the table and he switched it on, then connected to the internet. As he waited for the water to boil, he checked to see if any leads on Jordan's requests for information had come through. Sandor had told him to drop the search, but curiosity was a professional hazard. There were several messages, none related to his requests on James McHugh. He scrolled down, stopping at an e-mail from an unfamiliar source. The transmission was marked 'Urgent!'

He opened it and stared at the screen. The note read:

"The girl was a warning to those who interfere. You have been warned."

*   *   *

Sandor awoke in the unfamiliar surroundings of their room at the La Guardia motel. He quietly slid out from under the sheets, canceled the wake-up signal, then grabbed his clothes from the chair. He showered and dressed before she was up.

He had his leather bag in the bathroom, and carefully removed the S & W .45 and the Walther PPK with their extra clips. He wrapped each gun in a hand towel, stuffed them back in the satchel, then opened the door.

She was still asleep. He stood over the bed, watching her for a moment. He was a professional. She was a liability. He would take her to Florida and try to find Anthony Andrioli. After that, he would have to cut her loose.

"Come on," he said, gently shaking her by the shoulder, rousing her into consciousness.

Christine looked around, confused for a moment, then smiled at him as she raised her arms and stretched. "Oh God," she said. "I was having the strangest dream."

"Tell me about it on the plane. It's time to get ready." Jordan pulled on his jacket and picked up his bag. "I'll be back in a few minutes."

"Where are you going?"

"I've got to take care of something. I'll be right back."

She looked worried.

"I'll come right back," he repeated. "Bolt the door behind me." Then he left.

Sandor walked the five long blocks to the FedEx drop box he had called for late last night. The box was in front of one of the better hotels near the airport. He opened the top slot holding supplies, pulling out one of the large, Tyvek envelopes and a mailing label. He wrote out the address of the drop-box center in Fort Lauderdale he had also gotten last night, using the name from his second passport, "Scott Kerr", as the recipient. He used a false name and address for the sender, and checked off the box that read "Bill Recipient". Then he pasted the label to the envelope. Jordan stopped and had a look around. People were already coming and going at this hour, but no one was paying any attention to him. He pulled the two towels containing the automatics from his satchel, placed them in the envelope, sealed it with the adhesive strip, then dropped the package with a thud into the metal deposit box.

Sandor knew there was no chance to get these weapons past security at the airport, even if he checked the leather bag through. The high-resolution screeners would have their sirens blaring in an instant. It had been too late last night to get them out for delivery in Florida this morning, and he would not have been happy about giving up the protection anyway, just in case he had been followed to the motel. Sending them ahead was his only chance to get the weapons down south, although he would not be able to retrieve them until tomorrow, assuming they were not intercepted in transit. He would worry about that later.

He realized he could buy a gun when he arrived, Florida being a user-friendly ally of the NRA, but there could be a background check delay, and there would certainly be a record of the transaction, even though he would be using his forged passport.

Jordan's immediate problem was that he felt naked, unarmed now with so far to travel and so much ahead of him. He hurried back to the motel through the cold morning, mulling over what still remained in his leather case.

He had his real passport; the second passport, in the name of Scott Kerr, bearing his photo; two clean credit cards in the name of his alias; a dummy passport form that could be made up with a photo and name, as the need arose; almost ten thousand dollars in cash, which he had already been using, a hundred dollars at a time; both cell phones, one of which may or may not be compromised at this point; and a small address book, with names, phone numbers and a series of codes that might yet come in handy.

He inhaled deeply and exhaled slowly, his breath forming a small cloud in the cold air before him as he walked briskly along, wondering if he was already being followed.

*   *   *

Prescott and Covington sat down for an early breakfast in the hotel restaurant. Their meeting a few hours before, after losing Sandor's trail, had not satisfied the FBI man, and he demanded a full briefing.

"I've been authorized by the Agency to advise you of certain facts," Covington began. There was neither explanation nor apology for the deception he had employed up to that moment. "McHugh was wanted by our CTC group for questioning. Sandor is one of our former operatives who became involved, strictly by happenstance."

"Bullshit," Prescott said.

"Excuse me?"

"I said bullshit, and I mean it on at least two counts. First of all, you spooks don't have any 'former operatives.' CIA doesn't have a retirement plan for field agents. And his being here, it was no coincidence. I also made my phone call, and Homeland Security wants you to give me the full story. This is a domestic issue, Covington, CIA has no jurisdiction."

"That's your story," Covington said and picked up the menu.

Prescott reached across the table and pushed the menu aside. "It's a little late to be throwing your weight around. We lost this guy because of you. Your men interfered with our containment detail, and I need to know how you want me to fill out my report—should I say that you wanted him gone or that you're just a fucking idiot?"

Covington blinked. He was smaller and more narrowly built than

Prescott. He was not a man comfortable with physical anger. He placed the menu on the table. "Sandor is on the move because he stumbled onto something and we're using that to assist us. He and the girl may have a lead on someone we need to find, an associate of McHugh's. Whether you choose to believe me or not, Sandor is no longer working for us." As far as Covington was concerned, this was an accurate statement. At the moment, there was only one man in the CIA who knew otherwise. "The fact is, he and the girl are in grave danger, but we are willing to take that risk, given the serious matters at stake."

"You're willing to take the risk? You guys kill me. Did anyone ask Christine Frank if she's willing to take the risk?"

Covington stared back at Prescott.

"So that's it?" Prescott demanded. "That's the full level of cooperation we get?"

"That's all that I'm permitted to divulge at this time."

"I see. And are we supposed to be looking for them?"

"Yes. We are."

"Uh huh. So you gave them a lead, they spit the bit and now it's my problem, is that the way this is going down?"

Covington gave no answer.

"And where do we think they're ultimately headed? Paris?"

Covington's narrow eyes widened slightly.

"That's right. You're not the only one with intelligence sources. We know all about McHugh's plane ticket to France."

"Have you alerted the international airports?"

"I've made the necessary communications, yes."

"JFK, Newark?"

"Logan and D.C. as well."

"What about domestic flights?"

"We're working on that. A little tougher, of course, but doable."

Covington hesitated.

"What is it?" Prescott demanded.

"Is the Bureau ordering them to be picked up, or just followed?"

"You tell me, since this seems to be your show."

Covington looked away from him. "We want them out there," he said, then picked up his menu again.

*   *   *

If a manhunt had been mounted to find them, Jordan saw no evidence of it when they got out of their cab at LaGuardia.

He correctly guessed that Covington would thwart any attempts to apprehend them, at least for now. He was not worried about benign surveillance. His concern was enemy action. Amidst the busy, early morning pedestrian traffic inside the terminal, Jordan was alert to any indication they were being watched. He glanced at the faces of strangers, particularly those who were standing still rather than moving. He eyed guards and airline personnel that walked past or looked in their direction. He spotted nothing unusual as they made their way through the terminal to the automated ticket machine.

He felt particularly vulnerable without a weapon, exposed in this wide open area where anyone could be armed. He retrieved their tickets from the machine, using one of the credit cards in the name of Scott Kerr. For now, Christine would have to use her real name and identification. They would rectify that, once they got to Florida. For now, he could only hope that his name was the one they would be tracking, and that they would make their way through the airport security check.

They joined the long, slow line for screening. If they were going to be stopped, Jordan expected it to happen here or at the boarding gate. A man stood at the beginning of the queue, where Sandor displayed their first-class electronic tickets. Christine showed the man her driver's license. Jordan held up his 'Scott Kerr' passport, opened to the first page.

They moved ahead to join the line, waiting silently as the procession crept along. When it was her turn, Christine went through the metal detector without incident. Jordan placed his bag on the conveyor belt, removed his silver money clip from his pocket and the steel-banded Roléx Daytona from his wrist. He stepped through the frame of the machine and it made no sound. He was handed his money and watch, then waited for his bag to slide through on the conveyor belt.

"Could you step over here please," a small, Hispanic woman in a dark blue uniform said to him as he picked up the leather overnight case.

Jordan turned and followed her off to the side where she instructed him to place the bag on a Formica-topped table.

"Is there a problem?" he asked with a polite smile.

He received no smile in response. "Please sit down and remove your shoes."

Christine was standing twenty or so feet beyond the security checkpoint. Jordan gave her a reassuring look, nodding across the wide corridor at a man who was being put through the same drill. He sat down, removed his shoes, then watched as the woman had them passed through the scanner.

She brought back his loafers, then asked him to unzip the bag.

Sandor was pleased he had taken the time to secrete his additional passports in the false pocket along the inside of the case. The scanner would have picked them up as papers, but if the guard noticed them it could cause a problem.

The woman gave the contents a cursory inspection, then said, "You can go."

Jordan slipped on his shoes, picked up the bag and joined Christine.

"Oh my God," she said as he took her by the arm and they proceeded through the terminal.

"Routine," he assured her. "I'll probably get stopped at the gate too. Don't worry. Just a random check. Sometimes your number comes up, that's all."

They purchased magazines and coffee, then found seats near their gate. Christine said that she felt safe for the first time since they arrived at the airport.

Jordan nodded, not admitting that he would not relax until takeoff. All the same, it was mildly reassuring to know that no one other than airport personnel could be armed on this side of the security checkpoint.

When boarding began, Jordan was pulled aside again for a quick search. He chatted amiably with the security guard, all the while scanning the surrounding areas for an unfriendly face.

Once the cursory examination of his bag was completed, he and Christine joined the other first class passengers, settling into their comfortable, leather seats, then waited anxiously until the plane filled up and the door was closed. When the jet made its way to the runway and began its rapid acceleration along the tarmac, Jordan felt his body relax for the first time that morning. He knew they would be in danger again when they landed, but for the next couple of hours he could rest.

He wondered again how much of a risk his traveling companion might be, then let the thought go. He was asleep before the plane completed its ascent.

TWENTY-SEVEN

Fort Lauderdale was warm and humid, but Jordan was not slowed by the change to a tropical climate. They had disembarked without incident and, as they stepped out into the Florida sun, Sandor felt refreshed, his reserves of energy restored.

He removed his sport coat and took her jacket, folding them into his bag which he enlarged by unsnapping the sides. They took a cab and headed for the water.

The address Christine had for Andrioli—which Jordan would only have her tell him once they were on the plane—was a numbered boat slip along the intercoastal waterway at New River Drive. The taxi moved along the sun-bleached streets to Las Olas Boulevard, the main thoroughfare adjacent to the canal. Christine had directions that would lead them from there to the docksite of the boat where Andrioli was staying.

At Sandor's request, the cab driver let them out at a corner about a quarter mile from New River.

They stood there for a few moments, Jordan looking up and down the street.

"What are you thinking?" she asked him. "You didn't say a word the entire ride over here."

"I'm not sure, really. I guess it just strikes me as odd that you have his address, that's all."

"What's that supposed to mean?"

"Just what I said. This guy is in mortal danger. He's hiding from his own government, not to mention the people who killed your brother. It just seems strange that he'd be giving out his address like he was having a cocktail party. He could have given you a cell phone number, a contact address, that's what I mean."

"What you're really saying, is that you still don't believe me."

"Come on, we can't stand here all day. Let's walk."

Christine remained where she was. "Tell me. Do you believe me or don't you?"

"No," Jordan said. "Not completely."

Christine's angry look told him she was all done with sadness, at least for now. "Why are you here, then?" she demanded. "Why?"

Jordan's eyes narrowed. "The truth?"

"Of course the truth."

"Because it doesn't matter whether or not you're lying to me. You're the only lead I have right now. I'd just as soon not step on any land mines along the way, that's all."

The frankness of his response seemed to diffuse her anger. Her voice softened again, as she said, "I'm not lying to you. Jimmy didn't want to know where Tony was, just in case, in case . . ."

"I understand."

"I was the contact."

Standing there in the Florida sun, as the reflection of the bright morning danced off her sandy-colored hair, and her clear blue eyes gazed up at him, asking for his trust, he wanted to believe her. Too many years of training and too much experience in the field told him that he should know better. "It's all right," he said calmly. "We're here to find this guy. Let's find him."

They exchanged a momentary look that became a truce.

"Come on," Jordan urged her again.

She nodded, and they walked on to their unscheduled appointment with Anthony Andrioli.

*   *   *

Traiman's men were scheduled to arrive in Florida that evening. Their plane, having departed from Paris, was already cruising high above the Atlantic as Christine and Jordan were strolling along one of the streets that ran beside Fort Lauderdale's inland canals.

But the assassins sent by Traiman were not coming for Jordan. They were not even certain he would be there. The two well dressed men, seated comfortably in their business class seats were coming to find Anthony Andrioli.

They had been detached from one of the teams that Andrioli and McHugh had been training before they left Traiman's fold and returned to the States. Another of those teams had been captured in Washington yesterday afternoon.

Traiman did not like losing men, particularly those he had recruited himself. Particularly competent men. Particularly men who knew more about his plans than it was comfortable for them to know, now that they had departed his organization. In his world, there was no provision for early retirement, he agreed with Special Agent Prescott about that.

In the instance of the hit team in D.C., however, he had arranged to betray the men himself. They had been dispatched to Washington as part of a program of coordinated assassinations. They had been awaiting instructions on their targets, the dates for action and the precise plans for implementing the murders of several highly placed American legislators. Congressmen? Senators? The President? These assassins had not yet been informed. When they were arrested, they were still looking forward to receiving their orders.

But there were no orders coming. And there actually was no program of coordinated assassinations. Traiman had sent these men as a decoy, planning for Groat to turn them in as soon as his mission at Loubar headquarters was complete. These Arab hit men would be arrested, blamed for the explosion, interrogated. One or more of them would crack, Traiman was counting on that, and the Americans would then believe they had discovered the new al-Qaeda conspiracy, which involved several teams of political assassins being sent to the United States.

The authorities would run off in all the wrong directions, spending their energy and resources protecting Congressmen and cabinet secretaries, missing the entire point of Traiman's real plan. No one among the team of terrorists he sent in Washington knew anything about his Operation VX.

Unfortunately, Traiman feared, Anthony Andrioli might know.

When it became clear that McHugh and Andrioli had disappeared from Paris, Traiman began by making a conciliatory gesture. He offered special inducements, through an intermediary in France, if both men would return. McHugh and Andrioli were well aware of how generous such enticements could be, with supplies of money, women and drugs that were virtually without limit. They were also aware of how Traiman would make them answer for their betrayal.

When neither man responded to these entreaties, all indications were that they had returned home. Traiman assigned Rahmad and his U.S.-based espionage network to find and remove them. They were successful in locating McHugh, but McHugh was never as bright as Andrioli. McHugh made stupid mistakes, using the telephone, contacting people. Once they tracked him down, the methods employed by Kerrigan and Mustafa were direct and brutal—they needed McHugh to talk.

Under the torture they inflicted on him, McHugh admitted his suspicions that the assassination teams sent by Traiman were diversionary, that there was another offensive being planned for the United States and elsewhere. He lacked any knowledge of the details. He said nothing about Operation VX.

Andrioli was another matter entirely. He might know.

VX was a nerve gas developed by the British, just after the Second World War, which remains the most lethal weapon of its kind ever devised. Traiman's plan called for the simultaneous explosion of several large canisters containing this highly toxic substance in strategic locations around the world. The discharge of a vaporized form of VX, in American cities and the capitals of some of her allies, would be fatal to thousands, perhaps even tens of thousands of people in each location. VX had the consistency of motor oil, but a single milliliter became a fatal dose when spread through aeration or detonation. In a crowded train station, stadium, mall or arena, there would be no defense against the instantaneous cloud of death that would form. The result would be world-wide pandemonium. Suicide bombers would seem like nothing more than isolated acts of momentary terror. The attack on the *USS Cole* would be regarded as a single military strike. Even the destruction of the World Trade Center would pale in comparison.

The tragic effects of Nine-Eleven were dramatic, but the impact of Operation VX would be far more devastating. What would happen when hundreds of thousands of workers in these metropolitan centers refused to board the subways, buses or trains for fear of being murdered? Businesses would fail. Economic chaos would result. And Traiman was positioning himself to reap a financial windfall as these economies crumbled.

Operation VX had been carefully prepared, and Andrioli was far more likely than McHugh to have learned details of these plans before his disappearance.

Traiman was therefore obliged to put the mission on hold, until he could determine the extent of the damage the second of his two traitors might cause by revealing what he knew to American authorities. The interference of David Fryar at Loubar had caused another problem. As Traiman realized, his Arab associates were not patient men, and their intolerance of these delays was growing.

That was the reason Traiman summoned Rahmad to Tripoli. Every now and then, a face to face meeting was necessary, if for no other reason than to remind his subordinates of his influence.

Even though some time had been wasted on the journey east, it would be paid off in the effect of the visit. Mahmoud al-Rahmad needed to have the importance of this task emphasized, his own expendability underlined.

Rahmad would be sent back to New York to fulfill his other responsibilities and soon Anthony Andrioli and the growing stain of his disloyalty would cease to be a problem.

TWENTY-EIGHT

The boats on the New River canal were docked broadside, bow to stern, secured with lines, their hulls cushioned by bumpers against the concrete bulkhead. Jordan and Christine strolled along the northern embankment, silently reading the names on each transom, searching for the name Christine had for Andrioli's boat, the *Winsome II*. That was all she had. The name of the boat and the general location of the dock.

They walked without speaking, Jordan's sense of uneasiness amplified by the fact that he was unarmed. He had his bag slung over his shoulder, Christine staying right beside him as they passed an assortment of cabin cruisers and sailboats. As each boat came into view, their anxiety intensified. Perhaps Andrioli had abandoned the vessel, or moved to another marina. He might have put out to sea. Christine might even have the name wrong.

The midday sun now conspired to heighten their discomfort, the cloudless sky offering no relief. They were fresh from the chill of autumn in the north, and the early feeling of comforting warmth was replaced with a sweltering heat. Sandor found himself wishing he could change from his long-sleeved knit shirt.

They had just passed a two-masted sloop called the *Excess*, from Wilmington, Delaware, when the stern of the next vessel, a power boat, came into view. It was about forty feet long, of white fiberglass construction with teak trim. It bore the name *Winsome II*.

Christine stopped, but Jordan took her arm and urged her forward, the two of them continuing past the boat in silence.

Sandor was a stranger to Andrioli. He knew he could not step aboard the vessel without risking a sudden and violent reaction. Christine would have to make the approach, that much was certain.

As they moved past the bow of a cabin cruiser docked ahead of Andrioli's boat, Jordan said, "He knows you, right? You'll have to go first. I'll wait just off to the side. There," he said, pointing to a bench along the walkway. They stopped now. "Look, we have no way of knowing what the situation is in there. He may not be alone. He may not be there at all. He may have other visitors already, we can't be sure." He turned to have another look at the *Winsome II*. It appeared very quiet. "How well do you really know him?"

"I told you. I met him in Paris, with Jimmy."

"And he'll recognize you?"

"Of course."

Jordan knew they had already been standing there long enough. "All right, go to the stern and call for him. Quietly. First name only. And be careful. Any sign of trouble, anything that bothers you, you take off. Understand?"

She nodded, then turned towards the boat. Jordan stepped aside—if Andrioli looked through one of the portholes, he figured it was best for him to see Christine alone.

Christine turned back to him. "What should I say to him?"

"Say hello. Tell him you're in trouble and ask to come aboard. Tell him your brother's dead." The last statement sounded harsher than he intended. "I'm sorry. Look, just let him hear your voice, let him have a look at you. I'll be waiting right there."

Jordan walked away now, stopping beside the wooden bench, watching her. For a moment he considered making a call to Sternlich on his secure cell, just to check on Beth, but for now he decided he had better stay focused on Christine. *Damn*, he thought, *I would feel a lot better if I had a weapon.*

The *Winsome II* was a solid looking sport fishing boat, with an enclosed wheelhouse, flying bridge and deep sea rigs. There was no activity that Sandor could detect, no sign of movement above or below deck. Maybe Andrioli was out. Perhaps he really was gone.

He watched Christine lean forward and knock on the hull near the aft railing. She knocked again and, when she received no response, she moved forward to have a look inside, through a porthole of the main salon. She knocked again. There was no reply.

Jordan moved towards her now. Something did not feel right. When he moved up behind her, she nearly jumped with fright.

"My God, Jordan. You scared me to death."

"He's not answering?"

"I called his name, but I didn't want to yell it out."

Jordan looked behind them, up and down the quay. "Call your own name," he said.

"What?"

"Tell him who you are."

She leaned closer to the opening into the stern cabin. "Tony," she called out softly. "It's Christine. We're here to see you."

She said it again, then they waited.

A voice from somewhere inside the vessel responded now. "Move two steps back," they were told, "and keep your hands at your sides. Nice and natural now, the both of you."

Two steps back was going to put them squarely in range of the salon porthole. Jordan thought about diving to the ground before a shot could be fired, but that would leave Christine an easy target. He hesitated. Whoever was inside could have taken them out already, if he was willing to shoot them right there, in the open. He dropped his hands to his sides. "Come on," he said, taking her by the wrist and pulling back.

They stepped away from the railing, then heard, "Christine," in an astonished tone from the disembodied voice. "Come aboard, both of you, but leave your hands where they are. Especially you, cowboy."

"Hold it," Jordan snapped, taking hold of her arm again, before she could step forward. "We're not moving anywhere until Christine gets a look at you."

There was silence. Then a curtain was pulled back at the porthole of the main salon, below deck, and a face appeared. The man peered cautiously from beside the short drape. Even with a growth of beard and shaggy hair, Christine knew him at once.

"Tony," she exclaimed with relief.

"All right," he barked in military fashion. "Get aboard. And buddy, keep your hands away from that bag. Leave 'em out where I can see 'em."

They stepped past the opening in the railing, through the wheelhouse and down the stairs to the main sitting area below. If Andrioli trusted Christine, it was belied by the H & K USP9SD with the long, silenced barrel he leveled at them as they entered the cabin.

Andrioli was a wiry man of about fifty, although his age was tough to judge from the unkempt growth of grayish-black beard and his sloppy attire. His white polo shirt was dirty and wrinkled, and the khakis he wore looked as though they'd been slept in, and probably had been. He had sad brown eyes that warily studied Jordan and Christine as they stepped into the main salon.

"Sorry for my crude ideas about hospitality," he said. "Close that hatch behind you and latch it."

Jordan did as he was told.

"All right, lemme have a look see." He motioned Jordan to drop the bag, then pressed the barrel of the automatic into Sandor's back as he gave him a quick, but expert frisking. He inspected the contents of the leather case, mostly feeling around for anything sharp or metallic. Then he searched Christine, all the while holding his pistol at the ready.

"Not exactly a warm-hearted reunion," Jordan said.

"Afraid not. These are troubled times you know. Sorry Christine."

"It's all right," she said. "We understand."

"Whatever," he replied coldly, obviously beyond caring about anyone's understanding. "Go ahead, siddown."

Jordan and Christine sat on the settee facing their host, who settled into the captain's chair in front of the chart table. He laid the gun in his lap. "Smoke?" he asked them as he pulled out a pack of Marlboros. They both declined. "Filthy fucken habit, I gotta admit." He lit up and took a long drag. "So," he said to Christine, "who is this character and what's up with Jimmy?"

She looked at Jordan, asking him to respond.

"This character is Jordan Sandor," he said. "I'm the guy your friend Jimmy wanted to meet."

"You're Sandor, eh?"

"Right. And, in case you hadn't heard, your friend Jimmy is dead."

Andrioli's eyes moved slowly away from them, more pain in his expression than surprise. It was obvious he had not heard about McHugh which, in turn, was no surprise to Jordan. So far, the murders in Woodstock were not a national story. Prescott and Covington had seen to that. Unless Andrioli had an active source of information, which he probably did not, he would be in the dark. From the looks of the man, he was going it very much alone.

"Poor Jimmy," he said at last. "How?"

Sandor answered him. "Two men, one a small, dark skinned Arab, the other a tall, light haired American." Jordan searched his face for some sign of recognition. If Andrioli had any ideas, he wasn't sharing them yet. "They tied him to a chair, beat him senseless, then put two in his head."

Jordan's description was purposely harsh, but the vivid description of his comrade's death didn't seem to phase Andrioli. Instead, he turned to Christine and asked, "You all right?"

"I suppose so," she told him.

"Lousy sons 'o bitches."

"Jordan is the man Jimmy was going to talk to before, well, before . . ."

"I know that, assuming this guy is really Sandor."

"The same people who did this, they've also come after Jordan."

That got his attention. He shot a quick glance at Sandor, but said nothing. He looked back at Christine. "What about you?" Andrioli asked her.

"I'm okay. You mean has anyone . . ."

"Yeah, that's exactly what I mean."

"No. Not at all."

"Well then, what the hell are you doing here?" Andrioli's anger surprised them both. "Jimmy should never have gotten you involved in this bullshit. I told him he was wrong to have you come to Paris in the first place, the selfish little bastard. What in hell are you doing now, getting mixed up in this?"

"I wanted to help, that's all."

"Hold on a minute," Jordan said. "Let's back up here."

"Yeah," Andrioli agreed, "that's a good idea. Why don't you start by telling me what you know about all this."

"Funny, I was just about to ask you the same thing," Jordan said. "Of course, you do have the gun, so I'll go first."

*   *   *

Bill Sternlich sat at his desk, staring at the screen. He had received no reply to any of the inquiries he made for Jordan, except for the message that found its way to his personal e-mail address at home, telling him that the attack on Beth Sharrow should also be a warning to him. The lack of response from his usual sources was odd, to say the least. What was equally surprising, was the complete absence of any more news releases on the upstate murders, the shooting at Jordan's apartment or the subsequent disappearance of Sandor himself. He searched for any mention of the incident with Beth, but there was nothing about that either. Based on what Jordan had told him, he was certain there would have been some release in a Homeland Security report. He found none.

One thing was obvious—Jordan was back at his old job, Sternlich was sure of that, but the total information blackout was extraordinary. Whatever his friend had happened upon, it was bigger than either of them had first suspected. At least it was bigger than Jordan had told him.

He picked up the telephone and dialed Jordan's cell phone number for the fifth try that morning. This time, he didn't bother to leave a message.

TWENTY-NINE

Jordan described the events of the past three days, from the shooting in Woodstock and the murders of McHugh and Peters, to the attempt on his own life, the ransacking of his apartment and the apparent attempt by the government to hold Christine and him in protective custody. He had already concluded that Andrioli was no amateur, and if he wanted the man's help it wasn't going to work for him to hold out on what he knew so far.

Andrioli interrupted occasionally to ask for details. He wanted more precise descriptions of the two shooters in Woodstock. He was interested in the questions put to Jordan and Christine by Prescott and Covington.

Sandor answered everything, withholding only the fact of his former career with Central Intelligence. He also stayed with John Covington's cover story, that he and Todd Swedock were from the State Department.

The information Andrioli found most disturbing was the evidence that Jimmy had made arrangements to return to Paris. Was he planning to flip again? Was he going back to save himself and sell out his friend? It was difficult for him to contemplate any of that, especially in front of Christine.

Andrioli brought out some beers, passed them around and laid his gun on the chart table. He took two large gulps from his can, then eyed Jordan with obvious suspicion. "That it?"

"Those are the headlines and the back stories as far as I know," Jordan said. "Mind if I ask a few questions now?"

"You can if you want, but I'll tell you up front, the more you know, the more dangerous this gets."

"Your pal Jimmy didn't worry about that when he asked to meet me, which is why I'm here in the first place, right? And you two didn't worry about it when you got Christine involved in all of this." He let that thought linger. "Anyway," Jordan asked, "how much more dangerous can it get? They've tried to kill me twice already."

"You've got a point there," Andrioli conceded without a trace of sympathy. "But they failed. You happened to get in their way in Woodstock. That was bad luck. They tried to clean you up at your apartment, but they missed that chance. Maybe they'll let you be," he suggested, but there was no conviction in his voice. He sat back, slowly stroking his scraggly, auburn beard, drawing his hand across his mouth, thoughtfully, as if trying to convince himself that these killers might actually abandon their interest in these unclaimed victims.

Jordan could see in his eyes that he had dismissed the idea, so he decided to change the subject, try to get him talking about what he knew. "So, what made you choose a boat in Fort Lauderdale? It's pretty exposed for a man in hiding, isn't it?"

"Maybe." Andrioli permitted himself a brief smile that momentarily brightened his dark features. "Not exactly the old Hole in the Wall in Wyoming, is it?"

"Not exactly, no."

Andrioli took another long gulp of beer. "That's all right. Haven't you ever read 'The Purloined Letter'? I thought you're supposed to be a writer."

"Sort of a writer. I know the story."

"Hide in plain sight, right? When we split up, Jimmy ran for the mountains. Bad move, if you ask me. That's why I never told Jimmy where I was going. Jimmy was a good guy, but he wasn't the sharpest knife in the drawer." He glanced at Christine. "Sorry."

"I understand," she said softly.

"Look, I figured those sons o' bitches were gonna find us no matter where we hid. They trap you in the mountains, you got no one around and nowhere to go. I figured I'd be better off on a boat. I can take off, if I have the chance. Or I can slip over the side, into the canal. And I'm surrounded by a slew of people here all the time. These bastards are vicious, but they're not stupid. They're not sending suicide bombers after me, those kamikaze bastards are only good for random attacks. The two that took out Jimmy, they were pros, and they're not about to get caught or killed just to do a job. The more careful they have to be, the better chance I have to make a move. I came south, went to a broker and rented this thing for six months, paid cash in advance. Easy as that."

Jordan watched Andrioli throw back another mouthful of beer. Unremitting fear had taken its toll on this man. His eyes seemed constantly alert to peripheral dangers. Exhaustion lined his face. His body seemed permanently tense. Even worse, Jordan knew, was the realization that he had been the cause of his own inevitable destruction.

"Who were they?" Jordan asked him. "The two who took out McHugh. Were they Traiman's men?" It was the first time either of them had mentioned that name.

Andrioli managed a hearty laugh. "That's good, cowboy. Very good." He leaned forward in his chair. "Look, I didn't invite either of you to this party. You told me what you could. Best thing you can do now is blow the hell out of here and get as far away from me as you can."

"Thanks for the advice, but we're not going anywhere. We're here because Christine believes that you and Jimmy had something to tell me, and I'm not leaving until I get some answers."

"That right?"

"That's right. And I'll tell you what else. If we walk out of here now, and anyone catches up with us, they'll figure we know too much already, so we're cooked either way. Not to mention, we're now a danger to you, right? You think it'll be tough for them to force Christine to tell them where you are?" She winced at the thought, but the two men ignored her. "Even if you leave here today, you'll be a hell of a lot easier to track once they have a starting place."

Andrioli stared into Jordan's determined eyes. "So we're in this together, is that the deal?"

"That's the deal."

Andrioli considered that. "Tell me again about those names they ran by you."

"All right if I get the list from my bag?"

Andrioli grinned. "I'll get it." He picked up the bag, and Jordan told him where to find the list. He handed the paper to Sandor.

"Zagallai."

Andrioli nodded. "I know that name. Iraqi. Former Republican Guard, of the late Saddam Hussein regime. Recently joined up with Traiman, from what I hear."

"Mahmoud al Rahmad."

"Yeah. Saudi. Runs Traiman's operation in New York. Diplomatic pass-port. Friend of the al-Qaeda boys. Slimy bastard."

"Suaramar."

"Hmmm. Never met him, but I know the name. I think he works with Traiman, in Syria."

"Mustafa Tagliev."

"He's an agent for the CIA, NSA, some bullshit. They probably threw his name in there to keep you honest."

"American?"

"Nah. Works for the U. S., though."

"What about Tallal Abdullah Driann, you know him?"

"Sure. He's Qaddafi's liaison for everything Traiman was running out of Libya. Now that Qaddafi claims he wants to be a good guy, he'll sell out Driann in a heartbeat, especially if the world finds out what was going on over there."

"Plausible deniability."

"You got it."

"The last name is Ibrahim Abass."

"Yeah, I met him once. He's Traiman's direct liaison with al-Qaeda. Bad guy. Most dangerous guy on your list."

"Where is he?"

"No idea. Showed up in Tripoli once in a while, not often. Qaddafi's people are trying to move the entire Traiman operation out of the country. Traiman is not an easy man to push around."

Jordan nodded. "And this Rahmad, you say he's in New York."

"Usually."

They were quiet for a minute as Andrioli took a swig of his beer. "You know, no matter what they said, there's no way the feds wanted you two in protective custody."

"What makes you say that?"

"Come on, you seem like a smart guy. You think if they wanted to hold you, you wouldn't still be there?"

Jordan knew he was correct, of course. "I don't know," he said. "We made a pretty good run for it, right?"

Christine, who had been quiet for most of their long exchange, nodded.

"We did," she agreed. "You could see them on the street. They were looking for us."

"Looking, sure. But not holding you. See what I mean?"

Sandor nodded. Andrioli was a bit rough around the edges, but he was no fool.

"What does that mean?" Christine asked.

"Well," Andrioli said as he scratched his short, untidy beard, "it probably means they had you followed here."

THIRTY

Andrioli relaxed a bit from the beer and the company. He told them it had been a while since he had a conversation with anyone that lasted longer than it took to order a pizza. He described the solitary life he had been living for the past month. He said his only real sense of freedom came when he undocked his boat and set out for the calm, open sea. He was often tempted to keep going, he admitted. Only two things brought him back— the commitment he and Jimmy made when they decided to return home, and the uncertainty of where his journey would end.

So he would return to his slip, make midnight visits on foot to the twenty-four hour grocery store, then spend sleepless nights trying to sort out whatever future was left him. It was difficult to go it alone. No one else could understand the pressure or the fear. No one except McHugh. They were looking for the right approach, the right contact. Now that Jimmy was dead, there was no reason to wait.

Jordan let him talk, waiting for his monologue to lead back to Traiman and the work they did in the deserts of North Africa. But Andrioli was not so easily manipulated.

"If there's no reason to wait any more," Jordan said, "why not tell us what this is all about? What have you got to lose at this point?"

Andrioli stared at him again, then turned to Christine. "You believe he never met Jimmy?"

"I do."

"But you were on your way to see him," he said to Jordan. Andrioli was working it over one more time.

"McHugh asked to see me. Dan Peters put us together. I never got there." Jordan turned away, shaking his head. "How many times you want to go over this?"

"Your friend, Peters. He had to be working for Covington," Andrioli announced flatly. "It's the only thing that fits."

"Covington?"

"You said this guy Covington that you and Christine met with, up north, claimed he was from the State Department. Well he's not. He's CIA."

Sandor did his best to appear surprised. "Run that by me again."

Andrioli finished off his beer, set the can down and gave Jordan a dubious look that told him he wasn't buying his act. "John Covington is a CIA chief. He's been after Jimmy and me even before we got back. He was the man we got referred to when we first tried to make a deal from Paris. He didn't think we had enough to sell."

"Which leaves us where?"

Andrioli shrugged. "You know who Traiman is." It was a statement, not a question.

"I have an idea."

Andrioli smiled, as if he knew something else he wasn't ready to share. "Lemme help you out." He got up, taking his automatic with him, and brought them another two cans of Budweiser from the small refrigerator. He tossed one underhanded to Jordan. "Traiman used to be an American agent. I don't know what kind. Special Services, CIA, something. He took a powder a few years back, went turncoat on them. Now he runs a training camp for terrorists. He also brokers weapons and technology deals in the Middle East."

Jordan nodded. "So they say. Where did you and Jimmy fit in?"

"We were like instructors, basically. Trained all sorts of scum that Traiman brought into the fold from all over the place." He returned to his seat, placing the gun back atop the teak chart table. "It was wild, since we didn't speak anything but English. We had interpreters, never even needed to learn the languages—there were a lot of different nationalities, believe me. Like a bizzaro United Nations, a distorted universe, if you know what I mean. We were highly paid drill sergeants. More than that, even. We taught these sons o' bitches everything."

Neither Jordan nor Christine uttered a word in response.

"You hear about the explosion in Washington yesterday?"

"Covington told me about it yesterday, then I read the story in the morning paper," Jordan said, "on the flight down."

"Yeah, I saw it on the news. The company was Loubar," Andrioli told them. "Manufactured all types of para-military technology, bio-chemical stuff. If you saw the article, you know the deal. Anyway, president of the company died, along with his secretary and a couple of other people. The guy's name was Fryar, David Fryar."

"Should I take a guess?'

"Go ahead."

"He was Traiman's man in Washington."

"One of them," Andrioli said. "Probably stepped outta line. Asked for more money. Or worse."

"Such as?"

"Held up the shipments, maybe. Traiman's on a timetable right now. He needs to move his teams into the States, and he needs the equipment."

"What kind of timetable?"

Andrioli lit another cigarette and inhaled deeply before going on. "I'm not sure. In the spring, Traiman was assembling some of his best men for assignments in the States. Assassination teams, is what he trained them for. Here, and in Europe too."

"Who are the targets?"

"Who would you think?" Andrioli asked with a frown. "Heads of state, politicians, whatever."

"God," Christine said.

"And this wasn't coming from Qaddafi?"

"No way. Traiman is way beyond him. Old Muammar got religion after we bombed the shit out of Baghdad. He gave it the old "No mas" deal, threw in the towel, told Traiman his lease was up."

"So Traiman's not in Tripoli anymore?"

"Let's say if he is, he's not going to be welcome there much longer. He still has enough pull with the bad guys to buy a little time."

"Al-Qaeda?"

"Yeah. Especially now, because it's going to get really ugly."

"Worse than these terrorist hit teams?"

Andrioli shook his head. "Not sure, but I know they're moving something bad into place."

"Something bad?"

"Chemicals, biological weapons."

"When are they supposed to make this move?"

"Not sure of that either." Andrioli took another drag on the cigarette.

"When Jimmy and I split, we threw a monkey wrench into their scheme, if you see what I mean."

"I'm not sure I do."

"I have to paint you a picture?" He took another swig of beer. "When Jimmy and I took off, Traiman couldn't be sure how much we knew, or where we'd go with it."

Jordan waited, watching Andrioli take a puff of his Marlboro. When he lifted his can of beer to have another drink, Sandor lunged across the cabin, driving his right elbow into Andrioli's chest, grabbing at the automatic with his other hand. Beer splashed all over Andrioli's shirt and face as Jordan spun to the side, coming up with the pistol in hand.

"Nice move," Andrioli said as he righted himself and wiped some of the beer away. "Goddamn, I'm outta practice."

"Enough of this good old boy bullshit. Let's get some real answers about what you know, shall we?"

THIRTY-ONE

The jetliner landed in Miami, where Traiman's men disembarked and entered the international arrivals building. They stood on different lines, one an American citizen, the other a visitor from Great Britain. The immigration officers gave them and their papers a cursory once over. The passports were in order, and no questions were raised. They made their way through customs without incident, then into the arrival lounge where they were met by a driver holding up a cardboard sign with their assumed names.

They followed the chauffeur outside, to a waiting Lincoln town car being attended by a second man who took their suitcases and held the back door open. There were no greetings beyond an exchange of curt nods. When all four men were comfortably seated inside, the car took off for the ride up the coast to Fort Lauderdale.

"Where are the goods?" the American asked.

The man who met them in the terminal reached for the hard-shell case at his feet, then passed it to the back seat. The American flipped the latches and opened it, finding two SigSauer P228 9mm automatic pistols nestled safely in foam rubber. He lifted one out and handed it to the Englishman. He removed the second, checking the thirteen-shot clip. There were extra clips, fully loaded, and each man pocketed two. There were two small packets of C-4 explosive with detonators and two infrared remote devices.

"You have the address yet?"

"We have a lead on a boat on the canal," said the man in the passenger seat.

"A lead?" the tall Englishman asked.

"Don't worry," the driver said. "We'll get you where you need to be."

The two killers sent by Traiman completed their breakdown and inspection of the weapons, then stared out the windows as they motored north to the Fort Lauderdale exits, then circled around to Las Olas Boulevard, not far from the corner where Jordan and Christine arrived by cab earlier in the day. Once there, they turned from the main street into a public parking lot situated directly behind a low slung row of shops and restaurants that fronted on the main street.

It was growing dark now. They pulled to a remote end of the lot where the car came to a stop. The driver turned off the headlights and engine, then they waited.

THIRTY-TWO

"That's quite a move for a reporter, cowboy."

"United States Army, *cowboy.* I had training from a pretty good drill instructor myself."

Andrioli wiped his shirt with his hand, then drank off what was left in the can of Bud. "Yeah, I know."

"You know what?"

"I know you're not just some reporter. Why the hell you think Jimmy picked you, because you're fucking Ernest Hemingway?"

Jordan stared at him.

"We were with Traiman long enough, knew the old war stories. You were his fair-haired boy, back when he was doing his part for Uncle Sam. When he went AWOL, you were also the guy who got away."

"How's that?"

"Come on Sandor, drop the act here. Traiman tried to have you done four years ago. Then he almost had you in Bahrain. You were a heartbeat from being buried neck high in the Sahara Desert."

"That so?"

"Yeah, it is. So now what? You gonna shoot me?"

"That depends."

"On what?"

"On the answers I get."

"Shit, why not just shoot me? Probably be doing me a favor."

Christine began to stand up, but Jordan said, "Sit down," without taking his eyes off Andrioli.

"Jordan . . . ," she began.

Sandor cut her off again. "I said sit down, and I mean it." She lowered herself back onto the upholstered banquet. "So," Jordan said, keeping his attention focused on Andrioli, "the government wasn't willing to trade, based on what you know?"

"It's like I told you. We made calls from Paris, to people we knew, through contacts we had. We wound up being referred to Covington, and he told us to pound sand. To start with, he didn't seem to believe anything we said. Even if it was true, he said we didn't have enough to buy what we wanted."

"Which was what?"

"Money, immunity, witness protection. You know the drill." He looked at the empty beer can, then flipped it onto the chart table.

"Easy," Jordan warned him.

"Okay, okay. Don't get excited." Andrioli smiled at Christine. "He's tougher than he looks."

"Have you tried to speak with someone other than Covington?"

"Sure we did," Andrioli sighed. "Everyone we talked to figured it the same way—we were telling a tale just to make a deal, get immunity, whatever. How could we prove anything? What did we have to show them? We didn't have any hard evidence, dates, nothing. Covington was the only one who seemed interested in giving us a tumble, but then he turned to bullshit too. That's when we took off."

"And so I was another contact, is that the idea?"

Andrioli nodded. "Maybe the last one. That was the idea, anyway. Peters to McHugh and now to me. Tinkers to Evers to Chance." He smiled. "Did Danny tell you he knew me?"

Jordan shook his head at this latest revelation. Now things were beginning to make sense. "I never even heard your name until Christine gave it to me last night."

"Good man, Peters. Served with him for about six months. I'm sorry he got in the line of fire."

"Me too. So your the idea was what? To convince me to pitch it to someone for you?"

"That was one idea."

"Why me?"

Andrioli allowed himself a slight grin. "You know why. You've got an inside track. And you're the only person I know hates Traiman more than I do."

Jordan nodded. "You have another idea, if we can't sell the first one?"

Andrioli shrugged and offered a crooked smile. "Yeah. I figure if they don't buy what I have, I've got to get more to sell. I figure you're the guy to help me get it."

*   *   *

Traiman's men decided it was dark enough now. There was no one in view. This part of town was far from the night action along A1A near the Fort Lauderdale beach. Anyone they passed would pose little in the way of risk or subsequent identification. They got directions from the driver, then made their plan for where they would be picked up after they had completed their mission. They went over everything twice, then the two men stepped out into the balmy night air and made their way to the quay where they would find Andrioli's boat.

The American knew Andrioli, having spent time with him outside Tripoli during the operations briefings earlier in the year. The Englishman met him once. Traiman had selected these men for this 'clean-up' task, since neither was a friend of Andrioli's, but either could readily identify him. Prior personal contact was superior to a photographic survey, particularly since the target had likely altered his appearance. There were physical characteristics that could not be easily disguised, and these men were trained to penetrate such camouflage. The risk that Andrioli would recognize either or both of them was immaterial—everyone understood that Anthony Andrioli would be awaiting this appointment, that he was serving time on his own death watch.

There was no crisis of spiritual confidence for these two killers, no conflicting loyalties, no apprehension about the consequences of their actions. They were hired and trained as assassins, and the part they played in the rising tide of international terrorism, even when it involved a fellow combatant, was not their concern.

The American was a sharpshooter and, even by the standards of his trade, a particularly vicious killer. He had been schooled in the martial arts and could be as deadly with his hands as he was with a gun. If they took Andrioli alive, their instructions were to find out what he knew, using any means they chose. Then they were to eliminate him.

The Englishman, like his companion, was an expert marksman. He was also skilled in the use of explosives, hence the inclusion of C4 and detonators in their arsenal.

The two killers strode purposefully toward the canal, each intent on his responsibilities. Each understood precisely what had to be done.

They continued along the concrete dock without speaking. The American reached inside his jacket and made a slight adjustment to the angle of his automatic. The Englishman removed the safety clasp.

Sandor had often wondered at the blindness of such men, their inability to perceive the irony of their position—that some day their roles with Andrioli might well be reversed. Experience had taught Jordan that armed conflict has an immediacy that does not permit for reflection or doubt. Hesitation is fatal.

And so, these executioners moved on, any time for thought having succumbed to instinct, especially now, as they saw the transom of the *Winsome II* up ahead.

As they came even with Andrioli's cabin cruiser, the American gave a discrete signal to move on. Without breaking stride, they kept walking, coming to a stop after passing several more boats.

"Well then?" the red-haired Englishman asked quietly.

"I don't like it."

"The setup?"

The American nodded. "Bow to stern. Too open. We make a move to board, he'll feel us as soon as we step on deck."

The Englishman nodded. They were standing face to face, a hundred yards beyond the forward railing of the *Winsome II*. Even so, they spoke in a whisper.

"And we don't know what he has rigged up."

"What about blowing it?"

The American shook his head. "No good, not unless we know for sure he's inside. We can't be sorting through the pieces afterwards."

The Englishman frowned. "Agreed."

"We'll go with the plastique as a diversion."

"Good," the Englishman agreed. "I'll set a small charge up front, then place a full set-up at the rear as backup. Use the small blast to bring him out."

"And if he doesn't come topside?"

"If he doesn't, we're going in."

The American nodded. "The first blast'll have the whole canal in an uproar. There won't be much time."

"It's still worth the risk," the Englishman said, "if we don't have to board his bloody boat."

The American had a look up and down the dock. "Too bad we can't wait him out." He shook his head. "We have our orders."

"Orders?" the Englishman snapped. "The only order here is not to get ourselves killed."

The American stared at him for a moment, then said, "No one's getting killed except Andrioli. Place the charge at the bow."

"Done," said the Englishman.

THIRTY-THREE

When a soldier spends enough time in active combat, he develops auxiliary senses. Awake or asleep, he becomes alert to sounds that do not quite fit with the character of the other noises. Even an unusual silence can snap him to attention.

Jordan was asking a question, but Andrioli was listening to something else. He held up his hand, then rose slowly from his seat.

Sandor immediately sensed it also. He stood, turning to Christine, his finger to his lips.

There had been two sets of footsteps, shuffling by the boat, disappearing into the night. Then they heard the footsteps again, coming back the other way, not really conscious of them until they came to a stop.

Jordan moved next to Andrioli, who was checking to see that the blackout drapes on all of the portholes of this main salon were pulled shut. "You have any other guns here?" Jordan whispered.

Andrioli nodded, pointed to the aft cabin, then held up one finger.

"Get it," Jordan breathed in his ear.

Andrioli stepped quickly to the rear of the vessel, quietly unlatched the door to that cabin, went inside and then emerged with a Browning 9 millimeter.

The footsteps had ended somewhere near the bow. Andrioli pointed in that direction and Jordan responded with a brief nod.

Sandor saw that Andrioli was holding two extra clips for his Browning. Jordan held up the H&K with its long silencer and motioned to Andrioli's hand.

Andrioli disappeared into the aft cabin again, returning with a box of 9 mm shells. He handed it to Sandor. The two men were side by side, straining to hear what was going on above deck.

"They're either going to board us or blow the boat," Jordan said in a barely audible voice, his mouth close to Andrioli's ear. "We've got to move now."

Andrioli nodded. He tapped Christine's shoulder, then gestured toward the rear cabin. It would be the safest place for her, he told them, once the action began.

Christine turned to Jordan, and the steely look in his eyes told her not to debate the instruction.

As she started to move, he whispered, "Keep down, no matter what. Don't come out unless one of us calls you."

Christine hurried into the aft cabin, and Jordan closed the door behind her.

Andrioli held up two fingers.

Sandor nodded his agreement. There were two men. They were at the front of the boat right now, but would doubtless split up. Jordan knew that he and Andrioli were running out of time, but if they acted too soon, or moved in the wrong direction, they might be cut down before they had a chance to mount a counter-attack. He reached for Andrioli's arm and drew him toward the short stairway that led to the wheelhouse. "Open the latch as quietly as you can. I'll go forward, make some noise there. Just get it unlocked, then stand aside. When I come past, I'll blow through the hatch, you can follow me out."

Andrioli nodded.

"There's no margin for error. Shoot to kill."

Andrioli nodded again, then watched as Jordan moved forward in the salon.

*   *   *

The red-haired Englishman prepared the two explosive devices and handed the larger one to his partner. He fastened the C-4 near the railing of the bow, while the American stepped to the outside of the quay, taking a circuitous route to the rear of the boat where he attached the main charge to the aft hull, just behind the wheelhouse deck. Their plan was simple. The first, small explosion would bring Andrioli out. If they couldn't finish him off with a bullet, they would ignite the second charge and Andrioli and his boat would be history.

The Englishman stepped away from the front of the boat now, choosing a vantage point near a thick wood piling where he would have a clear shot at anyone coming through the main cabin or out through the hatch on the foredeck. He had his automatic in hand, keeping it under his jacket as he waited for the American to finish.

There was a noise from inside the boat, up towards the forward hatch. He snapped his head in that direction, then gave a quick whistle to the American, who jumped back and unholstered his SigSauer.

*   *   *

Jordan had smacked his hand twice against the inside bulkhead of the forward cabin. Then he sprinted back through the main salon, vaulting the steps to the pilothouse in a single motion, slamming his shoulder hard into the door that Andrioli had unlocked, bursting through in a sideward roll, hitting the deck with a thud. He scampered behind the instrument panel tower just as the Englishman detonated the small charge attached to the front hull, the explosion sending a spray of fiberglass, teak and other debris into the air and across the dock.

The American saw Sandor first, having the better angle from the rear, and opened fire immediately, sending three shots spitting through his silencer, shattering fiberglass and ricocheting inside the wheelhouse.

Jordan fired back at the American, who took cover to the side of the boat docked behind them.

Andrioli emerged from below, diving to a position alongside the wheel, firing his automatic at the crouching American to their rear. His weapon was the only one of the four not equipped with a silencer, and the reverberating report of the Browning echoed inside the wheelhouse.

The Englishman, seeing Andrioli emerge, sent two shots spitting through the plastic windscreen, whistling just above his target's head.

A woman in the sailboat to their stern let out a scream, and people along the canal began coming above decks to see what was going on, some shouting, others screaming.

In the noise and confusion, Sandor gestured to Andrioli to cover the forward shooter, then crawled on his stomach towards the transom. He climbed over the port railing, on the water side, now creeping along the catwalk until he came to the end. There, he spotted the second explosive against the side of the hull. He couldn't tell if it was set for remote ignition or a timing detonation, but he knew that touching the charge might set it off either way. He peered around the transom until the American, crouching behind the next boat, rose slightly to fire another shot. Sandor saw the man was holding something in his left hand and, figuring it was the remote, he leveled his gun and fired twice, hitting the American in the arm, then in the side of the neck, spinning him around until he was in full view, where Jordan fired again, the next shot striking him in the chest and dropping him to the ground, dead, before he could detonate the aft charge.

Sandor wondered if there was other plastique in place, or if the second shooter could set off the C4 against the transom.

When a fire broke out in the forward cabin, Jordan knew they had little time. Either another explosion would finish them off, or the flames on board would reach the fuel tanks. He had no line of sight on the man up front, but continued to move along the stern of the boat until he was at the corner of the starboard side, just along the dock. He heard Andrioli's Browning send off three more shots in rapid succession, using that cover to leap from the water deck onto the concrete path, firing at the Englishman who was squatting low, behind a bulkhead piling. Jordan squeezed off two shots, one that splintered the pole, the second glancing off the man's shoulder, moving him into a better line of fire.

When Sandor pulled the trigger again, however, he heard the nauseating, metallic click of an empty chamber. Goddamnit, he cursed himself.

The Englishman also saw what happened and righted himself for a shot at Jordan, who now jumped back towards the cover of the burning *Winsome II*, reaching in his pocket for the extra shells.

But Andrioli had also seen Jordan's last shot come up empty. He stood now, and fired off the new clip he had just slid into the Browning, driving the Englishman backwards with four bullets that ripped into his chest and face.

Jordan peered above the aft railing and nodded at Andrioli. He said, "Thanks, pal."

"Any time."

"Get Christine, my bag, anything you else need, then let's get the hell out of here. There's more plastic here, against the hull, more may be all over the boat. Don't know if it's on timers or what."

Andrioli leaped down the four steps into the main cabin, then rushed into the aft stateroom. Christine was standing there, terror in her eyes, her body rigid with fear. Andrioli pulled an attaché case he kept in the locker below his bunk, then grabbed Christine roughly by the arm. As they raced through the salon, he picked up Jordan's bag, then brought her above decks.

"Come on," Jordan urged them. "Let's move."

There was no way to know if these men had backup, or if the additional C-4 charge was about to blow. A growing crowd inched nearer the scene, but Jordan loudly warned them back.

"Someone call the police, call the fire and Coast Guard," he yelled at the crowd. "This boat is going to explode."

That sent the crowd scurrying backward.

Andrioli and Christine jumped onto the dock, even as sirens already began to sound in the distance. Andrioli walked up to the Englishman he had shot. He was face down, so Andrioli turned him over with the toe of his boot. "I knew this dirty sonuvabitch. I knew him. I recognized the other guy too."

"You've got nice friends," Sandor said. "Now let's get out of here before the police show up."

THIRTY-FOUR

Marty Koppel had seen better days. Back in the seventies, he emerged as a golden boy of American finance. He ran hedge funds that were among the darlings of Wall Street, helping to make any number of wealthy people wealthier than they already were. He then tried his hand at producing motion pictures, scoring a string of successes that elevated his status on two coasts. Whether he was financing dot com start-ups or pandering to movie audiences with deafening action and silicone cleavage, Marty Koppel knew what worked.

Then Marty lost his touch.

The eighties came and went, and so did the bull market. Regrettably, Marty was not a man who took short positions. He fought the current trends as long as his capital held out, then watched helplessly as his investments shriveled up as quickly as a winning streak at a Vegas craps table. When he turned to his Brentwood production company, he discovered that the self-indulgent excesses of his early successes had now become a kitschy joke. Unfortunately, however, Marty was not producing comedies. By the time the nineties rolled around, he felt his instincts had completely betrayed him, his golden sensibilities having morphed into a cluster of mistakes. The high-tech hedge funds he rode up the Nasdaq wave, and those slash and crash movies that played so well in middle America, had all turned to dust, taking with them his assets—and those of his investors. Marty was an instant dinosaur, a modern, up-to-the-minute, techno-age anachronism. He had leveraged everything he owned and lost it all. What was worse, he became a star in one of America's greatest sporting events—witnessing the spectacular rise and disastrous fall of a celebrity. The people who had enjoyed his Champagne and eaten his caviar, those who had clamored for invitations to his parties in East Hampton and his premieres in Hollywood, now found him a pathetic boor, avoiding him with the same energy they had once expended to court his attention, all the while bearing witness to his slide into oblivion.

There was a sad irony to all of this, since Marty had taken pains not to make enemies as his wealth and fame increased. Having grown up poor in the Kingsbridge section of the Bronx, he was mindful of the admonition about the people you meet on your journey up and down the ladder of life. It was a puzzle to him, therefore, that so many took so much pleasure in watching his demise.

Recently, through a friend of a friend, Marty had been touted to an opportunity for funding new investments, including a motion picture project. An admirer of his over-the-top film style was interested in teaming with Koppel on something new, something *au courant.*

There followed the mandatory string of telephone calls, lunches and a poolside meeting at the Beverly Hills Hotel. Then Marty was invited to Paris, to meet a man named Robert Groat. Groat claimed to represent a consortium of European investors. The principal money man, it was explained to Koppel, was a wealthy recluse who lived on a yacht in the Mediterranean. Marty was informed that Mr. Groat's client was particular about whom he met or spoke with, and that he regarded secrecy as the highest priority in his business dealings.

Koppel was not interested in the man's social idiosyncrasies, nor was he curious about his religious affiliations, eating habits or sexual preferences. Koppel readily vowed his discretion, asking only if Mr. Groat's client was serious about financing a new Martin Koppel production. When he was given that assurance, Marty made arrangements to travel to France.

It was only after those plans were made a month or so ago, that Koppel was contacted by someone else interested in his new opportunity—a representative of the United States government. Marty was invited to a meeting with the man the next day, the intimation being that his presence was required, not requested.

*   *   *

It was just a month ago, when Koppel knocked on the door of the room in the Mayflower Hotel in Washington. As instructed, he had come alone.

The man who greeted him was not at all what Koppel had expected. He was Koppel's age, nearly sixty, but unlike Koppel he was tall and trim and had a patrician bearing. He looked more like a highly placed corporate executive than a highly placed government agent, and his piercing gaze made Koppel instantly uneasy.

"So good of you to come," the man said, stepping to the side to allow Koppel inside.

Martin Koppel proceeded warily, having a quick look around, surprised to see that no one else was there.

Shutting the door behind them, the Deputy Director of the Central Intelligence Agency offered his hand and said, "I'm Mark Byrnes."

"You're the guy I spoke with on the phone?"

"I am."

"And we're alone here?"

"Absolutely."

"No tapes, no recording, just you and me."

"That's right."

"And you want to talk with me about what, exactly?"

Byrnes offered a tight smile. "I can see your reputation is well deserved. You're a man who likes to come right to the point."

"That's me," Koppel said, having another look around as if he expected a more lavish room to be provided for this meeting. "It's not exactly a thrill to have feds call you down to Washington, if you know what I mean."

"Of course," Byrnes said. He did not offer Koppel a seat. They were standing, face to face. "We have information that you're about to enter into a business arrangement. You have been asked to set up a domestically based fund for national and international investments, correct?"

"Who's asking?"

"I am."

"And who are you, exactly?"

"Let's just say that I represent the federal government, as you have suggested. That should be enough for now."

Koppel wasn't so sure, and he shook his head slightly. "Okay, let's say you're right, I'm starting a new company. That against the law or something?"

"Not necessarily."

Koppel didn't like the man's tone. He also didn't like that they were still standing. Marty was short, heavy and decidedly out of shape. He would be perfectly happy to sit down already. "What is this about, taxes?"

"No, Mr. Koppel. It's about the the fund you will be establishing. I'm informed that part of it will be used to finance a new motion picture production. Am I correct?"

Koppel saw no reason to deny what they obviously both knew to be the truth. "Yeah, you got it," he said.

"The other investments you are to make will largely be placed in short positions with respect to various commodities, stocks, derivatives and so forth. In common parlance, your investors want you to bet that the market prices will fall in the near future."

The extent of this man's information took Koppel back a step. That was exactly what he understood as the intention of Mr. Groat's client or clients, whoever they were. These investors were bearish, and were interested in betting on a downturn in the markets. How this man knew that was quite beyond him. "The plans of my clients . . . ," he began, but Byrnes cut him off.

"Of course. I understand. We have a matter of ethics to deal with."

"We sure do," Koppel told him.

"Good. I just wanted to be certain I was dealing with a man of character. Please," he said, pointing to one of the two chairs in the room, "have a seat. It appears we have a great many things to discuss."

*   *   *

The crowd along the New River Canal, gathering closer to the burning vessel, was too concerned with the dead men on the quay and the explosion of the *Winsome II* to pay much attention to the three people fleeing from the scene. Andrioli led Jordan and Christine up a short set of concrete steps, around the back of the dock and down the street to a nearby parking lot.

He led them to a beige Toyota Corolla, unlocked the door and told them to get in.

"Won't they spot us?" Christine asked.

Andrioli ignored the question as they climbed inside. He pumped the accelerator, turned the ignition key and listened as the old sedan shuddered to a start. "Don't worry about it," he said, then threw the car into gear and turned it out of the lot onto Las Olas Boulevard.

Once they were on the main street, Andrioli was careful to maintain the legal speed limit as the blare of sirens from police cars and fire engines grew louder. "Here they come," he said.

Andrioli was driving away from the commercial area of the city, towards the night action near the beach. He turned off Las Olas as soon as he could, the sound of the onrushing rescue vehicles receding now, as they headed for the canal.

"You've got a plan to get us out of here, I take it?"

Andrioli nodded at Jordan. "I do. Just chill out and let me handle this."

Christine was seated in the back, the two men in the front of the car. Even in the balmy night air, she began to shiver.

"You okay?" Jordan asked.

"I'll be fine," she told him.

"So," Andrioli said, not taking his eyes from the road, "way you handled that, I guess everything they said about you is true."

"I told you, I was in the military."

"Sure. I knew a lotta guys in the service, never coulda taken my gun from me, or moved like you did out there."

"That so? Well, just in case you forgot, I would have had my head blown off if you hadn't come up and taken out the second shooter."

"You counted wrong, that's all."

Sandor allowed himself a grim smile in the darkness. "I knew the H&K carried fifteen shots. You'd think I could have counted to fifteen."

"Uh uh," Andrioli said, allowing himself a smile. "Only fourteen. You counted right. Last chamber was clear."

"What?"

"An old trick of mine. Call it an insurance policy."

"Christ," Jordan said, shaking his head.

"Hey, only the paranoid survive."

"Seems I've heard that line before," Jordan said.

They reached the fringes of the town's main activity, where Andrioli turned into a small complex of low slung buildings, two blocks from the shore road. He pulled into an enclosed parking garage, coming to a stop just inside.

"This is what they call the moment of truth," Andrioli said.

"Meaning what?"

"Meaning, we're either going on together from here, or it's *hasta la vista.* Up to you."

"How about we make a call to Washington, first? We don't have to turn ourselves in, not yet. But we can tell them what you know about what's going down. I've got some friends I can reach."

"I'll bet you do," Andrioli replied. He stepped on the gas again, pulling around a cement post and coming to a stop in a parking space there. They got out of the car, the sickly glow of the weak, florescent lighting making Andrioli appear older and his eyes even sadder than before. "You just don't get it," he said, slamming the door shut.

"Get what?"

"Covington and his people. The way they're using you to get to me. What the hell," Andrioli said, as if speaking to himself. "You're probably part of this already."

"Part of what?" Christine asked across the top of the car.

"I don't know," Andrioli with a dismissive shake of his head.

"Look," she said, "if Jordan was here to hurt you, would he have risked his life just now?"

"He didn't have much choice, did he?"

"Of course he did. He had the gun, you didn't. He could have given you up to those men."

Andrioli was not convinced.

"I asked him to come here with me," she reminded him. "All this, this . . . whatever this is, it wasn't his idea, was it?"

The two men were staring at her now.

"So, wherever we're going, whatever we're doing, right now I think it's fair to say that we're going together."

Sandor and Andrioli looked at each other, not speaking.

"Well?" Jordan asked him.

Andrioli scratched his beard. "That car over there is mine," he said, pointing to a navy blue Chevy. "You and Christine take it, drive slowly out there, then wait on the street. I'll dump this car down the block, then come back to meet you." He opened his attaché case and removed a set of keys, then tossed them over the car to Jordan. "Go ahead."

Jordan caught the keys, still watching him.

"And then what?" Christine asked. "Where in God's name do we go from here?"

Jordan knew the answer. "Paris," he said.

Andrioli nodded. "He's right," he said to Christine, without taking his eyes off Jordan. "We're going back to Paris."

*   *   *

The driver and his companion were sitting in the Lincoln Town Car when they heard the explosion. Their orders were to bring Traiman's men to the canal, then take them back to the airport. They heard the gunfire in the distance, but did nothing. They had no instructions to interfere. For now they just sat there, waiting for two passengers who would not be returning.

THIRTY-FIVE

"Y̶ou ever wonder what they're thinking?" Andrioli asked. "In that last second? You know what I mean."

Sandor knew what he meant. "I have," he admitted.

"You seen a lotta guys die, have you?"

"More than my share," Jordan admitted.

"Yeah. Me too, goddamnit."

They were heading up the Interstate from Florida toward Georgia, Andrioli at the wheel. Switching cars had gotten them safely out of Fort Lauderdale. Even after Covington's men tracked them to the shootings at Andrioli's boat, it would be a while before anyone could identify and locate the old Toyota, and where would they look after that?

"I have no wife, no kids," Andrioli said into the darkness. "All that stuff about your life passing before your eyes. I always figured you would think about your wife and kids. I don't know." He pulled out a cigarette, lowered his window a bit, then lit up. "You married?'

"No," Jordan said. "Never."

"No kids then."

"No."

Andrioli took a long drag of the Marlboro and blew it towards the open window. "What the hell would you see, then, when the lights are going out?"

Jordan had a look at the man's profile, the uneven nose, the prominent, bearded chin. "I have no idea," he said. "Will it matter?"

"It might," Andrioli said. "If there's no God or anything, I figure those last seconds, that becomes your heaven or your hell, right then and there. It may be all you get."

Jordan peered over his shoulder. Christine had curled up in the back seat and was sleeping under his sport jacket.

"You have a passport?" Andrioli asked him.

Jordan told him he did.

"Your own name?"

"No, I'm covered, don't worry."

"What about Christine?"

Sandor had another look in the back seat. "We should leave her in Atlanta."

Andrioli nodded. "I guess so." He let another few moments go by before saying, "You came to see me without a weapon."

"I did."

"Kind of risky, wasn't it?"

"Too risky to try and get them through at La Guardia. Once we got here, we knew time was tight."

"No shit," Andrioli said, thinking of their narrow escape. "Turned out to be very tight, eh?"

"I sent a package to myself. Won't come until tomorrow morning, back in Lauderdale."

"Forget it. I can work it out when we get to France."

Jordan watched him drive the car, neither man saying anything as they covered a long stretch of highway.

Andrioli hesitated. "Who are you, really?"

"You know who I am. I'm a journalist, the guy Jimmy McHugh wanted to meet."

"Yeah, and I'm Kris Kringle."

"I was invited to this party, remember? All I'm trying to do is sort the bullshit from the buckwheat."

"So you think I'm selling bullshit."

"No," Jordan admitted. "If I did, I'd pull this gun again and take you to the nearest police station."

"If you could get the drop on me a second time."

They were silent for a while, then Andrioli took a long drag on his cigarette, blew out a cloud of smoke, and said, "Hey, about that thing that went down in Bahrain."

"What about it?"

"I had nothing to do with it. I mean, we heard about it afterwards, but McHugh and I weren't involved. Okay?"

"Okay."

"It's not like I even knew who you were, you were just the name of some guy from Traiman's past, but I wanted you to know I had nothing to do with it, in case you had any ideas about that."

"Okay," Jordan said again, taking a moment to have another look at Andrioli. "So why go to Paris? Why not just make a stand here?"

"It'll never be safe for me here, you just saw that. Jimmy already bought it. This is a business deal at this point. I've got something they want, which is information, and if I get just a little more of it, it might save my life. Strengthen my negotiating position, if you see what I mean."

"I'm listening."

"Traiman believes Jimmy and I knew more than we did. The government's not so sure. If Traiman gets to me first, I'm dead. If the government finds me, they'll see I don't have enough to deal with and they'll lock me up. Either way, I'm fucked."

"What do you really have?"

Andrioli turned to him. "I already told you everything I know, I truly did. And it's not enough."

"Okay. So, what's in Paris?"

Andrioli looked back at the highway and took a long drag on his Marlboro, then let it out slowly. "Answers, I hope," he said. "Answers."

THIRTY-SIX

John Covington had flown back to Washington for an 8 AM meeting with Deputy Director Byrnes the following morning. The DD was already in his office, waiting.

"Coffee, John?"

"No thank you, sir."

The Director removed his reading glasses and began gently massaging the bridge of his nose with his thumb and forefinger. "We may finally be getting someplace," he said with a weary sigh. "It's about time."

"Yes sir. Things developed quickly in Florida."

The DD nodded. "I received a call from the Bureau. Needless to say, they were not happy about your antics in New York."

Covington knew that Byrnes was sensitive to criticism about governmental agencies not sharing information in the post nine-eleven world. He was surprised at being awarded the blame, however, since he was following the DD's orders. "It had to be done."

"Yes, of course it did. There's too much at stake to risk their interference. In any case, there may be less of an issue than they think."

"Sir?"

"This matter wasn't going to remain within the Bureau's jurisdiction for long. That's what I explained to them."

"After the debacle in Fort Lauderdale, do you believe Andrioli will make a run back to North Africa?"

"France would be a better guess, don't you think?" The DD took a quiet sip of his steaming black coffee, effortlessly raising the cup to his lips without compromising his posture.

"They found a plane ticket at McHugh's house," Covington told him. "First class to Paris. It was in my report."

Byrnes nodded and Covington waited for him to say something. He did not.

"So sir, do you think he and Andrioli were planning to go back?"

"What do you think?" Byrnes asked.

"It doesn't make sense."

"It might, if they thought they could make a better deal there than they could get here."

"I suppose you're right."

"Perhaps there are others involved."

Covington nodded.

"What about Sandor?" the DD asked.

"We've pushed him this far. Knowing him, he won't be able to resist."

Byrnes nodded without taking his eyes from Covington. "I agree."

"You don't really believe Andrioli has enough information to interrupt Traiman's plans, do you?"

Byrnes leaned back in his chair. "Not based on the preliminary interrogation of the three men we arrested. We're not likely to get more from them at this point."

"Are they explosives experts?"

"There was no evidence of that in their Washington apartment. The arsenal we found in their apartment is designed for sniper attacks, not the construction of bombs. They've been questioned separately, of course. Each denies any involvement in the destruction of the Loubar office building."

"I see."

They discussed the implications of having apprehended this team of assassins. Then Covington returned to the subject of his assignment.

"Do you think we're wasting our time on Andrioli, then?"

"Not at all," Byrnes said. "Whatever he has, whatever he can get, we want it. We also want to see where he goes. The path he travels may have more value than anything he can tell us."

"If he has so little intelligence data on these ops, then why is Traiman so intent on removing him?"

"I believe it may have more to do with Vincent than with Andrioli." Byrnes had worked with Traiman for years. "Vincent was always a cautious man."

"And what if Traiman's people reach Andrioli first?"

"They'll kill him, of course. We saw that yesterday in Florida. That is, of course, unless he has something to trade."

"And the risk assessment?"

"We clearly stand to gain more by pushing him than bringing him in, at least for now."

"What about the girl?"

"The girl, yes." The DD raised his right eyebrow slightly. "What options does she have? She may be too frightened to move on her own."

"Yes," Covington agreed, "I suppose that's correct. They might even leave her behind."

"It's possible," Byrnes agreed. "I assume you've reviewed the CTC reports on the teams Traiman sent into Western Europe."

"I have," Covington said. The Counter-Terrorism Center had confirmed the movement of men believed to be involved with Traiman. They were currently running down the specific locations and identities.

"The press is going to get hold of this," Byrnes said. "There are leaks we can't plug. They may even be coming from the other side, as part of their campaign."

"You think al-Qaeda would use advance teams to advertise their plans?"

"Possibly. This is about terror, after all. The governments involved have increased security measures for the heads of state, particularly in the U.K. and Italy. The Secret Service is obviously on high alert."

"They believe this is for real?"

"We all do," Byrnes acknowledged solemnly. "Traiman is doing an effective job of gearing up without allowing us to pinpoint the source."

"Or the targets."

"Yes. The President has his hands full with Iraq, Iran and the rest of this mess. He can't afford another domestic catastrophe on his watch. The war, the stock market, the fear. The American people have had enough of this, and you never know how the Arab nations will align themselves."

"Petropolitics."

The DD permitted himself a grim smile. "Yes. The Arabs love to hate one another, but they're uniformly resistant to outside interference." He thought that over, then asked, "So, where are we on locating them?"

Covington shifted in his seat. "They left Fort Lauderdale right after the shootings. We're trying to pick them up now."

"What about the shooters?"

"Two of Traiman's men, or that's what it looks like. We sold it to the local authorities as a drug deal gone bad. The Bureau helped with that."

"And Sandor?"

"As I say, we're canvassing the airports. We assume he's with Andrioli and the girl. Got a lead on a car switch, trying to trace that now."

"Keep your eye on Paris," Byrnes told him again. The meeting was at an end, and the DD had mentioned nothing to Covington about Martin Koppel.

THIRTY-SEVEN

Morning broke in a glare of hazy sunshine that seemed to mock their loss of sleep. Night had become day, but it was less a transition than a milestone on their journey.

They stopped for breakfast at a Waffle House, just off the highway outside Macon. A short, unkempt waitress, who looked even wearier than they felt, took their order and brought them each a cup of steaming coffee.

"I heard you." It was the first thing Christine had said in quite a while.

"Heard what?" Andrioli asked, taking a sip from the heavy, ceramic mug.

"You expect me to stay behind, don't you?"

Neither man responded.

"When were you going to tell me?"

"Christine," Andrioli began, then stopped, not sure of what to say.

"You've seen how dangerous these people are," Jordan said quietly. She was sitting beside him in the small booth, and he turned toward her, placing his arm around her shoulders. "You wanted to find Tony, and we have. Why would you put yourself in any more danger?"

"Why would you?" she asked defiantly. "I'm involved in this as much as you are."

Jordan knew it might be useful to have a woman with them. He also knew the risks they would be taking.

"These people are killers," Andrioli said as casually as if he were commenting on the coffee. "You've seen it first hand. They murdered Jimmy, and they'll keep after me, wherever I go. If either of you are with me, you'll be in the line of fire."

"Don't you think I'm in the line of fire now?"

The two men exchanged a knowing glance. She was, of course, correct. Christine and Jordan had become targets, whether they went with him or not. Traiman's men would regard them as contaminated by the information Andrioli might have given them. Just as Dan Peters was terminated as a collateral risk, Christine would be in their sights, one way or another. Sandor also realized what they did not—Traiman would also have ulterior reasons for eliminating them.

"All right," Jordan said. "But any time you want to bail, you just give us the signal."

"Not me," she said. "I'm in this till the end."

*   *   *

After breakfast, they drove to Atlanta, where Andrioli located a shop offering instant passport photos. Christine had her picture taken, then got back in the car. Meantime, Andrioli used his passport and false credit card to buy a cell phone.

"I've got some arts and crafts to do," Andrioli told Jordan. "You drive." He climbed in the back seat, opened his attaché case and began working on a passport for Christine. Jordan got behind the wheel.

"You carry blanks?" Christine asked as she watched him applying her photo to the first page of a forged U. S. Passport.

"Comes in handy, as you can see. Not much trouble using one of them when you leave the country. Hassle getting back in with it, though." He looked up at her as they shared the obvious thought—that they might never get that far.

As Jordan drove, Andrioli went back to expertly affixing the photograph to the page, then applying a stamp. He handed it to Christine and had her sign.

"At least this way they won't be able to track us by our real names," he said as he took the passport back and finished his work. "The first thing they'll do is run flight rosters through the IATA computers. We'll travel separately, you two as a couple, I'll book as a single." Andrioli then used his new cell phone to make the reservations—two phone calls, different credit cards. Jordan had his Scott Kerr false passport and an American Express issued in the same name.

They made another stop, at a luggage store, where they bought a couple of suitcases. Jordan and Andrioli agreed it would be less suspicious if they checked in for an international flight with baggage. They purchased a few items in a clothing shop, then they left the city, resting for a few hours until dusk, in a park overlooking a small lake.

They arrived at the airport, left the car in the short-term lot, then went through the contents of Jordan's black leather bag and Andrioli's attaché case. They knew they had to leave the two automatics behind. As they walked to the exit, they placed the guns in a nearby trash can, making certain no one was watching as they covered the weapons with newspapers, then moved on.

"I feel naked," Andrioli said.

Jordan smiled. "Second time for me in two days. I've been throwing away some very nice hardware." He slapped Andrioli on the shoulder. "Come on, we had no choice."

His encouraging demeanor belied the tension he felt rising along the back of his neck as they approached the terminal. If anyone had followed them, or if there was someone waiting at the airport, he and Andrioli and Christine would be captured. Or worse.

"I think we should call Covington," Andrioli said.

Jordan stopped. "Covington?"

"I told you, he was the point man when Jimmy and I tried to come in."

"But you told me he wouldn't deal. He turned you down, right?"

"It's worth a try, if I can talk our way out of this."

"It won't work," Sandor told him. "And what makes you think we can reach him?"

"I've got a contact number for him."

"And as soon as we call, he'll trace us, they'll pick us up. You'll be done."

"They'll never trace this cell phone. Not if we're quick."

Jordan knew that whatever phone number Covington had given Andrioli, it would be hooked into the satellite links at the Global Response Center that could pinpoint their location within ninety seconds. He decided not to divulge his own knowledge of Covington's secure number. "All right," Jordan agreed, "but I think it's a waste of time."

"Why?" Christine asked.

Jordan was not prepared to give that answer, not yet. He understood that Covington wanted them in the hunt, that he would reject any deal Andrioli tried to make at this point. "Just a feeling," he said. "Let me do the talking. And time me. At seventy-five seconds, cut me off."

Andrioli's eyes narrowed slightly, but he handed Jordan the phone. They were at the edge of the parking lot, just across the access road from the international terminal. Andrioli opened his case and pulled out a number. Jordan recognized it as one of the sterile lines the Agency kept for outside contacts. As he had guessed, it was also a line easily tapped for tracing through GPS locators.

Jordan dialed the number and listened to it ring.

"Covington," the familiar voice answered.

"Jordan Sandor."

"You and who else?" he demanded brusquely.

"I'm standing here with Tony Andrioli and Christine Frank. Christine and I came to pay Tony a visit here in Fort Lauderdale."

"I heard about the shootings."

"Good. Then you know Andrioli is telling you the truth when he says he's got something to deal."

"Are we alone on this line?"

"Yes."

"I need to know where you're going."

Jordan didn't answer. Instead he turned to Andrioli. "Covington sends his regards."

Covington said, "I realize you can't talk, but just tell me if you're leaving the country."

"Of course," Jordan replied into the telephone. "That's why we're calling. We want to know where your agency stands on giving us some help. The three of us were almost killed last night."

"So you're on the move."

"Naturally," Jordan said. "You don't want us sitting out in the open for target practice, do you?"

"Are you going to Paris?"

"Look, Andrioli has information. He's willing to trade it for protection."

"You can tell Andrioli he can have the same deal we offered him in Paris. We don't bargain with traitors, and we're not convinced he has all that much to sell."

Jordan looked to Andrioli again. "Covington says you can have the same deal. Turn yourself in and they'll put in a good word for you at sentencing. They don't believe you know enough to be making demands."

Andrioli responded with a grim smile.

"My friend says you can shove it," Sandor replied to Covington. "If the best you guys can offer is the deluxe cell at Leavenworth, he'll take his chances on the outside."

Covington said, "Tell him he's got to give me something with real substance. If he does, I'll take it to the Director. Meantime, Sandor, I need to know where you're going."

Jordan only repeated the first part of Covington's remark, to which Andrioli just shook his head.

"Tell him to pound sand. That's what he told me."

"My friend says you should pound sand," Jordan said into the phone.

Christine pointed to her watch. She mouthed the words, "Fifty seconds."

Covington said, "This guy could be setting you and the girl up for trade bait."

While that thought had already occurred to Jordan, it surprised him to get the advice from Covington. He was not the type to caution his operatives, even former operatives, when it might scare them off. Perhaps it was that uncharacteristic gesture that gave Jordan the idea. Or maybe he had the idea already. "We just have one more question. Why did you send those two men to kill us last night?"

"What are you talking about?" The surprise in Covington's voice was as genuine as the look on Andrioli's face.

"They could have been your men as easily as the other side. Andrioli recognized one of them, said he was working for the Agency in Paris." Andrioli had not said any such thing, but he let Jordan run out the hand.

"What is this?" Covington demanded.

"Why would Andrioli lie to me?"

"I just told you why."

There was a short silence on the line, then Jordan said, "No deal then?"

"Sandor, where in hell are you? Are you going to Paris, just say yes or no."

Jordan hesitated. Covington had just confirmed what he had suspected since he managed to escape the hotel in New York. The Agency wanted Andrioli, not for what he knew, but as bait for bigger prey. "We're moving again, and you just blew your best shot to make a deal." Without a goodbye, he snapped the phone shut, disconnecting the call.

Andrioli was obviously disappointed.

"What did you expect?" Sandor asked.

"I'm not sure anymore."

"Come on," Jordan said, "let's go check in. We could all use a drink."

THIRTY EIGHT

Jordan and Christine checked in ahead of Andrioli. He stayed back, near a bank of phones, pretending to make a call as he watched them receive their boarding passes without incident. He then made his way to the First Class Check-In, and was quickly provided his ticket.

He was not far behind them as they stood on the long, slow security queue, another agonizing wait until they got through to the other side.

They found a small cocktail lounge near their gate and ordered drinks.

"Notice anything?" Andrioli asked.

"Not a thing," Sandor told him.

For now, Jordan believed that no one was certain where they were, or where they were going. Although Covington suspected they would soon be en route to Paris, and probably attempted to track the cell phone call through GRS, Sandor had to assume he was on his own. Jordan asked for Andrioli's phone.

"Who are you going to call?"

"What's the difference now?"

Andrioli didn't like the answer.

"A friend in New York. He's okay. We may need a contact person."

Andrioli reluctantly handed over the telephone and Jordan pulled a number from his pocket. He turned away from his companions and quickly punched in the numbers. A trooper in Woodstock, New York answered the call and Jordan asked for Captain Reynolds.

"Tell him it's Jordan Sandor," he said, then waited.

"Sandor," Reynolds growled in his best combat voice when he came on the line, "they tell me you've become a fugitive. Where the hell are you?"

"I can't tell you that Captain, but I have to ask you to do something for me."

194

"You are a brash young man," Reynolds said.

"Look, I have no one else I can trust. Is this line clean?"

"Clean? It better be, goddamnit."

"You have a pencil?"

"I'm listening," the Captain said.

Jordan quietly recited a phone number. "You got it?"

"I got it."

"It's a secure line. Call that number and just say that all three of us are on our way. Would you do that? Just say all three of us are on our way."

There was silence on the other end.

"Captain?"

"I'm here Sandor."

"Will you do that?"

"Give me one decent reason why I should."

Jordan shook his head. "Because I'm asking, that's all."

The Captain paused again. "All right."

"Thank you, sir," Jordan said.

"Be careful," Reynolds said, then hung up.

The next call Jordan made was to Bill Sternlich.

"Where are you now?" Sternlich asked, after Jordan briefly described the Fort Lauderdale shootings.

"It's better if you don't know. In fact, I've got to keep this call short so they can't run a trace. How's Beth?"

"Getting better. Pretty banged up, I can tell you, but they say she'll be fine."

"Is she under guard?"

"You bet."

"Good," Jordan sighed. He moved off to the end of the bar, away from his traveling companions.

"I finally got some dope on your pal McHugh. Guess it's too late to do you any good, eh?"

"Not at all. What've you got?"

"Not much, except he's a Code Orange on the terror alert barometer. Records sealed and all that, most of his dossier is classified, still regarded as a National Security issue. I even got a threatening little e-mail message, warning me off the search."

"Be careful Bill, these people are serious."

"I believe you."

"I'll call you when I can."

"Listen, Jordan, I did get one little tidbit you might find interesting."

"I'm listening."

"In the information I got, there's no record James McHugh ever had a sister."

*   *   *

Jordan and Christine were in Business Class. Andrioli was up front, in First.

An hour after they took off, Christine was already asleep. Sandor watched her, wondering again what she was about. Sternlich would be following up on her name and background, even though he told him not to, but whatever he uncovered might be just another fabric of lies devised by—whom?

Jordan stared out the window as the plane passed through the clouds in a darkening sky. He tried again to get some much needed rest.

It was just past daybreak when they landed. They navigated their way through customs and immigration, then met up on the taxi line. There, the three of them climbed into a cab that wound its way around the curves of the French *autoroute*, past the recently constructed multi-level buildings that had become part of the landscape of suburban Paris.

"No problems?"

Andrioli shook his head. "Customs opened the suitcase, but I told them I was here to buy some clothing. You know the French. They love that bullshit."

The cab cruised along the highway that belted the city in an uneven circle.

"What do we do first?" Christine asked.

"First, I visit an old friend," Andrioli said. Then, speaking French with an accent Jordan knew must be like fingernails on a blackboard to their driver, Andrioli told the man to stop on the Boulevard Raspail on the way to their hotel, the Pas de Tour on the Rue des Saint Peres. This was the small hotel on the Left Bank where Jimmy McHugh made a reservation the day before he died.

"Is it really such a good idea?" Christine wondered aloud. She was sitting between them, and looked to Andrioli for an answer.

Andrioli was thinking about something else, tugging on his scraggly beard, staring out the window. "Is what a good idea?"

"Going to this hotel." She lowered her voice, just in case the driver's English was more fluent than it seemed when they entered the taxi.

Tony smiled. "Are you worried about safety now?"

Christine nodded vigorously, as if to say how obvious that concern should be to both of them.

Andrioli responded with a short laugh. "By the time we reach the city, every CIA agent in France and half of Traiman's men in Europe will know we're here. Am I right, Sandor?"

Jordan gave no answer.

"Come on. Covington knew we were on our way to Paris, didn't he? That's what he said to you on the phone, right?"

"Yes," Jordan said simply.

Andrioli took Christine's hand and patted it gently. "I'm sorry, but we're up to our asses in alligators. Too late to be worried about jumping in the old swimming hole. The only thing we've got going for us is surprise, the oldest ally in the book of war. They don't expect us to be coming at them, which may be our best chance. If we try to run and hide, we'll wind up all over the front page of Le Figaro. Am I right, Sandor?"

"Right again."

"Good. So, if we're going into the trenches together, no more secrets among us, all right?"

"All right," Jordan said.

They turned to Christine.

"What secrets could I have?"

"Everyone has at least one secret," Sandor said.

She turned away from him without a response.

*   *   *

The cab stopped at the address on the Boulevard Raspail and Andrioli told the driver to wait. "I'll be right back," he told them, climbing out of the cab, taking his attaché case with him. Before he shut the door, he leaned in and spoke quietly to Jordan. "If you hear anything, any trouble, or if I'm not back in ten minutes, then get the hell outta Dodge, you hear me?"

Jordan nodded. Andrioli stood up, slammed the door shut and disappeared into a small apartment building just across the street.

When he was gone, Christine asked Jordan "What did you mean? About my having a secret."

"Just what I said. No one lives without a secret."

She shook her head, but did not speak. When she looked up at him, her sad, moist eyes were met by his cold gaze.

"It doesn't make you a bad person," he said with a grin that softened his features, but did nothing to hide the suspicion in his eyes.

She shook her head again, about to say something, then hesitated.

*   *   *

Andrioli removed a key chain from his case, used one of them to get into the building, then took the stairs two at a time, climbing to the third floor. There were four flats on the landing. He paused in front of the door on the left, listening.

Nothing.

He placed his attaché on the floor and, standing off to the side, knocked twice and waited.

Nothing.

If they were laying for him, he had no time to finesse an entrance. Using another key, he turned it in the lock, the click as loud as an explosion in the quiet. In one motion he turned the knob and thrust the door open, bursting into the small apartment like a fullback going through the line, low, hard and fast.

Nothing.

There was no one there.

He went to the kitchen, kneeled down and reached under the sink, where he detached a small package he had taped there two months before. When he heard something behind him he spun quickly, coming to his feet, not enough time to rip open the parcel, his hands at the ready.

Nothing.

He nodded at the dim silence, waiting, his muscles tense, his eyes alert. Then his friend Emil's cat scooted across the floor and jumped onto the counter beside him.

*   *   *

"There's something you're not telling me," Christine whispered.

Jordan shook his head. "There's a lot I'm not telling you, which makes us even." He checked his watch and had a look across the street. "Don't worry," he said. "We'll have time to catch up."

"Will we, Jordan?"

He looked at her again, wishing he could trust her.

"You still don't believe me, do you?"

"No," he said. "But I want to. I want to very much."

*   *   *

Andrioli emerged from the building, looked up and down the street, then hustled across, got back into the taxi and told the man to drive on. He placed the attaché case on his lap and opened the top, where the driver could not see what he had placed inside. He displayed the two outdated U. S. government issue Colt .45 automatics and a box of cartridges he had removed from the package upstairs. "My friends and I always kept at least one safe house," he offered by way of explanation. There were two other small boxes, still wrapped in paper, for which he offered no explanation.

"That was fairly dangerous," Jordan said. "What if someone was waiting?"

"What choice did we have? Unarmed, we're as good as dead already." He leaned towards them, and said, "Here's the deal. I'll get out on the Boulevard Saint Germain. There's a small café on the corner and I'll wait there. You and Christine take the cab to the hotel. When you walk in, you ask the clerk for a double room with a bath. He knows me, but he won't recognize you, which is what we want. No matter what he says, even if he's telling you he doesn't speak English, you interrupt him immediately and say 'Room forty seven.' You got that? Room forty seven."

Jordan nodded.

"He'll give you a key. The hotel isn't very big, but it's got two tiers and they're separated by an outdoor patio. When he gives you the key, don't hesitate. Pick up your bag and walk through the glass door out onto the patio."

"Where's the door to the patio? We want to look like we know what we're about, right?"

"It's just to the side of the desk. Small lobby, can't miss it. Walk across the patio to a second glass door, directly opposite. Take the stairway on the left up to the room."

"Forty seven."

"Not necessarily. He might give you another room in the back tier. Our best shot is if someone is already in forty seven."

"Why?"

"Don't worry, as long as you ask for number forty seven, he'll understand."

"What if there are no rooms available?"

"There's always a room. But if he gives you any bullshit, or gets on the phone, you just tell him you have no time to wait, then get the hell out of there. Don't run, don't act nervous. Just leave."

Jordan nodded. "Will he ask for our names, or our passports?"

"No. He shouldn't. Now, once you walk inside, the clerk will definitely call his contact to tell him one of Traiman's men has arrived. From that moment on, you're in danger. There are probably others in the hotel already. They tend to check each other out, just to keep score, if you catch my drift."

"Got it."

"Leave your suitcase in the room and head right back out. I mean right away. Leave your key at the desk and tell the clerk you'll be gone for a few hours. In case there are any calls for your room, you tell him they'll come in for Mr. Forest."

"Forest."

"Good. Then you go on over towards the church up the street, the St. Germain Des Pres. Everyone knows where it is."

"I know it," Jordan said.

"Good. I'll meet you there."

Jordan nodded.

Andrioli handed him one of the automatics, still hidden from the driver by the top of the open attaché. Jordan did a quick check of the weapon, then took an extra clip from the case. "I guess you expect a welcome committee to form right away."

"I do," Andrioli said.

"Then Christine should be out of the way."

Andrioli thought that over.

"I'll put her in a cab," Jordan said. "You can wait somewhere very public," he told her. "If one of us doesn't come for you in an hour, you head straight for the U. S. Embassy."

Christine saw that Jordan was not about to debate the point. "All right. Where?"

Jordan leaned towards them and whispered, "I'll pick a public spot, somewhere on the Champs d'Elysée."

She nodded.

"One last thing," Andrioli said. "The two towers are connected by a walkway on the top floor. Just in case you hit a snag in there, you may want to go up, across and down. It'll bring you back to the lobby, and at least you won't be pinned in the back of the hotel. It's pretty quiet back there, and help is hard to find."

"Thanks for the encouragement," Jordan said.

"Don't mention it. How's your French?"

"Dead awful."

"Good enough. When you walk in, speak English to the clerk. No problem. In the back of the hotel, if you can't fake the French, then both of you should keep your traps shut."

"Why does Christine have to come in at all? Why not let her out here?"

"If you go in alone, they won't be sure it's you, at least not right away. When you go in together and the clerk calls in, with the description they must have by now, they'll be sure. Help to stir things up, you see?"

Jordan was not so sure he saw, but it was Andrioli's show, and for now Sandor decided he would play it his way.

THIRTY-NINE

They turned past the Hotel des Invalides, then onto the Boulevard St. Germain. Andrioli told the driver to circle past the corner of the Rue des Saints Peres. There was a café there, busy with morning customers.

He told the driver to stop. "Now you two be careful," he said as the car came to a halt. Then he allowed himself a tense smile. "All of a sudden I'm Mother Goose." He turned back to the cabbie and told him to drop his friends at the Pas de Tour. The Frenchman was obviously annoyed by all the detours, so Andrioli paid the fare in advance and gave him a large tip, which managed to erase the frown if not to elicit any sign of gratitude. Andrioli took hold of his attaché case and opened the door. "Good luck," he said, then stepped out into the Parisian morning.

Jordan did not have time to watch Andrioli enter the café. As soon as the door slammed shut, the cab took a wild right turn across several lanes of the broad boulevard and lurched down a narrow street, stopping about halfway down the block, in front of the hotel.

Christine stepped out and Jordan followed. They took the two suitcases from the trunk while the cabbie, his fare already in hand, made no pretense at helping them with the bags. As soon as they slammed the trunk shut, he sped away.

The façade of the Pas de Tour was less than unpretentious. It was set in the middle of the street, a place one could pass again and again without even realizing it was a hotel. Jordan handed her the lighter valise, then picked up the other suitcase and, holding onto his leather bag, pushed through the wooden door and entered the lobby.

The clerk's desk was near the rear, over towards the left, the entry foyer surprisingly deep and rather narrow. That explained the two tiers, Jordan thought. One in front for the general roster of guests, the one in the rear reserved for special patrons. As he approached the desk he could see the patio and the glass door to the side, just as Andrioli had described it.

"Room for two," he said without offering a greeting. "With bath."

The clerk was a short, stocky, middle-aged man with an inexpressive face bathed in tedium. "I am sorry, monsieur, but . . ."

"Room forty seven." Jordan's brusque interruption was greeted by nothing more than a slight furrowing of the man's brow. Then, as the clerk reached below the desk, Jordan felt his body tense, the hard metal of the Colt pressing against his side beneath his sport coat. The suitcase was in his left hand, the black leather bag on his shoulder, his right hand poised to reach for the automatic. But the bored Frenchman brought up nothing more threatening than a key.

"*Cinquante sept, monsieur.*"

"I said forty-seven."

"I am sorry, *monsieur*, this is not available. Fifty-seven," he said in his heavily accented English and held out the key.

Jordan nodded and took the key. The clerk made no request for a credit card, identification or passport. Sandor motioned for Christine to proceed out the rear glass door to the patio. As he followed her, the clerk called after him.

"Monsieur. The messages. In what name will you accept messages?"

Jordan kept moving, letting the door swing shut behind him.

They stepped quickly across the tiled terrace, their footsteps echoing in the quiet of the enclosed courtyard. An elderly couple was having their morning coffee, not bothering to take notice of the new arrivals.

Once they reached the door on the other side, they found the rear stairway, just as Andrioli had described it. It was darker here than in the lobby.

"I'm afraid, Jordan." Her voice trembled in the dismal silence of the hallway.

"Come on," he said softly. "No English, not until we get to the room." He placed his arm around her shoulders, urging her on.

They headed up the carpeted stairs, finding there were only two rooms on each floor. When they got to the third landing, he heard the sound of a door opening, just above them. Christine froze, but he pulled her close to him, then let go of her hand and felt for the butt of the .45 in his waistband.

The staircase was narrow and winding, well suited to the belltower design of the structure it rose within, but not intended for people moving in opposite directions.

Two men were coming down from the landing just above them. As they approached, Jordan turned Christine toward the door to room 37. He bent forward, to disguise his height and cover his face, then made a show of looking for the key in his jacket pockets as the two men passed behind them without stopping. As they went by and took the stairs down to the next level, Jordan glanced quickly to his side.

Even in the darkness of the hallway, even as he caught only a glimpse of the man from his side and back, he knew him at once. The second man was the driver of the car in Woodstock. The tall, blond-haired American who had called for his Arab companion to end the attack and flee. Jordan knew him as surely as he felt his hand tighten around the cold handle of the Colt automatic.

The men did not pause or, if they did, Jordan had not seen it. Sandor waited to hear them reach the next landing below, then he grabbed Christine again and led her up the stairs to their room, two flights above, as quickly and quietly as they could move.

He never saw me in Woodstock, Jordan realized. *He was in the car when his Arab friend fired at me and Dan. He doesn't know who I am.*

But that didn't feel right to him. Wouldn't Traiman have circulated a photo to his battalion of assassins? Wouldn't they even know Christine by now?

Maybe Andrioli was right. Perhaps surprise was on their side. This man would never have expected to see them there. Why would he be looking for Jordan and Christine in the dimly lit hallway of his own hotel?

The two men gone, Jordan and Christine continued up until they reached room 57. As soon as they made their way inside and Jordan shut the door behind them, she broke down and began to sob. Jordan took her in his arms and held her to him. "Go ahead," he said, "I don't blame you a bit."

*   *   *

Deputy Director Byrnes was seated in the office of his boss, the Director of Central Intelligence. They were linked, by secure videoconference, with the Secretary of Homeland Security, the Secretary of Defense and the President of the United States. Byrnes had been given the floor, to provide a briefing on the current status of the counter-terrorist operation involving Vincent Traiman. When he concluded, the Secretary of Homeland Security began to speak, but the President interrupted him.

"I want to be sure I understand this, gentlemen, because a lot of this is news to me."

"Yes sir," Byrnes responded, knowing it would be his obligation to answer the President, and to take the heat.

"I've read the reports on this rogue agent, Traiman. I'm up to speed on that. Now you're saying he went after two reverse defectors, Americans, who flew the coop and wanted to come back here."

"Yes sir, they tried to make a deal."

"All right. But the deal failed, for reasons I'm not sure I comprehend, and then one of them is murdered in New York and the other almost gets blown to kingdom come in Florida. Have I got this right so far?"

"Yes, Mr. President."

"And all this time, these two men might have had valuable information, specifically related to movements of these teams of killers our ex-agent Traiman is running."

"We are not clear about the extent or accuracy of the information they possess. Or possessed."

"I see." The opportunity to watch the look of displeasure on the President's face made the interview far worse than a simple telephone conference would have been. The Commander-in-Chief was not a man who tended to hide his feelings, especially when he was dissatisfied with his subordinates. "So then, while we have a real and present threat to our national security being initiated by this sonuvabitch in Libya, or wherever he's hiding at the moment, not to mention the danger to targeted allies in Europe, you guys fiddled around instead of bringing these boys in. And now, one of them is dead and the other is on the run someplace in Europe."

"Paris, Mr. President."

"France. Perfect. Our ultimate fair-weather friend. Meantime, we've got an explosion here in Washington, a terrorist cell discovered down the block from the White House, the media demanding to know what the hell is going on, and I'm not sure about what in the name of God we're doing to defuse the situation."

"Yes, sir."

"And then, in the midst of this cluster fuck, we have one of our most capable operatives, who no longer works for us because we let him down a year ago, running around without giving us any idea about where he's going or how he intends to proceed, have I got this now?"

"Yes sir," the CIA man admitted.

"Well then, Mr. Byrnes, why don't you explain to all of us how you can justify these actions, with everything that's at stake here. I can't have my people raising the Terror Alert to another Code Orange with nothing but a hunch to back it up."

The Deputy Director took a deep breath. "Mr. President, please understand that I know full well what is at stake, and that I would never play fast and loose with the security of our country, or of my own men, for that matter."

"Thank you for the speech, Mr. Byrnes. Now, how about a straight answer?"

"Yes, Mr. President. First, our intelligence sources inform us that Mr. McHugh and Mr. Andrioli had incomplete data on the current offensive strike being planned by Traiman for al-Qaeda. Our hope was to follow these men upstream, to more informed sources. Second, we have reason to believe that Andrioli still has such contacts in Paris, who can provide the missing pieces to the puzzle on these threats."

"Is that it?"

"No, sir. We are extremely close now on at least two fronts. One is an operation intended to neutralize Traiman by bringing him out into the open where he can be apprehended. The other involves this man Andrioli and his efforts to obtain the additional, critical information on these terrorist plans."

"What chance does this Andrioli have, acting alone against al-Qaeda?"

"He is not alone, sir. I can assure you, Mr. President, as I have assured the Director, I have teams in place on these operations." Byrnes would disclose those arrangements, but he was not ready to divulge the full extent of Jordan's involvement, not even to the President. "For what it's worth," he said, "Sandor was one of our very best men, as you've mentioned. Whatever he's up to, I can vouch for the fact that he would never betray us."

"Well that's very comforting, Mr. Byrnes. Anything else on that score?"

"Yes sir. We have word that Sandor's with Andrioli now, in Paris, even as we speak."

*   *   *

Jordan held her for a few moments, until he felt her relax in his arms.

"I was scared to death," she said.

He gently wiped away her tears. "I was a little shaken up myself," he said.

She managed a smile, still looking into his eyes.

It really is a great smile, he decided. Then he pulled away slightly and said quietly, "Come on, I've got to meet Andrioli."

She nodded.

"You all right?"

"Sure."

"All right. But before we leave, I think you have a right to know something." He paused. "That man on the stairs. The tall one with blond hair." She nodded. "He was one of the men who shot at me in Woodstock. I think he was one of the men who killed Jimmy."

She recoiled from him, the stricken look on her face telling Jordan that she really was Jimmy McHugh's sister. Either that, or she was a lot better at acting than he had imagined.

FORTY

Vincent Traiman's office was crowded with people or, more accurately, was as crowded as he ever allowed his office to become. He was seated behind his large, contemporary glass and steel desk, silently surveying the group as if he were some benign corporate executive.

His key aides had been included in the conference, marking the significance of this meeting. Traiman would typically isolate his staff, doling out information on a need-to-know basis. Today, all of them needed to know.

Present was Tallal Abdullah Driann, Colonel Qaddafi's *Charge d'Affaires* for matters related to Libya's role as host to Traiman's operation, and Faisal el-Ridaya, the head of Libya's European propaganda lobby. The Colonel now steered clear of any direct communications with the terrorist cabal, limiting his involvement to the briefings he received at the Bab el-Azziziya barracks or his offices in the Villa Pietri. Having occupied the self-styled role as Great Leader for more than three decades, Qaddafi was working hard to revise his image as the mad dog of the Middle East, President Reagan's accurate judgment of him in the 1980's. Lately, he had adopted a lower profile, assuming the appearance of a mature and moderate statesman, undertaking a public relations push the liberal media in the West seemed to be buying.

As evidence that this image was a lie, his henchmen Driann and Ridaya were accompanied to the meeting by Ibrahim Abass, Traiman's direct liaison with al-Qaeda.

"I have handled the situation with Loubar," Traiman told the gathering. "Our current shipment has been protected."

"We understand that," Ridaya responded with a knowing look. He was an educated man, sophisticated and experienced in the world markets, with entrée to Europe's most exclusive circles in commerce, politics and society. In dealings on behalf of the Libyan government, he naturally gravitated toward the most powerful and influential men throughout Europe and the Middle East. He was well known for his observation that the character of a successful man was most easily identified by his women, an outlook that endeared him to Traiman. "The untimely death of Mr. Fryar was the subject of some discussion and speculation in the foreign markets," Ridaya pointed out to his host.

"Speculation is your area of expertise."

Ridaya nodded graciously. Grace was a necessary quality in his work. "Is it not, however, speculation to believe that Loubar will be able to fulfill the outstanding contracts?"

"No," Traiman replied. "The outstanding orders will be honored."

"Very well. We shall be guided accordingly."

"Now then," Traiman continued, "it appears our operations in the United States have been less covert than anticipated. The Secret Service has apprehended the team in Washington. Our men in New York and San Francisco are worried about exposure, and they await our further instructions."

No one inquired as to the reasons for the failure in Washington. No one asked how the team had been compromised.

"What of the preparations in Europe?" inquired the al-Qaeda delegate, Ibrahim Abass.

"We are moving our men into place."

"And the rumors of the two who defected from your organization?"

Traiman responded to Abass with an admiring nod. Other than Traiman himself, he knew that Abass was the most dangerous man in the room. "Your sources are to be commended."

Abass offered no reply.

"One of these men has been neutralized."

"Had he compromised your plans before he was removed?"

"No."

"And the other man?"

"We know that he has attempted to deal with the American government, but his efforts have been rejected. He lacks enough information to cause us any real problems. For the moment, he's nothing more than a nuisance that we are in the process of handling."

"A nuisance," Abass repeated angrily. "This sort of bungling is more than a nuisance, Mr. Traiman. We have worked too long, invested far too

much with your organization, to have it jeopardized at the last moment by a nuisance."

"The operation is not jeopardized," Traiman told them all, his tone calm and restrained.

Ridaya asked, "Why were these men not eliminated in the first instance, when they were located in the United States?"

"As I've said, one of them was removed as soon as we found him. The other eluded us, but has now returned to France."

There was some muttering around the room, and Ridaya's expression confessed his surprise. "He has come back to Europe?"

"He has. And we have our people working on the matter as we speak."

If Ridaya was satisfied with the response, the al-Qaeda representative, Abass, was clearly not. "These would not be the same men who have failed up to now, would they?"

"Of course not. The men who failed in eliminating Andrioli paid the ultimate price for their incompetence."

Abass stood up and walked towards the edge of the large desk. "We realize, Mr. Traiman, that you do not share the vision or the passion or the commitment of my people. For us there is the jihad, for you only a capitalist motivation which is foreign to our holy crusade. You are, what you Americans so quaintly call, a gun for hire, a necessary evil in our war against the greater forces of sin. When you speak of paying the ultimate price, you betray your misunderstanding of all we live and die for. Do I make myself clear?"

Traiman looked up at him, his dark eyes meeting the ebony gaze of the Arab terrorist, neither of them blinking. "I understand only this," Traiman said. "In this life, we are rewarded for success and punished for failure. In the new order, if and when it comes, I will have succeeded and my position will be secure."

"Perhaps so. For now, we need your teams to assume their positions and make ready for these assaults. San Francisco, New York, London and Rome. We need to confirm the timetable and we need successful execution of our attacks. We need assurances that the chemical shipments will arrive on time. Do I make myself clear?"

Traiman was not about to back down, but he knew well enough that this was no time to stand up and confront Abass. "What reason would you have to doubt us? Have we failed you up to now?"

"Up to now, you have provided munitions, technology and intelligence gathering. The raids you have organized were minor skirmishes. We are in a new arena, and we must have assurances that our operations will succeed."

Traiman was very much committed to the success of these operations, especially since he knew that he had worn out his welcome in Libya. The plans he was putting in place with Martin Koppel would assure him of wealth beyond any of their imaginations. Once these new rounds of attacks were launched in the United States, and the capitals of its most vocal allies, the world's markets would temporarily collapse in a heap. The release of VX gas would result in the death of tens of thousands of people around the world. Panic would be followed by economic chaos. However short-lived, Traiman would reap the benefits of this new economic fear. The funds being set up by Koppel, through the most legitimate of financial channels, would reap millions upon millions of dollars in the short positions they would establish over the next several days.

"Believe me, Ibrahim," Traiman said, addressing him in this familiar way, his tone becoming friendly as he reminded himself of his ultimate goal, "I am as committed to the success of these plans as you are."

FORTY-ONE

Christine was sitting on the edge of the bed. The initial impact had passed, the shock of having just seen the man who murdered Jimmy McHugh now replaced with a painful emptiness of fear and anger and hate.

"We've got to get out of here," Jordan said. "Are you all right?"

Christine did not respond, feeling that there was little difference now between moving and sitting still. She looked down at her hands, watching as they pulled at the hem of her jacket, staring at them as if they were not her own, as if someone else was busily yanking at the soft fabric of the suede top she had purchased the day before in Atlanta, half a world away.

Jordan kneeled before her, taking her hands in his, holding them still. "Listen," he said softly, "as soon as those men reach the front desk, they'll know we've just checked in. We've got to go."

She nodded, and Jordan watched her struggle to find her composure. She said, "He didn't seem to recognize you."

"I know. He never got a good look at me in Woodstock."

"By now, though, wouldn't they have a photo or something?"

"Yes, probably. It was dark, and this was the last place he'd expect to find me."

"But . . . ," she couldn't bring herself to finish the thought.

"Yes, once the clerk tells them we asked for room forty seven, they'll come back for us."

Her eyes widened, the pale blue swimming in a pink and ivory sea of concern. "We should go," she agreed in a hoarse whisper.

Jordan stood and moved to the window. They had a view of the court-yard below. He noticed that the old couple was gone and everything seemed quiet. He realized that was no reason to feel reassured.

Christine stood, smoothed out her jacket and said, "I'm okay."

They went to the door, turned off the light and stepped quietly out of the room. Jordan pulled his small leather bag onto his shoulder, then reached for the grip of the automatic, drawing it from his belt. He saw her stare at the gun, and he held his finger to his lips. Then he pointed up. His best move, he thought, was the secondary route Andrioli had described.

Christine did not speak. She walked ahead of him, quietly climbing the carpeted steps as he pulled the door to their room shut.

A brief moment of silence passed as Sandor remained alone on the landing, alert to anything that might pierce the stillness. This was Andrioli's scheme, that he and Christine would become the human decoys intended to flush Traiman's men into the open. How could he or Jordan have guessed they would run into them the moment they entered the hotel? Sandor knew he should count himself lucky for not being made right there, with so little chance to react.

He took off after Christine in a silent rush, two steps at a time, until he caught up with her on the next floor. He looked for the passageway Andrioli had described, then gave her a gentle shove, following her as they ascended the next flight of stairs until they reached a door on the right that led to a narrow corridor. He took Christine's hand and sprinted ahead, stopping at the archway to an enclosed bridge that connected the two towers of the hotel running the length of the patio below.

Jordan, holding the automatic in his right hand, thought of *Al-Sirat*, the bridge Muslims walk over to see if they will go to paradise or to hell. More slender than a spider's thread and sharper than a sword, according to Islamic tradition, it was a span only the good passed over swiftly.

He took Christine's hand and began running again, quickly traversing the length of the narrow overpass, reaching the door at the other end. He hesitated, listening. It was quiet, so he pushed it open, the gun at his side as he stepped out onto the top floor landing, looking quickly in each direction. No one was there, and the stairwell below was silent.

Now, as they raced downstairs, Jordan remained in the lead, prepared for any surprises that might be in store. He checked over his shoulder to ensure that she stayed close behind, attentive to any sound that might tell him Traiman's men had circled back to find them. The steep, winding staircase offered them no protection as they approached the end of each flight.

These small landings were the only places a pursuer could hide, unless they had positioned themselves in one of the rooms.

They came around the last turn without seeing anyone, but Jordan realized the gravest danger awaited them in the lobby.

Jordan stopped at the bottom of the staircase, behind the door that should lead directly into the deep, narrow reception area. Christine was right behind him, and they paused for a moment, Sandor visualizing the layout of the foyer, imagining how he would position a backup team if he were preparing the attack. One behind the counter, another in the corner, near the entrance. The two men they saw in the rear tower had likely gone in search of them by now, possibly with support. They could be anywhere in the building.

Jordan knew he should not delay his move.

"Stay low and close," he whispered to her, then pushed through the door in a running crouch, his gun extended, coming to a stop beside the desk where the wide-eyed clerk was handing a key to another guest. There didn't seem to be anyone else there.

"Don't make a fucking move," Jordan said, pointing the gun up at the clerk's face.

The guest, an Englishman who had either begun the day early or ended a long night with too many cocktails, had trouble getting his eyes to focus on the grey gunmetal of the Colt. "Say, what is all this?" the man asked unevenly.

"Shut the hell up and get on the floor," Jordan barked at him.

The Brit immediately dropped to his knees, either grateful to be taken out of the action or badly in need of rest.

"Out," Jordan ordered the Frenchman from behind the counter.

The portly man moved cautiously, his eyes on the gun still leveled at him as he moved.

"Keep watch on the glass door," Jordan said over his shoulder to Christine, referring to the entranceway to the patio behind them. "Come on," Jordan said, grabbing the clerk roughly by the arm, then twisting him around and using him as a shield.

"Jordan," Christine said. "I think I hear something."

Sandor stopped, the sound of footsteps in the distance coming from the front stairwell they had used. "Let's go," he said, pushing the clerk towards the front door, "you first." Then he shoved him through the wooden entry door to the hotel, out onto the Rue des Saint Peres.

As the door swung open, the man stumbled, and Jordan let him go. The clerk fell to the ground on his back. Christine had stood, petrified for an instant, before following them out into the street.

Jordan leaned over the stout little clerk, the automatic now hidden under his jacket. "Mr. Forest, you got that. Any messages for Mr. Forest, you hold them for me."

The man stared up at him, his look of bewilderment mixed with fear and rage.

Jordan pulled out their room key and dropped it onto the man's chest. "You fuck with me, I'll find out and I'll kill you. You got that?"

The man nodded without speaking.

Jordan stood up, took Christine by the hand, then began running towards the Boulevard Saint Germain.

At the corner of Saint Germain, Jordan flagged down a passing taxi.

"Take this cab to Foquet's," Jordan told her. "Sit there as long as you feel safe, but if Andrioli and I don't show in an hour, don't wait any more. Take a cab to the U. S. Embassy, tell them you've got to speak to someone at Langley about Jordan Sandor." He reached into his pocket and pulled out two phone numbers he had written out. "The first number is in Virginia. Just add 4-3-4 at the end. Tell them you've got to be connected to that number, it's an emergency. You got it? Don't write it down, just remember it. You add 4-3-4. Tell them everything you know."

"All right. What's the other number?"

"Add a 212 area code and a 5 at the end."

She nodded.

"That's my friend's number. Bill Sternlich. He'll help you."

The taxi driver was becoming impatient. "Monsieur," he said, leaning toward the passenger window. "Do you want the cab?"

"Yes, yes," Jordan said. Turning back to Christine, he handed her some folded one hundred dollar bills and said, "Now go."

"Will you be all right?"

He looked over his shoulder. He could not see very far down the street, as it curved in an arc before the hotel. "I'll be fine," he told her. "Now get out of here."

She took his face in her hands and kissed him. "I'll be waiting, don't worry."

Jordan smiled. "Don't you worry. I'll be there."

FORTY-TWO

The tall, fair-haired American named Kerrigan came into the lobby first, his smaller, darker partner right behind. The desk clerk, who was brushing himself off after shouting a loud string of French expletives down the street at Jordan and Christine, had lumbered back inside. The Englishman remained kneeling at the base of the front desk. He began to utter a rueful, "I say," but the effort was stifled at the sight of another automatic weapon, this one being brandished by the tall, blond American.

The concierge did not have to be coaxed into describing everything that had happened, including the message left by Sandor. Normally, he was paid for information, but this time he was only too pleased to help, giving every detail. "Mr. Forest," he said. "Lousy American." He finished by telling them the man and woman had gone off to the right, towards Saint Germain.

Kerrigan and his partner cautiously opened the front door and stepped outside the hotel. They moved slowly at first, looking up and down the Rue des Saint Peres several times before splitting up, each taking a side of the street as they began to stride purposefully towards the Boulevard. Kerrigan's partner, on the far side of the arched lane, got a look at Christine entering the cab and saw her pulling away. He was surprised to see Sandor remain behind.

He signaled Kerrigan, who crossed over just in time to spot Sandor, before he disappeared from view, off to the right. They saw that Jordan was alone, moving at a brisk pace, in the direction of the Rue de Rennes.

It was a chilly autumn day, the streets busy with the late morning traffic of students, artists, tourists and local habitués of the Left Bank. They needed to get to him, but a public scene would be a problem. They would have to find a better place to take him out.

When they reached the corner, Kerrigan saw him cross the wide Boulevard. They waited, giving Jordan a more comfortable lead, then followed him.

*   *   *

Andrioli nodded to himself as he viewed the proceedings from his ringside seat in the corner café across the way. Hiding behind a newspaper, he watched Christine leaving in the cab, Jordan heading off to their appointed meeting place and the two men following in a carefully orchestrated ballet of pursuit.

Andrioli waited until he saw Jordan safely cross the Boulevard in the direction of their rendezvous, the cathedral known as Saint German des Pres. He stood up, paid for his espresso and croissant, then stepped out into the brisk morning air. He did not recognize Kerrigan or his partner, but he made them immediately. He knew how Traiman worked, and expected a two-man team. Andrioli doubted they had backup in place, not if they were onto Sandor this quickly. Jordan and Christine had obviously surprised them by coming to the hotel, and there hadn't been enough time to put another pair of hitters in play, although there might be others on the way. He stood on the corner for a moment, watching, but saw no signs of anyone else in the hunt. Andrioli timed his move to cover Jordan's back. Left alone, the two assassins would surely kill Sandor within a matter of a couple of minutes.

Except that Andrioli knew where Jordan was going, which gave him the edge.

Rather than traveling along the bend of the avenue, where they might spot him, Andrioli walked quickly to his left, then made a right on Rue Jacob. He moved with purpose, criss-crossing the narrow street twice, prepared for what might still be coming from behind. He held his attaché case tightly in his left hand, his right already gripping the Colt beneath his coat.

After walking full circle around the church, Andrioli turned up the Rue Saint Benoit and stepped into a dark, quiet doorway on the side of the ancient, stone cathedral. From where he stood he could not miss them, not if they were led this way.

Sandor did not disappoint. As he hurried along the Rue Bonaparte, Jordan was in full view and did not break stride. If he stopped, or even hesitated, his pursuers would know Sandor had reached a meeting place or, even worse, an ambush.

Instead, Jordan continued past the side of the church and the small square, as if heading for the quay along the Seine. Andrioli waited, but no one appeared. He did not want to risk showing himself, but Jordan was leaving his line of sight now. He hesitated, knowing that he was certain to put them both in danger if he made a move from his doorway.

Jordan did not even glance in his direction as he walked by, keeping his gait brisk, passing within a few feet of Andrioli as he turned right, towards the back of the cathedral.

That was when the first of the two men appeared. Just as Jordan was entering the tiny Rue des Beaux-Arts, the smaller man came into view, around the far corner. He was pulling a gun from inside his jacket. He appeared to be alone.

It was the smart play, of course. His partner had likely circled back, anticipating Sandor's course. Or he might have gone toward the river, or even be hiding in one of the other recesses along the cathedral wall on the opposite side. Andrioli knew he was past waiting now. Once Jordan was completely out of his sight, Andrioli could not cover him.

"Traiman," Andrioli hollered, and the man on the Rue Bonaparte instinctively turned to the sound of the shout. It was all Andrioli wanted, just that moment to freeze him, and to give Jordan an instant to react. Andrioli stepped from the doorway, squeezing off two shots, the bullets whizzing through the silencer he had attached, finding their target, spinning the man and dropping him to the ground.

That extra moment was all Sandor needed. In one agile motion he drew his automatic from his belt and dove to safety in a nearby doorway. Quiet returned to the street with an eerie suddenness.

Jordan, squatting in the sanctuary of his portal, peered out at the small square adjacent to the church. Neither Andrioli nor Sandor could see each other now, and neither of them had a bead on the second man, Kerrigan. They were both vulnerable, since Kerrigan had surely spotted Andrioli, and certainly knew where Sandor had positioned himself. There was also the problem of the man lying in the street, dead or dying, with someone sure to happen by soon. The longer they waited, the worse their prospects became.

Jordan broke from his doorway, running toward two parked cars, hoping to draw fire and expose Kerrigan's position. No shots came.

He darted from between the cars, heading away from the church to create a crossfire with Andrioli. He stopped beside a small van, opposite

Andrioli's perch, and they exchanged quick nods. Jordan signaled that they should both break for the corner.

Andrioli gave him the thumbs-up, and Jordan did not hesitate. He moved first, rounding the turn in a tight, swift stride, Andrioli soon behind. Still there were no shots, no sign of the tall American. The only sound was a woman's scream from somewhere in the small square. She had discovered the body of the first man, lying in the street.

They raced the length of the Rue des Beaux-Arts, each taking a side of the narrow street, then turned up towards the Seine. There, they rested together in another entranceway, another unavailing haven from a danger that may or may not yet be in pursuit.

Andrioli was panting. "Man, am I outta shape."

"The American," Jordan said. "The one still out there. He shot Dan Peters, and the cop in Woodstock. And McHugh."

Andrioli nodded, still searching for air. "Good. We could use a little extra motivation right now. Revenge is good." His eyes were alert. "But I don't think he's out there anymore. He's a paid hit man doing a job, not a fanatic on a religious mission. He knows they blew their chance, he's gone by now."

"Maybe," Jordan said, still watching the street. "Let's take a minute and wait."

The two men stepped back into the vestibule of the apartment house overlooking the river. Andrioli leaned against the stone wall and Jordan watched him, smiling at the attaché case he still had clutched under his left arm, and had carried like a football as they dashed along the streets.

"Fond of that thing, are you?"

"You can laugh, if you want," he said, "but this baby is going to be the difference in us making it or not, believe me."

"Okay, so now what?"

"There are two guys who might help. I need to get with at least one of them. Word'll be out in five minutes that I'm back in town, so we should move fast. First I gotta ask you something."

"Go ahead."

"How deep are you into this mess? I mean, really."

Jordan sighed. "I'm in for the long haul, let's leave it at that."

Andrioli nodded his understanding that this was all he would be getting, and letting Jordan know that for now, it was enough.

Jordan said, "Mind if I ask you something?"

"Why not?"

"Did you meet Christine when she came to see McHugh in Paris?"

"Yeah," Andrioli said. "Why?"

"He ever tell you she was his sister?"

"Hey, that's two questions. I only got one."

"I owe you one."

"I'll remember that. Yeah, sure. He said she was his half sister, something like that. That's what he said, anyway."

Jordan nodded. "Okay."

"So," Andrioli asked, "where'd you send her?"

"Fouquet's."

He stuck out his lower lip and nodded. *"Tres touriste,* no?"

"Only place I could think of at the moment. I told her we'd meet her in an hour. Otherwise, she should get to the Embassy."

"And call in the cavalry, I suppose."

"Nuclear strike force."

"Well, we can't let her do that, can we?"

Jordan smiled. "Not yet." He paused. "But I do think it's time to cut her loose."

Before Andrioli could respond, a young Frenchman and his girlfriend strolled past, arm in arm. The two men tensed, and Andrioli leveled his automatic at the young man's head. The youngsters froze at the sight of two armed men in the doorway.

"Sorry," Jordan said to them.

They made some remark about crazy Americans, then hurried away.

Jordan laughed. "You really are out of shape."

"I guess I am," Andrioli said as he stuck the automatic under his jacket. "So what do you think? About Christine, I mean?"

"Were you serious about letting her go to the Embassy?

"Of course. If we didn't make it, what else was she going to do?"

Andrioli shook his head. "I don't like that sonuvabitch Covington, I gotta tell you."

"Neither do I," Jordan admitted. "Come on, let's go get her before she leaves, then we'll figure out what's next."

FORTY-THREE

Christine looked at her watch again, then had another sip of coffee. The waiter came by and asked if she would like something else, beyond the brioche and coffee she had been playing with for the past half hour.

No, she insisted, she was waiting for someone.

Of course you are, the waiter seemed to be saying when he responded with a sympathetic look.

Christine ignored him and checked her watch again, then lit another cigarette. Christine almost never smoked, but this morning she found herself anxiously working through a pack of Galouises.

Sandor and Andrioli arrived at Fouquet's, having taken the precaution of changing cabs in front of the Hôtel de Crillon, then asking the second driver to travel around Le Etoille and back to the other side of the Champs d'Elysée. When they stepped onto the street, they spotted Christine at a small table inside the glass-walled café, nervously puffing on a cigarette. She saw them and stood up.

Inside the restaurant, they embraced as if they had not seen her for years. The waiter, obviously surprised to find that not one, but two gentlemen had joined her, came by to take their order. Jordan asked for a round of cognacs and, although none of them had an appetite for food, he ordered sandwiches. Fouquet's more elegant cuisine would be wasted on them today.

After they told Christine everything that happened on the Left Bank, Andrioli wrote down the name and address of a hotel on the Rue de Rivoli. It was an elegant place, he told them, and they would be well insulated there. When they told the front desk they were not to be disturbed, they would not be disturbed. He would call and make the arrangements in the name of Jordan's alias, Scott Kerr.

"What about you?" Christine asked.

"I've got to pay a surprise visit to one of my friends." He thought that over as he sipped his cognac. "Might not be much of a surprise at this point."

Jordan agreed. "We've got to assume they're watching every one of your contacts."

"Yeah, well, nothin' to be done about that now. I gotta see him if we want the information we need."

"If you say so. But be careful."

"I'll be careful. First, we can all use some rest, so I'll hole up somewhere, then call the Pas de Tour, see what messages they have for Mr. Forest. Now that they know we're in town, Traiman'll probably have them try to set a meeting."

Jordan smiled. "Bet that clerk is going to be happy to hear from you."

"Don't you worry about that clerk. He gets paid by all sides. Typical Frenchman. Love the one you're with."

"You said you had two friends you wanted to reach."

"Yeah," Andrioli said, then took a bite of the baguette with ham and cheese they'd all been served. "I got a backup if Jackson doesn't come through."

They were quiet for a while, each of them sifting through their personal ordeal. Then Christine said, "I wish you'd killed the other man."

The two men looked at her, then to each other.

"It doesn't matter," Jordan said. "They're all interchangeable parts of the same machine."

Christine shook her head. "He killed Jimmy. The big one killed Jimmy, you said so yourself."

"I did, yes. But it might have actually been the little Arab who was there that day. What difference does it make now? What difference which one of them pulled the trigger?"

Andrioli put down his sandwich and looked across the table at them, his eyes ghostly sad now, the eyes of a man with a terminal illness. "He didn't pull the trigger," he said quietly. "Jimmy pulled the trigger. Just like I did. Sometimes the gun doesn't go off right away, that's all. It's only a matter of time."

Jordan reached out and gave Andrioli a friendly slap on the shoulder. "Come on, don't get all preachy on us now."

"Sorry, but I don't want Christine walking around all full of hate about this for the rest of her life. Truth is, Jimmy and I were stupid and greedy and selfish and we created everything we became. We couldn't see tomorrow for today. We were little boys who played soldier, just like a lot of little boys, except most of us grow up. Take responsibility. Care about something or someone, other than ourselves."

"What about us?" Christine asked him. "You're helping us, aren't you?"

"Helping you do what? Get yourselves killed? Jimmy never should have gotten you mixed up in all this to start with. Now you're stuck with me, a condemned man who wants to repent for his sins. What the hell is that all about? Nobody wants to die, that's all it is. If you two had an ounce of sense, you'd get up right now and walk straight to the Embassy. Period. You're nuts if you don't."

Jordan looked him in the eye and said, "That's not an option for me anymore, at least not until you get whatever you can get from your friends. You know it and I know it. There's too much at stake here for us to stop now, not to mention that we've aided and abetted a fugitive, traveled on forged passports and shot up the streets of Fort Lauderdale and Paris."

"Good point."

Sandor nodded slowly. "There really is too much at stake.

"More than you know," Andrioli agreed.

"So tell us."

"I will. After I find Jackson."

"Okay," Jordan agreed. He looked down at the drinks and food on their table. "It's been a while since I've flown to Paris for cognac and baguettes."

The three of them lifted their glasses in a silent toast.

*   *   *

Covington and four of his men, including Todd Swedock, were on their way to France. He had just received an e-mail, via satellite, describing the shootings near the Cathedral Saint German des Pres. It was not yet clear what happened, but one man had been found dead. Interpol identified him as a known terrorist. No one at the scene had been apprehended.

The Deputy Director told Covington it was time to shorten the leash on Andrioli and Sandor. Whatever Andrioli managed to find in Paris, he should be taken in for questioning. If Sandor was with him, Covington was instructed to bring him in as well.

Covington had other plans, but for now he would follow instructions. When he got to Paris he would make all appropriate inquiries.

FORTY-FOUR

On the way to their new hotel, Jordan and Christine stopped to purchase a few items. The suitcases and clothing they had picked up in Atlanta were abandoned in Room 57 of the Pas de Tour. Andrioli suggested the shops just off the Rue de Rivoli, near their new hotel, on a small street featuring an assortment of boutiques.

The shopping provided a welcome diversion. They visited a number of stores, replacing Christine's cosmetics and personals, choosing a couple of outfits for her, a pair of slacks and some shirts for Jordan and selecting the other sundries they would need for the next couple of days. By the time they were done, the two of them were laden with shopping bags and a large, signature khaki Longchamps tote for Christine.

"I don't think I can carry anything else," he told her.

The spree over, they found their way to the small but elegant hotel Andrioli had chosen for them, just a couple of blocks away.

The desk clerk greeted Jordan with a polite nod.

"I'm Mr. Kerr," Jordan told him. "I believe you have a reservation for us."

"Yes," the clerk said, "we received the call a short time ago." He asked for a passport and credit card, and Jordan signed the register and American Express voucher as Scott Kerr, then they followed the bellboy who took their bags, led them to the lift and escorted them upstairs.

The room was generously sized, with French provincial furniture and appointments, a view of the street below and a large bed that beckoned as they felt a wave of exhaustion wash over them.

Jordan tipped the bellboy and locked the door behind him. When he turned back, he found Christine had already pulled back the comforter, kicked off her shoes and was lying on the bed.

"I'm going to take a shower," Jordan said. "You want to go first?"

Christine shook her head. "I can't move."

"I won't be a minute," he said.

Inside the marble-walled bathroom, he removed the toiletry kit from his leather bag and had a shave, then stepped into a warm, steaming shower. He toweled off and pulled on the plush, terrycloth robe provided by the hotel.

Back in the room, he found Christine had removed her slacks and blouse and was curled up, under the beige coverlet, fast asleep.

He watched her for a moment, realizing that in the three days he had known her, it was the first time he had ever seen her lovely face at peace. He leaned over and straightened out the duvet to make her more comfortable.

Jordan considered dialing the front desk for a wake up call, then thought better of it. He knew he would not sleep for long, and if Andrioli needed him, he knew where to find them. He took off the robe and slid under the cover, on the other side of the bed, doing his best not to wake her. The satiny texture of the comforter felt good against his skin and, as he turned on his side, he was surprised to find that her eyes had opened. She was watching him.

"We need some rest," he said.

She nodded.

"You all right?"

She nodded again, then moved closer to him, placing her arm around his neck.

"Danger is an aphrodisiac," he warned her, then reached out to stroke her sandy-colored hair.

"Is it?"

He nodded. "It's not fair to take advantage of the situation."

She smiled, maybe the best of the smiles she had shown him up to now. "So if you frighten a girl to death, then what? Is that like getting her drunk at a party?"

"Never thought of it that way," he said, taking her by the shoulders and gently drawing her towards him. "I guess it's the right analogy, though. Just isn't done."

She kissed him tenderly on the lips, her legs now eagerly entwined in his. He pulled back slightly and looked into her pale, blue eyes. He saw a resolve that would have surprised him that first evening, at the cocktail lounge in New York where they met.

She reached up to kiss him again, pressing herself against him as she became lost in the moment.

Jordan held her, his emotions a mix of desire and doubt, passionate instinct and clinical analysis, wanting to trust her, but knowing he should not.

She felt his firm, naked form and moved away from him for a moment, remaining under the comforter as she slipped off her panties and bra, tossing them to the floor. She took his face in her hands and looked into his eyes. "You don't have to worry," she said with a slight smile, "this isn't because I'm afraid."

Their lips met again, mouths open, immersing them in a warm, moist flood of sensations, an enveloping wave that permitted no other experience but this embrace. He reacted to the feel of her firm breasts pressed against his chest, the taste of her, the reassuring suppleness of her body next to his. He felt her fingers dig into his back, pulling him closer and closer, until they were together, for the time being lost in the grand illusion.

*   *   *

Anthony Andrioli believed he understood things that his new partners in espionage had no way of knowing.

He understood the brutality of their adversary, Vincent Traiman, and how difficult that would make it for them to prevail, even to survive.

He understood that life cares not at all what you think of it, that that life rolls on with unremitting determination and uncaring inevitability, not requiring approval, not affected by the intent or purpose of a man's deeds. He understood that, as a result, life itself ultimately becomes the greatest teacher of how to live.

He also understood that for him, all that was left was the opportunity to stop Traiman, even if there was no valor in the deed. He had sacrificed his ideals long ago, saw them bleed to death with his friends in Vietnam, watched them tormented out of existence when he discovered how little remained for him back in the States. He had taken a handful of peculiar skills and become a traitor without a cause, a heretic with no religion to betray.

Now, after his years with Traiman, there was nowhere left for him to go. He had hidden in Florida, nearly staying there too long, as attested to by the pair of corpses left beside the New River Canal in Fort Lauderdale.

Now, at least, he had a reason to go on. He knew some of what Traiman meant to do, and he was determined to discover the rest. He gazed into the bathroom mirror in his small hotel room in Montmarte, his dark brown eyes staring back at him, wondering how far he would get—how far they would get—before Traiman stopped them. What the hell, he thought as he trimmed the edges of his beard. We've come this far. What else is there for me to do?

He turned on the shower, the rush of water quickly turning warm. He had very little sleep in the past couple of days, and he needed to wake up. He stepped into the tub, the Parisian shower fixture no higher than his neck. He bent forward, letting the soothing water cascade over his head and down his shoulders and back. He cupped his hands and splashed his face and hair, ducking his head beneath the shower again, until he felt renewed and alert and ready.

He dressed quickly in his wrinkled clothes, smiling at himself in the mirror. His rumpled appearance would be considered *tres chic* in Montmarte. He picked up his attaché case and made his way out of the hotel, stopping at a public telephone on the Rue Lepic.

Night had fallen, and Montmarte was alive with people bumping and bustling their way to the Metro, hurrying along the café lined streets, stopping to admire the local artists who displayed their work against the stone walls that climbed the hills of the area. Andrioli dialed a number and waited.

"Hello," the familiar voice answered.

"*Bon soir*, Steve. This is Forest."

"Jesus Christ," Steve Jackson gasped. "Forest?"

"Yes," Andrioli said calmly. "Meet me in five minutes at the Sacred Heart Church," he told him, using the English name of the famous cathedral.

There was a pause on the other end. "Better make it ten."

Andrioli didn't bother to answer. He replaced the phone on its hook and walked away.

He hadn't seen or spoken with Steve Jackson in more than two months, but he was still the only man in Paris Andrioli trusted enough to call. He knew that Jackson would not speak on the phone, that they would have to meet, which increased the danger. Any contact with Jackson was a calculated risk, but it was unavoidable. Andrioli had used his code name to tell him that his situation was serious, both realizing it was a superfluous gesture under the circumstances. Most agents in the system knew that their friends, Jimmy and Tony, had disappeared two months ago. They probably knew that McHugh was now dead, and had certainly been told that Traiman had declared open season on Andrioli.

Jackson received this information sooner than most. He worked the communications detail from Paris, the link between the free Western world and the dark operations that existed behind the veil of Arab protection. Jackson was a key man in the exchange of intelligence, and that was another reason Andrioli wanted to see him.

Andrioli never believed the story Traiman was selling, the placement of overseas assassination teams, that was being fed to the rank and file at Bab el-Azziziya. He didn't believe it any more than he believed that Qaddafi had become a moderate force for peace, or that Saddam Hussein had ever been committed to the dismantling of his weapons of mass destruction. There was another level to the missions being initiated by Traiman, Andrioli had heard enough about the Loubar shipments to know that.

Jackson was the logical connection, the man who should be able to give him vital information to piece it together.

Why, then, Andrioli wondered, *had Jackson seem so surprised to receive his call?* After the shooting this morning, a systems coordinator in Jackson's position would surely have heard that Andrioli was in Paris. And that he had survived the incident. Jordan had left the name 'Forest' with the clerk at the Pas de Tour. Jackson would have heard about that as well, probably would have been the man to relay the message to Libya. *What was so shocking about the call, then? Who else would I contact in Paris?* Andrioli had chosen a hotel just two blocks from Jackson's apartment, both of which were near the foot of the Sacred Heart steps. *Why did Steve need an additional five minutes to get there?* he asked himself.

These questions nagged at Andrioli as he climbed the mountain of steps that led to the imposing Basilique du Sacre Couer.

When he reached the top, he paused to view the surrounding area. This was a good meeting place. It was wide open and, now that he had ascended the long hill of stone stairs, he was afforded a fine vantage point for any possible approaches. As he looked around, he gave a subtle impersonation of a curious tourist. He pretended to be absorbed in the majestic view of Paris that stretches out below this centuries old cathedral, which is perched atop one of the city's highest points. He allowed himself a brief glimpse at those far reaches, then returned to the immediate area below.

He had arrived first, but had purposely given Jackson very little time to meet him there. Even with the additional five minutes, there was little opportunity for any covert placement of snipers. They would have to come directly at him, and so he turned and made his way up the final set of stairs to the front of the basilica.

He positioned himself beneath one of the cupolas, shielded from view by a large column, protected from the cold winds that whipped across the church's façade.

He stood there, opened the hard-shell attaché case, and waited.

FORTY-FIVE

Vincent R. Traiman made ready for his voyage north, across the Mediterranean, to meet with Martin Koppel. Everything was arranged, all precautions had been taken. The timing of Operation VX, which was being relentlessly pushed by his Arab compatriots, meant he could not delay his appointment. The trouble in Paris had to be addressed, of course, but he would rely on his men there to handle Andrioli and Sandor. If they could not, Traiman had an insurance policy in place that made his position fail-safe.

The most important thing was to finalize his financial arrangements with Koppel.

The production of a new feature film was the smokescreen Traiman had created. The plan was to bankroll an action movie where the Arabs were the heroes. His Arab benefactors loved the idea of countering Hollywood's pro-Jewish propaganda with a story of their own. Traiman marveled at their enthusiasm for the project—it bordered on the naïve. The true reason Traiman had arranged for Koppel to become involved was far more sinister.

Even though he had fallen from grace, Koppel still had an impressive background and a world of experience in the financial markets. His credibility could easily be restored, given the appropriate economic backing. His new production company would be funded through an investment firm Koppel would create. After nine-eleven, the United States regulatory agencies had become vigilant in watching over suspicious foreign investments. Koppel was decidedly American, a man with a reputation, having enjoyed great wealth and then having fallen from those heights.

Now, through a series of sanitized financial transactions, Koppel would be bankrolled, with an opportunity to repeat the success of his past. Except this time, his principal sponsor would be betting on failure. Koppel was as desperate as a man can become, and his cooperation would be easily purchased, even if he would never fully understand the extent of his complicity in Traiman's scheme until it was too late.

This was Traiman's grand plan, the payoff he had been working towards over the past two years. In the post nine-eleven world, he realized that his time had grown short. His welcome in Tripoli had come to an end, and the demands of his clients had become more insistent. Operation VX would generate the chaos his hosts desired and the conditions he needed to make his gambit with Koppel effective. After that, he would bid his Arab friends an amicable goodbye, then seek asylum somewhere in the world where his increased wealth would ensure him safety as well as great luxury.

Once his teams completed their lethal nerve gas attacks in the United States, England and Italy, panic would drive the financial markets to new lows. France and Germany, America's faithless allies, would be rewarded for their weakness by being spared these strikes. This would create an even larger rift between the Western powers, while generating a marked disparity in the economic reaction to these new terrorist assaults. Consumer and institutional confidence would plummet.

In the meantime, all of the money Traiman had funded in this new enterprise, the money belonging to him, would have been placed in short positions by Martin Koppel's new investment company. Traiman would be betting that those markets would collapse, while doing everything in his considerable power to create the panic to guaranty that result.

It would not be much of a gamble, and Traiman would be poised to reap the payoff.

*   *   *

Andrioli scanned the scene below, from the long stretch of ascending steps to the side entrances of the terraces just beneath him. He smiled at the grim irony of making his second visit to a church since arriving in Paris. The first ended with a body lying in the street. Steve Jackson was his friend, and he hoped matters did not come to that end this evening.

As soon as Jackson began climbing the stairs, steadily, slowly, off to the right, Andrioli spotted him. He appeared to be alone.

Jackson was younger than Andrioli, not yet forty. He was tall and slim, his long dark hair combed straight back in a fashionable, Parisian style. He moved cautiously and, when he reached the terrace level, he stopped and had a look around. His motions were deliberate, as if checking to see if he was being followed.

Andrioli was just above him now, standing beside a huge, marble pillar. He did not move yet, did not show himself. The section of terrace below was empty. The two men each stood, waiting. Then Jackson turned and began walking up the last set of steps, leading to the church entrance. He was near the center of the wide staircase, still to Andrioli's right. He climbed to the top, nearly reaching the tall doors of the basilica when Andrioli quietly called out, "Steve."

Jackson did not break stride. He continued to the entrance of the cathedral, turning around to look behind him again. Then he walked slowly toward the sound of his name, disappearing from the view below, facing his friend behind the width of the stone column.

"You think you'll need that?" Jackson asked, pointing to the automatic that Andrioli had drawn and ready.

"You never know," Andrioli said with a smile, then shoved the Colt back into his waistband.

"If I was going to turn on you, I wouldn't even be here. You'd be dealing with a team of snipers."

Andrioli realized he was right. "Yeah, well, I guess I should say thanks for coming."

Jackson took a moment to look at him. "What you should say, is what the hell you're doing in Paris?"

"Wish I had a smart answer for you."

Jackson hesitated, then said, "Well I've got some smart advice for you. Get out of here, and fast."

"And go where?"

"What do I know? China. Brazil. Look, Tony, you ran out on Traiman, wasted two guys in Florida, took out one of his favorite Arabs this morning . . ."

"Who was the other guy, the one who skipped?"

"Kerrigan. You ever meet him?"

Andrioli shook his head.

"Tall blond guy, right?"

Andrioli nodded.

"I. Q. about 54," Jackson told him, "and vicious as a snake. He was the one got to McHugh."

"So I heard." When Jackson responded with a quizzical look, Andrioli said, "Not important. I just heard it."

"What is this, Tony, you on a one man crusade?"

"Not one man, no."

"Don't tell me you're still dragging around the girl and that CIA washout."

"CIA washout?"

"Didn't you know? Sandor used to work for the Agency. Scrubbed a year or so ago."

Andrioli's eyes narrowed, then he gave a quick nod. "Yeah," he admitted, "I knew. One of Vincent's agents in the old days."

"Not just one of his agents, buddy, his best agent."

"So that's all good, have a top guy like that on my side. When did you find out he reached me?"

"When I was keeping them off your ass in Florida."

"What?"

"I screwed up a transmission when they first made you there a few days ago. Rode them off your tail for a little while."

"Thanks."

"Don't mention it. Sorry I couldn't get word to you."

"I understand. You guys in ground ops know how to play it safe."

"Communications is the place to be, man. No danger. Nice clean work."

"Yeah."

"Traiman offered to meet with you, did you get that message?"

"Oh sure, I got it all right. They tried to blow up my fucking boat, is how I got it."

"No, that was only after Jimmy told them to fuck off. He had a ticket back here, then changed his mind. He was supposed to get to you, set up a meeting."

Andrioli shook his head, wondering again about McHugh's intentions. He found it hard to believe his friend was going to flip again, but maybe Jimmy really did think about coming back here alone, hanging him out to dry.

"Look, Tony, you're a big boy, you do what you want, but this is too fucking dangerous for me to be standing around having a chat with you. You asked me to come here and I did. Now tell me what you want and then let me go into the church to pray for your immortal soul."

Andrioli uttered a hollow laugh. "I want to know what Traiman's got cooked up with these teams he's placing. And don't give me any bullshit about assassinations, okay?"

Jackson shook his head. "I'm here for old time's sake, but I'm not crazy."

"Come on, cowboy, time to give it up."

Jackson said, "Take a vacation in South America, will you?" Then he turned to walk away.

Andrioli grabbed him by the arm with his left hand and pulled out the automatic with his right. "I always liked you, Steve, but I got nothing left to lose. Now answer my question."

Jackson made a slight move with his free hand, but Andrioli jammed the barrel of the Colt into his ribs. Jackson stared into his friend's eyes. "You wouldn't kill me, Tony. Even if you figure you're dead already, you wouldn't shoot me."

"I'll tell you, Steve, I'm not sure myself, but I don't wanna have to find out."

They stood there in silence, each man measuring the other.

"All right," Jackson said, "for all the good it'll do you. It's Traiman's VX scheme."

"Get the fuck outta here."

"I'd love to, if you'd let go of my arm."

"Traiman's going with VX gas? That's fucken insanity."

"That's what I hear, and that's all I can tell you. Now get outta town, will you?"

Two gunshots, spit from a silencer, caromed off the stone wall behind them. Without the loud report, Andrioli couldn't determine the placement of the shooter. When two more shells blew chunks out of the marble column, Andrioli figured they were coming from below, just behind the balustrade off to their right. He yanked Jackson's arm and the two of them hit the cold, marble ground.

Andrioli turned to Jackson, to ask him if he had a gun. Then he saw the thick blood oozing from the side of his friend's head.

"Fuck," he said, wiping at the source of the bleeding to see how bad Jackson had been hit. "Steve, I'm gonna take a run at him. It may only be one guy." Jackson's eyes were nearly shut. "Can you hear me Steve?"

Jackson made a low, guttural sound. Then he muttered, "Must've followed me."

Andrioli had a quick look above the stone railing, then ducked again as another two shots took pieces out of the balustrade. "I'm sweeping wide, then coming back up the stairs at him. We need to get you help fast, and he probably has backup on the way."

Jackson's eyes opened now. They were the eyes of death. "Go on Tony," he urged him in a barely audible voice. "Just go."

The shooting had stopped, their attacker likely on the move. "Traiman," Andrioli said. "Is the VX assault for real?"

Jackson nodded weakly, then managed to say, "Go home."

"There's no way home for me. When is Traiman coming out again?"

Their eyes met. "Portofino," he said in a raspy whisper. "Tomorrow. Qaddafi's throwing him out. He'll be on the *Halaby* yacht." Jackson tried to draw a breath, to say something else, but a gunshot, from closer range now, hit him in the chest as he lay, propped up on his arm. His body convulsed for an instant, then he was dead.

Andrioli wheeled around, but it was too late. The sniper had come up the stairs on the far end, and Andrioli took the crippling blow of a bullet in the left side of his chest before sheer reflex caused him to squeeze off three rounds. The explosive sound of the .45 reverberated off the marble walls and ceiling. The first shot went high, but Jackson's killer was staggered by the second and third, then Andrioli fired a fourth, dropping the man to the ground, not more than twenty feet away from him.

Andrioli struggled to his feet. He stood there for a moment, leaning with his back against the pillar, bracketed by the bodies of Steve Jackson and his murderer. Both dead. But he was still alive, even as the searing pain of his wound nearly paralyzed him. He knew he might not be long for it himself. He also knew there might be a second hitter.

People were screaming now, the sound of Andrioli's gunshots creating mayhem along the steps and terraces below. He pulled out his handkerchief, reached inside his shirt and pressed it against his left side. He shoved the automatic in his belt, closed his jacket, then picked up his attaché case and made his way off to the left, wary of any other hitter that might have arrived, moving as quickly as he could as the pain staggered him, somehow making his way down the stairs, heading to the row of cabs near the Place du Tertre.

FORTY-SIX

Jordan and Christine were up and dressed when the clerk at the front desk rang them.

"Monsieur Kerr," the man said, "a Mr. Forest to see you."

"Right," Jordan said. "Send him up."

Jordan hurried to his bag and took out the Colt.

"What is it?" Christine asked.

"A Mr. Forest is coming up to see us."

"Wouldn't that be Tony?"

"Maybe," he said.

She nodded, then stood off to the side.

Jordan checked the clip, chambered a shell, unlocked the door, then moved against the wall, checking to see where he would have the best line of sight. "Lock yourself in the bathroom," he told Christine. "Don't make a sound or a move, not until you hear from me."

Christine nodded, disappeared inside and then Jordan took up his perch and waited.

He heard the knock, then said, "Come in," ready to take out at least the first two men through. The door swung open and Andrioli stumbled in.

"Jesus," Jordan said, helping him onto the bed as he called for Christine.

They insisted on taking him to a hospital, but Andrioli wanted to straighten some things out first.

He began to tell them what Jackson had said, his narrative coming in short bursts punctuated by long gasps for air and a look of pain that etched his features in dark relief.

Christine stopped him, pleading for them to get help.

"Listen, you take a foreigner to the hospital with a gunshot wound and they call the Sûreté, Interpol, the embassy. I'll be finished."

Jordan looked down at him. "You'll be finished anyway, if we don't stop the bleeding."

Andrioli motioned for his attaché case. Christine brought it to him, and he pulled out a number. "Call this doctor. Tell him you have a friend with acute gastric distress, he's got to come at once. He'll know what that means. He'll come."

Sandor nodded and dialed the number. "What about the desk clerk? Did he suspect anything?"

Andrioli offered a wan smile in response. "Whatever he noticed, a few hundred euros made him forget."

While they waited for the doctor, Andrioli did his best to explain what Jackson had told him. He was obviously in a lot of pain, his speech was halting and slow, but his mind was completely alert.

"VX is a lethal nerve gas developed by the British, about fifty years ago. It has the consistency of oil, but it's lethal. If you inhale it or touch it, you're dead. You can spray it, explode it, whatever, it'll wipe out a crowd in a minute."

"I've heard of it," Jordan admitted.

"That company, Loubar, they've helped with the delivery system. They might even be the means for transporting it into these countries."

"What countries?"

"Who the hell knows? The U. S. for sure."

"Where? Did he say where?"

"If he knew the targets, he didn't have a chance to tell me. Any place they can infect a lot of people at one time. Who knows? Can you imagine if they release this in a major city, kill forty or fifty thousand people in one shot?"

"And it's already in process?"

"What he said. I can't believe they'd go that far. The American response would be catastrophic."

"Yes," Jordan agreed. "It would take things to another level."

"As in all out war? Even a measured nuclear response is possible."

"Against who? That continues to be the issue."

"I don't know, but you're going to Italy to find out. Your old friend Traiman is on his way to Portofino tomorrow. He's going there to work out the final details."

*   *   *

Mahmoud al-Rahmad was feeling rather pleased with himself as he strolled down Fifth Avenue. He glanced at the window displays of the familiar stores, the upcoming holiday season another opportunity to treat himself to the finest of what New York had to offer. Bergdorf, Tiffany, Gucci, Cartier.

The meetings in Tripoli went better than he had anticipated. His failure to deal with the American, Sandor, had not been the problem he feared it might, and he certainly could not be held accountable for the failure of Traiman's men to resolve the issue down in Florida. In fact, if the rumors were correct, Traiman was falling out of favor with their Arab associates. The debacle in Fort Lauderdale might be another nail in his coffin.

On the other hand, the New York operations were proceeding smartly. It was true that he had exceeded his budget during the past few months, but he could not concern himself with those details. Results were all that mattered.

He had successfully coordinated the placement of the extraordinary team that had been hand-picked by Traiman himself. Two men were already in New York and the rest of the team would gain entrance to the country through Canada. Of those additional men, four would be sent to San Francisco. Two others were to be assigned to St. Louis and the final two would replace the men assigned to the mission in Florida, the two who had been killed in Fort Lauderdale. They would act as rovers. Together, these men would be the vanguard of the largest terrorist initiative since nine-eleven. Now that the Loubar Corporation was back on line, the return of the containers to the Port of New York would be as easy as sending an overnight package by Federal Express. The inspectors would never guess that they would be facilitating a transfer of VX gas from Europe back to the United States.

The disinformation being circulated, of assassination teams dedicated to the murder of key government officials, would keep the Americans busy with their useless Homeland Security efforts, moving ever further in the wrong direction. The team that had been arrested in Washington would resist any attempts to uncover the purpose of their mission. However, after a dose of sodium pentathol or some other cocktail mixed at the CTC, these zealots would reveal what they knew about a bogus assassination plot. They knew nothing of Operation VX.

Rahmad wondered if Traiman might have been behind the exposure of this team. He was certainly capable of such treachery, and Rahmad had long suspected that Traiman was responsible for the capture of Kahlid Sheikh Mohammed in Pakistan, dealing a crippling blow to al-Qaeda operations at the time, temporarily restoring Traiman's importance to the extremists. If either suspicion were proved to be true, Rahmad acknowledged to himself if to no one else, they were brilliant ploys.

Yet, even as Rahmad reviewed the progress of these plans, he knew he had one more hurdle to overcome. The meeting that awaited him at his office was not to be a mere debriefing session. It was, in fact, an important strategy session with representatives from Ibrahim Abass, his direct link to al-Qaeda.

When Rahmad arrived, his aides had already admitted their guests into the office. One was a Saudi in his mid-twenties, the other appeared to be Lebanese, about forty years old. They had come, they announced, from Washington. There they had attempted to gather information on the apprehension of the three-man team. There was great unhappiness about their capture.

The younger of the two emissaries explained this to Rahmad.

"I see," Rahmad replied, although it was not clear why they had come to him with this report. The team in D.C. and its exposure had nothing to do with him.

"Good," the younger man continued, "because we are here to discuss this recent interference with our activities."

Rahmad seated himself behind his desk. "Please, gentlemen, make yourselves comfortable." He nodded to his two aides, who were standing behind these visitors. No one sat, other than Rahmad.

"We would prefer to stand," the young man said. "What we have to tell you will not take long."

Rahmad looked beyond him, to his older assistant. "Interference?" Rahmad repeated the young man's word.

"Our team in Washington was betrayed," the young man continued. "We have been compromised by someone within our organization."

"How can that be?" Rahmad asked.

"It can be," the young man said, "when one of our own forsakes the integrity of Allah's mission in exchange for the comforts of Western comforts and depravity."

Rahmad felt himself stiffen. "Who?" he asked weakly. "Who would have done such a thing?"

"We think you know."

Now Rahmad sat up and nodded vigorously. "Yes," he said. "The American."

The older man, who had not spoken yet, broke into a smile, revealing a mouthful of stained, uneven teeth. "Why would Traiman destroy his own efforts?" His accent was much heavier than his younger companion's.

Traiman's intentional sacrifice of his own team seemed far-fetched, even to Rahmad. Still, he had long ago decided that Traiman could not be trusted. "These men were sacrificed in the name of a larger mission."

"What utter nonsense is this?"

"I'm certain of it. It was part of Traiman's plan. Don't you see? He is not one of us, after all." He attempted to go on, but the older man stopped him.

"No, Rahmad, we have learned the source of this treachery. Your name must now be added to the *Sijjin*."

The mere utterance of that word, meaning the scroll bearing the names of those Islamics going to hell, resolved any doubt or hope for the Saudi. Rahmad's epiphany was complete. Traiman had engineered things perfectly, arranging for the removal of anyone who was privy to or even suspected his real motives. These fools knew nothing of Operation VX.

"Wait," he said, "let me explain. You're making a mistake." But it was too late.

The next few seconds, the last of Rahmad's life, seemed to unfold in slow motion. He watched as the younger man drew a revolver, spun around, and fired shots into the chests of Rahmad's two aides.

The older Lebanese said, *"Allahu Akbar,"* God is great. Then he pulled out his weapon, smiled his filthy smile, and fired repeatedly into Rahmad's face.

FORTY-SEVEN

The French physician summoned by Andrioli had confirmed what they suspected. The slug had passed through Andrioli's side. The loss of blood was serious. If they did not get him to a hospital soon, he could slip into unconsciousness and might die.

The doctor was a distinguished looking gentleman, short and slender, with a thin mustache. He removed his jacket, folded back his sleeves and worked with meticulous care to treat the wound. First he swabbed the area, then injected Andrioli with a local anesthetic and an antibiotic. Andrioli almost passed out twice from the pain and blood loss, and the doctor gave Jordan more than a couple of looks, telling him he needed to get his friend a transfusion as soon as possible. After he closed the area with sutures, he handed Jordan a small vial of morphine capsules.

Andrioli had explained that the doctor was well known to his old cronies, so Jordan paid the man with a fistful of hundred euro notes from Andrioli's attaché case, then told him to keep his mouth shut.

"Monsieur," he said to Andrioli, "you know my reputation well enough to believe that I will exercise discretion," the doctor said.

"And you know me well enough to believe that I'll find you if you don't," Andrioli said.

They realized he could only be counted on to stay quiet for a few hours at best, but they hoped that would be enough.

Christine showed the doctor out. When he was gone, Jordan told them he had a plan.

Andrioli was in desperate need of a transfusion, so Jordan realized the first thing he had to do was contact John Covington. Since there was no reason for further pretense, Sandor pulled out his secure reach number. The operator promptly referred him to the United States Embassy right there, in Paris.

After being shunted from one level of bureaucracy to the next, he heard the familiar voice say, "Well, well, well. Jordan Sandor."

"Hello Covington."

"Good to hear from you again. I trust you and your friends are enjoying France."

Jordan was seated at the writing table. "One of my friends wants to say hello."

Christine handed Andrioli the phone from the extension beside the bed. "Covington," he said into the extension.

"Ah, Mr. Andrioli. Finding Paris to your liking, this time around?"

"Actually," Jordan said, "my friends are finding Paris a little tough to take. Thought we might get out of town."

"That so?"

"It is. And I'm going to make your life easy, so you can drop the trace on this call. We'd like to see you before we leave. This way, when you're trying to follow us, you won't be two days behind."

"How kind of you."

"I don't want you to think we're not flattered by the attention, but you're just not giving us much help, is all. We keep getting shot at, and there's no one there to cover our backs."

"That's not my job, gentlemen."

"We noticed," Andrioli said.

"You three are fugitives from the United States government," Covington said. "You're also wanted for questioning by the French authorities for a shooting that took place here in Paris today."

"Four shootings," Jordan interrupted, "just to keep your scorecard straight."

"Four?"

"That's right. Three dead, one injured. Check the evening news. Look, you want to see us or not?"

Covington said he would be pleased to meet with them, so Jordan gave him the name of their hotel and hung up.

They packed Christine's tote and Jordan's black leather bag.

"Get going," Andrioli said. "They'll be here any minute."

Jordan stood at the side of the bed, placing his hand on Andrioli's shoulder. "You're sure you're up to this?"

"Go, will you please?"

Christine came over and kissed Andrioli on the forehead.

"I'll be all right, as long as Covington gets here before Traiman's people do." He looked up at Jordan. "Right?"

Jordan nodded solemnly. "Either way, I'm worried."

"The government boys won't pull anything with me, not till I tell them what you're up to. I'll keep talking long enough to give you a head start."

Christine said, "Make sure they take good care of you."

"Sure thing." He pointed to his battered attaché case. "Remember that thing. And what I told you about the explosives."

Jordan nodded again.

"I guess you know more about those gimmicks in there than I do."

"We'll find out," Jordan said.

"So, you track him your way, and I'll have the cavalry right behind."

"That's the idea. I just want a little lead time."

Andrioli grabbed a cigarette from the nightstand and fumbled with the matches. Sandor took the pack and lit it for him.

"Not a great idea," Jordan said.

"What the hell." He took a long drag and blew it out. "Too late to be worried about my health." He looked at Christine. "You sure you don't want to sit this one out with me? Be a lot safer for you."

"He's right," Jordan said.

"No. If I stay, they'll just take me into custody when they get here. They need you, Tony, not me. I'm seeing this through."

Jordan nodded. "Let's go then."

Andrioli gave them a weak, narcotic influenced smile, then patted the Colt automatic that sat in his lap. "I feel kind of like Jim Bowie at the Alamo, you know? When Davy Crockett sets him up in bed for the final battle with a couple of pistolas."

Jordan nodded. "I remember. Hold a better thought for the outcome, okay cowboy?"

Andrioli smiled. "See you in Portofino," he told them.

Then Jordan and Christine left him alone in the room to wait.

*   *   *

About ten minutes later, the door burst open with a loud crash. Two agents lunged forward, guns drawn, ready to fire.

Andrioli was sitting on the bed, puffing away on another cigarette. He raised his head slightly and said, "Doesn't anyone just knock anymore?" He looked pale and, although the doctor had stopped the bleeding, he was badly in need of plasma. The gash in his side was throbbing, and he had yet to take any of the morphine, afraid to dull his senses before he knew which of his pursuers would get to him first.

The two agents remained poised and silent as John Covington and Todd Swedock came in behind them. Having a look at Andrioli's condition, Covington said, "Take his gun, but don't move him."

The first agent removed the automatic from Andrioli's lap, then backed off. Covington pulled up the desk chair and sat down beside the bed. Swedock stood behind him.

"Seems you got the worst of the action in Montmarte."

Andrioli slowly crushed his cigarette in the ashtray and lit another. "Not really. The worst of it is dead already."

Covington nodded. "You look better in your dossier photo."

"That so? Well, I probably hadn't been shot the day they took it."

"So where are your friends? Got tired of playing with you? No, hold on. Let me guess. They turned you in because they thought they'd be doing you a big favor. We'd get you a doctor and have that nasty little cut taken care of, am I right?"

"That's it." Andrioli shifted uncomfortably. "My H.M.O. doesn't cover foreign gunshot wounds, and Sandor told me what a sweetheart you are."

"Bad judge of character, Sandor."

"I'm not so sure."

"I think you'll have a chance to find out. First we should have a little chat."

"Suit yourself," Andrioli said. He was in no rush. He offered Covington a cigarette.

"No thanks, not one of my vices."

Andrioli felt the room starting to spin and planted his right hand on the bed to brace himself, in case he was about to pass out. "I sure could use a doctor, I'll tell you. Lost enough blood to be a Red Cross poster boy."

"We'll get to that in due course. First tell me where Sandor's going."

"I'm too weak to remember."

The CIA man glanced at Andrioli's bloody shirt. "Maybe one of my men can poke a finger into your side, perk you up a bit."

Andrioli took an uneven drag on his cigarette, then coughed a small cloud of grey brown smoke into Covington's face. "This your tough guy routine?"

"I thought you were the tough guy here," Covington said.

"Not me, not anymore."

"So, what do you have to sell me today?"

"Depends what you're after. I can give you Sandor. I can give you my life story as a bad guy in Libya. I can give you Vincent Traiman."

The last comment caused Covington a nearly imperceptible flinch. "You can't give me anything I don't already have."

"If I got nothing you want to buy, what the hell are you doing here?"

"Maybe I'm here to arrest you."

"You're a cop now? Hey, go ahead and arrest me, man. A prison infirmary sounds pretty good right now." He reached down and touched the bandage on his side. "I've got some stories to tell, if you're interested, but I'm running out of steam."

"You're just another sorry case of Vietnam burnout run wild. That's an old story, mister."

"You're not wrong about me, but you're wrong if you think I don't have something to deal."

"Suppose we're interested in your fairy tales? What do you want, other than the Congressional Medal of Honor?"

"I don't know. Immunity. Federal protection. A new identity. A girl with really big tits."

"Come on Andrioli, we sit here much longer you're liable to die in that bed. Where's Sandor?"

Andrioli took a deep, painful breath. "He's on his way to find Traiman."

"You're crazy."

"Maybe so, but here's what I really need. I need you to arrange a piece in the papers and on the wire services. Say two international businessmen and an American ex-pat were slain this evening in Montmarte in an exchange of gunfire. Something like that. Give them a good description of me, make sure they list me as dead. Got it?"

"I got it, but why should we do it?"

"Traiman's got to believe that I died with those two guys. This way I'd have no way of telling you what his man said, about where he's going."

"One of his people told you that Traiman is on the move?"

"Sandor told me you were an asshole. He never said you were slow."

Covington ignored the taunt "So what if I have Interpol make a release, the news services run the piece. Then what? Where's Sandor off to?"

"Not so fast. The immunity, protection, all that bullshit. I want it in writing. Official-like. For Sandor and Christine too."

"We'll get it, but right now my patience is running thin. Where are they?" Covington had his own information. He had to know if Sandor was headed in the right direction.

But Andrioli refused to answer. "Just a little while more, then I'll tell you." He took another puff of the cigarette, then dropped it in the ashtray. "Meantime," he said, "get me to a hospital." Then he fell to his side, face down on the bed. He was unconscious.

FORTY-EIGHT

Early the following morning, as Andrioli recuperated in the infirmary of the United States Embassy, Jordan and Christine were traveling to the port town of Santa Margherita on the Italian Riviera. They had taken an evening train from Paris, spent the night together in the Hotel Meridien in Nice, and now they were proceeding by rail into Italy.

The train rolled southeast along the Riviera coastline, racing past rocky beaches below and hurtling through cavernous tunnels that had been gouged from the sides of craggy mountains that rose defiantly above the blue Mediterranean. Jordan and Christine, alone in their compartment, paid little attention to the passing scenery. They were reviewing, yet again, the plans for their arrival in the village of Portofino.

"Maybe we should have listened to Captain Reynolds," Christine said with a wistful smile.

"What did he tell you?"

"He told me to stay out of it. He said I should leave town and let the authorities handle everything."

Jordan reached across and took her hand. "Well, you certainly left town."

Christine laughed. "I don't think this is what he had in mind."

"It's not too late," he told her. "You can turn around when we get there, leave this to me. Or just wait in Santa Margherita."

She shook her head, never taking her eyes from his. "I told you before, I'm in this to the end."

"I know, but by now Andrioli has told them everything we know. Covington and his men will fly out this morning, maybe even get there before we do. You don't need to do this."

"I really do."

Jordan sat back in his seat and studied her face, the pale blue eyes that had not smiled enough in these past several days. "Since everyone has fessed up, as Andrioli would say, how about you tell me the truth now?"

Christine also sat back, and they were as far away from each other as they could be in the small compartment. She looked out the window for a moment, seemingly lost in the majesty of the passing mountain range. When she turned back to him, some of the sadness had returned. "I'm not Jimmy's sister," she said.

Jordan nodded slowly. Whatever she was going to say next, whoever she was, regardless of the intimacy they had shared the past two days, his instincts were now in control. He thought about the Colt in his waistband, then felt his mind racing back to catalogue her movements since they left Paris. Did she have a weapon? Was she an enemy and not a friend? He hated himself for the inability to escape his own training, his innate suspicions. Still looking at her, he said, "I know."

"You know?"

Her surprise seemed genuine. "Yes. I've known since the airport in Atlanta."

Her wonder at his admission turned quickly to anger, and she leaned forward. "You knew, but you never said anything?"

Jordan responded with a puzzled look. "That's a strange reaction, don't you think? After all, you were the one who lied, right?"

"I had my reasons."

"Really? Then you'll have to believe I had my reasons too."

She appeared to be considering what he said, then waved it away. "You made love to me."

"Damn," Jordan said with a slight grin, "and I thought there were two of us there."

Christine responded with an embarrassed smile. "I guess we're a couple of liars," she conceded, "but mine was just a white lie. You never told me you worked for these government people. Or any of that."

"Uh huh. And telling everyone you're Jimmy McHugh's sister, that was a white lie?"

"You don't understand."

"Try me," he said.

She shook her head. "It all sounds so crazy, even when I say it to myself.

I mean, I really hadn't heard from Jimmy in years, that was true. But I'm not his sister."

"I got that part. So who are you?"

"I told you, I'm an assistant art history professor at Penn State. Oh God," she sighed. "Jimmy and I grew up together in Wilkes Barre. In Pennsylvania. He was much older. We were from the same town, neighbors sort of, and our families knew each other. Not much good to say about our families," she added with a dismissive shake of her golden colored hair. "Anyway, he went off to Vietnam."

"I'm listening."

She was staring out the window again, remembering. "He started writing to me from over there, chatty kind of letters, the kind soldiers write home. Jimmy never had a lot of friends and, like I say, his family wasn't worth writing to. So I wrote back. We knew each other for so long, it was no big deal for me to send him a note every now and then, tell him about this guy or that girl or what was new in town. But then his letters changed. They started sounding, I don't know, romantic or something. Not really romantic, that's not it, but he was writing to me as if we were, well, lovers."

"And you weren't?"

"Never. No. I mean, he was like an older brother or cousin or something. I don't think he ever really had a girlfriend before he went away, so he began making up this fantasy relationship between us that didn't exist."

"So what happened, you wrote him a 'Dear John' letter or something."

She turned back to him. "No. I should have, I realized that later, but I didn't. I was a kid, and it was nice, having this guy overseas sending me these beautiful letters, and I thought, if it made him feel better what was it to me? He was fighting in Vietnam for Godssake. From one letter to the next, I never knew if I'd ever hear from him again."

"So you led him on."

Christine shook her head back and forth. "No, I never did. I would keep writing letters that were like local news reports. But I never told him to stop being serious in his letters to me." She sighed. "I guess I liked the attention. If that's leading him on, then I suppose I did."

Jordan watched as she remembered. "Anyway, one day he came home."

She nodded, not looking at him. "He stayed in the service, stationed someplace overseas for a while. But yes, then one day he was back, thinking we had this great romance, that I was going to marry him or something. I was in high school, for goodness sake."

"How did he take it?"

"Not very well. And I guess I didn't handle it in the right way." She paused, and Jordan waited. "He became demanding, angry. It got really uncomfortable. He threatened my boyfriend. The police were involved. God, it was a mess."

She hesitated again. "Then what happened?"

"You know what happened," she said. "That's when he left, went back overseas. Disappeared."

"Which solved your problems with him, right?"

"That makes me sound so horrible," she said. "I felt really responsible. I still do. He was heartbroken when he left, and it was all my fault. It was like I cheated a friend, a friend who really loved me."

"Even if you didn't love him."

"Yes."

"But you were just one of the reasons McHugh left the States again."

"I know that, in here," she said, pointing at her head, "but not here." She held the palm of her hand over her heart.

"Guilt and affection are a lethal combination," Jordan said, thinking of Dan Peters and Beth, among many others. "So what's the rest of the story?"

"The rest of it is pretty much what you know. Some years went by and Jimmy began writing to me again. I don't even know how he found me. I was at Penn State by then. He apologized for everything, wanted us to be friends and all that. I was really careful this time, very particular about what I said."

"So, when did you decide to become his sister?"

"When he invited me to Paris." After the renewal of their friendship, she explained, McHugh asked her to meet him in Paris. It took some coaxing, but McHugh offered to pay for the entire trip, insisting it would be a 'brother-sister' visit. "I felt like I owed it to him, he made it sound so important. When I got there he explained what he was doing." She said that it was only when she arrived that he told her all of his friends believed she was his younger half-sister. "He said that if those people thought I was any sort of girlfriend, they might be concerned about him wanting to go home with me. So I became his half-sister. It didn't seem like a big deal to me."

"So he admitted it to you—that he was using you as cover to get him to Paris and then back to the States."

"Yes. He introduced me to Tony and some other guys. I can't even remember their names. After a couple of days he shipped me off to Madrid and disappeared."

"Until you heard from him again, when he was holed up in Woodstock."

She shook her head. "No, I heard from Tony. He wanted me to go to Jimmy, said he might need my help to get to Florida. I never spoke to Jimmy again."

"Didn't you have any idea how dangerous it could be?"

"Not then." She uttered a short laugh. "You people, you seem to live with all of this killing and craziness. It wasn't real to me, not until I got to Woodstock and found out Jimmy had been murdered and then they took me down to New York like I was some sort of criminal. Up to then, I actually thought Jimmy had been exaggerating, to make it all seem more romantic or heroic."

"Heroic?"

"You know what I mean."

Jordan watched her as she settled back in her seat.

"That's it, and that's why I'm here."

"Paying a debt to a dead man?"

"It sounds morbid, I know, but I guess that's it, yes."

"And you want me to believe all of this."

"Everything I'm saying is the absolute truth."

He stared at her for a while. "Then go back home. This isn't your fight. Go back as soon as we get to Santa Margherita."

She shook her head, very slowly. "No," she said. "I told you . . ."

"I know, you're in this to end."

She smiled now, that great smile he first saw in the hotel bar in New York five days ago. It felt like months. "Now you know who I am. And whoever you really are, Jordan Sandor, I feel like I'm part of the reason you've gotten mixed up in this, and I'm not leaving until we're done doing whatever it is we need to do."

"Right," he said quietly, "but remember—this may be your last chance to walk away."

"Do you want me to walk away?" she asked him.

Jordan turned away from her, gazing out at the hypnotic dance of the ever moving sea, the train swaying gently as it climbed another stretch of mountainside. He knew the answer he should give, but he said nothing at all.

"It's okay," she said. "The history of art will still be there when I get back."

FORTY-NINE

When Andrioli regained consciousness, the first thing he did was ask for John Covington. A few minutes later the CIA operative strolled into Andrioli's private room at the Embassy clinic.

"What time is it?" Andrioli wanted to know.

Covington told him it was almost seven in the morning. "How do you feel?"

"Seven? We better get going, man."

"I'm having some trouble getting those guarantees you wanted. It could take some time."

"Screw the guarantees." Andrioli was in no mood for an argument today. He was sore, and drugged, and worried about his friends. "They're on their way already," he said, searching his groggy mind for a sense of how far Jordan and Christine would have gotten by now. He had trouble clearing away his morphine induced confusion, then said, "No, they wouldn't be there yet."

Covington looked down at him, his thin lips approximating a smile. "When you say 'there', do you mean Portofino?"

Andrioli tried to sit up, a painful attempt that failed. As he grew more alert, the ache in his side became more acute. "Where'd you get that?"

"After a narcotic cocktail, a man can become more talkative than you think. Don't worry yourself, you only confirmed what we already knew. We're getting ready to leave now."

"I'm going with you," Andrioli told him, having another try at pushing himself up.

"I don't think so."

"Why not? What'd the doctor say?"

"Said you'll be fine, eventually. Some muscle damage, a fractured rib. Nothing that won't heal. Your biggest problem was the loss of blood."

"Fine. Get me something for the pain and I'm going back in the game."

"Why would we want to allow that?"

He made another attempt to sit up. "I can think of three reasons. First, I know exactly where Sandor is going and what he's doing. Second, I know Traiman's operation better than you do." He paused to take a breath, still trying to steady his thinking. "Third, I know what Traiman is up to."

Covington walked to the foot of the bed, where the two men had a good look at each other. "If I move you, you're likely to die before we get to Italy."

"Whatever. Let's get going." Andrioli again tried to raise himself, then buckled under the effort.

"I congratulate you on your tenacity, I really do. Your determination has exceeded our wildest expectations. Learning Traiman's destination was very resourceful. And then, having us plant that story with the press, so he wouldn't interrupt his plans, that was very clever."

"Is it in the paper today?"

"Of course. Just as you asked. Two international businessmen slain by an unidentified American who was also killed in the shooting. The description in the article didn't do you justice, but we included your name."

Andrioli drew a deep, uneven breath that hurt more than he would admit. The cracked rib, he thought. "You just told me you knew it already, that Traiman is headed for Italy."

"Let's just say our intelligence department does a fair job on its own. We planted the story for the same reason you requested it. We didn't want your clumsy interference to disrupt his appointment. We also happen to be quite anxious to have Traiman in Portofino."

Andrioli's numbed look phrased the question he could not ask.

"It seems we owe you an apology, Mr. Andrioli. It seems you have been used. You, that is, and your two accomplices. You've all played important parts in moving this forward. Unfortunately, you became more successful than we anticipated."

"Sorry to screw up your plans. Were we supposed to get ourselves killed along the way?"

"It was a considered risk but no, that wasn't it. We simply never expected you to learn of the meeting in Portofino. We never anticipated you and your friends getting in our way there."

Andrioli nodded. "Sorry to outlive our usefulness."

"So, when will they arrive?"

"I'm not sure. They should reach Santa Margherita by late this morning."

"Damnit," Covington said, expressing more annoyance than anger. "We'll just have to work it out."

As he turned and started for the door, Andrioli finally managed to sit all the way up, ignoring the searing pain that radiated from his side. "You said we were used, that you knew Traiman was heading for Portofino."

Covington stopped and turned back to him. "Yes."

"Without my help, Jordan and Christine might be a problem."

"I hope not. We're flying to Genoa right now. We'll find them and back them off."

"Sandor won't back off. You know that."

Covington hesitated, then walked towards the door. "I'll see you later," he said over his shoulder.

"No good," Andrioli hollered after him. "You need me there. You hear me Covington?"

Covington heard him, realizing Andrioli was correct even as the door to his room eased its way closed behind him.

*   *   *

Throughout his professional life, Vincent R. Traiman had always been just that—a professional. In his ability to separate emotion from reason, he was as clinical as a surgeon.

His current passage across the Mediterranean was a part of a plan shared with only a select few in his organization. His preparations and purpose were carefully guarded secrets. The death of Steve Jackson on the steps of the Sacre Couer, therefore, caused concern among Traiman's closest aides.

The accounts of the shooting were sketchy at best. Jackson, Andrioli and the assassin who followed them to the cathedral were all dead. Traiman had to assume that Jackson, in his role as communications coordinator, would have been able to decipher some information about the planned trip to Portofino. If Andrioli had extracted that information from

Jackson before he died, and if Andrioli had an opportunity to pass it on before he was himself killed, the mission might be compromised. Traiman therefore knew the Americans might be coming for him. He also suspected that Jordan Sandor would be part of the welcoming party, a collateral issue that could make for an interesting reunion.

And yet, Traiman went ahead with his plans.

His top assistant, Nelson, who accompanied him on the cruise, suggested the meetings in Portofino be postponed, but Traiman overrode his advice. Traiman kept his own counsel, realizing that time had grown short, particularly after the Loubar incident and these recent incidents of violence in New York, Florida and Paris. Matters had intensified; he was no longer welcome in Libya, and the resultant suspicions about him were also increasing. Traiman, however, had already arranged to minimize the risks.

As the luxurious, 132 foot yacht cut through the blue-green waters of the calm sea, Traiman satisfied himself that he had taken the appropriate precautions and had made the prudent decision. Martin Koppel would be there, in Portofino. It was an important meeting and, even if John Covington was bringing his men, Traiman already had his insurance policy in place.

Traiman saw himself as a consummate tactician, not offended when others compared him to a cold-blooded reptile who thrived in the ever changing environment of the desert. He felt flattered by the comparison, and viewed his personal pleasures in much the same way. Not inclined to the liquor or drugs favored by his subordinates, immune to romance, he enjoyed the anonymous privileges of his position, especially on those occasions when he traveled outside Libya. On the *Halaby IV*, the yacht owned by their associate Faridz, which was transporting him northward across the Mediterranean, Traiman could indulge his own preferred forms of relaxation.

"Come in," he said to the knock at his stateroom door. He was reclining on a large bed in the richly appointed owner's suite that Faridz had decorated in an opulent mixture of Arabian motifs, featuring rich fabrics, hammered brass and gold accents.

"Hello sir," the steward said. "We should be arriving in less than two hours. The captain is holding a conservative speed, as you requested."

"Good."

"Would you like to be entertained in here sir, or will you be using another cabin?"

Traiman's thin mouth turned up in his imitation of a smile. "This will be fine. Just send them in."

"Very well sir." The steward gave a short bow and retreated, off to fetch Traiman's entertainment, the two women who had been brought along for the ride.

Traiman got up and undressed, then slipped into a dark red satin lounging robe. When he heard another knock at the door, he was back on the king-sized bed. "Yes," he called out, and two young women entered.

Someone closed the door behind them and they slowly approached the bed. One was an Egyptian girl of no more than twenty, a tall, slim young woman dressed in a black silk dressing gown. She had smooth, olive-colored skin, long dark hair and a nervous look in her onyx eyes. The other girl was a black African of no more than eighteen, her voluptuous shape clad in a red peignoir. The black girl had been with Traiman before, and her apprehension was therefore all the more apparent.

Traiman believed that power was the key to sexual fulfillment. For him, violent rape was the most satisfying form of sexual expression. Even with these young women, who had no choice but to submit to his whims, he would engage in a brutal rite of passion, pursuing his illusions of sadistic conquest.

With a flick of his wrists he directed them to let their robes fall away. They followed his silent instruction, the firm, naked sensuality of their youth revealed. The Egyptian had small breasts, a lovely shape and silky looking skin. The African was a study in ebony, with a full bosom, rounded hips and narrow waist.

There was fear in their eyes as Traiman beckoned them forward. His pugilist's features were frightening enough, but from everything the black girl had seen and what the Egyptian girl had been told, their dread of what was to come was real. They wanted to recoil, to run, to escape, but had no choice, nowhere to go. They knew, regardless of their anxiety, they were there to provide whatever he demanded. Whatever pain or humiliation they were made to endure, they were there to suffer. The alternative, the consequence of his displeasure, was a far graver risk, not just for them, but for their families.

So they joined him on the bed, wordlessly attending to him, removing his robe, caressing him, clawing him, feigning desire and then resistance. The three of them acted out a deranged pantomime of his devise, the girls only praying that they would not be made too suffer too much pain as his excitement blended with anger.

They scratched at his thighs, rubbed his back, moistened him with their tongues, eager to rouse him and have it over with. He pinched them and then slapped them, abusing their firm asses, tender breasts, frightened faces. As his fury grew with his excitement, so did the viciousness of the assault. It was sex without intimacy or tenderness or compassion, culminating only when he had given full vent to the degrading cruelty and subjugation he chose to inflict upon them. Only then would he be relieved, only then would his entertainment be complete.

FIFTY

The path along the coastline from Santa Margherita to Portofino is a craggy run, a picturesque strip of narrow, twisting roadway. Small homes and large villas populate the green hillside in the distance. Small fishing boats and large yachts rock gently on their moorings in the harbor, or sit quietly against the docks tucked along the shoreline. It is at once provincial and affluent.

"You have been before to Portofino?" the Italian driver asked.

"No," Christine said. "I suppose this isn't the best time of year to visit."

"Ah, but you are wrong *signora*. This is the very best. Quiet. Not filled with so many *turisti*."

"Like us, you mean?"

The driver laughed. "No, no, *signore*."

"It's okay," Jordan said. "We could use some quiet."

The taxi hugged the sharp curves that ran above the coast en route to their destination, the Hotel Continental, chosen for them by Andrioli.

When they arrived, they found it to be a square, squat structure, considerably more modest than the promise of its title. It was located on one of the cobblestone streets towards the rear of the village, away from the sea.

Portofino is small, its compact geography defined by a tiny, horseshoe shaped seaport. On the edge of the Mediterranean, the front of the town faced the water, an inlet sheltered by the semi-circular protrusion of surrounding mountains. Adjacent to the modest harbor was a plaza paved in stone, ringed by a variety of restaurants, cafes and specialty shops. Behind these one and two story buildings were hotels and inns, each of which was more proximate to the real action, and with better views, than the Hotel Continental.

Further inland, at the foot of the mountains, away from the *trattorias* and boutiques, were the local merchants and private homes that stood in the shadows of the larger villas above. At the highest reaches, above the crowded quarters of the native Italians below, atop the overlooking hills, were the exclusive estates of the very wealthy, with views of the town, the sea and the beautiful yachts anchored outside the small harbor.

Jordan paid the taxi driver and they entered the lobby of the Continental. It was surprisingly airy, almost tropical. There were a couple of wicker chairs and a desk arranged in a sitting area. A large wooden table served as the registration desk. No one was there. Jordan rang the brass bell on the table, and a young man appeared through a side door.

"*Bon giorno*," he greeted them with a smile.

"Scott Kerr," Jordan said. "You should have a reservation for us."

The young man opened a cabinet off to the side of the desk, revealing a computer, a master telephone and some related office equipment. "*Si, signore*," he said, after punching a few keys. "*Signore e Signora* Kerr."

Jordan registered, then held up his black leather bag, Andrioli's attaché, and pointed to Christine's large tote from Paris, showing the young man that they could handle their own luggage.

The clerk frowned, then shrugged his shoulders. He was obviously a one man operation, which included check-in, bellhop and room service. When he handed Jordan his key, Sandor gave him a hundred dollar bill.

"Haven't had time to make change into *euros* yet."

The clerk's smile made it clear he didn't care.

"If anyone calls for me, put it through right away."

"*Si signore*," he said, still grinning as he pointed to the stairs.

*   *   *

By the time Jordan and Christine made it to the Hotel Continental, several field agents from Central Agency were converging on the area. Three were already in Portofino, another two waiting for instructions at an inn near the center of a neighboring town, Rapallo. These were not Covington's men. This team had been sent on the direct order of Deputy Director Byrnes.

Martin Koppel had also arrived. He was safely, if nervously, ensconced in a luxurious suite at the renowned Splendido, Portofino's finest hotel. He was alone, but not far from the watchful eyes of the three operatives dispatched by Byrnes. Koppel was instructed to stay in his suite and await his summons from Vincent Traiman.

Koppel was told that he would have his meeting tonight. Hopefully, before Traiman's men spotted a trap. Before Traiman turned tail back to North Africa. Before this transaction was left to one of his aides to negotiate or, worse, before the opportunity was lost altogether.

Byrnes had taken great pains to inform Koppel of the risks. *What the hell,* the financier thought as he paced the generous living room, waiting for the phone to ring. He had done everything, seen everything, run as far up and down the ladder as any man could travel. This was the ultimate challenge, dealing with stakes so high that life and death were part of the equation. *What the hell,* he told himself again. With all the financial deals he had created and motion pictures he had produced, he was finally starring in his own movie, produced and directed by the Central Intelligence Agency.

*   *   *

John Covington had no idea that Koppel and the other three agents were there. At the moment, his concern was Traiman and the terrorist teams that were being positioned in the United States and Europe.

He had flown from Paris to Genoa, and was now riding in the front of a car being driven by Todd Swedock. Another agent, Paul Bertram sat in the back seat beside Andrioli.

Covington had no choice but to bring Andrioli along. There was no way he could risk leaving him behind, not with what he knew, not with everything that would be happening today in Portofino. The doctors had another look at Andrioli's side, re-dressed the wound, filled his pocket with painkillers and authorized him to fly. The turbulence over the *Appennino* mountain range was painful, but Andrioli popped another pill and suffered through. Now they were traveling together by car toward the coast.

"Just so you're clear on this," Covington said over his shoulder, "I'm going to say it one more time. First, you're going to talk to Sandor. He might listen to you and get the hell out of our way before he screws up the entire operation. Second, we may need to keep Traiman off guard, and since you're so willing to get in his line of fire again, you're volunteering for that assignment too. You got that?"

"I got it."

Now Covington turned to face him. "Good," he said sharply. "Just remember, you're not here to redeem yourself. You're here to try and save your life. And Sandor's. And the girl's. Got it."

"I got it."

"Good. First we'll take you to find Sandor. The Continental, is that the truth?"

Andrioli was slumped in the back seat, trying to find a comfortable angle as the car jostled him painfully to and fro. He nodded.

"Okay." Covington faced forward again.

"Mind if I ask you something?"

"What is it?" Covington didn't bother to look back.

"How were you so sure Traiman was going to be here?"

"We have our sources. You confirmed what we suspected."

"No," Andrioli said. "I've been listening to you guys. The way you have this set up, it was more than a suspicion. You were sure of it before I told you anything. How is that?"

Covington turned back to him now, looking him square in the eyes. "You're here on a pass, not a fact-finding mission. Any trouble from you, I'll deliver you back to Traiman myself."

Andrioli answered with a grim smile.

Covington did not respond. He returned his gaze to the road in front of them, leaving Andrioli to stare silently at the back of his head.

FIFTY-ONE

Christine stood beside him as Jordan sorted through the contents of Andrioli's attaché. In addition to the Colt automatic and the extra ammunition, there were two small packages wrapped in paper. They contained C4 explosive. "You know what to do with that?"

Jordan nodded. "Yes," he said.

"So you really were an agent, or whatever it's called."

He nodded, then looked up from the material he was organizing. "I was," he said, "and I am."

Christine shook her head, a mystified look crossing her face.

Jordan took her by the shoulders and sat her on the bed. He pulled up a chair to face her. "I'm not here because of you. You're here because of me. I work for Central Intelligence."

"But I thought you said you left there, or something."

"Or something, is more accurate. I've been working on this mission for the past few months."

"So, what then? You were pretending to be a reporter all that time?"

"Journalist, and yes. After a mission went bad in Bahrain, I officially left the Company. Unofficially, I began working on a couple of different assignments."

"So when you agreed to go with me to Florida . . ."

"Yes, that was part of the deal. I needed to find Tony, and I needed to get here."

"So you lied to me. You were lying all along."

"Yes," he said.

"But you could have trusted me. You had to know that."

Jordan broke into a wide grin. "I do now," he said, "which is why I'm telling you. If you want out, you're out. If you still want to help, we need

263

to get to work." He stood up and went back to the two small blocks of putty-like substance. He held one up for her to see. "Things are going to get bad very quickly today. This explosive may be our last chance, depending how things play out."

"Isn't it dangerous, holding it like that?"

"No, not at all. It has to be detonated."

"Oh God. And you can make that happen?"

"I can, when the time comes. The tough part will be holding onto it, if they take us and search us."

"Take us?"

"Yes. Assuming we even get that far. It all depends how Traiman reacts. My guess is, he already knows I'm here. My hope is, he won't be able to resist the chance to meet with me."

"Then what?"

"Well, he isn't likely to be feeling very hospitable by then, I can tell you that."

"God."

"So, if you have any other questions, now's the time to ask."

She looked up at him. "Paris," she said, her voice softer now. "Was that, I don't know, was that part of . . ."

"No," he said. "That was about you and me."

She stood up and he took her in his arms.

"I told you to turn back," he whispered, then kissed her softly on the cheek. "You can still get out of here, it's not too late."

"I won't, not now."

"Okay then. Let's go for a walk, take in some of the local color, drop a few names."

He felt her nod, her head nestled in the crook of his shoulder.

"I don't know how much advertising we'll need to do, but word should travel pretty quickly around here today."

Jordan placed their key on the front desk and told the young clerk they were going out for a stroll around town. The boy replied with an uncomprehending look that Sandor figured was just a pose. Andrioli had chosen this hotel for a reason, and whatever that turned out to be, Sandor was beyond trusting anyone at this point.

He took Christine by the hand and led her into the fading, autumn afternoon sun. They headed on foot toward the main plaza, searching for a *caffe* Andrioli had named. The streets were virtually empty at this hour. They walked slowly towards the harbor, checking various locations until they found the place along the main wharf. They sat at a table inside and waited.

When their waiter approached, Jordan was pleased to find he spoke English, a bit of good fortune in a resort frequented more by Europeans than Americans. He ordered Camparis with soda and two *panini*.

"Beautiful ships here," Jordan said to the burly man as he returned with their drinks and set their glasses on the table.

"*Si*, from all over the world."

"Yes. We noticed the different flags."

The waiter did not reply. He went to the service bar and began working on the setups for dinner.

"Might have been too subtle, huh?"

Christine forced a smile.

There was only one other couple there. They looked to be Italian and were very involved in a quiet discussion at their table in the back of the room. Jordan watched the waiter slicing lemons and limes. A couple of minutes later he disappeared into the kitchen, then brought their sandwiches.

"Maybe you can help me," Sandor said to the man. "I'm supposed to meet some friends in town tonight. They're coming in on a yacht owned by Faridz."

The man set their plates on the table not looking at Jordan.

"They tell me it comes to Portofino quite often. I think it's called the *Halaby*."

Now the waiter glanced at him.

"I was wondering if you knew which boat it is. I wouldn't recognize it, I've never seen it." Jordan offered a short laugh as apology for his ignorance. "I'd like to know when it gets here, or if it's here already, for that matter."

The man just shook his head, saying nothing.

"That's too bad. I'd really like to know when they arrive."

"I am sorry, *signore*. Your friends, they will look for you I am sure." He turned to leave them, but Jordan reached out and touched his arm. The waiter looked down at Jordan's hand like it was something dirty that had just soiled his sleeve.

"I suppose you're right," Sandor said, keeping his tone friendly. "What the hell, I guess they'll find me all right. But just in case they stop in here, you can tell them I'm in town." Jordan held out a fifty dollar bill. "Jordan Sandor," he said. "At the Hotel Continental. Just in case anyone asks for me."

The waiter began protesting in rapid Italian, pushing the money away, in a loud voice saying something about never having heard of the *Halaby* yacht. An older man emerged from the kitchen. He could have been the waiter's father by the looks of him. He strode towards the table and stepped in front of the younger man. Without speaking, he took the fifty dollar bill from Sandor's hand and placed it on the table.

"We know nothing about this *Halaby*, *signore*. We don't know who comes in and goes out. This is not our business." His countenance bore a severe look that told Sandor the conversation was at an end.

"That's too bad," Jordan persisted. "This was the place my friend told me to come." He waited, but there was no further response in the offing. The waiter had already walked back to the bar and now the older man turned and went back into the kitchen.

"What now?" Christine asked quietly.

"I guess I didn't make much of an impression."

She forced a smile.

"We did just fine," he assured her. "I may run for mayor here, when this is all over."

They finished their drinks and sandwiches and left, leaving the fifty dollars on the table to cover the bill.

They stopped at two more *caffes* along the dock, and each time Jordan asked about the *Halaby* yacht he received the same sort of reaction. If anything, the responses were even stiffer. As soon as the name of the yacht was mentioned, it was clear Jordan was no longer a welcome patron. He knew that, by now, his own name would already be burning up the local telephone lines.

"At this point," he told Christine, "they'll know where to come for us."

"Jordan," she said as they walked back to the hotel, "I feel like we're being followed already. I suppose you're going to tell me that's good. I mean, that's what you want, isn't it?"

Sandor shrugged. "Depends on who's doing the following."

They retrieved their key at the front desk and found their way back to the small room upstairs. Jordan went to work immediately, first closing the shutters and pulling the drapes tight, then moving the table and two chairs.

He answered her puzzled look by saying, "If we're going to have company, we better see them before they see us."

He went about rearranging the pillows on the bed, adding two from the closet and using a chair cushion, lining them up, then plumping them and pulling the covers over them. In the darkened room, his soft sculpture appeared to be two bodies between the sheets.

"That's supposed to be us?"

"Go ahead and laugh," Jordan said as he fluffed the pillows again. "Art was never my strong subject."

"And where are we going to sleep tonight?"

He looked up. "I won't be doing any sleeping, not for a while. For now, let's just sit here and see who shows up." He put down a blanket and pillow on the floor, then sat beside her, their backs to the wall, out of view from anyone coming through the door.

"It's siesta time for you," he said.

She moved close to him, resting her head on his shoulder. "I am a little tired."

"Let's be quiet, then, see who comes for a visit."

FIFTY-TWO

As soon as the imposing *Halaby IV* dropped anchor in sight of the Portofino harbor, four of Traiman's men set off in the power launch. Once ashore, they split up. The first team would make contact at a few locations in the center of town. The other two men would generally canvass the area.

All four quickly learned that an American couple had been making the rounds, asking for the *Halaby IV*. The man had identified himself as Jordan Sandor.

The town seemed otherwise quiet, exuding its normal level of casual charm and studied indifference, particularly in the middle of autumn. Sandor's brazen arrival had served one of his intended purposes—to distract attention from the other, more covert activities initiated by Byrnes' agents. The three advance men Byrnes dispatched had not caused a ripple in the placid waters of the peaceful village or, if they had, it was obscured by the loud splash made by Jordan. The second reason for his approach was more than an intrusion by an unexpected visitor. It left Traiman's advance teams, with whom their leader shared only minimal information, to worry over why and how Sandor came to Portofino.

Precisely one hour after their arrival on shore, the four Traiman scouts regrouped at their launch. The two men who made a general survey of the area reported that Koppel had checked into the Splendido. They also shared the news that Sandor was in town, staying at the Hotel Continental. He and the girl had been announcing their presence and leaving his name, asking for the *Halaby IV*, claiming it carried an old friend, acting as if they expected to be invited aboard. The second pair of Traiman's scouts confirmed the information.

As they motored back to the yacht to report their findings, they debated how Sandor's presence might affect the plans for that night and the next day. He had proved himself an elusive target up to now, but Andrioli was dead, and that might make it easier to take him out. They had heard enough about Sandor, and they were eager to be rid of him as soon as possible.

*   *   *

Andrioli was not dead, however. He was seated in the back room of a small restaurant in Rapallo, under the close watch of Covington, Swedock and agent Bertram. The two other operatives who had been waiting now joined the group.

"Let me get this straight," Covington said. "He's going to try and get to Traiman himself? Is that the plan?"

"That's the plan of last resort, if he doesn't hear from me."

"He's going to try and board the yacht and take Traiman alone?"

"Not exactly. We discussed some variations on that theme."

"Wonderful."

"Look," Andrioli said, "we came after Traiman. It's that simple. How were we supposed to know what you expected us to do?"

"I expected you to get yourselves arrested in Paris."

"Sorry. You might have given us a better signal that we were on the same side, you know?"

Covington shook his head, worried he might have misplayed his hand. "All right, tell me how he expects to get on the boat."

"Don't know. He said I should leave that to him."

"I see. And I don't suppose, then, he gave you any idea about how he intends to get off."

Andrioli shook his head. He was not going to explain any of the details, not to Covington. He reached into his pocket and popped one of the painkillers they had given him at the Embassy.

"Better go easy on those."

Andrioli smiled. "Yeah. Like it matters."

Covington watched him for a moment, thinking. "We've got to stop him," he said. "He'll never make it alone."

Andrioli shook his head. "That's the funny part, isn't it?"

"What is?"

"He really is alone. I mean, you used us to get here, I understand that. But now that we're here, you have no use for any of us anymore."

Covington did not answer.

"Sandor is no goddamned reporter. You sent him to find me, right?"

Covington actually laughed. "The day I can get Jordan Sandor to do anything for me, you'll be the first to know."

"That doesn't answer my question. He's one of yours, right?"

"Once upon a time. Not now. But it's a little late for you to be worrying about Sandor, unless you're going to help us move him out of the way."

Andrioli muttered to himself.

"What's that?"

Andrioli grinned. "I said it's not like me."

"What isn't like you?"

"Worrying about someone else."

*   *   *

An hour or so after Jordan and Christine returned to their hotel, the desk clerk received a call. It was a familiar voice, one of the local men who specialized in providing personal services to wealthy tourists. His instructions to the clerk were clear. Do not put through any incoming calls to the American claiming to be Mr. Kerr. Get the caller's name, then say you have instructions not to disturb their room. Notify me of any calls. And notify me immediately if either the man or the girl leaves the hotel.

The clerk knew he was to follow these directions. He would receive an appropriate reward for his cooperation. More important, there would be no recriminations so long as he complied.

As Jordan and Christine waited in their room, the clerk intercepted Andrioli's third phone call in the past twenty minutes, telling him that Mr. and Mrs. Kerr were not to be disturbed. Once again, the caller refused to leave a message.

The clerk recognized the caller to be the same all three times. He did not have a name, but he picked up the switchboard phone to report it each time, just in case.

*   *   *

"Damnit," Andrioli said as he slammed the phone down. "They won't put the call through."

Covington turned to his agent Swedock. "Come on," he said, "three strikes and you're out. Let's go."

FIFTY-THREE

Darkness was descending on the Mediterranean coast, and Jordan knew it was time to make his move. They had waited long enough for Andrioli's phone call. They were on their own, at least for now.

Christine had dozed off, curled up on the floor with her head in his lap. He gently roused her. They needed to get ready to leave.

"It's time," Jordan told her.

She sat up and rubbed her eyes.

"Come with me," he said.

He took Andrioli's attaché case and she followed him into the bathroom. He placed the case on the counter and removed the two packets of explosives. He removed the paper and carefully molded two pieces of the C4 plastique. He smoothed the first piece and taped it against the small of Christine's back. The second he fixed with adhesive along the inside of his upper thigh.

Hiding the detonators was more difficult—the remote, electronic device in Andrioli's case would be found in the most cursory frisking, leading to strip searches and discovery of the plastique. The remote would have to be left behind. Sandor needed to rely on the magnesium strips, not as reliable, more difficult to gauge the response time, but certainly easier to conceal. He placed two strips in the lining of his jacket, then wove two under the collar of Christine's blouse.

When he was done, Jordan checked the clip on the Colt and pocketed two spares. At some point tonight, he expected to be taken by Traiman's men. Once captured, he knew the gun would be the first thing they would take from him. When they searched him and found the extra ammunition clips, it might be enough to satisfy his captors that Jordan was otherwise clean.

It was a theory, anyway.

"What about me?" Christine asked as he jammed the automatic into his waistband.

"What about you?"

"You know, like in *The Wizard of Oz*. Don't you have anything in there for me?"

Jordan smiled. "Are you looking for courage, my dear?"

"I was thinking more about a gun."

"Sorry, Tony only brought the two from Paris, and he's got the other one."

She nodded, forcing a brave smile. "I'll be right behind you then, all the way."

"Oh, you'll be doing more than trailing me around." Jordan told her what to do when they left the room, then took the remote detonator and hid it between the towels that were stacked on the ledge of the tub. Then he went back to the bedroom and placed the attaché case in the closet. When he turned around, she was standing there watching him.

"Well, it's time to go for it."

Christine walked towards him slowly, the unsteady rhythm of fear. "I'm ready," she said, then held herself against him.

"Don't worry," he told her. "We'll just have a quick drink on Traiman's yacht, then I'll get you home early so your mother's not upset." He stepped back and looked into her pale blue eyes. "You know what to do?"

She nodded.

"It'll be all right. Come on."

"I'm ready," she told him.

They stepped into the quiet corridor just above the small lobby. Christine handed Jordan her jacket and then, as calmly as she could, descended the steps leading to the front desk.

As she walked downstairs, Jordan took a small piece of paper and wedged it against the jamb at the lowest hinge, closing the door on it. He moved to the edge of the landing and listened.

Christine was doing her best to explain to the clerk that they were expecting a package that should have come already, doing everything she could to give the young man a reason to check in the back room for a delivery. "Maybe it came yesterday. Or before you got to work today."

She was at her most charming, even trying some Italian as the clerk pretended to struggle with his broken English, insisting there was no package. *Not a very polite young man,* Jordan thought, as the unhelpful clerk refused to check for her. It confirmed Jordan's suspicions, that the boy was on watch, and that he had probably intercepted Andrioli's phone calls.

The clerk finally relented. *"Aspete,"* he said, *"aspete."*

Christine nodded, which was Jordan's cue. As the clerk disappeared for a moment into the storage room behind his desk, Sandor stole down the stairs and hurried into the street.

A moment later, when the clerk returned empty handed, Christine expressed her disappointment, but thanked him all the same.

"Si, si signora. Prego."

Christine showed him her smile, then turned towards the stairs, as if she were returning to her room. As soon as she rounded the corner, she stopped and listened. She heard the young man making a phone call, which meant he had his back to the front door. She turned and hurried across the small, carpeted lobby and outside.

The clerk spun around, having heard something, but she was already gone.

Jordan was waiting at the corner. "All right?" he asked as he helped her on with her jacket.

She nodded, although her heart was beating faster than she would have liked. "I think so. He seemed so nervous. I was just asking him to check for a package."

"I noticed. I don't know what he's up to, but I think it'll help if he believes we're still in the room." He placed his arm around her shoulder, felt her trembling as they began to walk.

"You think he saw you leave?"

She shook her head.

"Good. Let's take a stroll." He led her down the stairs, around the perimeter of town, toward the private docks where they arrange daily rentals of small power boats. "Take a couple of slow deep breaths," he told her. "The night is young."

*   *   *

Martin Koppel received a phone call from Mr. Groat. There was a change in plans. The dinner, scheduled for a cozy restaurant in town, had now been arranged on the yacht. Two of Mr. Groat's associates would be by at seven to pick him up and take Koppel by launch to the *Halaby IV*.

Koppel nervously put down the phone, standing there, numb.

This was not the deal. He was supposed to have dinner at a restaurant, where he would be watched. And protected.

Koppel felt he should call someone, but he was warned not to make any phone calls. They would contact him, they said, and he reminded himself that they had his line tapped. They had certainly heard the call, and they would tell him what to do next. Otherwise, he would be having dinner on Traiman's yacht in less than an hour.

FIFTY-FOUR

Traiman was standing beside the bed in the teak lined stateroom. The comforter and pillows were on the floor, the sheets in disarray. He pulled on his robe, giving the two young women a last, dispassionate look. They were naked, lying face down, their fleshy, rounded asses bearing the marks of the lashes he had inflicted on each of them in turn, while the other was obliged to attend to him until he became bored and forced them to assume new positions.

"Get up," he ordered them, having spent himself, knowing he had already wasted too much time at these games.

The women slowly turned and rose. The face of the Egyptian girl was marked and red, the mouth of the African woman swollen and slightly bloodied. Traiman took no notice. He waved them towards their dressing gowns, then dismissed them, sending them off to another cabin where they might rest and heal. He was having guests, and their services might be needed again.

After bathing and dressing, Traiman met with his four scouts in the main salon, where they briefed him on their reconnaissance in town.

"And is that all?" Traiman asked.

"Sir?"

"Is that all you know?"

The men from the advance party looked from one to the other, then back at Traiman. "Yes," the senior agent replied. "That's all we learned so far. There doesn't seem to be any other unusual activity. Sandor and the woman are still in the hotel. No calls are being allowed in or out of their room. We know that someone was trying to get through to them from a location in Rapallo. We've been waiting for you sir, for further instructions."

Traiman responded with a malevolent smile. "That's always a safe bet, isn't it? 'We've come back for orders'. What an excellent way to shun responsibility. 'We were awaiting your pleasure, sir'." His voice mocked them, but they offered no reaction. "Get Kerrigan in here."

They waited through an uncomfortable silence until Kerrigan was shown into the room. The tall, blonde-haired American was usually one of Traiman's favorites. Former Special Ops in the U. S. military. Recently the murderer of James McHugh.

"I hope you enjoyed your trip to the City of Lights," Traiman said. "It's been a long time since I've been able to promenade along the Champs d'Elysée."

"It's the same," Kerrigan replied sullenly.

"Well, that's good to hear. We were just having an unscheduled convention of incompetents, and I felt such a gathering wouldn't be complete without you. Please," Traiman said, pointing to a chair, "sit down." He waited for Kerrigan to ease his large frame into the seat. "Now then. It appears fate has provided you an opportunity to atone for your failures."

"How's that?"

Traiman stood and began slowly pacing the large salon. "Your inability to resolve a nagging problem will be tested once again. My old friend Jordan Sandor seems to be visiting us here in Portofino."

Kerrigan's eyes widened, but he did not interrupt.

"Isn't it amazing? My former comrade-in-arms, the man with the most annoying, overdeveloped sense of patriotism I have ever seen, he haunts me still." He looked around the room at his five men. "Sandor's morality can be an insufferable pain in the ass, let me tell you, but he's worth more than all of you combined. I have to admit, it'll be good to see him again. Pity it'll be such a brief get-together." He paused. "All right, here's the situation. Our associate, Faisal el-Ridaya, has contacted me from Paris. It seems that Anthony Andrioli was picked up there yesterday morning by his own countrymen." He let that sink in for a moment. "Yes gentlemen, Faisal's inside source assures him that Mr. Andrioli is quite alive, although wounded. The shooting at the Sacre Couer was apparently not fatal. At least not to him. In any case, he is yet another burr under our saddle. In fact, at this moment, he is also en route to Portofino."

Kerrigan spoke up. "You should weigh anchor and leave right now," he said. "It makes no sense for you to risk being here another minute. Leave this to us, we'll handle it."

"Thank you, Mr. Kerrigan, I appreciate your concern. However, I have already anticipated certain of these developments, and I can assure you that there is no need for us to leave this lovely setting, not yet." Traiman seated himself behind the captain's table again, his eyes moving from one to the other of these five men. "Before we act, we must consider each of the distressing possibilities we face." He picked up the phone and called the steward, ordering sparkling water to be served. "Jordan Sandor left the Agency after he had a difference of opinion with his superiors over the operation in Bahrain. You remember Bahrain, Mr. Kerrigan."

The American nodded.

"It is conceivable that Mr. Sandor has by now learned his true adversary in those proceedings was none other than his former field commander. Add to that the death of Mr. Peters in Woodstock and the unfortunate assault on his former lady friend in New York and one might believe that he is hell-bent on revenge. In short, he may have journeyed all this way to find me for personal reasons."

None of the five spoke.

"As appealing as that theory may be, it is the least likely of the three I have considered. Jordan Sandor is an able and tenacious operative, not a reckless fool. It is more likely that he is in league with Mr. Andrioli, attempting some maneuver we have yet to fully discern."

Four of the agents were nodding their heads, but Kerrigan was not.

"What is it, Mr. Kerrigan? Aren't you enjoying my speculation?"

"You said there was a third alternative."

"Option, Mr. Kerrigan, option. There can only be one alternative to a proposition, but there can be many options."

"Option, then," the American said with a disgusted look.

"And so there is. Care to have a guess?"

Kerrigan had enough of Traiman's pedagogy. "Sandor is still an American agent."

"Very good," Traiman said, slowly clapping his hands. "Go to the head of the class."

"If that's what you think, why stay here in Portofino?"

"If this is a CIA trap, you mean? Because, gentlemen, when you play chess, the key to success is planning several moves ahead. In this case, I have taken precautions to protect our position. What we need to determine is whether the financial arrangements I have begun to put in place with our friend, Martin Koppel, are authentic or part of this so-called trap. That is an answer I do not yet possess."

They listened in silence.

"As a consequence," Traiman continued, "I have insisted that the meeting with Mr. Koppel will take place here, on the *Halaby*."

They waited for more, but Traiman was done. Only Kerrigan, of the five men, knew of the plans with Koppel. Only Kerrigan understood what Traiman knew—that their days as trusted allies of the Arab extremists were at an end. The successful completion of Operation VX was not only critical to Traiman's personal financial scheme, but also necessary to an amicable parting from their Islamic hosts. If all went well, it would be an amicable, but final, parting.

"Should we go ashore and take out Sandor?" Kerrigan asked.

"You have not managed that up to now. We might as well make use of your failure. You will take him alive and bring him here. Perhaps he can supply some of the information we need. You two, start at the hotel. Find Sandor and bring him to me. Mr. Kerrigan, you take Mr. Fraser and revisit the issue of whether there is other surveillance in town. I need to know if Sandor is truly alone. Then you can bring Mr. Koppel for his dinner. You," he said, pointing to the fifth man, "you stay with the launch unless we radio you other instructions."

"What about the woman?" one of the men assigned to the hotel asked.

"She's of no use to us, except as leverage." He offered his thin smile again. "Jordan always had a weak spot in that regard, so she might provide some opportunity for persuasion—that is, if he is still his old, stubborn self."

"So we should bring her too, then?"

"Yes," Traiman said, "that would be best. But if she gets in your way, kill her."

*   *   *

As Traiman's men were heading for shore, Jordan and Christine were negotiating with a local man for the use of his small boat and outboard. The man was finishing up for the day and was not pleased to be bothered with them.

"No, no to start at night," the man said in his best English.

Jordan gave him a wink, then nodded in Christine's direction. "It's romantic at night," he said with a smile.

The Italian shook his head. He was short, with unruly black hair and an unhappy look on his face. *"Freddo,* no? Cold."

Jordan pulled out his cash and peeled off five one hundred dollar bills. "Just a couple of hours," he promised.

The boatman looked from Jordan's money to the small wooden vessel. "No. No at night. You get killed. *Domani. Domani.*"

Jordan pulled out another five bills from his sportcoat and placed them beside the five he was already holding. "This is it," he said, peering over the man's shoulder. "For a thousand dollars, I'll buy a damn boat from someone else. Just two hours."

The man snatched the money and shoved it in his pocket. *"Due oras,"* the man repeated.

"That's all," Jordan said. "We'll come back for it in a little while, just leave it right here."

The man looked confused.

"I've got to buy a little wine, you know. *Vino.*"

The man shook his head, as if to say he felt crazier than the American for allowing this. Then he showed Jordan where he would leave the ignition key, beneath the board that served as the aft bench in the boat.

"No," Jordan said, bending over and grabbing the key. "I paid in advance, right. This way I know I have the key when we return, *capisce?* Wouldn't want someone to steal it before we get back." He smiled. "Don't worry, I'll leave it under there when we're done."

The man frowned, then said, *"Due oras,* eh?"

Sandor nodded. "We'll be back in less than an hour," he assured him, then looked at his watch. "We'll take a quick ride, *tutto finito en due oras.*"

"Bene," the man said, then turned and walked away, up the hill past the concrete reinforcement that ran beside the dock.

Jordan made a pretense of taking Christine back into town. Once he was certain the fisherman was out of view, they doubled back to the spot where the small boats were set aground.

"Now what?" Christine asked. "We've got ourselves a little dinghy for a thousand dollars, and pretty soon everyone in town is going to know about it."

"Exactly," he said. "That's just what we want." He gazed out into the moonlit night, the sea lapping gently at the shore just a few yards from where they stood. "We want them coming for us. We also want them thinking we'll be gone for the next hour."

He led her to a spot behind some dry-docked skiffs and they made themselves as comfortable as they could for another long wait ahead.

FIFTY-FIVE

Traiman's men came ashore at the main wharf, on the end of the harbor opposite from where Jordan and Christine were hiding along the rocky beach. They tied up the launch at the main dock, then prepared to split into two groups as instructed.

Kerrigan told Fraser they would start in the main plaza. Fraser was also American, an athletic looking man with an uneven nose earned in too many fights, and the bow-legged stride of a horseman that belied his New Jersey upbringing. Like Kerrigan, he was a veteran of the Gulf War and had been in Traiman's employ for the past three years. He had never seen Sandor but he had met Andrioli.

"We'll see you back here in an hour," Kerrigan told the others.

The two men assigned to the hotel were Iraqi, survivors of the American war of liberation in their homeland. Having been members of Saddam Hussein's Republican Guard, they did not remain in their country to celebrate the new freedom. They recently joined forces with al-Qaeda, presently taking their orders from Traiman. The taller of them was Zagallai, the assassin whose name Jordan had written on his list, the name Andrioli had recognized. He was carrying a canvas duffel bag, with their automatic weapons and extra rounds of ammunition inside.

"We'll start at the Hotel Continental," Zagallai told Kerrigan in his heavily accented English.

The fifth man in the group had been appointed to stay with the motorboat. He was a short, trimly built Syrian, whom Traiman often used as a lookout. He found a bench on the pier where he sat down, placing his cellular radio beside him. He lit a cigarette and prepared to wait.

*   *   *

A short time later, Covington arrived in Portofino with Andrioli, Swedock and Bertram. They had driven along the same winding route Jordan and Christine traveled earlier in the day. They parked away from the Hotel Continental and set off on foot. Covington had left his other two men back in Rapallo, as their control team.

Covington and Swedock walked ahead, Bertram guarding Andrioli as the wounded man limped along, trying to keep pace.

"You going to make it?" Bertram asked.

Andrioli made an effort to steady his gait. "Probably not."

"How's the side?"

"Sore." The surgery on his chest seemed a long time ago, mainly because he was in a continual fog induced by the painkillers. "I almost forgot about it, till you reminded me. Thanks."

"Don't mention it," the agent replied.

They trudged down a hilly walkway, where Andrioli pointed to a set of ancient stone steps. "That's the place, right around the corner."

Covington held up his hand and the four men came to a stop. He said, "Andrioli goes in first. Swedock and I right after him. You stay outside and back us up, Bertram."

Bertram nodded, happy to be relieved of trailing Andrioli.

"I'm not even armed," Andrioli said. "Why should I lead?"

"Sandor's your friend, he's not going to shoot you, is he? Don't worry, we'll be right behind you."

"What if Sandor's not in there? Lemme have a gun, for Chrissakes. You afraid I'll take the three of you out?"

Swedock and Bertram looked to Covington, but he shook his head. "You've got your orders," Covington barked, "Now let's go."

They negotiated the steps, Bertram lagging further behind now. When they reached the street, Bertram took a position along the stone wall. He watched as Andrioli, Covington and Swedock entered the hotel.

Inside, the three men found the young clerk behind the desk.

"We're looking for our friends. Mr. and Mrs. Kerr," Andrioli told him.

The young man eyed them suspiciously, then said something in Italian none of them understood.

"Kerr," Andrioli repeated. Then, in response to the look in the clerk's eyes, he leaned forward slightly and said, "Now, fella."

The clerk stared into Andrioli's eyes and saw the man meant business. He nodded slightly and told him the room number. Then, in his broken English, he explained nervously that he didn't think Signore and Signora

Sandor were in their room. Two men came by just a little while ago and went upstairs, but there was no answer.

"Where are those two men?" Andrioli asked.

The boy told them they were gone, but the way he said it caused Andrioli to turn to his two companions. "I don't believe him."

"Ring their room," Covington said.

The clerk shrugged. "I try before," he said. "No answer."

"Try again."

The three men watched as the boy placed a call. No one picked up.

Inside Jordan's room, Zagallai and the other Iraqi were waiting. They had already removed the two H&K MP5 submachine guns from their satchel and chambered the first rounds. The guns carried 10 mm shells, with the option of single shot, three round bursts or continuous firing. The SMG was designed for a magazine with 30 rounds and a replacement clip attached, carrying the same load.

Each man occupied one of the far corners of the room, facing the door. When the phone rang they tensed, glancing quickly at each other, then bringing their weapons into position.

When the clerk finally hung up the phone, after half a dozen rings, Covington asked, "You been at this desk all evening?"

The young man became agitated, insisting that he never leaves the desk, just like a good soldier, ever at his post.

"I think he's full of shit," Andrioli said.

"We'll have a look for ourselves," Covington agreed.

The clerk understood their comments, as well as the demand. He was definite in his refusal. "No, *signore. Impossibile.*"

Now Swedock stepped forward, pulled out his 9 mm and pointed it at the clerk's face. "Key," he said in plain English.

The clerk turned slowly to his side, grabbed a spare key to the room, then held it out in a trembling hand.

"*Grazie,*" Andrioli said.

Swedock stepped behind the desk and grabbed the young man by the arm, pulling him forward. He held his finger to his lips, then motioned with the gun for the clerk to lead them up the stairs. The four of them proceeded in single file up to the first landing. Once again, Swedock put his finger to his mouth. This time the clerk pressed his lips tightly together to show that he understood.

Andrioli held out his hands, palms upraised, and the clerk pointed across the corridor, to one of the doors.

Swedock took the clerk by the shoulders and spun him around, facing him against the wall. "Shhh," he whispered in his ear.

Andrioli noticed the small strip of paper on the floor near Sandor's door. When Covington motioned him forward, Andrioli shook his head and pointed to the paper.

Covington nodded his understanding, then mouthed the words, "Call his name." Swedock had walked silently past the door, Covington standing on the near side, beside Andrioli.

"Jordan," Andrioli called out. It was a raspy whisper, but in the quiet of the hallway it was like a shout, sure to be heard inside. "Jordan," he said again. "It's Tony."

There was no answer.

Covington motioned for Andrioli to open the door with the key. Andrioli responded with a look that told him he must be out of his mind. Covington reached out and took hold of the knob. He could feel it was unlocked. He turned it and pushed at the door as he moved quickly two steps back down the hall.

A splintering crash of gunfire erupted before the door had come all the way open, shattering the wood and piercing the opposite wall. The fusillade, coming at crossing angles, struck Andrioli and dropped him to the floor before he could move aside. Covington and Swedock refrained from firing, just for an instant, giving the shooters enough time to think that Andrioli might have been alone. Then Swedock took a step forward and began firing.

The men inside responded with another hail of shots. The walls of the hotel were old and wooden, and easily gave in to the powerful explosions being launched from the automatic weapons. Swedock was hit in the side of the face, spinning him sideways as another series of shots killed him before he hit the floor.

As Swedock's lifeless body collapsed at his feet, Covington hollered out, "Hold your fire. It's Covington." He had yet to fire a shot.

Traiman's man, Zagallai, who was off to the right, hunkered down behind the bed, took a quick look, his weapon at the ready.

"It's Covington," the CIA man repeated as he stepped into view in the open doorway. "Hold your fire."

The two men inside the room stood up.

The sound of the gunshots had already brought Bertram racing in from the street. He took the stairs two at a time, coming around the turn in the corridor at a crouch, just in time to hear Covington use his own name to bring the exchange to a halt. He froze, his gun in hand, staring at his operations chief.

He saw that Swedock and Andrioli were down, the clerk was huddled against the wall, and Covington was standing there, in the middle of the corridor with his weapon at his side.

There was no time for Bertram to comprehend the treachery. Covington answered his agent's startled look by raising his automatic and firing three rounds into his chest. Bertram crumpled to the floor.

Traiman's men came slowly to the door, their SMG's still in position.

"It's all right," Covington told them. "That's everyone. They're done."

The second Iraqi followed Zagallai into the hallway.

"What the hell are you guys doing here?" Covington asked. "Where's Sandor?"

"We don't know," Zagallai said. "We came here looking for him. We had an hour before we meet Kerrigan, so we waited here, in case he came back."

"What about him?" Covington asked, pointing to the Italian clerk who was crouched against the wall, not looking towards them.

"He works for the locals," Zagallai said. "Let him go."

"No," Covington said. He turned, extended his arm, then fired two shots into the back of the boy's head. "We're not leaving any loose ends this time."

Traiman's men stepped over Swedock's body, then stood alongside Covington, who was staring down at Andrioli.

Andrioli was covered in blood, his breathing uneven and shallow, his eyes still open. He had fallen with his head propped against the baseboard of the corridor wall. He stared up at Covington.

Covington smiled down at him. "You just refuse to die, don't you?"

Andrioli struggled for air. "It was you all along."

Covington said nothing.

"You miserable fucking traitor," Andrioli managed to gasp.

"That's kind of the pot calling the kettle black, don't you think?" Covington said. Then he took the H&K from Zagallai and fired several shots into Andrioli's chest.

FIFTY-SIX

Jordan and Christine had no way of knowing what occurred at the Continental. They were still waiting near the shore, in the cold, damp evening, Jordan sensing that the time for action was near.

A few minutes later, they heard footsteps coming down the long wharf, firm and unhurried. It was the confident gait of men who believed they were too early to be concerned about concealing their arrival. They had obviously learned of Sandor renting the boat, then bought the story that he was leaving to get something and would be back in an hour. Jordan had told the fisherman he would be off to buy some wine. These men probably assumed he was going for help, and they intended to get there first.

The sound of the water sloshing against the rocky beach made it difficult for Sandor to determine how many there were. It was certainly more than one. Three or more coming for them would make it considerably more difficult. All he had was the one pistol and the advantage of surprise.

As the men drew nearer, he was able distinguish their steps. There were two men approaching, he decided, then they came into view, silhouettes set against the misty backdrop of the growing darkness. One man appeared to be broad, of average height, with an athlete's bearing. The other was tall, the swagger of his stride now recognizable as Kerrigan.

Jordan and Christine were silent as they watched the men slow, then step down onto the beach. They passed directly in front of them, just a few yards from the stacked skiffs that provided their cover. They watched as the men turned toward the water, trying to identify which of the boats Jordan had rented.

"This must be it," one of them said.

Jordan stood, rising above the pile of inverted boats, his hand gripping Andrioli's Colt .45. "Sorry boys, you guessed wrong, but thanks for playing. Now, under the rules of our little game, if either of you so much as twitch, I'll shoot you both."

Kerrigan, the tall American, wasn't waiting to find out what came next. He dove to the ground, reaching for his gun.

Fraser, with no warning that Kerrigan was going to make a move, was a split-second late in reacting. As he turned to his side, trying to pull out his weapon, Sandor squeezed off two shots. The first hit him in the shoulder and spun him around. The second tore into his chest.

As Fraser collapsed onto the sand, Jordan turned to Kerrigan, getting a bead on the large man as he scampered on his hands and knees to find cover behind a nearby rowboat. Kerrigan had unholstered his pistol, but Jordan fired, hitting him with a shot in the back of the thigh, a second ripping through his side. Kerrigan lurched forward, sprawling face down on a rocky outcropping, his gun sliding out of his reach.

Sandor stepped cautiously from behind his makeshift barricade of wooden boats, his Colt trained on Kerrigan's back. He had a quick look at the other man. Fraser appeared to be dead.

"I said I'd shoot you if you moved. You've got to learn to trust what people tell you, Kerrigan. Now I've got this gun pointed at the back of your ugly head. You move again, you die."

Kerrigan groaned something that Jordan could not understand.

"Whatever," Jordan said. He circled slowly, keeping his distance as he retrieved Kerrigan's Glock 9 mm and shoved it into his waistband. Now Jordan was standing in front of him. "If you want to have any chance at all of living past the next few minutes, you have to tell me where I can find Andrioli."

Kerrigan made a move, trying to roll onto his side.

"No, no, no," Jordan said. "Talk first, move later."

Kerrigan fell back on his face, uttering another painful moan. Then, as he attempted to speak, Christine cried out, "Jordan."

Sandor turned to see Fraser trying to raise himself, his gun in hand.

Jordan's instincts prevailed. He fired three rapid shots, one after the other causing the man to jerk back in a convulsive pantomime of death.

Jordan swiftly turned his attention back to Kerrigan. "I asked you something."

"Dead," Kerrigan grunted.

Sandor glanced briefly at Christine, then asked, "When?"

"Tonight." Kerrigan managed to turn his head so he could look up at Sandor. "You just can't seem to keep your friends alive, can you?"

Sandor resisted the impulse to kick him in the head. "Where?"

"Right here, in Portofino," Kerrigan said, then his face twisted up in a contortion of pain.

"Does it hurt?"

"Fuck you," Kerrigan spat at him.

"Witty reply. So, where's Traiman?"

Kerrigan managed a grin. "Traiman? He's having a little party on his yacht tonight. And his guest of honor is another friend of yours."

Jordan kneeled down, so Kerrigan could have a good look at the barrel of the Colt pointing at his face from just a few feet away. "Do tell."

"Yeah, our men buried that rat bastard Andrioli. Then they took an insurance policy."

"Bullshit."

"You think it's bullshit?" Kerrigan started coughing. Jordan couldn't tell how bad he had been hit. He didn't want to lose him before he got some more answers.

When Kerrigan stopped choking, he said, "They took Covington?"

Kerrigan took a couple of uneven breaths, then said, "That's right. Traiman's got your CIA man, and what the fuck are you gonna do about it?"

"Where's your launch?"

He hesitated, so Jordan waved the gun at him. "I asked you a question."

"Main dock."

"Which yacht out there is the *Halaby*?"

"I'm bleeding to death here."

"Which one is the *Halaby*?" Jordan repeated.

Kerrigan said, "Fuck you," then resumed his coughing. This time, as he made a show of trying to hold his wounded side with his right hand, he slid his left arm down towards his ankle.

Jordan watched, letting him get just far enough. As Kerrigan went for his ankle holster, Sandor said, "Nice try," then fired two shots into his face.

Christine turned away, but Jordan watched the man's head snap back in a bloody spasm, then fall lifelessly forward onto the rocks.

Sandor stood up. Staring down at Kerrigan's body, he said, "Thanks for giving me the excuse."

FIFTY-SEVEN

Jordan put a fresh clip in his Colt, then checked the magazine of Kerrigan's Glock. It was full, a cartridge already in the breech. The man had never gotten a shot off. He handed the gun to Christine.

"You're going to tell me you've never shot one of these, right?"

She nodded, holding the butt of the gun like it was covered with dirt.

"All you've got to do is point and pull the trigger." He turned it in her hand so she was holding it properly. Then he gently pointed the barrel to the ground. "But you probably won't have to. If they take us, you just need to have a weapon. Once they find it, they probably won't search you beyond a frisking."

She responded with a look of fear and confusion.

"Trust me," he said, taking the gun and placing it in her bag. Then he took her by the hand and started off for the center of town.

The gunfire at the Hotel Continental had caused neighbors to call the police. The shootings of Kerrigan and his partner were going to raise even more local activity.

Sandor hurried along with Christine at his side. He had no way of knowing what, if any of the things Kerrigan had said, were true. He only knew that he needed to get to Traiman.

As they neared the center of the town, he stopped beside a short, brick building. "Come here," he said.

She followed him into the shadows, where he took her by the shoulders and looked into her frightened eyes. "We've got to split up. I'm heading for the main dock. I want you to go into the café near there, the one closest to the water. Go inside, order something and don't come out unless I signal you." He took the Glock from her and placed it inside her bag.

"You're going to leave me behind," she said.

"No," he lied, "but I need to try and get to the launch alone. If they see us together, they'll make us from a hundred yards away. If I'm on my own I'll have a chance."

She stared into his dark eyes, understanding. "Everything I told you is true. Do you know that?"

He nodded.

"No, really Jordan. I need to know that you believe me."

He took her in his arms and kissed her tenderly on the cheek. "I believe you," he said. "Now please, believe me when I say that I know what I'm doing."

"You're going out there alone."

"Please," he said, "leave it to me."

She lowered her head, then nodded.

"Good. Now wait here just one minute, then go right to the café, the first one we visited today. And hold onto that gun, we may need it."

He kissed her again, and she held herself against him for what she feared would be the last time. Then she watched as he walked towards the sea and disappeared from view.

*   *   *

Jordan stole his way around another row of powered skiffs, sunfish and rowboats that had been pulled ashore for the night. As he came closer to the pier, he could see in the distance a man seated on a bench, directly across from what he assumed would be the *Halaby* launch. Obviously Traiman's lookout.

Jordan had taken Kerrigan's radio from the dead man's pocket, to see if he could confirm what Kerrigan had told him about Andrioli and Covington, but whoever else was in town was obviously now observing radio silence. He turned the two-way off, then headed for the underside of the quay.

He mounted a support post underneath the dock, then climbed from strut to strut. The old, wooden beams were wide and round and slippery with years of the ebb and flow of the sea. He moved carefully and quietly, making his way by stepping inside the joints of the crossbeams. When he reached the white power boat marked '*Halaby IV*' he continued past it, then carefully traversed from the interior supports to the outside piling where he climbed atop the dock behind Traiman's sentry.

Sandor pulled himself up, finding that he was just beyond the bench where the guard was seated. He placed his foot on a rounded wood brace and drew the Colt from his belt, then he yanked himself higher, climbing over the railing, his weapon pointed at the back of the man's head.

"*Buona serra,*" Sandor said.

Traiman's scout turned, his hand about to draw his weapon.

"Uh, uh, uh," Jordan said. "Stay right there."

The Syrian did not move as Jordan came over the railing and stood above him.

"I'm going to need your help," Jordan said, "but first I'm going to need your gun."

The man smiled, his white teeth in stark contrast to his swarthy complexion. "I don't think so," he said, motioning with his head at what he had been watching when Jordan appeared.

Sandor glanced down the length of the pier. Coming towards them were four men and a woman.

The Syrian said, "I think you better give me your gun instead, unless you want us to kill you and the girl right here."

Jordan had another look at the approaching group. Two men he did not recognize were walking close behind Christine, John Covington and a man Jordan knew to be Martin Koppel.

He bowed his head at the sight of Christine and exhaled slowly. "Goddamnit," he said, then let go of the butt of his automatic, the pistol now hanging from his index finger by the trigger guard. He extended his hand and the Syrian stepped forward and took the gun.

"Now you will get in the boat," the man ordered.

"Not without her," he said, "and him," gesturing to Covington.

"Don't be concerned, Mr. Sandor. Everyone is invited."

The party of five had almost reached them. The only one speaking was Martin Koppel.

"What is this with guns?" he was demanding nervously. "I'm a businessman. I'm here for a business meeting, for godsake. What's with these guns?"

No one was paying any attention to Koppel. When they were only a few paces from Jordan, one of Traiman's men told the group they had gone far enough.

"Who are you?" Koppel asked Sandor. "Do you have any idea what this is about?"

Jordan ignored him. "Hello Covington," Jordan said. "I see you're also having a bad night."

"Extremely," he replied grimly. "Lost both of my agents. And Andrioli."

"I heard," Jordan said. "Where?"

"At your hotel, where you should have been."

"I'm not sure how to take that, John."

Zagallai barked at them, "Enough. Enough talking. No more talking from any of you." He turned to the Syrian, who was now holding out his Glock, as well as Jordan's Colt. "Any sign of Kerrigan and Fraser?'

The man shook his head.

Jordan said, "I'm afraid they won't be joining us, if that's what you're waiting for."

Everyone looked at Sandor.

"Yes," he said, "I'm afraid they've gone off to join the foreign legion in the sky."

Zagallai raised his hand to strike Sandor with the butt of his pistol, but his partner stepped forward and stopped him. "Not now. We'll have time for everything. Let's get them on the boat."

*   *   *

The three men dispatched to Portofino by Deputy Director Byrnes were now gathered in the room they had taken at the small hotel, just behind the shops on the edge of the harbor. One of them had been on watch and saw Traiman's man come and collect Koppel from the Hotel Splendido for his meeting. He followed at a safe distance into the center of town. There, the other two CIA agents, seated in the *caffé* near the main dock, witnessed the second Traiman henchman arrive, accompanied by John Covington. There, they met Koppel and his escort, and the four of them proceeded to the dock. It was at the entrance to the pier that they encountered the woman, who was standing alone, gazing out at the pier. They took her, just moments before Sandor appeared on the wharf and went face to face with Traiman's operative at the power launch.

The three agents then hustled to their hotel where they convened to make arrangements for their next move.

As two of the agents stood at the window, using binoculars to monitor the activities at the power boat, the third called Byrnes and reported these developments.

"They have Covington, then?"

"Yes sir."

"And the girl?"

"Yes. They're with Koppel now, and two of Traiman's men. They also have Sandor."

"Good," Byrnes said.

The agent asked if it was time for them to move.

"Not yet," the Deputy Director told him.

"Sir, I must report the situation is grave."

"I know," Byrnes replied.

"The risks are extreme, sir. If I may say . . . ," he attempted to go on, but the DD cut him off.

"We all appreciate the risks."

"Yes sir."

"You go to the fallback position, just as we planned. And remember what's at stake. We need the information more than we need the kill. Sandor is just where we need him."

FIFTY-EIGHT

Any prospects for a celebration on the *Halaby IV*, with Martin Koppel as the guest of honor, had evaporated with the radio transmission from the launch. Traiman, however, was not entirely displeased. He was disappointed perhaps, that his conference with Koppel would not go as smoothly as he would have liked, but he was determined to conclude their financial venture. Or to discover that it was a ruse.

Traiman was awaiting their arrival in the main salon. He was accompanied only by his top aide, Nelson, a former British commando with broad shoulders, a thick neck and a bald, bullet-shaped head.

"Once they're aboard," Nelson was saying, "we should weigh anchor and leave."

"There appears to be no sign of backup. This is Covington's mission, and he's on his way here. Where's the concern?"

"What if there is backup? What if Koppel was followed? If we move right now, they'd never chance an attack in open waters."

"Perhaps not," Traiman said. "I'm not so sure."

"The Americans would never be that reckless, not without confirmation that you're aboard. And how will they get that? They'll also know we have Covington, Sandor and the girl."

"You may be right. On the other hand, they don't need to launch missiles or torpedoes to mount an attack."

Nelson shook his head.

"We need to conclude our business with Koppel," Traiman said, "then put him safely ashore. If there's any sign of a problem, we can make the appropriate arrangements then. Meantime, our security details are in place."

There was a knock at the salon door, followed by the entrance of one his guards. "They're approaching, Mr. Traiman."

"Good, good." Traiman remained seated while the man went back to meet the boat. Traiman turned back to Nelson. "If we run, we'll surely be at risk. Consider it. As long as we stay right here, the chance of an assault is less likely and more manageable."

"And if it isn't? Time will work against us."

"Perhaps so, but I think our guests will ensure a measure of safety. Remember, our Arab clients will prove even more difficult in the event we fail to deliver."

Nelson knew he was right. He knew that this was Traiman's final opportunity to square himself with those who believed he had betrayed Kahlid Sheikh Mohammed in Pakistan and the assault team in Washington—which, of course, he had.

There was another knock at the door. The same guard appeared to say, "They're aboard."

"Fine," said Traiman. "They've been disarmed?"

"Yes sir."

"Show them in."

He and Nelson waited a few moments. Then Jordan walked into the spacious salon, stopped, and had a look around at the opulent décor. "I'm glad to see you're doing so well for yourself, Vincent."

Sandor was followed by Christine, Koppel, Covington, the three men who had been ashore and two more from Traiman's on-board security force.

Traiman remained seated. He pressed his hands together and brought them to his lips. "Jordan. My God, Jordan. You can't imagine what a pleasure it is to see you again. And Ms. Frank. Your photograph doesn't do you justice."

It was Koppel who spoke first, demanding to know what the hell was going on, again asking, "What's with these guns?"

Traiman ignored him, looking instead to his men. "You say they've been searched."

All five men nodded.

"And frisked? My friend Jordan has carried some interesting toys with him, from time to time."

One of the men from the shore detail said, "Yes sir." He had searched them, but so far had not discovered the C4 Jordan had taped to Christine's back and his own thigh. The man held out his hand to Traiman. "We took their guns and an extra clip. He had one of our radios. Here are the papers and other things we found on them."

Traiman took what the man offered and placed it on the table without looking it over. "No portable laser beams, Jordan? No nuclear devices? What a disappointment." He turned away and faced his other guests. "John Covington. So good to see you again, too. And you, sir, you must be Mr. Koppel."

"Damn right I am. See here, . . ."

Traiman held up his hand, palm forward, then rose from his chair. He was dressed in a dark suit, white shirt with French cuffs bearing gold links, and a grey Charvet tie. He appeared every bit the successful businessman. "I truly apologize for all of these theatrics, but you see, a man in my position has many enemies. I'm sure you understand. Corporate espionage has become a ruthless game." Traiman's congenial tone seemed to nonplus Koppel, if only long enough for Traiman to add, "I assure you, our meeting will proceed as scheduled. Gentlemen, please show Mr. Koppel to the forward dining salon, and get him anything he wants."

"What the hell . . . ," Koppel started up again, but he stopped as Traiman again raised his hand.

"Please indulge me, sir. I'll only be a few minutes," he said and, with that, two of the security detail politely, if firmly, escorted Martin Koppel from the cabin.

As soon as Koppel was gone and the door closed behind him, Traiman's tone became more severe. "Where are Kerrigan and Fraser?"

The dark-skinned Syrian, who had acted as scout on the pier, said, "They never made it back. He," gesturing toward Sandor, "claims they're gone."

"Gone?"

"Afraid so," Jordan told his old mentor. "A Viking funeral may be in order."

Traiman turned his steely gaze on Jordan. "I was very fond of Kerrigan. He was a good soldier."

"Ah," Jordan said. "Only the good die young, Vincent."

Traiman responded by issuing several commands. Covington was to be detained in one of the guest cabins and kept under guard. They were to make ready for the dinner with Koppel. He would take a few minutes with Sandor and the girl, then they would also be held, for further interrogation, as he put it.

Two men grabbed Covington by the arms and led him away. That left only Traiman, Nelson, and one security guard with Jordan and Christine.

"Sit down," Traiman told his two guests. "And Jordan, please believe me when I say that in the event you make even the slightest untoward move, these men will kill you without another warning."

The guard lifted the submachine gun he was holding and pointed it at Sandor, just to reinforce the warning. Nelson removed a pistol from his shoulder holster and laid it on the table before him.

"You see, Jordan, in addition to the loyalty I command among these men, several of them were quite friendly with Mr. Kerrigan and Mr. Fraser."

"Thanks for the deep background, Vincent."

"Now do me a favor, please," Traiman said as he resumed his seat. "Begin by explaining why on earth you're here. Other than a burning desire to get together with me to reminisce."

"Well Vincent, it all began when your people began shooting at me in Woodstock New York—by the way, how far back do you want me to go? You want me to talk about how you screwed me when we were in Kuwait? Should I get into the Panana gambit?"

"No Jordan, not that far back. You see, I don't have much time for this interview, and if you insist on wasting it on the tiresome sarcasm you find so amusing, I'll be left no choice but to turn you over to more persuasive members of my staff. Am I clear?"

"As always."

"So then, let's conduct ourselves as professionals and get to the point."

"Professionals?"

"Oh no, I feel it coming. We're about to move from sarcasm to jingoism, am I right?"

Jordan stared across the cabin without giving a response.

"Ah yes, Jordan Sandor, fighting for paychecks and patriotism while I, the mercenary, opted for wealth and power."

Jordan still refused to reply.

"Propaganda and peanuts, that's what you've risked your life for, Jordan. You've always been supremely talented, but incredibly naïve."

"You consider morality naïve?"

"Ah, morality. Tell me, Jordan, what gives the United States the moral high ground, when it aids and abets the assassination of leaders in third world nations, or promotes civil war in those countries, or invades them when their internal politics become distasteful to the American administration *du jour*? How many died in the fields of Afghanistan or the streets of Tel Aviv? How many are slaughtered every day in the wars that rage endlessly Africa, where no one in New York or Los Angeles can even name the countries? No one cares about those tens of thousands that die of poverty, starvation and internecine battles, not really. So where is it written that only the United States cannot be attacked or invaded without provoking a world conflict? Why, when someone blows up a building in New York in protest against its policies in the Middle East, must the entire world be made to pay? Spare me your sanctimonious patriotism, Jordan, and tell me—which of us is the mercenary here?"

"In answer to your first question," Jordan said slowly, "I came here because I wanted to see you again. And to kill you."

No one in the room moved or spoke for a moment. Then Traiman began to laugh. "You see," he said to Nelson, "do you see why I've always loved this man so?"

No one else seemed to find it funny, except Sandor. He was smiling.

"So that's why you let my men take you without a fight. You actually did want to come aboard?"

"No. To be accurate, Vincent, I gave up my weapon because they had Christine and Covington."

"Of course. You gave up your weapon to protect the damsel in distress and your old boss from the CIA, a man you don't even really like, if memory serves."

"Not much, no."

"Always the hero. You just can't seem to help yourself, can you?"

Jordan watched him without answering.

"All right. And now that you're here, and we still have your lady friend and our old crony from the Agency—not to mention you, dear man—what did you really want to see me about? Before you kill me, that is."

"One of the items is moot, since I understand Tony Andrioli is already dead."

"I see. You came to argue for clemency."

"That's true, yes."

"What else, then?"

"I would like you to leave Christine alone."

Traiman turned his attention to her now. "I am sorry about Mr. McHugh. Not about his death, you understand. That became unavoidable. It is his disloyalty I regret."

Christine did not speak. She stared at him with obvious loathing.

"So then," Traiman said as he got to his feet again. "You have set your sights rather low, Jordan, and failed in all respects. Mr. Andrioli is dead, and there is nothing you can do to save Ms. Frank or Mr. Covington. You should have never left the game, Jordan, it appears you've lost your edge."

"There is something else."

"Yes?"

"I want to know why you betrayed your own people?"

"Why I left the CIA?"

"No, of course not. I mean the people you work with now. I mean, I thought I had you all figured out, Vincent. The money, the power, that whole cynical speech you made, it all fits. But then you torpedo your own team of hit men in Washington. For the life of me, I can't figure out why."

Traiman could feel the gaze of his Syrian security man bear down on him as he stood there. "Don't be ridiculous."

"Ridiculous?" Jordan smiled again. "Look, everyone in the business knows you've worn out your welcome in Libya. Qaddafi is playing the moderate now, and he's giving you the heave ho. He might even turn you over to us, offered the right deal. So why risk antagonizing your chance at a safe haven somewhere among your Arab friends by screwing them now? Especially now, when you're about to launch your VX project?

Traiman's eyes flashed with anger.

"Vincent Traiman, always the traitor. I guess you just can't help your-self."

"This discussion is at an end," Traiman said. "Mr. Nelson, take them to the library and keep them there. I'm going to meet with Mr. Koppel. I'll deal with them later."

"Leaving so soon?" Jordan asked as Traiman made for the door.

"Don't worry, Jordan. I'll be back."

FIFTY-NINE

Deputy Director Byrnes gave the order to move out. The agents who had been waiting for instructions in Rapallo were now on board a thirty seven foot Italian made *Cranchi Smeraldo* speed boat that would travel a course around the point on a southeastern bearing into the Mediterranean. The three men in Portofino were taking a larger craft, cruising at a slower speed, due south.

A Black Hawk helicopter crew had taken off from Genoa, and were out of sight and earshot, just beyond the ridge of the *Appennino* mountain range.

Meanwhile, the *Halaby IV* was anchored in the distance, gently rocking on the calm sea.

*   *   *

Traiman was in the private dining salon, doing his best to calm Martin Koppel's frayed nerves. He explained that the man and woman who had come aboard were rivals of his, and his bodyguards had been overzealous in protecting him. "Their presence here has nothing whatever to do with our arrangements."

Koppel told him that he did not buy any part of that story. "What about the other man?" Koppel asked, referring to Covington.

"He's an associate of mine," Traiman told him confidently. "United States government official."

"Is he involved with our project?"

"No. Knows nothing of our plans."

"Why is that?" Koppel asked.

Traiman leaned back and had a good look at his guest. The more they spoke, the more relaxed Koppel appeared. "I have always made it a policy to segregate the data and people involved in the different aspects of my business life."

"Need-to-know basis, eh?"

"That's one way to put it." Traiman lifted his glass of Pellegrino water and took a sip. "So, I assume that by now you've researched the matrix set up by Montana Management in Switzerland."

"Yes, I have. You know whose money that is?"

Traiman's thin lips parted in his imitation of a smile. "Of course, Mr. Koppel. Together with the MidCo Finance group, these companies possess the riches stolen from the people of Iraq by Saddam Hussein and his minions."

Koppel nodded.

"My aspirations are not that grand, Mr. Koppel. Have you organized the investment funds we discussed?"

"Everything is set to go," Koppel told him. "But I don't like all this gun-toting nonsense. What kind of man are you? Are you kidnapping your goddamned competitors, is that what's going on here?"

Traiman liked the questions Koppel was asking. They were the logical questions of a man who was here to do business, not a CIA plant. He was particularly relieved to have witnessed the fact that Covington and Koppel did not know each other, or about each other. Traiman had never entrusted Covington with any information about his investment plans with Koppel. Covington was told that there was a scheme in place that would generate enormous profits in which he would share. Need-to-know basis, just as Koppel said. If Koppel was part of a CIA gambit, Traiman reasoned that Covington would surely have known about that by now.

"Please, Mr. Koppel, don't allow your Hollywood inspired imagination to run wild. There's nothing so theatrical at play here as kidnapping. Save those creative concepts for the movie we will ultimately produce together. After we have dinner and conclude our business, we will put you ashore. My associates and I will then address the matters we have to discuss with these . . . competitors. It's as harmless as that by now."

"Whatever," Koppel replied, proud of the acting job he was doing. *Maybe I should take a part in my next picture,* he thought. "It's none of my business, right? I just don't like the bullshit with the guns. Let's wrap up the details so I can get the hell out of here."

"Of course." Traiman held up his glass again. "We are going to be very wealthy men, you and I, and very soon."

*   *   *

Jordan and Christine were sitting side by side in the library. The walls of the cabin were lined with oiled walnut bookshelves, many of the volumes bound in leather. There was a campaign style captain's table in the center of the room, several club chairs set around the table and a settee against the wall that Jordan and Christine occupied. Directly across from them, Nelson was comfortably seated in one of the arm chairs, his weapon resting in his lap. The security guard had stepped outside, waiting on deck near the door.

"Hey Nelson," Jordan said. "That's your name, Nelson, right?"

Nelson did not answer.

"All right if I have a cigarette?"

"You move your hand and I'll shoot your arm off."

Sandor nodded. "That's okay, I don't really smoke."

Nelson glared at him. "Traiman said he wants you alive for now, but he didn't say anything about what condition you need to be in. Don't press your luck."

Jordan nodded again, studying the man, taking the measure of his options, and gauging the eight feet or so that separated them.

*   *   *

The first mate, noticing something on the radar screen in the wheelhouse of the *Halaby IV*, was the first to see them. The speedboat was just a blip on the screen, but it was moving quickly. He radioed the man on the foredeck and asked him to have a look through his night vision binoculars. The man obliged, scanning the dark sea to the west. The boat was not yet in view.

The lookout on the port side of the stern deck heard the radio communication from the wheelhouse and signaled back that a cruiser was moving south from the Portofino harbor, still a long way off their stern.

Neither activity was unusual in this area, but with Traiman aboard the yacht, the security detail was on high alert. When the cabin cruiser began to circle on a course slightly to the east, the man on the port side of the ship hurried to the dining salon. He knocked, then entered at Traiman's bidding.

"Yes?"

"Sir, may I speak with you, please? Privately."

Traiman was annoyed by the interruption, but knew his team well enough to appreciate that the man would not have intruded if it was not important. "I'm sorry, Mr. Koppel. I'll be right back."

Traiman followed the guard onto the deck, closing the door behind him.

"I'm sorry sir, but there seems to be movement. It may be nothing, but . . ."

"Details," Traiman demanded.

The man explained what they had noticed to the west and the north.

"Stay here," Traiman told him, then hurried forward along the teak deck.

*   *   *

John Covington was enjoying a drink in a guest cabin with one of Traiman's men, the man who sometimes called himself Groat. His real name was Richard Dombroski.

Covington was having a scotch. Dombroski was having mineral water. The two men knew each other, but they were not friends. Theirs was an association forced upon them by circumstances.

"That was a rather dramatic exit you arranged for David Fryar at Loubar, wouldn't you say?"

"We needed to make a point," Dombroski replied in his monotone.

"You certainly accomplished that." Covington took a sip of the fine, aged single malt scotch. "So, who is this Koppel character? Isn't he that financier, lost his shirt a few years back?"

Dombroski looked at Covington, his hooded gaze giving the impression that he might be falling asleep. "I don't ask questions," he said in his flat affect.

Once he arrived on the yacht, Covington was looking forward to abandoning his role as a double agent, anticipating a warm greeting from Traiman. He expected to be the guest of honor, the completion of the mission in Portofino his coming out party. Covington's days as a mole within the CIA were over, and he was disappointed to have his reunion with Traiman upstaged by a broken down Wall Street investor and Jordan Sandor.

He was obliged to continue playing his part a little while longer.

He took another drink of the smooth, oaky-tasting scotch, left to bide his time with the man he knew to be Traiman's number one enforcer, wondering why Vincent had chosen Richard Dombroski as his chaperone.

*   *   *

Deputy Director Byrnes arrived in Portofino to coordinate the mission himself. He already had word from the men on the water that they would be circling near the *Halaby IV* within a few minutes. They would be approaching the yacht from two directions.

Byrnes warned them again that the *Halaby* was likely to be well armed and staffed with experienced military personnel.

The crew on the attack helicopter was standing by, but the DD wanted to hold them off as long as possible. If there was any chance at all that Sandor could get the information they needed, Byrnes was going to wait.

SIXTY

Traiman threw open the door to the cabin where Covington and Dombroski were waiting. If Covington was expecting this to be the moment for an appreciative greeting, he was wrong.

"What goes on here, John?"

Covington was too dumbstruck by the anger in Traiman's voice to frame a suitable reply.

"There are two boats approaching. What goes on here?"

"What?"

"You told me your detail was the only one trailing Sandor, that it was clean behind you."

Covington nodded. "Of course."

"Then who the hell is out there?"

"Out where? Let me go with you to have a look."

Traiman shook his head. "No. No, it's better if you continue to pretend you're our prisoner. We may still get some mileage out of that." Traiman was thinking now, calculating the probabilities of his situation. "Koppel. You never met him before?"

"Never."

"Never saw a file on him at the Agency, no mention of him?"

"Nothing."

Traiman nodded to himself. "Fine," he said. "You wait here. Richard, you come with me."

Dombroski followed Traiman out onto the deck pulling the door closed behind him.

"We may be going seaside," Traiman said to Dombroski. It was all the man needed to know. Traiman had an emergency escape plan that was arranged for only two. Below decks were scuba gear and two motorized underwater props fitted with lights and a range of more than an hour. In the event all other options were foreclosed, he and Dombroski would enter the water through the transom hatch and head for safety.

Dombroski nodded his thick head in understanding.

"Hopefully it won't be necessary, but get it ready all the same."

As Dombroski went below to make the preparations, Traiman hurried aft along the teak catwalk. When he passed the guard and burst into the library, his entrance was so abrupt that Nelson quickly came to his feet, his automatic aimed at the door.

"Sorry, sir," he said.

Traiman waved at him with the back of his hand, and Nelson sat down. "What the hell is going on here, Jordan?"

"We were just in the middle of a staring contest."

Traiman turned to Nelson. "The next wise answer he gives me, shoot the girl in her knee. Shatter it completely, one shot, you understand?"

Nelson responded with a satisfied smile as Jordan felt Christine stiffen.

"Now," Traiman said, turning back to Sandor, "let's have it. What are you doing here?"

Jordan looked from Traiman to Nelson, then back again. "I told you my reasons for being here. What else do you want to know?"

Christine was so frightened, she couldn't even breath. She took hold of Jordan's wrist, digging her nails into his flesh.

"There are two boats approaching. Your friend Covington knows nothing about them. What do you know?"

Jordan had never told Christine anything about Deputy Director Byrnes or their plans to take Traiman. Her look of astonishment was therefore genuine. Sandor did his best to look just as bewildered.

"I was with Andrioli and Christine. You knew that. I figured Covington was on our tail, but you know I wouldn't count on him from here to there," he said, pointing across the cabin with the hand Christine was not squeezing.

"Watch it," Nelson told him.

"Right," Jordan said, placing his palm back on the sofa. "Look Vincent, Andrioli told me about your plans to place hit teams in the States and in Europe. That's as much as I know."

"You're lying, Jordan. You mentioned VX. Tell me what you know about Operation VX."

"VX? I don't know much. Somebody mentioned it to Andrioli in Paris."

"Shoot the girl," Traiman said.

Christine screamed.

Jordan hollered, "Wait," just as Nelson was leveling the automatic at her knee.

Traiman raised his hand to his aide. "Well then?"

"I've heard rumors about a terrorist assault involving VX. I realized later that was what McHugh wanted to talk with me about." Sandor gave him a look that suggested he had just pieced together the last part of a puzzle. "That's it, isn't it Vincent? That's what Andrioli was after. The assassinations are bogus. The team they took down in D.C., that's a disinformation ploy, am I right?"

"Yes, yes, yes," Traiman intoned impatiently. "But what about you? What have you cooked up for me, my old protégé?"

"I told you, Vincent. I wanted to see you, face to face."

"Well then, you have your wish."

"Look, if these boats are really heading for this yacht, what would I be doing here now? What kind of idiocy would that be?"

Traiman thought that over. "I wonder."

"So what are you really up to? VX nerve gas, that's not your style, Vincent. And Martin Koppel, what's that all that about?"

Traiman scrutinized him closely, Jordan's gaze never leaving him now.

"I recognized him, of course. What would you be doing with him?"

Traiman took a step back and sat in the arm chair to the side of Nelson. "Since you claim to have nothing more to tell me, I may satisfy your curiosity."

Christine felt all the breath go out of her.

"Such as your plans for VX nerve gas?" Jordan asked.

"A fascinating substance. Unctuous, like motor oil, more toxic than serin, with a longer effective life. Spread a few hundred liters in Grand Central Station or Times Square at rush hour and thousands upon thousands will die. Then New York will come to a standstill—even more so than after nine-eleven. The destruction of those towers was a devastation to be sure, the deaths of two thousand people a catastrophe. But remember what happened next. In a couple of days everyone else went back to work. The tragedy lingered in the American consciousness, but the actual terror was remote to most people. My goal is to reach further, you see? Take away the hub of a city's transportation system, what have you got? You have hundreds of thousands, maybe millions of people, not willing to go to work for fear of their lives."

Jordan shook his head slowly, the solemn look in his eyes not lost on Traiman.

"Of course you see it, Jordan. We'll have the same result in the BART in San Francisco, Paddington Station in London, the center of Rome. And on and on," he said, as if the subject was beginning to bore him.

"How do you get that much VX into the country?"

Traiman smiled. "You're always on duty, my old friend. Well," he said with a slight shrug, "since you have very little time left, regardless of the exploits being planned out there on the water, I suppose there is no harm in sharing the cleverness of my plan with you." He looked at Nelson, who had his gaze trained on Sandor. "You are one of the few men I know who can appreciate the genius of my approach."

"Thanks."

"You recall the explosion at the offices of the Loubar Corporation the other day."

"Of course."

"Such a tragedy. A nice man, Fryar. In any event, an investigation had begun, all of that bureaucratic rot you and I so despise. After the explosion, the authorities will increase their vigilance. The shipments from Loubar that arrived in France last week will all be impounded and returned to the United States. The government will insist upon it. What they won't know, however, is that these shipments, which were already at dockside in Marseilles, have been fitted with the chemical solvent that will wreak a holocaust on the United States."

"Fucking French."

"*Quel dommage.*"

"How will they get it through customs? Those shipments are going to be examined left, right and sideways."

"Of course they will. That is, once they've arrived and are taken off the container ship. Before that, however, the barrels of VX will be separated and set aside. As you and I often told those dolts in Washington, the harbors of the United States are the most vulnerable danger points in America, not the airports. We told them that for years. But does anyone listen?" Traiman stood up, a professor having concluded his lecture.

"What about your men?" Jordan asked. "Where are these people, the ones who are going to plant the VX?"

"You're asking for names and addresses, I presume."

"It would be a start."

Traiman allowed himself a heartfelt laugh.

"The team that was arrested a couple of days ago in Washington, they weren't part of it were they? They were a decoy you set up, then sold out, right?""

Traiman's smile faded as he glanced at his man Nelson. If he realized his gaffe in having gone this far, he quickly recovered. Turning fully toward him now, he said, "You see, Nelson, you see why I've always loved this man? Not only a patriot, but one of the world's great optimists. Just moments away from death, and he's still planning to save the world. Ah, Jordan, if only you were ruled by a little more sense and a little less emotion."

They stared at each other for a moment. "I don't suppose there's any sense to my mentioning the loss of innocent lives or any of that."

"Don't be absurd."

"It's like you said, Vincent, I just can't help myself."

"Yes, I realize it's true. It may be your epitaph." He looked to Christine and said, "Ms. Frank, I am truly sorry you have to be involved in this, but you should have chosen your friends more wisely. Now I must go. I cannot be here to see a lovely young woman and my old comrade face such grisly deaths." He turned for the door, then looked back at Nelson. "Dombroski is below decks, he'll be back in a moment if you need him. And Mr. Nelson, please try to handle this outside, where you don't make a mess of the library."

Traiman was almost at the door when they heard a knock. He opened it and his lookout from the port side said, "They've thrown a floodlight on us forward."

"How far off are they?"

"A couple of hundred yards. The cabin cruiser is off to the west, but seems to be circling towards us."

"Prepare for an assault," Traiman snapped. He was standing in the doorway when he turned back. "You were the most talented agent I ever had the privilege to work with, on this side or that, Jordan. Even though you've become a horrible nuisance, I will truly miss you."

SIXTY-ONE

Traiman pulled the door shut behind him. Jordan could hear his voice trail off as he walked forward, barking orders to his men. Whatever the outcome of the action going on outside, Jordan knew he and Christine had little chance of surviving unless he moved now.

Nelson said, "You heard the man. Stand up. Nice and slow."

Nelson was already lifting himself out of his chair when a burst of automatic weapons sounded from the front of the ship. In that instant, as Nelson's eyes momentarily moved toward the direction of the gunfire, Jordan had his opening. He acted at once.

He grabbed Christine's sleeve, dragging her to the floor as he lunged to his right, flinging himself at Nelson's feet.

Nelson tried to retain his balance as he squeezed off three rounds, all of them high. "Hold it," he hollered, "I'll kill the girl," but Jordan had already rolled into Nelson's shins, knocking him backward onto the chair. Sandor sprung up, driving the heel of his right hand into the point of the man's nose, breaking it with a single blow, blood covering Nelson's mouth and chin. Nelson still clutched the automatic, but Jordan came with his left hand, hitting him under his chin, snapping the man's head back, the gun clattering to the floor.

Sandor hit him twice more, short chops to his throat that left Nelson gasping for air. Jordan pushed himself backwards now, falling to the floor again as the armchair flipped over with a thud. The door had swung open and the guard from outside stepped forward, measuring his shot as Jordan rolled to his side. Christine, who heard the doorknob turn, grabbed a heavy ashtray and flung it towards the door. It glanced off the guard's arm, but was enough to give Jordan the additional moment he needed to reach Nelson's gun, turn and fire.

310

Bullets flew back and forth, the guard taking cover behind the bulk-head, outside the door. Christine yelled out a warning as Nelson made an effort to get to his feet. Jordan aimed over his shoulder and shot Nelson once in the chest, sending him reeling against the bookcase, then falling across the table. The guard sent another barrage of SMG shots into the library, but he was still hidden. Jordan had no clean shot at him, but the man was not exposing himself enough to get a line of sight and take dead aim inside the cabin.

Sandor motioned for Christine to stay off to the side, behind one of the chairs. He clambered behind the dead body of Nelson, using him for cover as he searched his pockets for another clip to the automatic. A replacement magazine in hand, he fired a series of shots through the wall, then dry-fired several times, to let the guard know he was out of ammunition. Sandor dropped the spent clip to the ground with a press of the release button, then replaced it with a fresh one, pulling back the slide just as the guard peeked inside. Jordan fired two shots, but the first one was enough. It caught the man in the forehead, killing him instantly.

"Get ready to go," he called to Christine. "I just need a minute."

"What?"

The din of gunfire at the front of the yacht had increased, which made it unlikely anyone would be checking on them right now. Jordan went through Nelson's jacket and came up with another clip. "What a boy scout," he said as he pocketed the ammunition.

Then he went to the captain's table and lifted the top, exposing various nautical charts, maps and information on the tides. There was also in a translucent yellow plastic cover holding several sheets of paper. Jordan smiled.

"What are you doing?" she asked anxiously.

"Old habits die hard," he told her. "I've known Vincent a long time—he still writes everything out by hand."

"Traiman?"

He nodded, quickly riffling through the pages, then sticking them back in the folder. "Doesn't trust computers, doesn't trust anyone."

"What is it then?"

"Whatever he was going to put in place tonight," he said, holding up the file, "some of it is right here."

She watched as he rummaged through the desk, pulling out a waterproof chart cover. He placed the file inside, zipped it tight, then opened his jacket and stuck it inside.

"Jordan," she cried, noticing the growing stain of blood on the side of his shirt.

He looked down. "No time for that now," he said.

Panic was etched across her clear features.

"Hey, you did a pretty nifty job with that ashtray." Then he paused. "You feel that? They started up the engine. They're going to move out."

"What should we do?"

"If we don't jump now," he said, "we won't have a chance later."

"Jump? The water will be freezing."

"No, it won't."

"We'll drown."

"Maybe, but if we stay here they'll kill us for sure. Turn around."

She obliged and he pulled her blouse out from her slacks. Then he tore off the C4 he had placed there.

She let out a painful gasp.

"Sorry." He reached under her collar and took out two fuses. "I've got to get below decks to plant this and set it off. After that I'll use the charge I'm carrying."

"What about me?"

"I told you, I think you should jump and head for one of those other boats at anchor. You won't need to get all the way to shore."

She looked up at him, then said, "I'm staying."

They went to the door, where Jordan had a quick look outside, then pulled the body of the guard inside, together with his Uzi submachine gun, then closed the door.

He took the Uzi from the dead man, checked it, then handed it to her. "If you need to fire, just point and shoot—but not anywhere near me."

She frowned.

"It's not very accurate, is what I mean. Now keep low, and if I say jump, you go for a swim. Agreed?"

She nodded.

Jordan switched off the lights in the library and opened the door again. There was now action to the stern of the yacht. He could feel the boat moving, the anchor already up. They bent down and hurried along the walkway toward the bow. For the first time, the gash in his side began to ache.

He couldn't even remember being hit, what with the hand to hand struggle with Nelson and diving back and forth across the floor. He wasn't concerned about the pain, he just didn't want to become lightheaded from a loss of blood. He also knew that if he stayed aboard too much longer, with the yacht heading out to sea, Christine might be able to swim to another boat, but he would not.

He stopped and listened at the next cabin. He heard nothing, then quickly opened the door and stepped inside. He found John Covington standing there alone, his drink in hand. Covington could do nothing to conceal his astonishment. He recovered enough to say, "Jordan, thank God it's you. I thought you were dead."

Sandor made a quick survey of the cabin. "Keep that pointed at the door," he said to Christine. "Anyone walks in, anyone at all, you shoot them dead. We have no friends here, you got that?"

"I got it," she said nervously as she clutched the submachine gun.

"What's going on out there?" Covington asked.

"Not sure, John, although at the moment I'm even more curious what's going on in here. I mean, no guard, the door unlocked, you standing here having a polite cocktail. Scotch, that still your beverage of choice?"

He nodded.

"Well, why not finish your drink, then you and I can go outside and have a look?"

Covington placed his glass on the bar. Sandor's cold gaze told him everything he had to know. "You've been hit," he said casually, dropping his guise as the nervous prisoner.

"You worried about me, John?"

"Not really."

"I believe you." He watched as Covington's hand moved a little too close to his side. "Uh, uh uh," Jordan said. "You make another move like that and I'll have to get nasty."

Covington's pressed his thin lips together, then said, "So you know."

"Oh yes. I know, and I knew."

"You knew nothing."

"I knew you sold us out. Why do you think I'm here?"

Covington said nothing.

"You gave them McHugh and then you took care of Andrioli. That's how Traiman's men found Tony in Florida."

"We didn't count on you becoming such a problem."

"You didn't count on me still working for the Company," Sandor said.

"No," he admitted grimly, "I didn't."

"What about Andrioli? Was it a fair fight, or did you give it to him in the back?"

"Collateral damage."

"Right, like my team in Bahrain. That was you and Traiman too, right?"

"Yes, if that makes you happy. You're a dead man anyway."

"Humor me, then. You came here to meet Traiman, get rid of Andrioli and me, tell the Agency that Traiman got away, and then you were going to take the information back to the States to set his Operation VX teams in motion. How am I doing?"

Covington said nothing.

"Come on, John, how long did you and Vincent think it could last?"

Covington said, "A lot longer than this." Then he spun quickly to his left, reaching for a pistol holstered at the small of his back.

Jordan reacted instantly, lashing out backhanded with the automatic he took from Nelson, smashing the butt of the gun into the right side of Covington's jaw. Covington fell sideways, still trying to pull out his weapon as Jordan kicked him in the throat with the heel of his shoe.

"I told you, John, you desk jockeys should never play field agent games." He knelt down and picked up the gun and tossed it on a chair across the cabin. Covington was gagging. "Oh, Jesus, John, I didn't crack your windpipe, did I? Not with one kick."

Covington made an effort to lunge at him, but Jordan responded with another swift blow from the butt of the automatic, striking him square in the forehead. Covington fell backwards, gasping and moaning, still struggling to breathe.

"Don't be throwing up all over the place now, John. We don't have much time and I need some answers."

"Go fuck yourself," Covington panted.

"Hey, there's a lady present," Sandor said, this time bringing his left heel down into the man's midsection.

Covington doubled up on the floor. "You're going to kill me anyway," he wheezed.

"Not me, John, I'm one of the good guys, remember? You tell me what I need to know, then I'm gone. I'll leave you to Vincent and his merry men."

Covington's mouth was bloody, his jaw broken and he was still having trouble getting a breath. He stared at Jordan's face. "I'm dead either way."

"Maybe," Jordan said with a nod, "but I can tell you, you don't answer me right now and you're dead for sure."

Covington stared at him without moving.

Christine said, "I think I hear someone."

"Keep that thing pointed at the door," he told her without taking his eyes off Covington. "So John, what are you trying to protect? Traiman's plans? He didn't even tell you about Koppel coming here, did he? Come on, I saw it on your face. You had no idea about his scheme with Koppel. You thought this was only about Andrioli and me."

Covington tried to look away, but Sandor grabbed him by the hair and yanked his head back.

"That's why Byrnes never let you in on the Koppel play. This way Traiman would buy the whole show and come out to make his deal."

Covington stared up at him, realizing the truth. He was just another Vincent Traiman casualty.

"So let's have it, John. Who's your contact?"

Covington did not answer.

"John." Sandor pushed the barrel of the automatic against Covington's bloodied forehead. "I keep telling you, desk jockeys shouldn't play field games. Now who are you supposed to contact?"

Covington looked up at him. "I'm not sure. That's why I'm here."

Sandor figured it was true, and now he had Traiman's papers. Hopefully, the answers were there. "Who's been your go-between up to now?"

When Covington hesitated, Sandor pressed the metal a little harder against his head.

"Figueroa," he growled, giving Jordan the name of the other traitor inside the Agency.

"Thanks pal," Sandor said.

"Drop dead."

Jordan nodded. "Not yet, John." He pulled the gun back and stood up. "You hear anything else?" he asked Christine.

"Yes," she said, giving her head a nervous shake, still watching the door. "I think someone just ran past."

Sandor stood there for a moment, listening. The intermittent sound of gunfire outside had not relented. He turned back to Covington. "Just so you know, we had you in our sights the whole time I was on the move. The DD figured you had to be the leak. You iced it when you got the call, that anonymous message exposing Traiman's team in D.C. Typical Vincent, that move, giving up some of his own men, the old Queen's sacrifice. I played too much chess with him to miss it."

"And he usually beat you, didn't he? Traiman has every option covered," Covington said, his voice raspy with pain. "You'll never get off this boat."

"Maybe not, John, maybe not." Sandor walked toward Christine, purposely turning his back on him, listening for him to make his move. When Covington went for the gun Jordan had tossed aside, Sandor turned and fired two shots into his chest. "But neither will you," he said as he watched Covington collapse, struggling to draw his last breath before he fell over, dead.

SIXTY-TWO

Jordan led Christine out of the cabin and down the steps, below decks. The bleeding from his side had increased again after grappling with Covington, but he felt clear-headed enough, and quickly found his way to an aft compartment. Almost all of Traiman's men were above, and he moved swiftly to place the plastique against the bulkhead and set the makeshift fuses he had taken from Andrioli's attaché case.

"This'll blow quickly," he said. "Let's get the hell out of here."

*　　*　　*

Traiman was on the bridge, directing the captain on the path of the yacht, as well as the flow of the action. He was on the radio, ordering his men to keep the smaller craft at bay while he led them into the open sea. Thus far, neither had come close enough to attempt boarding. Heavy fire had kept them away.

He picked up the intercom and called Nelson in the main salon, receiving no answer. "Damn," he said, returning to the walkie talkie.

"Dombroski, this is Traiman. Where the hell is Nelson? Come back."

Dombroski replied immediately. "Main salon, with Sandor and the girl."

"I'm getting no answer. Check it out."

"Over," Dombroski said.

At that moment, the yacht was rocked by the explosion Jordan had set just below.

Traiman grabbed a handrail and steadied himself as the captain was thrown against the control panel.

"What the hell was that?" Traiman hollered into his radio.

"We're not sure," his man on the foredeck responded. "Explosion below."

"Send two men down there to find out. And protect your flank. It could be a diversion."

"Yes sir," the man said. "Over."

Traiman stared out at the dark sea ahead.

"Stay the course?" the captain asked.

"Yes, yes, push it," he said. Then he slammed his fist down. "Damnit," he said. "Push it."

*   *   *

Byrnes' lead agent radioed back to shore. "We just heard an explosion on the *Halaby*, sir. How much longer?"

The DD knew that it would become more dangerous as the yacht led them further out to sea. He also knew that Sandor should be given as much time as possible to complete his mission.

"All right," Byrnes said reluctantly. "I'm calling in the chopper. Give it three minutes, then get on the bullhorn."

*   *   *

Jordan and Christine were hiding in the companionway, outside the entrance to the engine room, which was another series of steps beneath them. They listened as Traiman's men scurried towards the site of the first blast.

"I'm going below one more level," he whispered. "Alone."

She began to say something, but he put his finger to his lips.

"I need you here. Anyone coming this way, you fire. "I'll be right back."

Sandor did not wait for a response. He lowered himself down the metal steps, facing forward, one hand on the rail the other holding the automatic. He moved as quietly as he could but, as soon as he came into view from below, one of the ship's mates spotted him.

Jordan could not afford to hesitate. He fired, hitting the man in the shoulder, then leaped to the deck and dove for cover behind one of the huge diesel engines that powered the ship.

He heard men hollering, then the sound of several pairs of feet scuffling on the other side of the room, but no answering gunfire came. He had already removed the C4 he had hidden along the inside of his leg. Now he rigged it with the detonator fuse and secured it against the side of one of the huge diesel engines.

Judging from the first charge, he would have less than sixty seconds to get out of there. He looked towards the metal steps, listening for the movement of the others as they were pulling the mate to safety.

Jordan started the fuse, then bolted, firing his pistol behind him, aiming under his left arm as he rushed toward the metal steps. He was halfway up when his clip made the awful metallic sound that told everyone within hearing that the chamber was empty. A series of gunshots followed, one of which caught Jordan in the right calf just as he made it to the top of the stairs. He clung there for a moment, almost falling backward, then sprung upwards, collapsing beside a startled Christine.

"You've been shot," she said as he slammed the metal door behind them.

"Again," he said, trying to force a smile that didn't work. He struggled to his feet. "That charge is about to blow," he told her. He dropped the clip in his automatic to the floor and inserted the final replacement, then drew a round into the chamber. "Let's go," he said, taking her hand and leading her back toward the set of steps to the main deck, limping forward as blood ran down his leg.

The second explosion was more powerful than the first, the C4 positioned as it was beside the engine. The ship shuddered, a violent quake that thundered throughout the yacht. Jordan and Christine held on as the boat shook, then ran to the corner of the passageway, where they came face to face with the two men Traiman had sent below.

Both men had their guns drawn. Sandor responded by shoving Christine back, the two of them tumbling behind the corner of the bulkhead as the two guards opened fire. Jordan grabbed the Uzi from Christine, scrambled to his hands and knees, then pointed the weapon around the turn and answered their fire.

In the small area, Traiman's men had no chance, falling under a barrage of rapid and ricocheting shots as Jordan emptied the submachine gun at them. He got to his feet and, holding Nelson's automatic at the ready, made sure they were finished.

One of them was the tall Arab, Zagallai.

"We owed him that one," Jordan said. "For Andrioli."

He leaned over and picked up the man's H & K MP5 submachine gun.

"Come on," he called out to Christine, and they hurried to the main deck.

*   *   *

Traiman was still in the wheelhouse. He ordered the captain to go full throttle, but the explosion in the engine room had slowed the boat to only a couple of knots.

"We've suffered some real damage down there," the captain told him after speaking to his engineer on the intercom.

Traiman got a call on his radio from Dombroski. "Nelson and the guard are dead," he reported.

"Damnit," Traiman said through clenched teeth. "Sandor." He knew it was getting close to the time when he would have to exercise his emergency escape plan.

"Prepare for seaside," Traiman said.

"Copy," Dombroski said.

*   *   *

Jordan led Christine to the port deck. They were squatting below the steps to the pilot house. "I want to try and get Koppel out of here," he whispered.

Just beyond the main cabin structure they could still hear gunfire on the starboard side.

"Where is he?"

"No idea. They said the dining salon or something. Come on."

He moved along the deck, checking a series of empty cabins, ready with the SMG as he threw each door open. They found Koppel in the main dining room, hiding in a corner, beside a large breakfront.

"Come on," Jordan said. You two are going for a swim."

Koppel responded with a stunned look.

"Come on," Jordan growled at him, "I'm the good guy. Let's move it, right now."

Koppel stood up, more dazed than afraid, and came to the door.

"Drop over the side here," Jordan told them. "Push as far out to sea as you can, away from the ship, then just tread water. This boat's moving fast enough, it'll go by you pretty quickly. Then the cruiser to the rear should spot you."

"Should?" Christine asked

"Just do it."

"And if they don't see us?"

"Keep your head down as much as you can until this boat is gone, then swim for the lights on shore or one of the boats anchored between here and there. And whatever you do, stay together."

"What about you?" she asked.

Jordan looked down at the large stain of blood on his shirt, then gingerly touched his leg. "I'm okay for now. I've got some unfinished business. Then it's man overboard for me too." He checked the two clips in the weapon he had taken from Zagallai. There were several rounds left.

They were kneeling beside the main bulkhead. He pulled out the rubberized, waterproof chart cover that held Traiman's file. He handed it to Christine, then helped her tuck it inside the waistband of her slacks and pulled her blouse over it. "This is important," he said.

"I know," she said, then leaned towards him. "You're going after Traiman."

Jordan looked beyond her, down the length of deck. "Go on," he told her. "Don't make me push you overboard."

"Be careful," she said.

He kissed her on the forehead, then watched as she and Koppel climbed under the rail and slipped, feet first, into the pitch dark Mediterranean.

SIXTY-THREE

If Traiman was still on board, Sandor knew he would be on the bridge. It was his old partner's style, always the admiral or the general, depending on the circumstances.

Once Christine and Koppel were in the water, Jordan stole up the stairway in a crouch, staying so low he was practically crawling. The ache in his side was not as bad as the debilitating pain in his leg. He pushed himself, knowing there was only one more thing left for him to do. He nearly tumbled as he quickened his pace, then steadied himself with the heel of his left hand, the H&K SMG securely in his right.

As he came to the top of the companionway, he realized he had already gone too far. His head was in view of the glass enclosed wheelhouse and he froze, but it was too late. The captain spotted him and pointed. As Sandor pulled back, he caught a glimpse of Traiman.

Traiman responded with a rapid fire explosion from his MAC 10 repeating automatic that shattered the glass and sent it in a spray across the foredeck and into the sea.

Jordan held his position, just beneath the sight line of the bridge. He extended his arm, peered up swiftly, then squeezed off two rounds. His shots were answered by another burst from Traiman.

"Get to the port foredeck," Traiman hollered at his men into the radio.

Sandor acted quickly, diving across the fiberglass foredeck, firing up at the pilot house, striking the captain, who Traiman was now using as a human shield. As the captain slumped, Jordan ignored the blast from Traiman's gun, knowing this might be his last and best chance. He came up shooting, catching Traiman in the shoulder, then the side of the neck, sending him reeling backward against the wall on the starboard side of the pilot house.

Jordan, on his feet again, moved cautiously forward. Traiman was barely standing, leaning against the control panel, his submachine gun now lying on the deck at his feet. Sandor moved slowly inside, checking behind him, then kicking the door shut.

"What a bore you can be, Jordan." Traiman coughed.

"Every party has a pooper."

"I hope you don't expect me to answer any more of your endless questions."

"No Vincent. As it turns out, I got everything else I needed from Covington."

"That sniveling bureaucrat?"

"I never liked him, you know."

"Neither did I," Traiman said with a slight laugh that became a throaty cough. When he caught his breath, he said, "Dead?"

"Very," Jordan told him.

Traiman nodded slowly. "Probably deserved it."

"That's how I saw it."

Traiman had a look at Jordan's blood stained shirt and trousers. "My men will be here in a few moments, but it appears I may not need their help. You're already done for yourself."

Sandor steadied himself, grabbing hold of a handrail. "You may be right, but you're not looking too swift yourself."

"So then, we old comrades end up dying together."

"Don't flatter yourself, Vincent. We're not comrades and we're not going to die together."

In that instant, Jordan saw the flicker in Traiman's eyes, even before he heard the movement behind him. Sandor turned and moved to the side in one fluid step, firing a long burst at Dombroski. The man staggered backwards, down the steps to the wheelhouse and over the railing. Given the moment, Traiman dropped down for the MAC 10 that had fallen to the deck. He looked up, straining to reach the weapon, his gaze now met by Jordan's.

"I can't say I'll miss you, Vincent."

Traiman forced a grim smile. He said, "I suppose not, old friend," then lunged forward the last foot or so, in an attempt to reach the gun. Jordan did not hesitate. He fired a series of shots that sent Traiman sprawling face first across the deck of the bridge.

Sandor leaned over to make certain he was dead. He kicked aside the SMG, stood up and stared down at Traiman one last time. He shook his head sadly, then made way to the foredeck.

*   *   *

The *Halaby IV* held its course, cutting through the calm waters of the indifferent Mediterranean, the speed cut well back due to the damage Sandor caused in the engine room. The sound of gunfire had subsided, the two crafts piloted by Byrnes' men having moved out of range. The remaining force on the yacht could see the helicopter approaching through the dark from the east.

Jordan saw the Black Hawk, knowing he had run out of time if Traiman's men refused to surrender. The *Halaby IV* would be pulverized, along with everyone on it.

Sandor had come aforedeck, and was standing in the cool night air, in front of the enclosed bridge. He saw two men running fast along the starboard walkway. He was too weak now to chance another battle, especially if they sent a second team up the port side, which was more than likely.

Jordan held the H & K out beyond the cover of the wheelhouse and sent a barrage of shots at the two approaching gunman, holding them off for the moment. Then he hobbled to the railing and dropped himself overboard.

*   *   *

The Black Hawk attempted to radio the yacht, but the two men on the bridge, Traiman and the captain, were both dead. The men aboard the helicopter watched as the yacht limped slowly through the calm sea, it's course set, its engines damaged.

The next option would have been to send a warning shot alongside the ship, a small missile that would explode in the sea, sending a huge spray of water high into the air.

However, Byrnes ordered the co-pilot to hold off, instructing him to shine two large spotlights on the deck of the ship, then using the high-powered loudspeaker, telling the men remaining on the *Halaby IV* that they had exactly ten seconds to come on deck with their arms raised and to kill the engines. The Black Hawk had to be concerned about the launch of a hand-held missile, so no further warning would be given.

By now, the men aboard knew that Traiman was gone. They also knew the Black Hawk could fire a charge smack into the center of the ship that would end the debate in one shot. One of the men argued that they could use a shoulder mounted stinger to take out the chopper, but the others shut him up. There was more artillery where this Black Hawk came from.

They marched onto the main deck, threw down their weapons and held up their hands.

"Into the spotlight," the loudspeaker ordered them, and the men complied. You will be boarded now. A hostile move by anyone on the ship will be an act of war by all."

The co-pilot radioed the larger boat and told them to take the *Halaby*.

The pilot of the smaller, faster boat had spotted Christine and Koppel when they went over the side. He had circled back to pick them up. Now he was looking for Sandor as the larger cabin cruiser headed straight towards the *Halaby IV*.

Even with the aid of their night vision glasses, it was Christine who saw him first. "Jordan," she cried out, pointing at him.

The speedboat swung sharply to the port side and came around to where Jordan was struggling to stay afloat, then motored swiftly to his position, reached over the side and hauled Sandor to safety.

SIXTY-FOUR

Jordan Sandor, his left arm in a sling, a cane resting against his chair, sat at a small table in Doney's on the Via Veneto in Rome. He was sipping his second cup of espresso with anisette, looking out the window at the stream of inevitable pedestrians that crowd this famous boulevard on a sunny afternoon.

"Listen to this," Christine said, reading from the International Herald Tribune. She recited another account of the capture of terrorists in New York and San Francisco, together with the interception of a shipment of potentially dangerous chemicals in Marseilles. There were no details, no mention of VX gas.

"Potentially dangerous," Jordan repeated with a shake of his head.

The Deputy Director walked through the front door, spotted them and came to their table. He held out his hand to Christine. "Hello, Miss Frank. I'm Mark Byrnes."

"Excuse me if I don't get up," Sandor said.

"Good to see you haven't lost your sense of humor."

"Along with all the blood, you mean?"

The DD sat down, taking a chair across from them, his back to the street. "It was a good job, Jordan."

Sandor nodded. "Too bad about . . . ," he began, but Byrnes cut in.

"We stopped them. You stopped them. It was important, and you got it done."

"Yeah. Stopped them for now."

"We can only fight one battle at a time," the DD said. It was one of his favorite sayings.

"Koppel okay?"

"He's fine, thanks to you. He'll wind up the hero, of course. Probably get funding to make a movie about his own exploits."

"One of the sweet ironies of life."

"So it would seem."

"No glory for us, right chief?"

"Not if you're true to the code."

"Right."

Their waiter came by, but Byrnes said he would not be staying. The man ambled away, muttering something in Italian.

"I just wanted to meet Miss Frank, to thank her personally. And to tell you to take as much time as you need."

"And then?"

"And then you're coming back, aren't you?"

Jordan smiled. "Where else have I got to go?"

Byrnes looked at Christine now. "The world can be a pretty lousy place, young lady." He stood up and extended his hand. "Thank you for your courage."

Christine was not sure how to respond, so she shook his hand and said nothing at all.

"The name Covington gave me," Jordan said. "Was he telling the truth?"

"Unfortunately," Byrnes. "Figueroa was a good agent, or so we thought. Smarter than Covington. We had no idea he was involved. I'm surprised John gave him up."

"Covington was a coward," Jordan said.

"I suppose you're right."

"So what happens next?"

"We've got another lead, we're about to take Traiman's last team, here in Rome. Then I'm going home and do my best to wrap up this mess."

"One battle at a time."

"Goodbye Miss Frank. Sandor, I'll see you in D. C."

Jordan sighed. "Yes sir," he said, "you will."

They watched as the Deputy Director walked through Doney's front door and strolled along the Via Veneto, lost among the tourists and locals, on his way back to the Embassy. When Jordan picked up his espresso again, it was cold. He signaled the waiter to bring them two more.

"You're thinking about your friends, about the people, all of that, aren't you?"

"Yes," he said.

"What you did," she said, "it needed to be done, didn't it?"

Jordan stared at her. "Yes," he said at last. "It did."

The waiter brought fresh coffee and Christine topped them off from the bottle of anisette. "Let's make a toast," she said.

"To what? The end of tyranny? Peace for all time?"

"To Tony," she said solemnly.

Jordan nodded. "Sure, and to doing what needs to be done."

They touched cups before drinking, then were silent for a while.

"Well, let's look on the bright side," he said. "At least we didn't catch pneumonia in the Med."

"Or drown."

"That's true."

"Next time we tour the world, let's make our plans a little more carefully."

"Fair enough," he said.

They paid the check and set off for their hotel, Jordan hobbling along on his cane as they walked slowly along the ancient streets of Rome.

The End

For sales, editorial information, subsidiary rights information
or a catalog, please write or phone or e-mail

ibooks
1230 Park Avenue
New York, New York 10128, US
Sales: 1-800-68-BRICK
Tel: 212-427-7139 Fax: 212-860-8852
www.ibooksinc.com
email: bricktower@aol.com.

For sales in the United States, please contact
National Book Network
nbnbooks.com
Orders: 800-462-6420
Fax: 800-338-4550
custserv@nbnbooks.com

For sales in the UK and Europe please contact our distributor,
Gazelle Book Services
Falcon House, Queens Square
Lancaster, LA1 1RN, UK
Tel: (01524) 68765 Fax: (01524) 63232
email: gazelle4go@aol.com.

For Australian and New Zealand sales please contact
Bookwise International
174 Cormack Road, Wingfield, 5013, South Australia
Tel: 61 (0) 419 340056 Fax: 61 (0)8 8268 1010
email: karen.emmerson@bookwise.com.au